All That Was Taken

LISETTE BRODEY

Published by:

SABERLEE BOOKS
Los Angeles, CA
United States of America

Copyright @2023, Lisette Brodey
Published, January 2023

Copy editing: D.L. Savvides, Kenneth Brodey
Cover design: The Cover Collection

ISBN-13: 978-1-7340894-5-5 (paperback)
ISBN-13: 978-1-7340894-6-2 (e-book)

To Lisa Wentworth,

Thank you for all you've done over the years to support my writing. And, if not for you, this book wouldn't be.

"In order to understand the world, one has to turn away from it on occasion."
— Albert Camus, *The Myth of Sisyphus and Other Essays* *("The Minotaur")*

"Solitude sometimes is best society."
—John Milton, *Paradise Lost*

ACKNOWLEDGMENTS

To D.L. Savvides for being such a great editor;

To Kenneth Brodey for his superb preliminary edits and brotherly support;

To Lisa Wentworth for being such an amazing friend over the past twelve-plus years, and doing so much to support the writing and production of this novel … and always believing another book will follow;

To Charles Roth for his endless love and support over the many years;

To all of the following people who lent a hand with my research: Stephanie Bauerlein, Mark Cote, and Cynthia and Mike Pecoraro.

To Deborah Nam-Krane for being an invaluable beta reader and friend;

To Stephanie Bauerlein, Shykia Bell, Dody Cox, PattiAnn Cutter, Dionne Lister, Tonya Staufer, Virginia Talamantes, and Sheri A. Wilkinson for their ongoing support and kindness;

There are so many people who have supported me in so many ways. I wish it were possible to thank each and every one of you. I hope you all know who you are. And last, but not least, thank you to my fellow authors for your support, advice, inspiration, and friendship. You all mean so much to me.

Crooked Moon
Squalor, New Mexico
Molly Hacker Is Too Picky!
Mystical High (Book 1, The Desert Series)
Desert Star (Book 2, The Desert Series)
Drawn Apart (Book 3, The Desert Series)
Barrie Hill Reunion
Hotel Obscure: A Collection of Short Stories
Love, Look Away
The Sum of our Sorrows
The Waiting House: A Novel in Stories
All That Was Taken

All That Was Taken

CHAPTER ONE

The cold hand on his left shoulder startled him. Jolted awake, no longer holding the hand of the auburn beauty he walked the beach with, he sat up as unease hugged his consciousness. Pained by the dissipation of his dream, his eyes cautiously adjusted to the early morning light as he turned to see a spiky-black-haired woman with large bare breasts sitting next to him in her bed. As her tongue slid over her top lip, signaling her desire to ravage him, his gut churned. Disgust scribbled on his face, he jumped out of bed, ending her show of seduction more quickly than it had begun.

Keeping his back to her, intentionally obscuring what she most wanted to see, he stepped into his jeans, shoving his underwear in one pocket. Hastily, he stuck each arm through the sleeves of his gray-linen shirt, not caring if it was buttoned.

"Are you effing kidding me?" she said, climbing out of bed. Within seconds, the naked woman stood before him.

Averting his glance, the fifty-something-year-old man ran his fingers through his shoulder-length salt-and-pepper hair, but said nothing.

"Do you even know my name?"

"Sorry. I shouldn't have had so much to drink last night."

"'Sorry' is not my name. It's Shelley. You're John, right? Or so you said."

"That's my name. What of it?" He exhaled in frustration. "Look, I'm sorry, okay?" He paused, allowing a painful "Shelley" to fall from his lips.

"What? You're leaving? Just like that?" Her defiant stare met only a mediocre oil painting on a nearby wall of a basset hound crossing a sand dune.

Looking down, he slipped on his shoes. "All I remember is having parked my car outside of this house because the Barelli's lot around the corner was full. I had way too much to drink, and I recall chatting to you briefly at the end of the night. When I said I was unfit to drive and mentioned where I'd parked my car, you offered to let me crash here. I was hesitant but thought that was way better than crashing my car and hurting myself or someone else. Not into driving under the influence. So I agreed. How I ended up without my clothes on, that's a mystery … a rather frightening one at that." He unhooked the car keys that were attached to a belt loop with a climbing hook, patted his back pocket to make sure his wallet was there, then turned to go.

Shelley blocked his way by scurrying around until her naked body was only inches from his clothed one. "You took a shower because you didn't wanna reek of booze, and you said you felt sweaty because of the crowd. I thought we'd have some fun when you got out—and I led you to my bed. That's when you promptly passed out. I pulled the towel off you so you'd be ready for me when you woke up." She huffed in disgust. "Well, you're awake now, and I'm tingling in anticipation."

"You might want to anticipate and tingle for a different man. I'm not interested, and I've never been more grateful to my body for rendering me unconscious."

She snarled at him. "You know what, I'll bet you don't even

remember we almost spent the night together five years ago in 2008. But after we got outside and stood under the street light, you all of a sudden felt sick." Regret distorted her face as the truth slipped out. "My hair was blonde then, so not surprising you can't place me. You had more of a beard, as opposed to that five-day macho stubble you have now. We met in Barelli's, same as last night, and yeah, your name was John then too. Only I don't remember you being the rude SOB you are right now. Just that I was pissed you didn't come home with me."

"Could you please not stand in such close proximity?"

Her eyelids fluttered like an overgrown coquette. "Why? Is there some arousal happening that you don't want to credit me for?"

He grunted. "No chance in hell. And sorry, I don't remember you."

"Yeah, I know you don't." Shelley took two small steps back. "What do you do for a living, John?"

"I'm a map maker."

"Really?" She scratched her crotch. "Five years ago, you told me you sold hot sauce."

"Impressively creative of me, wasn't it?" He suppressed a disgusted laugh. "But the only thing you need to know now is that I'm outta here. Sorry to disappoint, but like I said, I only came here to crash. Should've called for a ride, but you know what they say about hindsight."

Shelley licked her top lip again. "Oh, come on. That's what you say now, but you know you wanted me." She fondled the rhinestone star that hung from her naval piercing. "Sexy huh?"

John had no words.

"Lots of men tell me I'm tight for fifty-four. *All* the time."

Then give one of them a call. Mumbling expletives under his breath, John walked out of the bedroom and flipped the lock on the front door and pulled it open. "When you're blitzed—or horny, the Brooklyn-Battery tunnel seems tight. Give up. Will you? Don't degrade yourself like this." He sighed in revulsion as he pushed open the security screen door and walked outside, turning to her one last time. "I don't know when I'll be back in Long Beach, but when I am, kindly expect to never see me again—anywhere. And if you do, look the other way. Because I promise you, that's exactly what I'll be doing."

Undeterred and full of rage, Shelley followed him outside as he walked quickly down the driveway of her small Spanish-style home situated on a busy residential street that ran through the southern California beach city. "Don't degrade myself?' This coming from you, Mister high-and-mighty-map-making-hot-sauce-selling god of nothingness."

John turned to speak to her. "That's me." Seeing his well-loved navy-blue Subaru Forrester on the street, he hurried toward it as she followed.

While she traipsed and jiggled to the sidewalk, a black Jeep, with a barking brown-and-white pit bull in the back seat, came to a screeching halt. The young driver lowered his window and gave her the once-over. "Señora, por favor. You're making my dog upset. He just ate. Don't want him losing his breakfast on my new 'pholstery job. Don't exactly wanna lose mine either, yanno?"

"Kiss my fifty-four-year-old ass!" she shouted back, turning as she bent over to display her goods.

"Dios Mio. No gracias, puta! Hope lightning don't hit ya where the good Lord split ya." As the Jeep drove away, the white Honda Civic behind it slowed to a crawl, but didn't stop as several passersby on foot, along with neighbors tending to their front gardens or other business, craned their necks to gawk at the unclad spectacle.

John turned to her. "Really, demeaning yourself in private wasn't enough for you?" He pointed to her hair. "Your spikes are drooping. Why don't you go inside and make yourself decent before you get arrested? If that's even possible." He sighed and nodded toward the end of block. "Pretty sure that white car with the bright blue stripe is LBPD. Go on, get inside."

"I'll do what I want, you condescending bastard from one-night-stand-with-no-benefits hell."

"Suit yourself." John snickered at the unintentional humor. "Or don't."

"Loser. You fell asleep before we could … ugh."

"Never would have happened."

Defiantly, she watched as he smiled in relief, got into his car, turned the key, waited until the looky-loo vehicles passed, then carefully pulled into the driving lane. Squinting, she committed his license plate to memory as he drove away, unfazed by all of the eyes committing her exhibitionism to their respective memories, whether they wanted to or not.

Seven minutes later, John pulled into the driveway of his friend Ben Rockley's Long Beach house, and within seconds, the front door opened, and a brown Siberian Retriever came bounding out to greet him as if years had passed.

"Hey, Kono, how's my boy? Believe me, I'm every bit as happy to see you too."

Ben, a forty-four-year-old man, his muscular arms displaying several nautical-and-music-themed tattoos, sporting a long blond ponytail with a purple tip, stepped outside. "Yo, John. You disappear for twelve hours, but damn if Kono didn't miss the heck outta you. I think he was actually worried."

John scratched Kono's neck and hurried to the house. "Poor guy. Need to hit the head something fierce. Be right back."

A few minutes later, John entered the living room, greeted by Kono a second time, as well as by Dodger, Ben's Airedale mix. After playing with them both for a moment, he sank into his friend's old couch as Kono jumped up next to him, nuzzling his side.

Sitting in his recliner, Ben smiled. "You know Kono isn't used to being without his dad. Who'd you hook up with, anyway?" He laughed as he saw the look on John's face. "That bad, huh? Didn't even wanna take time to whiz in her bathroom, did ya?"

"Whoa, you know me too well. Benjo." John shrugged off his disgust. "Is it that obvious?"

"Yeah, helped by the fact that your drawers are sticking out of your side pocket. My dude, you were in one hell of a hurry."

"I was. And just for the record, it wasn't exactly a hook up."

"Right. Well, help yourself to the shower. Scrub her off if you have to. I've got some heavy-duty exfoliant soap in the dish." A smile appeared on his lips. "So what exactly was it?"

"I got way too drunk and met this woman at the end of the

evening. I lamented that I wasn't fit to drive home and that I'd left my car around the corner. When she discovered I'd parked in front of her house, she used that as an excuse to tell me I could crash there."

"Crash and burn sounds more like it." Ben smiled as the dog rested his head on the armchair and looked up at him for attention.

"I was stupid enough to ask to use her shower. Next thing I know, it's morning and I'm naked in her bed. Me and my hangover."

"Headache pills are in the medicine cabinet. Who was she? If it's chill to ask, of course."

John fortified himself before answering. "Let's just call her Spiky Shelley." He paused. "I need mouthwash. It feels like that name will be forever stuck in my throat."

Ben groaned. "Noooo way. Tell me you didn't wake up with that crazy bitch with the black-spiked mop on her head. Does hair and nails in some shabby storefront, I hear. Used to have a nice salon until her husband divorced her for whoring around Long Beach, Seal Beach, Laguna—you name it.

"My buddy Ken, you've met him, brought her home one night—about a year ago. And yeah, he'd had too much to drink as well. They *did* take a shower together, got into bed, and her freshly dyed black hair transferred onto his sheets like a press-on tattoo." He smirked. "Didn't notice the black residue in his shower until it was too late. Anyway, he told her to vamoose and the bitch started screaming her head off at 3:00 a.m." As he spoke, Ben grabbed one end of a rubber tug-of-war toy that Dodger had brought to him and began to pull." Not a good look for a cop, but because Ken *is* a cop, he managed to threaten her if she didn't leave. Called a car service to haul her ass home."

"Sounds just like her. Doesn't like to take no for an answer." John smiled as the dog licked his face. "Love you, too, Konhead."

Ben continued pulling on the toy as Dodger growled playfully. "Speaking of friends who are cops, I was walking these guys when my friend Ken pulled up alongside us in the squad car. Just then, a call came over the radio that some crazy woman was standing naked on Granada screaming at her neighbors and at the drivers who were slowing down for a peek at the freak." Ben looked at the horror on John's face. He gulped. "Oh, no. Nooooo fuckin' way." He let go of the dog toy. "You win, Dodger." He looked at John. "Tell me I'm adding two and two and getting seventeen."

John met his friend's eyes. "I'm afraid you get an A in math." He sighed. "And yeah, she followed me outside to read me the riot act for rejecting her. Surreal."

Slapping his forehead, Ben fell back onto his chair. "Sorry. I just gotta ask this, but why didn't you call a cab last night? And why the hell did you drink so much? That's not like you. Not even close. I'm the one who used to party too hard, not you."

"Short answer. You were out last night, and I was restless, especially thinking about this move and all of the bullshit that's been going on. You know, the uncertainty of what lies ahead just got to me, not to mention the undercurrent of something I can't really describe. So I went to Barelli's where I had too little to eat and way too much to drink. I was also exhausted when I agreed to her offer, and my better judgment became temporarily estranged from my inebriated self. Trust me, it'll never happen again."

"Did this unfortunate event have any connection to your move?" Ben crinkled his forehead. "Between my schedule and your random visits, we haven't had any time to talk. The last two times you stayed over, I was at my ex-wife's place visiting with Avery."

"I'm glad you're getting more time with her."

"Me too. Love that kid. And believe it or not, things aren't so bad with her mom. I kind of visited with her too." He grinned. "So listen, back to you. Are your nerves doing a number on you, seeing that you're moving to a new town after eight years on Catalina Island?"

"I'd say so. Something's been way off, and I'm not as coolheaded about everything as I gave myself credit for."

Dodger, who was having no part of being ignored, stood on his hind legs, the toy in his mouth, and his front paws on Ben's lap, making it clear that they were not finished playing. Ben grabbed the proffered end of the toy, only to find his palm instantly coated with dog saliva. "Man, Dodger, you did that on purpose, didn't you? Gave me your end of this slimy thing." He smirked and resumed playing with the dog, this time with his right hand as the left rubbed the saliva onto his well-worn jeans. He laughed as he saw John watching him. "Don't judge, man. Not after …." He laughed again. "So, listen, I was going to ask you about the move last night when I got home … but you weren't here … so …."

"Don't remind me." John lay back and closed his eyes. After a moment, he looked up. "I can't wait to move to Teal Beach and find my solitude again and shed this dark aura that's suddenly wrapped itself around me. Glad I'm buying this time. Don't want anyone to have access."

"That sounds heavy. Is there something in particular going down?" He thought. "Guess there has to be."

"For starters, because I'm a magnet for crazy women … as last night clearly illustrates." He sighed. "As you'll remember, when I moved to Two Harbors from Avalon six years ago, this nice old man, Sergio Sabelli rented a cottage to me. All was good. People left me alone, I took my night walks on the beach without disruption, and I did my work during the day."

"I do." Ben lurched forward as Dodger, ever determined, took advantage of his lack of focus and pulled the toy from his grip. "I gotta stop feeding you so much spinach, Popeye." He laughed and redirected his attention to John. "Then Sergio died not too long ago and his daughter, I forget her name, inherited the cottage you lived in along with his. Right?"

"Renata Sabelli. And yeah. What you just said."

"Nice name."

"And I hoped she'd have a personality to match. I was picking up the Konhead's food one day at the pet store and overheard two people talking about how they hadn't ever seen her on the Island, and how Sergio preferred to visit her in Tuscany, where she's lived since graduating college in LA years ago." He shrugged. "I kept my distance. No desire to get pulled into conversations with strangers."

"As if I don't know that, dude."

John smiled. "You do."

"So what's she like? How old is she?"

"I'd say late fifties. A real piece of work. Looks like she was transported here from another era: a flower child, spiritual guru, and very aggressive human being—all in one confusing package. I can't quite read her, but I'm not trying to. So there's that. You'd think she'd be staying in Sergio's cottage, since it's hers now, or will be, but no, she's sleeping at the Two Harbors campground. Says her father's spirit is far too overwhelming for her psyche to handle now." John rolled his eyes. "Told me her parents were divorced, which I knew, and her mother had died a few years prior and she was an only child. I never asked; I didn't want the information, but she offered. Even showed me her passport when she first came to my door to 'identify and introduce' herself. I'm sure she was hoping that I would share personal details in return. No dice there."

"Trippy. Something sounds way off."

"You think?"

"What happened next?"

John exhaled his revulsion. "She began invading my life in little pieces. Insidious as they come. First, she was just checking out the cottage because … supposedly, her father had become lax in his old age and let things slide." He twisted his lips. "So she said. Nothing I saw. All of a sudden, I started noticing things needing repair that I'd never had a problem with."

"She was sabotaging her own property?" Ben pointed to Dodger's bed as the dog reluctantly settled into it.

"Not in any serious way. Nothing she couldn't fix. That was the point. It didn't take long for me to realize she was finding excuses to come inside. When she started asking me questions about my work and personal life, I had to make sure to close everything up before I went anywhere. I assume she has a key and didn't trust her not to snoop. All the incessant questions were just more than I could endure."

"That's gnarly."

"Yeah." John smiled as Kono lay his head down on his lap and closed his eyes. "She didn't like that I had little or nothing to say to her. Just kept pounding me with questions and I kept not answering. I won't go into it, but you know me, Benjo, and she's everything that I can't tolerate and then some."

"So what was your breaking point? Or when?" Ben stood and walked into the nearby kitchen. "Got some banana-nut and carrot muffins from Danzinger's Bakery. Want one? I know you haven't had jack to eat."

"Sure. Carrot, please. Don't really want to stop for breakfast once I hit the road."

"Want me to make you some coffee?"

"No thanks. Waking up next to that … uh … female … roused me out of my sleep in a way no caffeine ever could."

Ben laughed, then looked at Dodger who was now sitting beside him in the kitchen. "I didn't offer you anything, doggo. Put your tongue back in your mouth." He placed a muffin on a piece of paper towel and walked over to John. "Hope you're okay with Bountyware."

"Same dinnerware chic I use." John laughed as he took the muffin and immediately broke off a piece, then shoved it into his mouth.

Ben sat in his recliner and slowly peeled the red muffin liner away, unlike his ravenous friend. "So it was Renata … her snooping, her questions … that's what triggered you to move?"

"Pretty nearly, but not quite." John looked into Kono's eyes. The dog was now sitting upright and staring at the muffin, then at John.

"No need to be stingy. Share with the Konhead. I'll give you a couple for the road. And whatever else you want."

John smiled. "Thanks. Don't think the road is quite as starved as I am." He fed a generous piece to Kono, who promptly scarfed it down. "I'd already been wanting to move … for several reasons. But I was still deciding on whether or not to buy the Teal Beach cottage. He took another bite of the muffin as Kono stared at him. "The final straw was several months ago when I went into the grocery store. A new person was working the register. Young woman, maybe twenty-three, tops. When she heard someone call my name, just to say hello, she said, 'Oh, you must be Renata's soulmate. She was telling me all about you. How miraculous it is that you two found each other right here on Catalina Island.' Then, she went on about how there's nothing like a good love story to make her day. Thirty seconds later, an older couple walks over to tell me they heard the 'whole love story.' Unnerved me something fierce."

"Oh, hell no."

"Damn straight hell no. I went home. Made a call to buy the Teal Beach cottage I'd been coveting, then had my attorney move on the sale at breakneck speed. Finally closed the deal last week. I'm having work done … new floors, painting, etcetera, so I can't move in immediately, but that's okay. It's more important to move *out*." He rubbed Kono's head. "I'm sorry I didn't tell you any of this was going on, Benjo. I just didn't want to jinx anything before closing."

Ben nodded. "It's all good. But yeah, I thought you were making more trips onto the mainland than usual. When you said it was because Kono loves the ferry rides, I knew there was something you didn't want to talk about, and you know I don't pry. Only on the dumb stuff like where you might have spent the night."

John tried to laugh. "And I appreciate that. It's why you're one of the few people I trust."

"Okay, so when my guys transported your stuff here the other day, you booked a time for us to move the rest, correct?"

"It is. I'll understand if you won't be able to fit me in when I'm ready."

"No worries. You know I'll spin magic for you. Just like you've done for me."

"Thanks, friend." John popped the last bite of muffin into his mouth, much to Kono's dismay. and curled the wrapper around his index finger. "I appreciate that. But don't sweat it. The only items left waiting to be picked up for delivery from Two Harbors to Teal Beach are two end tables that I made and several sealed boxes of non-personal items. I've ordered new furniture. Most everything in the Two Harbors place came with old man Sabelli's cottage anyway … not that I'd want the stuff if it did belong to me. Need a new start. As you saw, all of my equipment and personal files are in your guest room. It's not your freight service I don't trust; I just feel better having the things that matter with me. I hope Renata won't snoop, but if she does, there's little to find."

Ben pulled his cellphone out of his side pocket to see who was messaging him, quickly texted a response, then shoved it back inside. "So nothing in what you left behind that would reveal—"

"Nothing."

"Good. He laughed as Dodger's expectant eyes bore into his own while a jealous Kono watched from across the room. "Okay, last piece is yours for being a good dog." Ben stood. "I've got to get going. That was Jimmy. I finally hired a new guy, Mateo, and he's waiting for me to show him the ropes. I'll catch up with you soon, though. I'm gonna miss you being just a boat ride away. Gonna miss your car in my driveway for all of these years."

John got up and walked over to him. "You're one of the only real friends I have in this world. You've been a port in a storm. Thanks for everything. And the parking spot is no small thing. You gave me freedom to leave the island and get lost when I needed to. Speaking of which, I'll have to rent a spot in Teal Beach. The cottage is only accessible by footpath or the beach. Exactly as I like it." He sighed. "But moving is complicated even for a no-frills person like me."

Giving his friend a hug, Ben took a good look at him. "You know all of the ways you've helped me. You still do. I'm every bit as grateful to you. The only change is that your car is leaving my driveway, and you'll be farther north."

"True. Very true." John laughed as Dodger ran to the door. "I think your assistant is telling you it's time to go. As for me, I'm going to scrub off the slime, pack up the car, and get moving." He smiled. "You might want to wash your hands."

"I've got handwipes in the truck. Give me dog saliva any day over—"

"Yeah, yeah. I know, and I agree." John offered a reluctant chuckle.

Both men watched as Kono ran over and stood by Dodger.

"Kono knows something is different," John said. "I can only hope that one day I'll be as smart as he is."

"Should have taken him with you last night," Ben said as he pushed open the white security screen door with Dodger behind him, laughing loudly as he walked to his truck. "Lock up when you leave."

A broad smile on his face, John yelled through the screen. "I'll get you for that. You know I will."

CHAPTER TWO

"What do you think, Konhead?" John asked the dog as they pulled into a parking space outside of the Teal Beach Sundial Inn that sat on one of the smaller cliffs in the area. The main building, once a large home now renovated and expanded for commercial use, boasted teal-stained wood with French-shuttered windows. A wrought-iron fence adorned with flower boxes enclosed the balcony on the second floor. On the ground level, an inviting porch offered teal Adirondack chairs, a cream-colored wicker sofa, assorted succulents in large clay pots, and hanging baskets of cascading foliage.

To the right of the hotel's main building, there were several matching cabins in full view and glimpses of several more, mostly obscured from sight. The ground between the cabins, landscaped with stones, various cacti, and assorted wildflowers, suggested a property well maintained throughout the year.

John noticed a restaurant across the small unpaved road, Dodo Deen's, and made a mental note not to worry about dinner as he looked over at Kono. "This hotel is our new home, boy. A temporary one, but nice. You think? Just a short walk downhill to the beach and our new cottage is about a half-mile west of here on elevated ground. Just five steps down and the ocean is in our front yard. Everything we love, right? I hope you've memorized all of this. Pop quiz later." He laughed to himself. "Meaning your pop will be quizzing you."

Kono cocked his head and gave John a suspicious look.

"You are one smart dog. Always know when I'm messing with you." Once out of the car, Kono on a leash, John checked to make sure the car was locked. Looking around, he saw about twenty people, several walking or sitting down on the beach and some going into the nearby restaurant. "Looks about right for mid-March. Good thing we're not moving in summer. Would've been a whole lot more hectic. Come on, let's see what awaits us inside."

As soon as they stepped onto the porch, John could hear Phil Collins's "In the Air Tonight" playing. "Whoever is inside has excellent taste in music. That's a good sign, Kono." He pushed open the large carved wooden door with the embedded beveled-glass oval.

"Welcome, friends," the cheerful woman with wavy blonde hair watering a plant arrangement at the receptionist desk said. "Let me turn down the music. Sorry, I'm a pop and rock nut. Especially from the 70s and 80s. Can't get enough of it." She rushed to lower the music, then raised a counter panel, pushed open a lower gate, then closed it before walking into the lobby. Her floral-and-paisley crushed velvet cardigan draped beautifully over a black top and pants. Taking a closer look at John, she stopped, as if seeing him for the first time in that moment.

As his eyes soaked in both her physical appearance and shining countenance, he realized he was feeling something he'd convinced himself would never exist again. Because he wouldn't let it, and because that part of his life was over. And he was way too intuitive not to see that she was looking at him the same way, and like him, she was taking pains to hide it.

"You must be John Hennessey." She broke eye contact as she admired Kono. "But I don't know the name of this handsome fella by your side. I'm Sunny Harrison, the owner." She smiled as she nodded toward a teal couch with a wicker table in front of it. "The lobby is empty at the moment. You mentioned on the phone that you're moving to Teal Beach, so I'm wondering if you'd care to have a quick get-to-know-you chat before I sign you in." She gulped as if she wished she'd swallowed her words before speaking them.

"Oh, I'd—"

"Perhaps you'd prefer to be off to your cabin and settle in. I'm sure it's been a long day for you. By the way, there's no rule that says you ever have to get to know anyone—including me."

She was as nervous as he was. "Don't be silly." John tried to silence his jaded inner voice. "That sounds nice."

"If you're sure then. After you." Sunny gestured for him to sit.

Kono, who was usually content to be wherever John was, stared at the reception desk and began to whimper and growl as he pulled toward it. In seconds, his vocalizations were met with whining.

"His nose knows. And now his ears hear. That's my Miggy. She's a mid-size brown labradoodle. Very playful. Okay for her to come out and meet Kono? Is he good with other dogs?"

"A gentle soul." John took a seat on the couch. "Far more open to new friends than his old man, I'd say." *Why did I have to say that?*

Sunny eyed him curiously, then offered a gentle smile. "You have a beautiful and benevolent spirit. I saw it the moment you walked in. I meet a lot of people, and I often know who they are before they utter a word."

John ignored the awkward lump in his throat.

"Oh, I'm sorry. I didn't mean to make you uncomfortable. Just the opposite."

"I know. And I appreciate the kind words." He smiled. "I do."

Sunny lifted the panel again, and the spirited brown

labradoodle came bouncing through the gate as John unhooked Kono's leash. After introductory butt sniffs, the dogs began to play, initiated by Miggy who ran to the other side of the lobby and pawed a yellow-and-brown rubber giraffe from underneath a chair where she'd left it.

"I was wondering where that chewed-up delight had escaped to." Sunny laughed as she sat on the teal couch next to John. "Her pink elephant toy has been missing for a week, but I think the poor thing escaped. Can't say as I blame it. I'd fly the coop if someone had put that many teeth marks into *me*."

"I hear you." Afraid his face gave away his unexpected attraction to her, he took a moment to look at the dogs. "So, you're Sunny, and this is the Sundial Inn. Named after yourself, I presume?"

"Actually, the other way around. My father collected vintage sundials." She paused. "Well, that came out funny. It's not as if there are any that *aren't* vintage."

They shared a laugh.

John noticed her gray eyes shined as she spoke. *You're quite beautiful.*

"He was a history professor at Berkeley. He developed an interest early in his career while preparing a lecture that included the first use of sundials, somewhere around 1500 BC—"

"Your father must have been quite old to have been preparing lectures in 1500 BC."

As her embarrassment coupled with her mirth, Sunny laughed heartily. "I'm a real flubbermouth today. My goodness."

"Not at all," John said, feeling a refreshing departure from the toxic women of his past as the presence of the extraordinary woman he was speaking with threatened more. "Please, go on."

"Miggy, play nice with Kono," Sunny called out as the labradoodle's over-enthused manner caught her attention. She turned back to John. "My father fell in love with sundials—everything about them. And so he became a collector. That glass case behind the front desk houses a few of them. The most precious ones I keep elsewhere, and my brother has several."

"Fascinating. Not what I expected to hear." John glanced at Kono, happy to see him interacting so well with his new friend. "So, is Sunny a nickname?"

"It is. He wanted to name me Sundial Serena, but my mother told him there was no way under the blazing hot California sun that her child's first name would be Sundial."

He laughed. "I can kind of understand your mother's thinking. So what happened?"

"Well, she finally agreed, albeit reluctantly, on Serena Sundial. You can understand her hesitance."

"I can. But it's uniquely you."

"Thank you. But it's also pretty bad as names go. She said the hospital nurse was trying not to laugh when she filled out the birth certificate, then profusely apologized for being so unprofessional. My mother told her, 'Don't worry, I'd laugh too. My daughter will have her father to blame for this. I'm only compromising on the lesser of two evils.' Then they both laughed. As it turned out, I wasn't called Serena for long. When they saw I was such a happy baby, they decided to call me Sunny. Harrison is my late husband, Grey's, surname."

"Oh, I'm so sorry. About your husband."

"Thank you. Me too." Sunny paused. "Grey ran this hotel with me, along with another property we own, a house, about two miles away, high up on a cliff. My husband was captivating, but a dark, brooding poet as well. Very multi-faceted to say the least. There was always a little piece of him I couldn't reach, but I was more intrigued than disheartened. He never bored me, always challenged me, and he loved me as passionately as I did him. He died tragically at fifty-two."

John watched as she fought to hold the tears back. "May I ask how long ago he died?"

"Nearly six years ago. It was ...." She stopped to compose herself. "On the outside, I'm still the bright, shiny Sunny everyone's come to know, but many days, I weep inside."

"Speaking for myself, and of the best people I know, I think we all weep inside to varying degrees. Some people hide it better than others."

There are only a handful of people who see the real me, but only sometimes. I philosophize way too much, but like my crying, I do 90 percent of that in my head. My daughter, Jess, told me I come off way more 'light and fluffy' than I am."

"That's so ... laundry-ish."

Sunny laughed. "Isn't it? I told her she made me sound like a freshly washed towel." She turned a light shade of pink. "I'm good at fooling people, and I have no idea on God's green earth why I'm telling you all of this. I *never* tell anyone this. I'm a happy person by nature, so I let the façade thrive. I mean, it's not as though sadness will bring him back, so I try to enjoy life. But still, there are some days I can only pretend."

"I hear you. Facades are often easier than truths. I'm very sorry you lost Grey. Love like that doesn't come along often, and it's frightening how quickly it can slip away when it does." John surprised himself by asking to hear more. "So, tell me more about your children."

"I have two. Jess, who I just mentioned, is a production assistant in LA, and my son, Alex, is an environmental lawyer up north in Marin County. I'm very proud of them both. How about you?"

"Uh … guess that would be a no." Noticing that Sunny was eyeing him curiously, he shot another glance at the dogs. "I think it's love at first sight."

"I think so too. And I'm rather amazed." Sunny looked away and rearranged two California travel magazines sitting on the table that had been thriving fine on their lonesome.

Feeling his heart beat in a way that was almost unrecognizable, he turned to the desk, as if he were speaking directly to the music that was playing. "Phil Collins, Queen, Peter Gabriel. Is this your own mix?"

"It is. I've got every artist. Pink Floyd, Bon Jovi, Heart, R.E.M. and so many more. Just wish my favorite artist had recorded more music. He would have been a superstar if—"

John glanced at the wall clock and stood, the intensity of what he was feeling finally overwhelming him. "Sorry for being so abrupt, Sunny. I'm just a bit nervous about my life sitting outside in my Subaru. Didn't mean to cut you off; I should probably sign in and start taking care of business."

"Of course," Sunny said as she rose from her seat. "Here I am just gabbing away—"

"Not at all. You're charming." *And so much more.* "But I

should unload the car, feed Romeo over there, and make a call before it's too late."

Looking embarrassed, Sunny patted her thighs for Miggy to come, then hurried behind the counter with the dog. Quickly pulling out a register and putting on a pair of tortoise-shell reading glasses, she smiled at John as if he'd just walked into the hotel. "So, all I need from you is ID and a credit card. I have you booked in cabin eleven. If you leave through the side door, just make a sharp left, and walk all the way back. If you're by your car, though, just walk to your right and down the stone path. I think you'll find the cabin quite roomy. And it has a kitchenette area where you can cook a decent meal, if you're so inclined. Speaking of food, from seven to ten every morning, we have a continental breakfast buffet in the nook to the right of the gift shop.

"Nice."

Sunny, as if trying to disguise her nervousness, shuffled a few papers around. "As for your cabin, yards away from the front door, you'll see a laundry facility for our guests. And no doubt, when you pulled up earlier, you likely saw there are wooden steps on the west side of this building that go down the side of the cliff to the beach. It can be kind of a steep walk, and a tricky climb back up. So be careful."

"I will. Thanks. Anything else?"

"Yes, actually. I've given you a deluxe cabin and it comes with a jacuzzi." She paused to think. "Oh, one more thing. If your cabin loses pressure, oxygen will drop from overhead. Be sure to securely put your mask on before helping Kono with his."

Startled, John looked at her, then laughed. "Was that to make sure I was paying attention?"

Sunny brightened. "Believe it or not, I've never said that to another guest. Just now, as I was giving you all of the directions, I felt like a flight attendant again, something I was for three years in my twenties. Just couldn't resist. Odd how that's never happened before."

"That was funny. You got me." John called Kono to his side, pulled out his wallet, and handed her a card. "By the way, when I reserved the cabin, not sure if I mentioned that I'm not one-hundred-percent positive when my cottage will be ready. I was told it should be about a week. Is that okay?"

"It's the off season, and it's fine. Even if it were the dead of summer, I'd work something out for you." As she processed the card, she looked up at him and smiled. "I must tell you, the cottage you bought is magnificent. The owner actually had a couple of offers before he sold it to you. He didn't want just anyone to buy it. It was a special place for him and his late wife, and he was adamant that it wouldn't be sold as a party house or to anyone he thought wouldn't respect the solitude and beauty that is Teal Beach. He wanted to make sure it would go to the right person."

"How did he know I was the right person? He never met me."

Sunny handed him his credit card and ID along with a key. "The person who showed you the cottage, Landon, that's his son. He knows what his father wants and doesn't want. He's very wealthy and the highest bid wasn't necessarily the best bid."

"Ah, I see. That explains things. Honestly, I was rather surprised it hadn't been snapped up. I was afraid I'd waited too long after seeing it."

"Well," Sunny said, opening the gate and returning to the lobby area. "Now you know. It was meant to be." She paused to switch gears. "Also, while you'll find most everything you'd need in town, I should mention that a few of the more high-end stores and restaurants close for the winter, but you won't have any problems with everyday needs. There are several stores within walking distance of here where you'll find your basics—groceries, hardware, pharmacy, and more. Just down the road a half mile, by the other inns and motels, there are several more restaurants and a gas station with a convenience store. All of them open year-round. You'd have passed them on the way here. If you need a doctor, there are a few practices in town. And an excellent hospital only five miles away. I hope you won't need that."

"Hope not. My most pressing need at the moment is a good dinner. Only had a couple of muffins today as I was eager to get on the road."

Sunny regarded him with a curious but bright smile. "Dodo Deen's is across the street. It's a family slash Cajun Southern seafood place owned by my assistant manager's brother, Rolo Gardet and his wife, Clarissa. I met them all in New Orleans fifteen years ago and we've been a team ever since. Rolo and Clarissa live above the restaurant with their two children, and Ty lives in a backhouse here on the property. Usually, he works from nine at night until whenever I relieve him in the morning. Our hours are flexible. And he helps out his brother from time to time." She laughed awkwardly.

He wanted so much to ease her nerves, but he was having too much trouble with his own. All he could do was smile, leaving Sunny to talk some more.

"Again, this isn't information I ever give anyone, but I feel like we're old friends somehow, and as you're a new resident of Teal Beach, I want you to feel as comfortable as possible with your surroundings. Oh, and Miggy and I live behind that back wall, which is part of the original house."

"All good to know. Thank you." John put the receipt in his wallet and the key in his side pocket. "So, if I read correctly on the Internet, you have three suites and five rooms in this building in addition to the twenty stand-alone cabins outside."

"That's right. Also, as your cottage is inaccessible for the mail carriers, I should tell you my hotel is the designated postal annex for Teal Beach." She pointed to her left. "Right behind our little gift shop is Sunny's Post Office. Once you move, I can set up a P.O. box for you. You told me you were moving here from Two Harbors, right?"

"I did."

"You might have had a similar setup with postal delivery there."

"I did, but I made no use of it. I used my friend Ben's address in Long Beach. It was just easier. I don't get much physical mail that needs my immediate attention. Anyway, the system is just fine and exactly as I expected. I do know that nobody in Carmel has home delivery."

"That's right, "Sunny said as she handed him a folded map of Teal Beach. "They set it up that way to force the residents to get to know one another when they pick up their mail. Carmel also requires a permit to wear shoes with heels more than two inches."

"Don't I know it," John said with a grin. "Last time I was there, I made the mistake of wearing my three-inch spiked boots and spent a harrowing night in jail."

Sunny looked at him blankly, then burst out laughing. "You had me going there for a moment."

"I was pretty convincing, wasn't I?" He chuckled. "Payback for the flight-attendant joke. Seriously, I didn't know that."

"It's true about the ordinance, but they don't enforce it. At least that's what I've been told."

"Well, you never know when that information might come in handy." John picked up the map. "I'm sure I'll see you soon. Think I'll try out Rolo's place for dinner."

Sunny laughed to herself.

"Oh no. Is there something you're not telling me?" he said, moving away from the gate so she could re-enter the lobby.

"Not at all. The food is excellent. It's just that a few locals stubbornly call it Rolo's Place because Dodo Deen's sounds silly to them. You see, when Rolo was a boy, he had a stuffed Dodo bird toy that he loved. He wanted it to have a last name, but Dodo Gardet didn't sound right to him. Too grown up and like a real person, I think he told his mother. That's when she suggested her maiden name, Deen. He loved the alliterative sound and kept it." She smirked. "Of course, he had no idea what an 'alliterative sound' was back then. Decades later, the restaurant is named after his childhood toy."

"Great story. I did notice the Dodo bird on the signage. A wonderful way to cherish the past. I'll be heading over there as soon as I unload the car and tend to the boy. Thanks for everything, Sunny." Looking her in the eyes, he believed they were asking to join him for dinner. He told himself he was imagining things, but he feigned obliviousness for good measure. Feeling every emotional scar he carried, he attached Kono's leash and hurried out of the lobby just as Sunny was blasting the volume on "Total Eclipse of the Heart."

He stood on the porch and closed his eyes for a moment. Looking at the front door, he considered asking Sunny to join him, but he brushed the thought away as he walked toward the car.

With Miggy behind her, a bit after ten o'clock, Sunny opened the back door of her home to the small, private, and beautifully landscaped yard behind the hotel that offered a vista to the sea. It was "last call" for Miggy and a special time for Sunny, who loved to look down at the ocean's dark waves as if they were saying goodnight to her. On some nights, she believed her beloved Grey was there with her.

With a smile on her face, she glanced down to see one of the overhead lights shining on something pink in the grass. "Look Miggy, Mr. Elephant!'

Wagging her tail, the dog put the toy in her mouth and continued to sniff around the yard.

Sunny smiled, but as she looked over the fence and out to sea, it was then that she saw something out of the ordinary. A tall man in a long dark coat, hands in the pockets, was walking close to the water's edge as a dog followed by his side.

"What in the world? Who's that? I don't know anyone …." She focused on the solitary figures. "Oh, my. It's John and Kono," she mumbled to herself. *This walk isn't the result of a whim; it's a ritual. The longing for peace is there; the momentary surrender to pain is there, yet still fighting against the odds. The feelings of overwhelming loss powers his movement. Even though I'm far away, I know there isn't any sound.* "Oh, Miggy, tell your silly mother to stop watching and overanalyzing this lovely man. It's not right."

The dog eyed her curiously, then looked away as Sunny's thoughts continued to taunt her. *His spirit screams to be rescued while simultaneously begging to be left alone. This nightly walk is every bit as necessary to him as breathing. And I feel so guilty for watching him.*

Sunny looked down to notice that Miggy was now standing by her side, her shaggy head tilting from one side to the other, a movement the dog made only when she sensed something was off kilter. "You *are* reading my thoughts, aren't you, girl? You're wondering how I know what I do?" She kneeled down and kissed the top of the dog's head. "Don't you see, down there on the beach? That's you and me, my love. It's pretty impossible not to recognize oneself in another, especially when what you see is nearly a mirror image. I wasn't crazy when I saw something special in Mr. Hennessey. Everything I sensed was real. And sadly, my furry sweetheart, because of that, I know that the closer my approach, the farther he will run. The most ironic part of it all, is that part of me wants him to do exactly that."

CHAPTER THREE

"Hey, there! John!"

Having just shut the cabin door, John stood with Kono as the tall, muscular, bald, forty-something Black man approached him with a smile. "Hello. You must be Tyler. I think I saw you for a minute last night when I was having dinner at your brother's place."

Kono, wagging his tail, greeted Tyler by standing on his hind legs.

"You did. And please, call me Ty," he said with a smile as he extended his right hand to John while his left forearm served as a landing place for Kono's front paws. He looked into the dog's eyes. "Kono, I presume. So, I hear you might be sweet on Miggy."

"They had a passionate first meeting." John shook Tyler's hand. "Okay, down, boy. Give Ty his arm back."

Tyler smiled. "I'm guessing he needs to empty his tank. Mind if I walk with you a bit?"

"Sure thing."

The men walked only a few steps down the path before stopping when Kono found a large succulent to water.

"My brother said he had a nice chat with you last night while you feasted on his gumbo."

"We did. And he's one hell of a cook."

"Sure is. Family recipe. Speaking of family, you've probably noticed I'm much better looking." He grinned. "Which is why he got the hair and I'm bald."

John laughed. "You actually look quite similar. Hair aside."

"Yeah, we do. And I've never minded being bald. My girlfriend, Imari, tells me I've got that raw machismo Rolo can only dream about. Can't disagree." He laughed. "You met Rissa, Rolo's wife. She maintains those long braids for him. Used to be a hairdresser early on in her career. That was long before she became a wife, mother, and restaurant owner."

John felt momentarily sickened as the word "hairdresser" was mentioned as he pushed the unwanted vision of Shelley out of his head. He stopped at the end of the path as they reached the driveway. "You must be exhausted. I hear you work overnight and also help out your brother sometimes, yes?"

"Right on both counts. I'm also an artist and handyman. I'm plumb tired right now because I haven't slept. But don't let my all-nighters behind the desk fool you. Pretty much no action at all. I often lock the lobby and side doors and go to sleep if I'm not working on a wood carving. If people need something or other, they ring the bell or call."

"I hear you."

"Sunny hates that I do this. For years, she's wanted to install a new security grille around the reception area—the old one broke years ago. She wants to close the lobby at night, and modernize the front door so guests only need a code to get in. But I can't quite get there yet."

John saw the torment in his eyes. "So you're there every night?"

"I make alternate arrangements here and there, but most times I am. Sunny, Imari, and my family *hate* that I do this—with a passion. And that's putting it mildly."

"Then why torture yourself and those you love? The new setup you mentioned sounds like a plan."

"I know. I know. Just can't quite get there. See, Sunny's the best people I know." He stopped and twisted his mouth. "Mind if I say a few words? Got a good reason for it."

"Oh, okay. Sure."

Tyler's eyes made a quick sweep of the area before he began. "See, about fifteen years ago, Sunny was in New Orleans with her husband, Grey. Rolo, Clarissa, and I were going through some real tough times with family—won't go into that now. We met them at a restaurant in the Quarter where the three of us were working. They'd come in for dinner. Long story, but we hit it off something fierce, and the five of us went out together after the restaurant closed. Next thing you know, we'd moved from Louisiana to Teal Beach. Sunny and Grey sold the restaurant to Rolo and Rissa and gave me a job and a home. I'm also part owner of Dodo Deen's. But it's their baby."

"They've done an amazing job. One of the best meals I've had in a long time." Noticing Kono was impatient, John motioned for him to sit. "Sorry to interrupt. Go on."

Tyler smiled as he checked his surroundings again. "Thanks, man." He exhaled. "Anyway, meeting the Harrisons changed our lives forever—better in every way. Been in Teal Beach ever since. And when Grey died … uh …." His face tightened, and he exhaled. "Well, let's just say I can't help but give Sunny some extra looking out for. She keeps telling me it's not necessary, but I don't take no for an answer. She's family to all of us. Me, Rolo, Rissa, and their two kids, RJ and Jacie. She's Aunt Sunny to them."

"Nice." As Kono stood and pulled forward, John turned to

walk across the lot to the steps that led down to the beach but noticed Tyler standing in place, not wanting to follow. "Is there more you want to tell me? Something specific?"

"There is." Tyler nodded to his left. "Before you head to the beach, mind if we go in the opposite direction for just a few?" He looked down at the dog. "Just give me a minute, okay, boy?" He met John's eyes. "Just don't want Sunny to see us through the windows."

Confused, John narrowed his eyes a bit. He paused as an older couple smiled and walked toward the hotel, then followed Tyler as he walked away from the main building. He looked at Kono. "Sit." As the dog responded, John gave Tyler his full attention. "I'm listening."

"One of the reasons I wanted to talk to you is because you're going to be a permanent resident. We don't get a lot of new people moving to this part of Teal Beach. Up in the hills, where most of the homes are, where Sunny rents a house, well, people come and go there all the time. But to the man who sold you the cottage, Edward, that cottage was his second home for forty years. One he probably spent more time in than his house. Like I said, not a lot of traffic in and out here, except for the tourists who prefer a sleepy, scenic beach town over the ones with more nightlife."

"That's exactly why I bought this place." John eyed him curiously. "My days of being around a lot of people are far behind me. I'm a bit of a loner. Maybe even a hermit most days."

Tyler put his palms up. "Oh, sorry, man, not trying to pry. Hope I'm not coming off that way. Your business is your own. But I know Sunny took a liking to you, and her people radar is rarely wrong. Neither is Rolo's. Or mine. Don't want to burden you on your second day here—or any day for that matter. You haven't even moved to your cottage yet."

"I'm not feeling burdened. I'd tell you if I were."

Relief washed over Tyler's face. "Good to know. So, I just wanted to tell you that Sunny—well, she went through some serious trauma when Grey was killed and that kind of suffering doesn't just walk away. And things that cause trauma aren't always as gone as they should be. Problem is, you just don't always know." He shook off his unease. "Not trying to be cryptic or play any guessing games. It's Sunny's choice to tell you what she wants." He sighed. "Not trying to pull you into anything, either. Or take you down a path you don't wanna walk." He took a deep breath, then exhaled. "It's just that I'm passionate about protecting her. So, just trying to say—if you ever see anything that doesn't look right, or just get a feeling that doesn't sit well with you, I'd appreciate it if you'd tell me or Rolo, or do whatever is comfortable for you. We protect each other around here. Have each other's backs—if that's clear."

Kono lay down on the ground. John, knitting his brow, bit his lip and said nothing as he processed all that Tyler had said.

Tyler, who John noticed had been carefully watching his expression, slumped his shoulders in defeat. "Just to be clear … 'having your back' doesn't mean 'in your business,' John. Far from it. We're not the nosy-ass neighbor patrol. Not even close. Everyone's business is their own. We work hard to keep it that way. If I've overstepped or given you the wrong—"

"We're good, Ty." John gave him a quick smile. "In fact, I'm not only on board, I appreciate you telling me. Your words were just a shift of the winds for me, and I didn't want to misinterpret."

"You sure about that? What I just read on your face told me

something different."

"I'm a careful person. Have been for a long time. Let's just leave it there."

"I'm down with that." Tyler looked down at his tight gray T-shirt and work jeans. "Gonna take a shower, toss these grimy clothes in the laundry, and get some serious shut-eye for a bit. Nothing about me in good shape right now. I can't burn the candle at both ends the way I used to. Worked on carving a small sailboat last night and didn't get a wink."

Both men turned sharply as a bleached blonde in a hot fuchsia leisure suit, matching sun hat, and giant pink sunglasses, who had come from one of the cabins, was speaking loudly into her phone. "Yeah, so I booked this place for some peace and quiet but don't know what I was thinking. A cemetery would be more fun. I'd give new meaning to 'jumping someone's bones.'" She burst out laughing, then listened for a minute. "Yeah, yeah, I know it's March, but does that mean all of the hot guys have to hibernate? Even on a Saturday night? I came across one fine hunk of a man, but he ignored me. Probably gay seeing how uninterested he was." She paused. "I don't know why I thought listening to my iPod and looking at the ocean would do eff all for me. I should have gone to Santa Barbara. Got lucky there the last time. Bet those boys come out to play year-round."

Tyler made a face and looked at John. "She strolled into the restaurant last night after you left. Hit on Rolo with all the force of someone pounding a hammer at one of those high striker games at the carnival. Told him she wanted a nice piece of chocolate for dessert—and could he deliver it to her cabin. Damn. Lucky Rissa didn't hear her. Bro just ignored her, played dumb, and went back into the kitchen. Piece o' work that horny chick."

"I'll say." *At least this one is keeping her clothes on.*

Both men looked at the woman as her voice got louder.

"So, yeah," she said. I'm gonna hit the road. Don't worry, I'm going to feed my face with a big old breakfast before I do. I deserve it, dontcha think?" She stepped onto the porch. "Hope they've got sausage and hash browns to go with the eggs."

"Ain't gonna find any of that in the lobby," Tyler said, shaking his head as she disappeared into the building. "Hope she doesn't make a scene."

John put a comforting hand on Tyler's shoulder. "Get some rest. Kono and I will make sure everything's okay."

Kono's ears perked up as he stood on all fours.

"You sure?" Tyler wasn't convinced. "You almost look a bit triggered."

"And you're scary perceptive. For a second I was, but I'm cool."

Tyler bent down and petted Kono's head. "Hope you have a good walk." He regarded John with a comforting smile. "Thanks again for listening to the mumbo jumbo—or as Imari says, 'mumbo gumbo' that came outta my mouth. Hard to focus when I'm tired. I appreciate you listening and hearing me. Not always easy. Y'all take care."

"You too." John watched as Tyler disappeared down the path. Suddenly, the woman's loud voice startled John again, only now it was coming from the lobby, and he was way too far away to hear anyone speaking in remotely normal tones. "Come on Kono. Let's make sure all's good with Sunny."

"This is not breakfast!" the woman screamed at Sunny as John and Kono entered the lobby. "Swiss cheese chunks, bagels, Danishes, cut-up fruit, and orange juice don't do it for me. This is so prissy. Like what some skinny rich Beverly Hills bitch would eat to keep her size-zero figure. Minus the Danishes. It's not real food."

Sunny and five of her guests stood in horror as the shouting began. John saw the frustration on Sunny's face and the subsequent swell of relief as she noticed him.

"As I told you at check-in, and as is written clearly on our website, we offer a continental breakfast."

The woman made a dramatic shift with her hips. "Hullo? Are we not on a continent? North America, I think. At least it was the last time I looked."

"That's not what continental breakfast necessarily means," Sunny said delicately.

"*Necessarily?*" She huffed. "It means you get the food of the continent. Otherwise they'd call it something else. Like Skinny Bitch breakfast or Cheapskate's Delight."

John watched as the older woman who'd passed him outside, stepped away from her husband to confront the fuchsia nightmare. "Dear, this is exactly what a continental breakfast is. Believe me; we're world travelers."

"Hullo! You travel the world, and you're in Teal Beach eating scraps? Don't BS me, lady." She looked at Kono. "I think there's something here for you, *dog.* Woof." She turned to Sunny. "I want fried eggs over easy, hash browns, bacon, and sausage. That's the kind of breakfast people eat on *this* continent. Oh, and good old American white bread—toasted."

"Oh, dear," the woman murmured as she walked back to her husband. "Incorrigibly crude and hopelessly gauche."

"I'm sorry you're disappointed," Sunny said to her. "But as I explained, what you see here is exactly what I promised. As you can see, this is a hotel lobby and not a restaurant. You're in luck, though, as there are several places up the road where you can get exactly what you want. You might try the diner."

"Are you gonna pay for it, lady? If I go somewhere else?"

"No, I'm not."

The woman eyed the food. "I've already decided not to stay in this mausoleum another night. So maybe I'll just take *all* of this crap with me."

John walked over to the woman. "No, you won't do that either." He followed her glance to the spread. "This is quite a nice selection. I see there's some yogurt too."

"A nice selection for your *dog*!"

John sighed as if he were bored. "I can make a quick call to a fellow officer who's on duty now. I think they serve bacon and eggs in the local jail." He pretended to be having a good think about it. "Or maybe just oatmeal. Yeah. Pretty sure the latter for disrupting the peace."

The woman snarled at him. "Oh, so that's why you have a dog. You're a cop, and you need him to sniff around for clues that you're too lame to find yourself. Or maybe to protect you because you're really a wuss."

"Everything you just said." He smiled. "Would you like to see how I work? Meet the sheriff? Or would you like to leave?"

Sunny's face relaxed as did the customers who'd been watching.

"I'm leaving. But first I'm going back into the cabin to pick up the two bucks I left for the maid. Not spending one more dime here that I don't have to."

"I'll tip her for you," John said.

"Loser cop, loser hotel, and super loser food." She looked at the older couple. "I'd use stronger words, but I don't want to offend you."

The older woman smiled. "Exactly why I didn't use stronger language with you. Only we wouldn't have minded offending *you*, but not everyone else. Having traveled the world, I can curse people out in many languages. So can my husband."

"Ugh!" She walked out the front door as a rumble of laughter made its way around the room.

As the guests went back to eating, Sunny hurried over to John. "Thank you so much. I'm capable of saying more than I did, when necessary, but I'm not the same person I used to be before—you know. I just don't have the stomach for ugly. Not that I ever liked it, but it hits me harder now."

"Same here. More than you know." John reached into his pocket and pulled out a ten-dollar bill. "It was my pleasure, Sunny. You didn't deserve that." He handed her the money. "I'm not sure how many people you have working for you, but please, do give this to whomever is cleaning up after that woman."

Sunny smiled. "There are two sisters who work for me:

Miranda and Larae. They live in town. You'll meet them. Larae is married to the chief of police, Rafael Lanza. Aside from the housekeeping, they're both fully trained to fill in for me and Ty at times, which really comes in handy. Miranda is working today, and I'll see that she gets this. But really, you don't have to—"

"It's no trouble. I want to. She deserves to be tipped. Listen, Kono needs his walk, and I'm going to see the cottage and attempt to assess how everything's coming along. Maybe we can have a chat when I get back—and if the lobby is empty, Miggy and Kono can have some quality time."

"I'd love that."

An awkward pause hung between them as they looked at one another.

Not wanting to expose his feelings or make Sunny uncomfortable, John spoke first. "If you could put a garlic bagel aside for me, I'd appreciate it."

Sunny winked. "I've got some cream cheese with chives and onion in my mini-fridge behind the desk. Would you like that as well?"

"Absolutely. Used to have that at my favorite deli in New York."

"Oh, are you from the East Coast? I didn't know that."

"I am, but California's my home now." John looked uneasy as he turned to go. "See you a bit later, Sunny."

As she forced a smile, John surmised she might herself be chastising herself for thinking she'd asked too much. He wanted to make her feel better, but the reassuring words didn't come.

"You'll know the lobby is empty if the music's loud," Sunny

called after him.

Unable to say anything, John offered a thumbs up and headed outside with Kono.

CHAPTER FOUR

Three hours later, before he reached the porch, John could hear Smokey Robinson's "Tears of a Clown" blaring from inside the lobby. Instantly, he recognized the song's theme as the nearly identical sentiment Sunny had used to describe herself when they met: crying on the inside while wearing a facade on the outside. He related to it all too well but didn't know if he could—or should—break through and offer her any needed comfort. The part of him that used to be so good at consoling others felt irrevocably broken, but it also shielded him from getting close to people.

As soon as he and Kono stepped onto the porch, the dog pulled John until they were inches from the door, looking up as if to say, "Open it."

"You win, boy. This time." Wearing a smile, he walked into the lobby.

Sunny's face lit up when she saw them, and Kono went crazy when the counter gate was unlatched and Miggy came racing out into the lobby. After a sniff exchange, Miggy ran as Kono chased her.

"It's like they've known each other forever. I've always thought that dogs feel a soulful connection just like people do." Sunny turned the music way down, neatly pushed the small pile of mail to the side, then lowered herself behind the counter. "Am still here, John. Just getting your cream cheese and breakfast from my minifridge." She laughed. "Just hoping I can stand up again. It's never guaranteed."

"I know the feeling."

Sunny popped up a few moments later. "Here I am. Not too

worse for wear." She put a plate on the counter with a bagel, sliced cantaloupe, strawberries, and grapes, and reached down for the container of cream cheese. "You must be hungry. If this doesn't do the trick, I can cook you something else. I can toast that bagel as well."

He walked to the reception counter to pick up the items. "Thanks for this. Looks perfect."

"Not without these." She winked, then reached below and placed a napkin and silverware next to the food.

Opening the gate, Sunny came into the lobby. "Just let me scoot past you, and I'll get you some orange juice and coffee from the nook. First, let's set you up here." Grabbing the plate before he could, she put it down on the coffee table as he picked up everything else.

"Please. Sit."

A moment later, they both broke into laughter as they saw the dogs had obeyed John's unintentional sit command, yet were staring at them as if they were crazy.

"Oh my!" Sunny walked to the dogs and scratched each one on the head. "At ease, silly ones. As you were." She continued to the breakfast nook as the dogs resumed their play. "That was hilarious. I don't think we could have convinced them to do that if we had a million bucks at stake."

"I don't either." John picked up a piece of melon and bit into it. "I've trained Kono better than I thought I had."

"I guess they're both on their best behavior. Not sure which one wants to impress the other more."

John watched her pause as if she were playing the words back in her head, feeling the sentiment she'd just described.

"How do you take your coffee, John?"

"A bit of milk, no sugar. Thank you."

After pouring the juice and coffee, Sunny walked to the coffee table, placed them down, and sat in the chair across from him.

"Nothing for you?"

"I have the pleasure of your company. Another cup of coffee and I'll be circling the room like Miggy and Kono. Speaking of our wildly active canine children, I have a lovely backyard with a tubular picket fence. The dogs can look through it to see the ocean below, but it's way too high to jump over. Lots of toys out there as well … and way more space to run. Would you be okay if Kono went outside with Miggy?"

"If he's good to go with you, then I'm fine with it."

Sunny called the dogs, and both came running through the gate as she re-opened it. "Be right back, John."

Three minutes later, she returned. "Kono looked like he'd seen paradise when I opened my back door. His tail was wagging so hard it looked blurry. Then again, I didn't have my glasses on." She laughed. "So, tell me. How's the cottage coming along? I hope you're happy with it."

John picked up the small knife and spread a healthy dollop of cream cheese on the bagel. "This is such a treat. It's been a long time." He took a bite. "Spent a good hour and a half in the cottage talking to the guy. The new floors are in and look better than I expected. They're making some repairs and tomorrow the painting begins."

"I'm glad you found people to work on a Sunday."

"They used to do work for the previous owner. So I'm getting special treatment."

"Ah. Okay. I know them then. Great guys. Superior work

ethic."

"Wes was very thorough. Walked me through the place and showed me everything he and George had fixed in both bedrooms. As promised, Edward left the washer and dryer for me. Almost new. I hadn't paid much attention to the appliances when I saw the place, but I was happy to hear the stove and fridge had been replaced only eight months ago. Really, everything was in good condition—well cared for. But as you know, there's no stopping the wear and tear that the years will inevitably bring."

Sunny touched her face and sighed. "Don't I know it."

"Nothing wrong with how you look. You're beautiful." Stunned at the words he spoke, John smiled awkwardly and filled his open mouth with a large bite of his bagel, guaranteeing no other thoughts would dare reveal themselves.

Her face reflecting awkwardness while being simultaneously showing elation at his words, she jumped up and walked over to the nook. "Thank you. I'm flattered. And while I don't need any more coffee, I could use a glass of orange juice. And that's not pulp fiction." She laughed nervously.

As Sunny returned to her chair, John wiped his mouth with the napkin and continued speaking. "After we left the cottage, Kono and I took a long walk. This area is exquisite. Extraordinary cliffs. Did you say you own a house up there?"

"Yes, I do. The current residents will be moving in two days. Thanks for reminding me to prepare for the vacancy. It's wonderful that the area is so pleasing to you."

"More beauty than I realized, now that I live here and have the time to explore more thoroughly." He took another bite of his bagel.

"It's been so long since I last moved that I've forgotten all of the things I need to do. Once you give me an official address, I'll take care of the changes, but I was hoping you could recommend a garage in town or somewhere I can rent a parking space. I've been spoiled, keeping my car at my friend Ben's place for eight years."

"And so you shall continue to be spoiled. I have four spaces in my driveway behind the building. We had it built that way for me, Grey, and the kids when they started driving. It's just me now, and my Honda CRV gets lonely."

"You'll have to let me pay you."

"Don't be silly. It costs me nothing, and I'd feel awful taking money from you. Just consider the price included in the post box rental. And I'll have that set up for you by Monday morning."

John finished the bagel and smiled. "Okay, but you'll have to let me do something for you."

Sunny's face became solemn. "There is something actually. It's nothing I want you to do per se, just a story I feel compelled to share. Only I'm sort of between a rock and a hard place. I'm thinking maybe I should just zip it, you know?" She picked up the glass of juice from the small table next to her and took a few sips.

"If you really want to tell me and feel that strongly about it, you should." John's words surprised him. "I'm happy to listen."

She expelled a nervous breath. "Okay. Thank you, John. First, I need to make it crystal clear that what I am going to share with you is nothing I would *ever* think to tell someone on the second day we've known one another, even someone like you who I connect with. Absolutely never. In fact, I rarely tell this story to anyone. But circumstances have changed my thinking, and I hope you'll understand."

"If you're good with sharing, I'm listening." He paused. "I truly mean that."

"Thank you." She squeezed her hands together. "Well, this morning, I'd opened the side door for a guest, and I saw you and Ty having a chat on the far end of the cabins. He's like a brother to me. I see him every day, and I didn't need bionic ears to know what he was talking about."

"Ah, okay." John's face tensed.

"For the past several hours, I've been worried that what he said might have been awkward for you. I want to tell you the whole story so things will make sense, but at the same time, I'm concerned you might wish to just keep your distance from my tale of woe. And if you do, I'll understand completely."

As he finished the last morsel on the plate, a strawberry, John pushed it to the side and settled comfortably to listen. "So much of my life has made no sense at all, Sunny, so please, feel free to fill in whatever blanks you wish. It's clear how much the Gardets love you, but I did sense Ty felt torn about talking to me, yet at the same time, unable to stay silent."

"That's about as spot on as it gets. Knowing Ty, he outlined the situation for you, but said little, as he's not one to talk about my personal business."

"He said as much."

Sunny took another sip of her juice. "I'll be as brief as I can. Sure you're okay hearing this?"

"I would never say yes if I weren't. Not how I roll."

She smiled. Good to know." She shifted nervously. "So,

yesterday, I told you I was a flight attendant for three years in my twenties."

"You did."

"You see, I graduated from college with a degree in business. I'd wanted a liberal arts degree, but my father wisely encouraged me to study something I could actually use. And he wasn't wrong. But once I graduated, the idea of a job in business bored me to tears. I was only twenty-two and wanted to spread my wings, and one day, after saying exactly that to my mother, my words gave me the brilliant idea of becoming a flight attendant."

"Ah, sounds like your inner voice was prodding your outer one."

Sunny brightened. "I think you've got something there. Long story short, I was lucky enough to get a job, and I flew out of LAX. Just before I turned twenty-four, after two years, I met Grey on a flight to Chicago. The chemistry was instant for both of us, and he asked to call me when he was back in Los Angeles. After a year, we both hated that I was flying off so regularly, and he proposed. When I was twenty-six and he was thirty-one, we were married.

"I'll skip over the next several years, only to say that our children were born. In 1992, two years after our youngest, Jessica, came into the world, my father died and left me three pieces of real estate: the home on the cliff we just spoke about, this house, before it became a hotel, and the house across the street, which was a different restaurant and also the home it is today."

"And a collection of sundials, yes?"

Sunny laughed and John felt pleased that he instinctively knew how to settle her nerves.

"Yes, the sundials. My brother inherited real estate in the Bay area, where he lives now. I always feel awkward when people learn how wealthy my family is."

"Mine was too. And I did everything I could not to make it obvious. Never wanted to be stereotyped, and to this day, money has never been my guiding light."

"We have that in common. My family was so unassuming. Actually, it wasn't until I saw what I had inherited that I realized how special the properties were. My father always downplayed his wealth."

"Mine didn't." He paused to tamp down his regret. "Go on. Tell me more."

"Well, when Grey and I came to look at the properties, everything fell into place for us. My business degree, which had been lying dormant in the dark recesses of my brain, emerged with both hands waving. 'Hey, Sunny. Remember me?'"

"You're very funny."

"Funny Sunny." A sad smile took refuge on her lips. "Grey used to call me that."

"Oh, I'm sorry."

"Don't be. I love that you said that. Where was I?"

"Your business degree was waving at you."

She laughed. "It was. I never had what it takes to run a restaurant, so I just continued to rent to the family who ran a seafood restaurant. Grey and I moved into the house, and it didn't take us long to decide that expanding the property to become a hotel was the perfect fit for us. In 1993, we opened this place."

"I take it this is the background for what you really want to tell me."

She lowered her eyes. "It is."

"You okay?"

"Not so much, but I need to do this." She paused as if she were unsure how to begin. "When Grey and I were dating, he told me about a pretty awful thing that happened when he was nineteen." She looked at John as if waiting for permission to continue.

"Go on. All's good here. Say what you need to say any way you can."

Relieved, she continued. "It was his first year of college, and he met this girl, Nancy Nestor, at a local bar where he and his friends hung out. After the second so-called date, really just a hook-up at the bar, he'd had a bit too much to drink and made the mistake of sleeping with her."

John winced.

"Immediately, she became obsessive and possessive—like someone flipping on a crazy switch, he said, and he ended the relationship. Only the termination was one-sided. She stalked him, called his dorm multiple times a day, spied on him from behind trees, followed him, and did pretty much everything else stalkers do. Then, one day, she stopped hiding and stood in the hallway outside the door of his Spanish class and waited for him to come out. When class was dismissed and he saw her, he pulled her outside, not wanting his classmates to hear whatever she was about to ramble on about. That's when she told him she was pregnant."

"Oh, my."

Sunny held up the palm of her right hand. "But Grey's smarts kicked in and he simply didn't believe her. He asked for the name of her OB/GYN, and she said she'd taken a home pregnancy test. When he asked her how she knew it was accurate, she said she'd had it confirmed at a clinic out of town. No matter how hard he pressed, she was vague at best, tripping over her own words. He knew she was lying, told her as much, and walked away."

"A trick as old as time. To be told you're the father when you're not." John looked away, his face becoming rigid with pain.

"I can stop this story, John. Just say the word."

The faraway look in his eyes dissipated with a blink. "No. Go on. Please."

"Eight months later, she showed up at his dorm room with an infant in her arms and told him to meet his son, Greyson Alexander Harrison, Jr."

"I'm afraid to ask …."

Sunny put her hand to her chest and paused. "Grey didn't believe it was his, not for a moment, but he did think it was hers with another man. After he told her to leave, he mentioned the incident to a close female friend, and she told him that a newborn boy had been stolen from a local hospital the night before. He cut his next class and went straight to the police."

"Good for him." John winced. "Stealing a child; what a horrific thing for her to do. How long did she have him?"

"Three days. An eternity for the parents."

"Absolutely. What happened next?"

"There was a trial, of course, and Grey testified for the prosecution. She ended up getting eighteen years. Not sure how many she served."

"Whatever the number, the sentence was well deserved."

"It was. And you know what, she wasn't only obsessed with

Grey. She was obsessively stalking a female classmate, I heard, because the woman was wealthy, and Nancy thought she deserved a heap of *her* money because they had lunch together twice and 'best friends' share. Crazy." She took a moment to collect her thoughts. "Sorry. I really am straying from the story a bit."

John leaned slightly toward her. "I know this isn't easy to talk about. Are you okay to continue?"

"I think so." Sunny paused, took a long breath, then continued. "Back to my life with Grey. We'd had this hotel for five years. We never wanted to leave for vacation, but my brother and his wife begged us to take a trip and let them handle things in our absence. So, in February of 1998, we decided to see our first Mardi Gras. Things were slow at the hotel in the off season, and the family who'd been running the restaurant had closed shop and left town.

"As I'm guessing Ty has told you, we met him, Rolo, and Clarissa in a restaurant they were all working at in the French Quarter. We hit it off so well that we went out together after their shifts were over. Then, we learned that Rolo and Ty's parents had tragically died, that they were estranged from their family, and because of emergency circumstances, they'd all found work at this Cajun restaurant—and hated the people who owned it." She paused to finish her juice." Ty can tell you the details, but when it later came up in conversation that we were looking to sell the restaurant property, they said they'd just inherited some money, then jumped at the chance to come to California and see the area and the property. Just like with Miggy and Kono, it was love at first sight."

Right. Just like Miggy and Kono. John smiled, knowing she was trying to take the edge off her pain and determined not to let any current emotions interfere with her tale of the past. "Take your time."

He saw the gratitude in her eyes.

"We immediately set the sale in motion. The Gardets took a few months to take care of business in Metarie, Louisiana, where they're from, and then they moved up here. It took more time for the deal to close, but they stayed in the cabins until everything was final.

"Rolo was a chef by trade, and Clarissa loved the business, so it was a natural fit. Like me, Ty isn't a restauranteur. He's an artist, so although he's part owner, he didn't want to be part of the everyday operations.

"Also, Clarissa was pregnant with RJ, and the idea of living in a quiet beach town, right by the ocean, thrilled her to no end, especially knowing that the neighboring town was much larger and had wonderful schools. When I told Ty that I needed an assistant manager and handyman, and could provide him the two-bedroom backhouse to live in, it was a 'done deal' as they say." She smiled. "Bringing the Gardet family to Teal Beach was truly serendipitous, John. I love them all so dearly."

He could only search her eyes. He knew her forthcoming words would bring inconsolable pain, but he couldn't change that. Her sadness touched him more intensely than he imagined possible. "The next part of your story—it's the hardest to tell."

"Yes."

A long minute of silence rested between them. Finally, Sunny spoke. "Ty, Rolo, and Rissa were always so grateful to Grey and me, not that they needed to be, and it was rare they ever left this property to do anything more than enjoy a day's outing somewhere. When they learned that some friends from back home were vacationing in Pismo

Beach for four days, they really wanted to go but didn't want to leave us." She drew a pained breath. "I told them it was crazy, and I insisted they go and live their lives. They didn't have the additional staff they do now, but closing the restaurant for a few days was no big deal. There are others nearby and as it was a weekend in the off-season, just like now, there was no possible reason to hang around. They'd been in Teal Beach for nine years, and a four-day weekend was ridiculously overdue—at the very least."

John opened his mouth to speak, but feeling his emotions twisting and tangling, he said nothing.

"Their reluctance to leave may sound a bit extreme, so let me explain. You see, before this particular weekend, I'd been getting some strange hang ups at the hotel. I could hear someone breathing, or at least I thought I did, but I wasn't sure if it was my imagination. For two years prior, guests had reported to me that they'd seen a woman sneaking around, but Grey and I never did, and had to assume they were probably just spotting one of our more colorful guests." She made a face. "Like the one you met this morning."

Shaking off a chill, John looked at her. "This isn't a good story."

"No. It's not." Sunny wiped a few tears away, clearly steeling herself to prevent any more from running down her cheeks. "You see, Nancy Nestor had been out of prison for quite a while. And like all psychos do, they find someone to blame for their actions."

"Oh, no."

"That night, about thirty minutes after the sun had set, she showed up in the lobby. Grey was panic-stricken as he recognized her right away, and before he spoke her name, I'd figured out who she was."

"Awful."

"Being such a smart, intuitive man, Grey knew that confronting her with kindness was the best possible thing to do. Only it didn't work. She pulled out a gun and trained it on me. Told Grey he would pay for her years in prison by watching me die right before she took his life as well." She stopped talking as more tears fell. "I had never been more terrified in my life. My husband was so amazing. I don't know how he did it, but he was unrelenting in his kindness and words. She had finally agreed to put the gun away, when a road-weary traveler who'd spotted our vacancy sign, opened the lobby door, saw the gun, and screamed bloody murder. And in that instant, her scream so spooked Nancy that the gun went off, and to my horror, killed my beloved Grey instantly before my eyes."

"My God." To his surprise, John stood and put out his arms. "I'm so sorry, Sunny. That's horrible. I'm truly sorry." She rose, fell into his embrace, buried her head in his chest, and cried for several minutes. Finally, regaining her composure, she thanked him, and, sat again in the chair with a look that said she was determined to finish.

She sniffled. "I won't go into the details. For one, because I can't do it without collapsing in pain, but what I need you to understand is that when the Gardets came back, aside from their shock, horror, and agonizing grief, Ty, most especially Ty, never forgave himself for going away. He just clung to his guilt, and I couldn't convince him to let it go, no matter how hard I tried. He was certain that his having been here would have stopped this tragic event. I don't think it would have. How can any of us know? Even so, he had every right to go away."

"It all makes sense now."

"That's good. Anyway, to finish this monstrous story, Nancy went back to prison. But because of the 'accidental' way things happened, her second sentence wasn't as long as the first one. The thing is, John, for several months, I've felt that she's been stalking me again. Hang up calls, but only in the day when *I* answer the phone, and just some strange things which I won't go into. Absolutely nothing I can prove. But Ty is freaked, as am I. And that poor, dear man, who blames himself for a family vacation many years ago, is hell-bent on never leaving my side and protecting me at all costs. There's no reason for Ty to cover the front desk all night long, especially in the off-season, but he can't help himself. He insists on doing the job and won't let me streamline operations in the same manner other places do. It's not good, John, because he's giving up so much of his life. I've been wishing for years that he and Imari would marry, but he can't do it. He's afraid that if he stops protecting me, something horrible will happen."

John wiped the sweat from his brow, his face twisted with pain.

"So, when I saw him talking to you this morning, knowing you were strangers, I knew that he was telling you to watch over me. Of course, I'd told him you were moving to the cottage, and that I found you to be a fine man. And apparently, Rolo had spoken to you last night for some time and quite liked you. That was enough for Ty to enlist you in his never-ending 'Protect Sunny' army. You can tell me if I'm wrong about anything, but I don't think I am."

"That pretty much covers it. It's what you said. He was desperate to tell me, but at the same time, was very reluctant and apologetic in his nature. I knew there had to be more to it all, but I couldn't pin it down. I'm not one to ask a lot of questions. Probably because I don't like answering them."

She smiled. "I get that about you. And it's fine. I just wanted you to know why Ty told you what he did, and to let you know that you're under absolutely zero obligation to protect me. None. Please hear me."

"I hear you, Sunny, but—"

She stood. "Oh my. I should check on the lovebirds—dogs. I think they've probably had more fun than the law allows. Time to bring them in. And no doubt you and Kono need to be on your way."

Before John could say another word, Sunny had risen, opened the gate, and disappeared from his sight as she passed through the door to her private residence and closed it behind her.

CHAPTER FIVE

The crashing sound of the waves, louder when other sounds have gone to sleep, reminded John that waves never cease to cry out in their everlasting and cyclical existence.

Wearing his long black coat, the one his nineteen-year-old girlfriend, Juliana, had given him the night she called their relationship off, he could never forget how she implored him to wear it, to bury his hands deep into the pockets as her grandfather had done when he wore the coat on Cape Cod during his nighttime walks. It was a time, she said, when clarity embraced him. Only she didn't use those words. "Hugged him tight" was the closest he could remember. Normally, every word she spoke would have been etched in his memory, but those particular words were obscured by, "I've met someone, and I'm going to marry him. I've got to say good-bye." And then, in the muddle of his agony, she handed twenty-one-year-old John an old black coat, told him to put it on and repeated the bit about her grandfather—the absolute furthest person from his mind. But there was something about the torment and urgency in her voice, about how she vehemently implored him to emulate her paternal grandfather, that haunted him for decades. Why? What made her so insistent that he do so? At nineteen, what possible significance could her grandfather's solitary actions have had on her young life?

With Kono off leash, he walked on. As it always did, the white foam of the waves took center stage while the dark blue of the water became one with the night sky. Every time John would stop to look out into the expanse, or at the sky unencumbered by light pollution to see the stars, Kono would do the same.

John's previous dog, Zivar, had died at sixteen and left him heartbroken. He never believed he could find another companion as loyal or as intelligent. But one day, when he was traveling to Long Beach to see Ben, he'd just gotten off the ferry at Catalina Landing, when he noticed a woman hysterically begging everyone who would make eye contact with her, to help the Siberian Retriever puppy that some man had purposely abandoned in the crowd, with only a leash tucked into his harness.

Without giving it a second thought, he walked up to the woman with the words, "I'll be happy to take him," and that was it. As soon as John spoke softly to the frightened puppy, petted him, and properly attached the leash, he saw the gratitude in the dog's eyes and believed that Zivar had arranged for them to meet. He knew his faithful companion hadn't wanted to leave and believed that he had sent Kono to take his place. Even on the first night walk, as a playful pup, Kono was attached to John as if he'd always been with him.

As he reached into his coat pocket to pull out a bag to collect Kono's business, he felt around frantically for his lucky silver dollar. With extreme sadness, he realized that it was gone. Just like with the front hem of the coat, and a few of its buttons, the pocket stitching was loose. He made a mental note to have them fixed, or better yet, to do so himself. After all of the years, the coat was a part of him, and the thought of leaving it with a tailor bothered him. He would only have it dry-cleaned by businesses that offered same-day service. How people would laugh if they knew the coat was family to him. Or that he carried the silver dollar he'd found on the streets as a young teen, believing it would always protect him. It was like losing another part of—devastating for a man who had already lost so much.

Though able to present himself amiably when connecting with the world, he was most secure in his seclusion, where his eccentricities could run free, and he answered to virtually no one but himself. But despite living a life he had shrunk down to almost nothing, every day was not the same. The betrayal cast upon him by so many was unshakable, but by controlling his surroundings, he had become capable of managing his heartache. Most of the time.

Relationships were out of the question. Having a car on the mainland enabled him to drive all over Los Angeles to meet women, but even on the rare times he felt the possibility of a connection, he never saw any of them again. A mutual agreement for a one-night stand was all he could handle, but hurting someone, or being hurt, was not something he would consider.

He had moved past the pain of being left by his young auburn-haired beauty, (though never forgotten it), but the hell that rained down on him in the years after was the motivating force that changed him.

And so, while he found Juliana's words about her grandfather baffling, they were also intriguing. When he left New York and moved to California eight years prior, he began walking the beach at night, as her final words had compelled him to do. Instantly, he felt at one with things greater than the daylight world could offer. Trusting only his closest friend, Ben Rockley, and a handful of others, he embraced his new life, and within the boundaries he set, however constrained, he felt content to be the man he had become, and was determined to remain so.

But now, even with his blinders on, he couldn't help but see the kindred spirit in Sunny. Earlier that day, she had shared the worst horror of her life. She had accepted his comforting embrace, and it had not escaped him that for a few minutes, he felt her pain and passion simultaneously. Then, when her tale was finished, she fled to the backyard to retrieve Kono, and after thanking John again when she returned to the lobby, almost abruptly, she then dismissed him with a frightened smile and went back to work.

It took every cell of his being to fight the urge to comfort her again, to strip her unease away and let her know she had done nothing wrong in sharing the worst day of her life. But any more soothing sentiments would have been from the old John. The new John made himself vulnerable to no one.

As he felt his heart beat more rapidly, there, under the moon's light and guidance, he decided to do the opposite of what felt right and steer clear of her for a couple of days. He wondered if her abrupt end to their conversation was for her benefit or his. But what did it matter if they were more alike than he'd thought? Or if they were instantly attracted to one another? Living life on the precipice was difficult; but it was home to him now. He wouldn't fall again. He couldn't.

He walked on as she stood on the hill above, watching his every move and imagining his thoughts.

When he awoke the next morning, as the sun streamed through his window, he realized how cruel it would be to hide away for two days. He couldn't allow Sunny to believe she'd made a grievous error in judgment with her confidence. The fact that he was pulling himself in two opposite directions ceased to be important for the moment.

John had already purchased breakfast food at the local grocery store to eat in the cabin. He didn't want to socialize with the other guests, nor did he want Sunny going to any special trouble for him.

After toasting an English muffin and brewing coffee, he and Kono went down to the beach to check on his cottage, waving to Tyler as they passed at a distance. At noon, when John had climbed the steps from the beach and stood in front of the hotel, he remembered Sunny was going to give him a new address so he could make all of the necessary changes.

Hearing Queen's "Somebody to Love" blaring from the lobby, he walked in, unable to miss the way Sunny's face lit up when she saw him. Before Kono could utter a whimper, Sunny opened the gate, let an ecstatic Miggy loose, then turned down the music before she came out to speak with John.

"They're at it before I can even say hello." Sunny smiled radiantly.

"Kono was still smiling when we left yesterday. I've got to wonder what happened in your backyard."

"We'll never know. If you have a few minutes, I'd kind of like to put them there right now. I have guests checking in today, and not knowing what time, I'd prefer not to have dogs running in the lobby."

"Sure." He took Kono's leash off and put it around his neck. "Go with Sunny and Miggy, boy."

Kono looked at him as if to say thank you, then disappeared behind the gate and into Sunny's home again.

He took a seat on the couch as he waited.

In no time at all, she was back. "What can I offer you, John? Are you hungry? Thirsty?"

"I'll take one of those bottled waters you've got behind the counter. That's all I need."

Grabbing two bottles, Sunny handed him one just before taking her seat across from him, as she had the day before.

"Thanks. Hey, you shouldn't have turned Queen down. I spend so much quiet time on the beach, so immersing myself in good music is a treat."

"Actually, right before you got here, I was listening to my favorite artist from the 1980s."

"Our taste seems to be in sync. I'll bet I like him or her too."

"It just kills me that he's not making music anymore. His one and only album was such a hit. Do you know who I mean?"

"Can't say that I do."

"Whisky Devers. The song was 'Someone Who Looks Like You.' Do you know it? 'Someone who looks like you, told me we were through, and someone who looks like me ….'"

"Didn't wanna be that kind of free."

"You do know him!"

"Yeah, rang a bell after you mentioned the album. He was pretty good. Kind of a vague memory now. Ancient history."

"Not for me. I still listen to him all the time."

He smiled awkwardly and let the small talk fade.

"I need to apologize to you, John."

"I can't imagine for what." He twisted the sports cap on his water bottle. "You've been nothing short of wonderful to me."

"I was rude yesterday. After I told you my story, I all but

dismissed you. And it wasn't because I wanted to, but I felt that maybe you were overwhelmed. First, Ty unloading on you, then me."

He bent his head down. There were several answers he could give her, and he was tempted to give the easiest one. The most shallow and specious thing he could say was that he was fine on all counts. But in only a short time, his respect and admiration for the woman who looked at him was greater than his proclivity to fabricate a response. "I'm a loner, Sunny. To varying degrees, I have been for a quite a while. I'm not going to tell you differently. I have a tendency to separate myself from society … and from most people, but that's not written in stone. As reclusive as I've become, I'm not shy. If I didn't want to hear what you had to tell me, I would've let you know. And I think that if you hadn't figured that out about me, we wouldn't even be having this conversation. Am I right?"

"You are. I hope we'll be friends. If it's not too forward of me to say, I hope we already are. I just need you to know that I respect a person's privacy—and boundaries." She thought for a moment. "I guess I'm more intrigued by people who have boundaries, or maybe 'secret places' would be a better term. I'm not sure how to phrase it."

"The first day we spoke, you told me that Grey had places you couldn't reach. I believe you said he was a poet." He watched the light dance in her eyes.

"I did. You see, he was an extraordinary man and quite a gregarious one. You would never have guessed that his poetry took him to another place—an unreachable one."

"What did he write about? Don't tell me if it's too personal."

"Well, early on in our relationship, he told me he had an alter ego, one who didn't come from wealth. Please don't misunderstand,

Grey always recognized the advantages he grew up with and didn't feel he had any right to complain. But there was always another person inside of him, one who wanted to be anonymous and not have all of the labels and expectations that can come with privilege."

John nodded without even realizing he was doing so.

"And it was the alter ego who wrote the poetry. On the nights my heart can take it, I settle in my easy chair and read his words. I never really understand them because he wrote in such complex symbolism. Way above my pay grade, I'm afraid, but that's okay. I never believed that I need to know everything about everyone, even those closest to me."

Just as John was about to respond, the phone rang. Sunny frowned. "Sorry, I need to get that." She jumped up to go behind the counter and answer it. Cheerfully, she took a reservation for a new guest, then picked up a second line and asked the caller to hold. She smiled and looked over at John. "When it rains ..."

As he sat there, John felt an odd sense of relief they'd been interrupted. She'd made him so comfortable that he'd been about to share one of the many parts of himself that had long taken asylum deep inside.

Immersed in thought as Sunny spoke to the second caller, he was startled when he looked up and found Tyler smiling at him. John stood and shook his hand. "Good to see you again."

"You as well," Tyler said, taking a seat next to John as they both sat. "When I waved to you earlier, I was hoping to talk, but you were too far away. Hey, glad to catch you alone while Sunny is on the phone. She told me that she explained things to you." He sighed. "I feel way better that she did. I hated that our first conversation was so intense

… at least my side of it. Must have seemed off the wall to you. Didn't plan to do it. Surprised my damn self that all of that came out." He looked over at Sunny. "Just can't tell you enough how much that woman means to us and—"

John put his hand up. "It's okay, Ty. Don't wrap yourself up in knots over it. I get you. More than you know."

Tyler relaxed his shoulders and smiled. "Thanks for that. So listen, my bro and Rissa just made a whole heaping lot of food for a catering order. There's a bunch left over. Food so good, as they say back home, you'll be happy as a pig eating slop."

"Quite the endorsement." John laughed.

Tyler leaned closer. "They're wondering if you and Sunny would like to have lunch together. I can take over here while she's gone. Slept all night, so I'm good. Anyhow, didn't want to ask you in front of her, so you wouldn't feel pushed into anything."

"I must say. I've never met people so tuned into my eccentricities as I have before I came here. Thanks. Yes, I think that sounds nice, but only if Sunny is okay with it."

A huge smile crossed Tyler's face. "Great. I take it the doggos are in the yard. I'll check on them as well. Wanna give me that leash around your neck, or is that a new fashion statement?"

"Oh, yeah. I forgot all about this." He handed the leash to Ty. "Not much of a tie guy. Never was."

They both laughed and continued to chat while Sunny picked up a third call.

Ten minutes later, she'd finished and came into the lobby. "Like I said, when it rains it pours. Even in the off-season." She eyed Tyler curiously as she handed John a small envelope. "Here's your new post office box address as well as the street address if you need it. Silly me, you already have the street address or you would never have found the hotel." She laughed nervously. "The key to the box is in the envelope as well. Taped to a piece of paper."

John tucked the envelope into his side pocket. "I'll take care of this tonight. Thank you." He smiled. "Ty just told me that Rolo and Clarissa need us to come eat up some of the extra food they made. Care to have lunch with me? I hate to see good food go uneaten. I think that's a crime in some places. In fact, you can get more hard time for wasting food than you can for wearing three-inch heels in Carmel."

Sunny laughed, but her radiant smile needed no words.

Tyler looked confused. "You can explain that one later." He turned to Sunny. "Go on, then. Don't be taking your sweet time. Fam and food waiting."

As John crooked his arm for Sunny to loop hers through, it slipped his mind that he'd just broken every rule in his book.

CHAPTER SIX

As John walked the beach with Kono that Tuesday afternoon, only a half an hour after a rare morning of heavy rain had claimed the skies, he felt a renewal of his spirit, and a nascent appreciation for the cottage and the town he now called home. Earlier, when the rain pelted his roof and the drops slid down the bay window of his not-quite-ready-to-move-into cottage, a rare nirvana had been created. His favorite sounds—the rain and the ocean—were like nature's finest musicians performing a rare gig together. Putting aside everything he'd planned to do, he sat on his newly delivered chaise sectional, enjoying hot tea with lemon, and fell into a welcome trance.

Now, Mother Nature's second act was every bit as enthralling. The rain had refreshed the air. The hillsides and cliffs, their greens, oranges, purples, and yellows brighter than ever against the deep gray-blue, cloudless sky, welcomed him outside. He was acutely tuned in to the bird calls that he didn't normally hear and could see the soft sway of the foxtails, purple Echium flowers, and the orange poppies on the side of the cliff. The light, hitting the water just so, gave it the beautiful teal color that the beach had been named for.

As he embraced the beauty of his surroundings, Kono began to bark, and within seconds, began running east.

"Hey, boy, where are you going?" Knowing that Kono wouldn't leave his side without good reason, he ran after him. After a quarter of a mile, John could see Kono was headed toward the steps from the cliff outside Sunny's hotel. A dog he presumed to be Miggy was barking by the base. A few minutes later, seconds after Kono arrived on the scene, John's guess was confirmed. Fearful, he ran even faster.

As he approached, now able to hear the sound of sobbing, John walked under the cliff steps to find Sunny sitting in the small cave, tears running down her face. "Sunny!"

Her startled eyes looked up at him as she quickly wiped the streaks from her cheeks. "Oh, John. I came here so nobody would find me. Except my four-legged town crier decided to bark my distress—and her own. She never barks unless something is urgent. I guess her mother crying in a cave fit the bill. Do you know dogs can hear way farther away than humans?"

Miggy, now content that John was there, walked out on the beach with Kono while John sat by Sunny's side and put his arms around her, finding no resistance.

"I do know that. Why are you hiding away in this cave?" John took his index finger and softly wiped her tears away.

"I'm so scared, John. I got a very upsetting call just before Miranda covered for me. Normally, I just eat lunch behind the desk, but today I was going to run some errands in town, so having her there was pre-planned. Or maybe I should say pre-ordained. I don't know." She sniffled. "It was just hard for me to hide my anxiety, but I pulled together some nonsense about needing a beach walk more than a trip to the hardware store and the bakery. I feel like a criminal hiding in here, but if any of the Gardets see me like this, they'll ramp up their worrying several notches."

"What happened? Who was on the phone?"

She lowered her eyes. "I told you what happened to my Grey and that I've been getting hang-up calls for several months. Well, not only do I think Nancy, that monstrous woman who killed him, has been making the calls, today I believe she stepped up her game. There was this loud heavy breathing, and every hair on my body felt like it was standing on end. That's why I bailed on my errands and tucked myself away here. Note to self: when distraught, do not hurry down steps wet from the rain."

"Oh, no!"

"Oh, yes. I tripped coming down the last three of them, fell onto the sand, hit my forehead on a piece of driftwood, and then I crawled like an injured animal into the cave, crying like a fool. That's why Miggy was barking—she wanted someone to help me."

John smiled sympathetically. "Well, it worked. Are you hurt?"

"No. Only embarrassed. I've sprained my ankle before, actually on these same steps, and I'm certain this is not that. I just have a bad feeling about that call, but at the same time, it could be something else. At least I keep telling myself that."

John held her hand as the dogs entered the cave, each one resting on either side of them. "You know you can always call me. You don't ever have to worry alone."

Biting her lip, Sunny squirmed uncomfortably. "I didn't think …."

"Sunny, I had a wonderful lunch with you at Dodo Deen's on Sunday. After we said good-bye, I walked away feeling happy because I knew you that much better, and, to be honest, because I liked you even more."

"Oh, I'm so relieved."

"Did you think otherwise?" He put his hand under her chin and lifted it.

"I was just worried that you might have felt pushed into the lunch and—"

"And that's why you haven't seen me for two days?"

An uneasy look landed on her face. "Something like that. And it hasn't even been forty-eight hours, so that's embarrassing. But I didn't want you to think that every time I have a problem, I going to try to draw you into my drama."

John negated her worry with a shake of the head. "Nothing of the kind. And after what you've been through, your reaction to a call like that is nothing I would classify as 'drama.' Remember that. As for the past two days, I just had a lot of work to do, and more so, I needed time to process all of the changes in my life—emotional and physical. And the changes that are still to come, whatever they may be. Oh, and yesterday I was waiting for the couch delivery. Today, my friend Ben's men are picking up the last of my belongings from Catalina Island, and they'll be here next Monday with all of that. The rest of the furniture I bought from another store is scheduled for Saturday delivery." He looked into her eyes. "Well, that was probably way more than you needed to know."

"No, not at all."

"Good." He smiled. "I think I unintentionally rambled to get your mind off the call and anything else upsetting you. Not to mention that moving arrangements make for riveting conversation."

She averted her eyes and tried to smile. "I really did want to know your plans, John."

Noticing her unease, unsure of how to handle it, he absentmindedly twirled his finger in the sand. "I know you received my text on Monday because you responded to me." Before she could say anything, he continued. "But you worried because you thought I was being polite while simultaneously evading you. Am I right?"

Sheepishly, she made a face that told him his assessment was correct. "You're insanely intuitive, John." She smiled. "I think that's a good thing, but I'll have to mull it over and let you know." She winked, then her voice became serious again. "As you know, I've been a loner too. Just a more visible and less-obvious one. I haven't made any new friends because I have everything I need right here in addition to friends and family elsewhere. I meet people all the time, and most are very nice, but I wasn't expecting a wonderful new friend, someone I would like so very much." A long sigh escaped her lips. "I had those silly thoughts about our friendship because I forgot how to think straight."

"So you had crooked thoughts?"

She smiled. "A bit zig-zaggy, I'll give you that. I'm so embarrassed about the tears. You see, right after I got the creepy call, my son, Alex, called me to tell me his legal team won a huge and very important case. It's quite a victory, and even though I'm thrilled and proud, he could detect that something in my voice wasn't right and asked me what was wrong. I had to pull it together and make up some story. I hated lying to him and even more so that I wasn't fully there for his shining moment."

"He's an environmental lawyer, right?"

"Exactly, and what he and his team have just accomplished is truly a victory for us all. I'll share it another time." She slowed her breathing. "I'm sure he'll understand, but I felt so frightened, and then angry, that I let that horrid call work me into this lather. It's a good thing that it stopped raining when it did, or Miranda never would have bought my I-need-to-walk-on-the-beach story."

John laughed. "It *was* coming down hard."

"In buckets. Not to mention the thunder and lightning earlier."

His visage turned serious. "What can I do to help make all of this better?"

"Just be you. Continue being the wonderful man that you are, and don't worry about my sometimes-muddled brain. I know you're being honest. I can accept that and not torture myself." She took a measured pause. "And please know that you can always call me as well—for anything."

"I'll remember that. But please, Sunny, if you get any more unsettling calls, don't keep it secret. Tell *me* if you can't tell anyone else. I just can't bear to see you go through this again."

"I was tempted to knock on your cabin door, but I didn't. And you wouldn't have been there."

"No. The cottage is my home, and I'm preparing it as best as I can. When I heard the storm was coming, I saw no reason to leave since I had a place to sit and a few essentials in the kitchen. The rain was beautiful— exhilarating, really."

"You did find the perfect home for yourself. I can't wait to see it."

"Me too." John started to play with a lock of her hair, then stopped, realizing what he was doing. "Monday will be my official move-in day. I've got a lot of busy work to do in the next three days before, but if I don't see you, I'll call you. Things should settle by the weekend. I'll be around." He smiled. "No one will be the wiser about the call, though I think you *should* tell your closest friends. That's your choice, of course. But I'm begging you: never go through any of this alone. That said, I hope there's nothing to 'go through.'"

"Me too." She pulled a tissue from her pocket and blew her nose.

"Now, may I walk you back to the hotel?"

"Yes, I'm feeling much better. Thanks to you. I would appreciate that."

As John helped Sunny to her feet and she took a few easy steps, Miggy's joy overcame her. She wagged her tail so hard that it smacked Kono hard in the face. Instinctively, he turned to respond appropriately, but reassessing his options, his instinct for retribution disappeared with one look into her big brown eyes.

Smiling, Sunny and John exited the cave, breathing in the fresh ocean air that greeted them.

Walking into the diner down the road from the hotel, John debated whether to sit in the booth or on one of the stools.

"Hello, there!" said the chubby strawberry blonde woman behind the counter as she cleaned the coffee machine.

John sat on the stool closest to her. "Hello to you too."

"I'm Lucy, the owner. You're a new face. Off-season visitor?"

"I'm John. I'm moving into the cottage."

"Oh, you're the man who bought Edward's place." She replaced the old coffee filter with a new one, then stood in front of him.

"That's me."

"Can I get you something to drink? Are you ready to order?" She grabbed a menu from under the counter. "Being new, I guess you'll need this."

"Actually, I'd like a nice bowl of soup." He nodded toward the sign on the wall. "It says 'Ask about our soup du jour.'"

"It does. Today is Friday, and we have homemade vegetable or split pea."

"Vegetable, please."

"That comes with poppyseed bread. Sound good?"

"Perfect. And I'll have a cup of herbal tea."

Lucy turned to go into the kitchen, then stopped. "My goodness. I should tell you. There was a woman here the other day asking if the cottage was still for sale and where it might be."

Trying not to show alarm, John managed a brief smile. "Who comes into a diner to ask about a cottage being for sale?"

"One moment." Lucy hurried to the end of the counter to refill a customer's glass of soda, then came back. "It was one of my staff, Bethany, who spoke with her. I was busy waiting on a booth. I didn't really pay much attention."

John wrinkled his brow. "Did she say anything personal that should concern me?"

"Only that she was too late and should have looked at it sooner and that she wanted a 'look-see' so she could compare it to other properties still for sale. I only heard that snippet of conversation as I passed them. Maybe she just thought that being locals, we'd know."

"Makes sense, but still, seems a bit odd."

Lucy's face fell. "I suppose so. I'd call Bethany to ask for more details, but her mother is gravely ill, and she just flew to Illinois to be with her." She recovered with a smile. "The woman sounded friendly though. And I didn't get the idea that she had any ulterior motives." She reached for the pot of hot water. "Maybe she'd never been a prospective buyer. Who knows? Could have just wanted to sell you something—you being new to Teal Beach and all." She nodded in agreement with herself. "Yeah, that could be it too. I probably shouldn't have mentioned it. Me and my big mouth."

"I'm glad you did."

As Lucy poured a cup of hot water for him, pulling a small basket filled with herbal teas from under the counter, John maintained a pleasant smile. But the second she excused herself to get his lunch and pushed the large swinging doors into the kitchen, his stomach soured. Remembering that Sunny hadn't had another call in three days, he tried to convince himself he felt a little better. "Maybe this is just all a coincidence," he mumbled to himself. "But I'm not liking it."

CHAPTER SEVEN

Sunny smiled and handed the amorous honeymoon couple a card key and a map of Teal Beach. "Suite one." She pointed. "That dark wood door will take you upstairs, and you'll find your suite on the right. There might be a little something from me waiting for you in the room." She winked. "Congratulations again on your marriage."

John watched as the couple thanked Sunny and walked away with their luggage. Once they were out of sight, he walked up to the reception counter. "Good morning." He looked at the wall clock. "Or should I say good almost afternoon. And how sweet that you leave gifts for honeymooners."

"I do. A bottle of champagne, a modest cheese-and-crackers platter, and a small bouquet of artificial flowers. The latter is kind of a souvenir to take home for the sentimental types like yours truly."

"So, loners like me don't get anything, huh?" He smiled. "Seriously, that's lovely and so are you."

"I try." She blushed ever so slightly. I can't believe a week has passed since we met. It seems like I've known you much longer, yet at the same time, it's like you first walked through that door five minutes ago." Sunny shooed away the emotion that crept into her voice. She lowered her reading glasses, looked down at the hotel register, and made some notations. "On Tuesday, in the um … cave, you mentioned that the rest of your furniture would be delivered today."

"They said Saturday, and they meant it." He smiled. "My new furniture is beautiful."

"And the delivery went well?"

"It did. They parked on Seascape Highway and carried it down the footpath with no problem. That's why I'm here. Just wanted to let you know that all is going according to plan, and I'll be moving Monday." He smiled. "And to say hello. I was hoping to sneak in a visit these past three days. Just a lot of 'stuff.'"

"Moving is always more complicated than we expect. So I take it your friend Ben brought the last of your belongings from Catalina Island on Wednesday?"

"He did. I'm completely moved out of Two Harbors now."

"You look concerned. Maybe a bit rattled. Nothing unpleasant, I hope."

"Just happy to cut ties with people I never want to see again. One in particular. All good."

Sunny looked over the counter and realized Kono was missing. "Miggy is sleeping in the living room, but where's the boy?"

"Oh, I ran into RJ a while ago, and he offered to walk him while I get ready for Monday's move. Kono loves him. Great kid."

"Isn't RJ terrific? I think I told you Clarissa was pregnant with him when the Gardets moved to Teal Beach. And now he's almost fifteen. Speaking of time sprouting wings and flying by."

She reached over to turn up the music, then proceeded to finish checking the paperwork. "Don't you love this music? The amazing Whisky Devers. This is another of my favorite songs: 'I Wish I Knew the Woman I Love.' Do you know it?"

"Actually, now that I hear it, I remember it rather well."

"Just like Leonard Cohen, he had a quality that no other musician … hold on. Darn. I'd better turn the music down before I answer the phone. Don't want people to think they're calling some smoky coffeehouse from another era." She spoke brightly as she lifted the receiver. "Good morning. Teal Beach Sundial Inn."

John watched as the sunshine in her expression turned to a dark cloudy day. Her face froze as she hung up the phone and put her glasses on the counter. For a moment, she said nothing and stood in place.

John lifted the gate and stepped through, as if he'd done it many times before, escorting her into the lobby and to the couch so he could sit next to her. "Are you okay? What was that?" He took her hand and looked into her eyes. "Did you get one of those calls?"

She nodded almost imperceptibly.

"Do you think it was Nancy?"

"Yes."

"Oh, shit." John bit his upper lip. "What did she say?"

"She whispered, and it was very faint, but I think she said 'bitch' and then she just stayed on the line, probably hoping to hear me moaning in fear—or hoping I'd say something."

"But you just hung up."

"Yes." She clasped her hands over John's. "I'd like to tell you I'm not worried, and I know I underplay my fear to the Gardets, especially with Ty, but Nancy *is* someone who stole a newborn baby, wanted to kill me, and *did* kill my husband. Also, this is the first time she's said anything—if it was indeed her. Like she's stepping up her game and testing the waters. At least that's what my gut tells me. So there's that."

John pulled her to him as the tears ran down her face. "Try to slow your breathing, Sunny." As he rubbed her back, Clarissa, dressed her in embroidered Dodo Deen's polo shirt and jeans, walked into the lobby.

Alarmed by the sight of Sunny in distress, Clarissa stood still and made eye contact with her, just as she'd reluctantly pulled away from John.

"Oh, no, girl. Oh, no, no, no, no." Clarissa turned to John for clarification.

"Yes. Sunny got another call."

Mumbling expletives under her breath, Clarissa took the closest chair. "The breathing thing again? She hasn't done that for a while now." Her eyes widened as Sunny's face gave her the answer. "No way! She spoke this time?"

"Yes, and I didn't tell you before, but she called me on Tuesday with just the breathing."

"You should never keep that from us, Sunny girl. So tell me what she said just now."

Sunny's face contorted in pain. "She just said 'bitch' and then stayed on the line. Like I told John, I think she wanted to me say something back."

"Yeah, a make-my-day kinda thing so you could give her a reason to eff with you some more. You know what the Rolo-man and Ty are going to say when they hear this, right?"

"Please, Rissa. It'll be okay. I just freaked out for a moment there. You know I have an alarm under the counter now. And the police regularly drive by and check on me. Besides, the voice was so faint, it might have been someone else. I can't know for sure."

"Sugar, even if it wasn't her, anyone calling to whisper 'bitch' at you isn't a good thing. And heavy breathing isn't so cool either. You know all this, right? And you answer by saying the name of this place, so it couldn't have been a wrong number. You hear me? I don't trust that raving lunatic. People like her hold grudges until the cows come home—and they're the ones who have no business being grudgy with anyone but their damn selves. I know you don't want to hear this, and I remember how hard you fought us on it before, but it's long past time for security cameras so we can watch the place from across the street, so you can see the lobby from your home, and also be able record what might be happening live."

"No, absolutely not." Sunny stood and began pacing.

In seconds, Clarissa was right behind her. "Honey, I know it's an invasion of your privacy. Most of the time, this is like your home. Well, it *is* your home. Just the open-to-the-public part of it. My point is, no matter what you call it, you need to be safe here. And you're not always behind the desk with your fingers a hop skippety jump from the alarm. You hear me? We just love you so much and want you to be okay. And you know we can't be monitoring the lobby every minute, but it's one more thing to give you better protection. Not to mention if someone else reports seeing a suspicious person, isn't it a good thing that we have some kind of CCTV footage?"

John watched from his seat. He wanted to say something, but to do so at that moment felt like he would be interfering with a family discussion.

Sunny stopped. "I'll think about it. Can we just table this discussion for now? Please. I'm too overwhelmed and I feel like anything else now will put me over the edge."

Reluctantly, Clarissa nodded.

And you know I'm always happy to see you, Rissa, but you almost never come for a visit until the afternoon. What's up?"

"What if I said my psycho radar was doin' overtime." She looked at John. "Not talking about you." She turned to Sunny. "If I told you I just felt compelled to pop in, would you believe me?" Clarissa offered a playful smirk.

"That would be a no."

Putting her arm around Sunny's shoulder, Clarissa returned to where John was sitting. "Rolo Junior just brought Kono over for a visit and told us that John's move is on for Monday. So, we were hoping that the two of you would come for dinner after you lock up tonight. We'll put the sign on the lobby door. Anyone needing to get in can call Ty's business cell and we'll transfer the hotel phone, just like we always do on the rare occasions that we can pry Mr. Tyler Gardet away from the desk at night."

Sunny squirmed uncomfortably, trying to gauge John's reaction with only a sidelong glance. "We were your lunch guests only six days ago, on Sunday—"

"I know, honey, but this is sort of a farewell to John leaving the hotel after a week, and simultaneously a welcome for moving to Teal Beach. All rolled into one tasty feast cooked by my smokin' hot husband who will have the staff wait on us so he can be part of the celebration. And yes, I know we recently hauled the two of you over there, but really, can anyone get too much of the Gardet family? Don't answer that." She smiled. "Besides, this is different. That was the two of you. This is a family party. Ty's invited Imari to join us as well." She looked apologetically at John. "This isn't how we usually do things— having the guest of honor be the last to know and all. Not even close. It's just that we got the idea when we heard you were moving to your cottage Monday, and we ran with it, bumbling track stars that we are.

Translation: in typical Gardet fashion, we were a bit overenthusiastic. But it's what y'all love about us, right?" She paused. "But you can say no and there won't be any hard feelings. No BS. We're not in the business of ambushing dinner guests." A mischievous smile landed on her lips. "Although not a bad idea, but the advertising, not to mention the implementation, could get a little tricky."

Through her rattled nerves, Sunny laughed. "Your sense of humor was the first thing I liked about you all of those years ago."

"It's gotten me through many a hard time." Clarissa smiled at Sunny and John. "Well, what do you say to dinner? C'mon. It's Saturday night."

John looked at Sunny. "I'm in if you are."

"Sure." She let out a sigh of relief. "Sounds like a welcome distraction. If nobody mentions the calls, or anything remotely related to them, then I'm good. Just for this evening, I'm asking for a moratorium on the subject."

"I'll make sure that promise is kept." Clarissa sighed. "Great then. We've got ourselves an exclusive dinner party." She looked at John. "Fair warning: if you don't come over now and get that gorgeous and lovable dog of yours, we might not be able to let him go."

John stood. "I'll get him right now." He looked at Sunny. "Think Miggy would be up for a backyard playdate?"

"She's missed him terribly." Sunny reddened as John pretended not pick up on what she really meant.

"Okay, Clarissa, lead the way. I'll pick up the boy and then Sunny and I will see you all later this evening. He smiled at Sunny before he turned to go, hoping that he could somehow distract her from the ugliness of the call.

"This was the nicest evening I've had since Grey was still in this world." Standing outside of the hotel, Sunny waited for Tyler to go inside before she continued. "I know that dinners like this aren't your thing. I hope you didn't feel pressured to accept."

John smiled awkwardly as Kono pulled toward the front door. "No, boy. Miggy's asleep in her home. We'll see her tomorrow. Sit."

Kono gave him a defiant stare.

"Sit, *please.*"

Kono obeyed, but banged his tail on the ground three times in defiance as Sunny and John shared a laugh.

John met Sunny's gaze. "No, I didn't feel pressured to accept. And you're right. I don't socialize like this. Not ever. Not in a very long time—because—well, I just don't. But you and the Gardets are tough to say no to." He managed a warm smile. "And I'm quite good at it. Saying no." He paused to search for words. "No regrets, Sunny. It was a great evening."

"I'm so glad."

He turned to watch the ocean for a moment, his eyes longing to be down on the beach, then remembered he'd taken his attention from Sunny. "Sorry about that. My mind wanders. Just like I do."

She offered a gentle smile. "I understand. Very much so. By the way, I *am* going to get security cameras put in. For everyone's sake." She looked at the door to the hotel. "I wish Ty wouldn't insist on sleeping in there at nights. It's not necessary."

"Seeing how you got that call earlier, I'd wager a guess that tonight isn't the optimal time to talk him out of it."

She frowned. "I know. But he can't keep sacrificing the quality of his life for me. You saw what a special woman Imari is. They're so much in love. He should be with her. Not on a cot behind the reception desk. For all of the guilt he has about me, I have just as much regarding him." Her shoulders dropped. "That's why I'm going to agree to the camera system. If there's a way to find out if Nancy or someone else is behind the calls, despite the few I've gotten, then it's time to make that happen so we can all go back to living without fear, guilt, or whatever other unwanted emotions routinely take hold of us. I hate being captive to past horrors." She looked at John in mortification. "Oh my goodness. I don't know much about your life, even though I do believe I know something about the man you are, and what just I said, I'm sure, even though I can't articulate why, was an appalling choice of words. I'm so sorry."

Pained, he looked toward the beach again, then down at Kono, who was now lying on the ground, bored with human conversation. After a moment, John surprised himself by putting his hands on her shoulders. "No apologies, please." He thought for another moment. "Sunny, I'm not trying to play the mysterious stranger who appears in town with a suitcase full of secrets, intent on making everyone tiptoe around him so as not to set off landmines. That's a pretty messed-up equivalence, but I hope you get my point." He took his hands away. "I wish security cameras could fix what haunts me. But they can't. Over the years, I've just worked out a lifestyle that suits me the best. Once in a blue moon, like right now, I wish I were different, but still, I don't want to make a change. Being vulnerable is a bitch."

"I understand. And I wanted to die on the spot when Jacie asked what kind of work you do."

John turned toward the beach again. "Clarissa deflected her question like a pro, but none of you should have to do that. Look, between you and me, I write songs for popular artists—under another name. My love of music goes way back, as I know yours does. That's really all I want to say about it, but I want you to know I'm not into any illicit activity. And sometimes I play music, but only for Kono. An audience of one."

"I see. Have you ever wanted to widen your fan base?"

He spoke softly. "I've had a lot in my personal life to contend with, so I just keep it simple. No, I don't, actually. And I write what I'm asked to write. Not necessarily my taste or desire. The songs I sell for other artists are not works of art by any stretch of the imagination. Just commercial garbage a lot of the time."

"I'm sorry, John. I shouldn't have asked."

He turned again to the ocean. "Do you ever think about what's under the surface of the water? An entire civilization. What they call the 'deep ocean' accounts for something like sixty percent of it, or so I've been told. The diversity there is extraordinary, and in so many ways, I think it must parallel life on land. It's not without predators, not without problems and as beautiful as it is, it can be ugly. But that underwater civilization needs to be preserved, just like ours. On land, it's even more difficult. There are just too many people who will destroy everything for their immediate gain, ego, vindication, revenge, money—you name it."

Feeling her eyes on him, he turned around. "I know the wheels must be spinning in your head, wondering what the hell I'm on about.

Sunny, I meant it when I said it isn't my aim to make you or the Gardets walk on eggshells around me. And I know I was rambling, battling with past demons. I didn't mean to do that. What you just heard was not a trailer for Mystery Man Theater. Just me mumbling aloud. And yeah, I suppose I *was* avoiding an uncomfortable subject by talking about another one, but I didn't mean to intentionally digress like that. Here I am telling you not to worry about what you say, and then I'm taking mind trips to avoid what's uncomfortable for me. That's messed up, I know."

She crossed her arms and rubbed them to take the chill off. "I want you to be exactly who you are, John. I can't say that more strongly. And yes, I'm human—sometimes strong and sometimes fragile. I think about everything. I wonder about people. I have questions, but that doesn't mean anyone needs to change for me. If you can't be yourself around a person, you'll never truly care. I mean—be comfortable with that person. I do hope we'll be friends."

He took a step closer to her to take over the rubbing of her arms. "We already are. And it's cold outside. You should go. I'm going to take Kono for a walk and then get some sleep."

The dog stood and wagged his tail.

Sunny smiled, wanting to say so much, but settling for two words. "Goodnight, John."

"Goodnight." As he walked a fair distance away, he spoke to the dog. "Just let me grab my coat and we'll go to the beach."

Ten minutes later, Sunny, now wearing a brown winter parka, stood in her yard with Miggy at her side and watched John and Kono down on the beach. "I almost feel guilty, John. Watching you every night as I do, so high up that you never know I'm here. A large part of me feels as if I'm invading your privacy, and maybe I am. But when I see you next to the ocean, I understand you, and I'm right there with you. And that feels so good."

CHAPTER EIGHT

After nearly knocking John onto the floor with his enthusiasm, Dodger gleefully reunited with Kono who'd just finished greeting Ben.

"My dude," Ben said, giving John a hug. "Good to see you. But honestly, I was happier to see the Subaru. I mean, she was in my driveway for eight years, whereas you just popped by occasionally. Oh, and she never tried to steer me wrong."

John laughed. "Well, I hope you two had a warm embrace in the parking lot. As long as you kept it PG. And when did I ever steer you wrong?"

"Never. Just didn't want to pass up the car joke, lame as it was." He petted Kono who had come back for a second round of affection, while a jealous Dodger nuzzled his way in between them. "I'll tell you something, though. I think having your car in my driveway protected me. The reason I'm an hour late is because I had a flat. Found a couple of tacks under the back right tire when I went to check it out."

"If I was the kind of guy to make lame jokes like you just did, I'd say that was a tacky excuse. Aren't you glad I'm above that kind of thing?"

Ben laughed. "Touché!"

John shuddered, his palms beginning to sweat. "Yeah. Score one for me, but, I'm not happy to hear that. Where do you think the tacks came from?"

"Someone put them there. Could've just been random, meaning kids or something. I'm not gonna worry about it. Still got here way ahead of Jimmy and Mateo, as I'd planned, though I did call and tell them to take their time. They should be here in about an hour, and we'll move everything outta this cabin and into my truck while they unload the stuff from theirs. And you'll be good to go." Ben sat on the bed. "So, I see you've met a woman. One who is definitely not your type."

John leaned against the wall, his expression more serious. "What the hell are you talking about?"

"Sunny Harrison. I met her in the parking lot. She'd been watering plants on the porch and came to say hello. 'Dark Side of the Moon' was blasting in the lobby. Could hear it from the lot, and so we talked about Pink Floyd, Queen, and some other groups for maybe fifteen or twenty minutes. Even told her I played drums with the band in Long Beach. When I said I was here to help you move, and that you were my closest friend, for real, dude, her hundred-watt smile ratcheted up a few notches. Not messing with you. Her eyes told me everything I needed to know." He studied John's face. "Sort of like your eyes are telling me now. Damn, you couldn't have overcorrected more after that accidental one-night-sleepover last week with the spiky-haired exhibitionist. Only I know you, John, and when I say Sunny's not your type, I mean that she's fucking perfect for you, and that means you're probably keeping an emotional distance, and definitely a physical one, because everything in me says you like her as much as she likes you." He paused to take a breath. "Okay, tell me what part I got wrong."

John said nothing for a long minute. "Oh, I don't know. The part where you just opened your mouth to speak."

Ben smiled crookedly. "That's the man I know. Confirmation by way of an absence of denial."

"Smart ass." John bent down to give Kono some human attention as Ben did the same with Dodger. "So, do you want to see the cottage or wait for Jimmy and Mateo to get here?"

"Let's wait for the guys. I need to eat first. But I know I'm going to love it." He sighed. "Seriously, man. This is the perfect town for you. I hope you'll take the armor off and let yourself feel again."

John walked over to the kitchenette to wash out the coffee pot.

Still sitting on the bed, Ben swiveled around to face him. "I wouldn't have even touched this subject with a ten-foot pole if I hadn't met Sunny. You know that. But the minute I met her, I just knew. And you both confirmed it in your own ways. So, that said, I can't watch you sabotage your happiness, and I might have to be a pain in your ass."

John rinsed out the pot a few times until all of the soap was gone, then laid it back on the coffeemaker. "You might find yourself *having* a pain in the ass. You hear me?"

Ben waved off the remark. "I'm trembling in fear." He laughed. "So where are you going to keep your car now? Did you find a space in town to rent?"

"Found one closer." John walked away from the kitchenette and stood by the cabin door.

"Where?"

"Somewhere nearby."

"What's the big secret? Why can't you tell me?"

"It might be in Sunny's driveway behind the house. She insisted." He looked at Ben and smirked. "Wipe the damn grin off your face. Come on, I'll take you across the street to Dodo Deen's and buy you lunch. Put something in your mouth to keep the drivel from pouring out."

Ben chuckled and looked at the dogs. "I might have forgotten that Sunny offered to keep these canine dudes in her backyard while we were moving. Sounds like we should take them over there now if we're going to chow down, huh?"

"Yeah. If you lose the grin." He turned to Kono. "Come on, boy. Let's go see Miggy."

"Who's Miggy?"

"Sunny's labradoodle. Kono's new girlfriend." He stared at Ben, twisting his mouth. "You know, Benjo, you've got the loudest damn thoughts I've ever heard. You want to ask them to pipe down."

Ben laughed. "I just love that you've met someone. Best news in a very long time."

"Well, gentleman, how did it go?" Sunny asked, standing behind the reception desk, as Kono and Dodger reunited with their respective fathers.

"Quick and easy," Ben said. "Most of the time we move people, it's far more complicated. But we'd already moved John's things from Two Harbors, so getting to the cottage without any large furniture was a cinch. Not to mention he doesn't own a lot."

"Thanks, my friend." John patted Ben on the back while giving him a knowing look not to say anything.

Ben smiled to taunt his friend. "I think this move is the best thing you've done in a long time. And now I'm going to hit the road.

Taking my daughter and her mother to dinner tonight." He addressed Sunny. "We've been estranged for years. My ex and I are trying to get over past hurts and put our family back together."

"Oh, that's lovely to hear." Sunny smiled. "How old is your daughter?"

"Avery's eleven. And I really want to be a full-time father to her. Tearing down walls has been harder than I imagined. But I realized they were crumbling to bits, and so, hey, why not rebuild, I told myself. You know? Anything's possible when you want it enough. Even when you gotta do it brick by brick." He shot John a look but turned back to Sunny before John could return it. "Anyway, Dodger and I need to hit the road. Sunny, it was really nice meeting you."

When Ben and Sunny exchanged good-byes, the two men, with the dogs now on leashes, walked out to the parking lot and over to Ben's truck.

"You've come up in the world with this cottage, John. Way nicer than Sabelli's. The kind of place you can really build a life."

"Brick by brick?"

"I was just messing with you. I don't think Sunny picked up on that or in any way thought I was also talking about you."

John's eyes narrowed. "You don't, huh? She's way smarter than you're giving her credit for. Nuances don't escape her notice. You think she didn't know you're putting your stamp of approval on something that's not likely to happen? Or trying to forecast the future as you imagine it?"

Ben opened the door of his truck. "Hop in, boy." As Dodger took his seat and Kono whined at the separation, Ben leaned against the door. "I seriously suck. I wasn't trying to do anything that would cause a problem. But hey, just the fact that you know that much about her after such a short time says something. You never have that kind of insight into any woman you meet, and that's mostly because you're more comfortable scraping the bottom of the barrel."

"I'm a regular scum connoisseur. Tell me something I don't already know."

"I didn't mean—"

"Thanks for moving me, Benjo. For *most* everything you do. And when I get my computer set up, I'll be sending some new songs your way. But please, don't push me with this nonsense, because you know I'll go in the opposite direction. Just because Sunny is an amazing woman, that doesn't change *me*. And if anyone in the world knows that, it's you."

Ben looked at the ground, then at John. "You're right. I messed up. I'm sorry. I was just so blown away by Sunny, and picturing the two of you together, that I flipped the off switch on my common sense for a moment or two. My bad. For real, but I still believe everything I said. Just gotta be quiet about it. Oh, yeah. One other thing. I told her you saved my life all those years ago, but I didn't give her any details. You're free to share, if you want, if it comes up in conversation down the line. You know, when you open up to her. I don't mind." He scratched the top of Kono's head. "I know *you* still love me." He put out his hand to John. "We good?"

John responded with a warm hug. "For the record, I have no plans to open up to anyone. Drive safe, big mouth. I'll talk to you tomorrow. Have a good night with Avery and Kathryn."

When John and Kono returned to the lobby, Sunny was sitting on the couch, listening to Aerosmith, much lower than normal, and sipping a cup of tea. "Let me get you a cup, John."

"No thanks. I'm good." He sat next to her. "I'm only going a half mile, but it feels strange."

"It does. And I hear whimpering in stereo. Let me free Miss Miggy from the dungeon behind the desk." She laughed as she rose and walked over to open the gate. Within seconds, the dogs were racing around as if they'd been parted for years.

"Nothing in the world like happy dogs."

John nodded. "I agree. And hey, I want to show you the cottage—after I unpack and have it looking like a home."

"Take your time. This will be a hectic week for me, and I know you've got a lot to catch up on after having your life packed away in boxes." She smiled nervously. "You know the home I own, up on the cliff?"

"Sure. You've mentioned it a couple of times."

"Well, the previous tenants vacated on Thursday and it's been cleaned, so I'll be showing it to a few interested parties. If you see Miranda or Larae at the reception desk, it'll be because I'm out showing the place. Also, I've got a new guest moving into one of the suites and several more cabin rentals. And the security people are coming to install cameras. Just a lot of busy happening." She reached in her pocket and pulled out a card. "This is the hotel number, of course, you have my cell, and the house phone is on the back." She smiled at Kono. "And yes, you're welcome to call Miggy."

"Thanks." John took the card, glanced at it, and put it in his shirt pocket. "I gave you my cell number when I reserved, yes?"

"You did." She turned to watch the dogs play—an uneasy expression on her face.

Damn, Sunny. Benjo scared you with that brick-by-brick, crumbling-walls crap. I knew you picked up on it. I can't even tell you I'm sorry without making things more uncomfortable for us both. "Well, you take care of business, and I'll see you sometime next week. Thank you for everything. Your friendship, your hospitality, your understanding, the parking space—just being you."

She gulped, then smiled as if, suddenly shy, she didn't wish her words to be heard.

As John stood and motioned for Kono to come, Sunny also stood and called Miggy. In that awkward moment, he could only thank her again, and she could only think about watching him walk the beach, her secret place, where she could always speak freely and walk alongside him.

CHAPTER NINE

"I'm so happy you had this system installed," Clarissa said as two men from the security company walked out of the lobby with their gear. She took a seat on the couch. "You can't be too safe in this world, and I don't say that expecting anything to happen to you." Her eyes swept the lobby. "Sunny, sit for a moment while the place is empty, will you? You haven't stopped moving. Please, chill for a few."

"Sorry, Rissa." Sunny sat in the chair on the other side of the coffee table. "I'm glad the cameras are in as well. I just wish it wasn't necessary. This whole thing has frazzled my last nerve."

"You know what they say, honey, about bringing an umbrella so it won't rain? That's the way we need to look at this."

"I suppose."

"Only you're not only thinking about the security cameras. You've got John on your mind as well. Yes?"

"Am I that pathetically obvious?"

"Let's take that *p* word out of the question, okay?" Clarissa offered a sympathetic smile. "When's the last time you saw him?"

"Three days ago. Monday. When he moved out. He finally texted me this morning. He said he's not feeling great, hasn't forgotten me, and will be in touch soon." She let out a long sigh. "I don't know why I was hoping he'd find a reason to be back here Tuesday or Wednesday. I guess it's all for the best. I was out showing the house and would've been so frustrated if he'd stopped by when Miranda was filling in for me."

"From what you told me about the man, and from what these

eyes see, he doesn't socialize with anyone. Yet, twice he said yes to my offers for lunch and dinner. Gotta wonder why. Hmm. Let me see?" She pretended to caress her chin in deep thought. "I know. Could it be because he *really* likes you? My oh my. I think I'm on to something."

Sunny made a face. "So both of those meals *were* to get us together?"

Looking around as if she were searching for an answer or someone else to blame, Clarissa shrugged, suppressing a smile. "Maybe. But we really like John. A lot."

Sunny's eyes smiled. "You need a good scolding, Clarissa Raye Gardet. Anyone ever tell you that?"

"Just my mama. And not for years. It was when I was sixteen and we were living in a rental home in Fat City. I put pillows under the covers to make it look like a body was sleeping. Then, I climbed out my bedroom window and tried to scale the trellis. Would have gotten away with it too if the darned thing didn't bust on me as soon as I stepped on it. Fell on my ass and wailed like a baby. Better that I almost broke my butt because the boy I was escaping to see would have broken my heart and something else. I was fixing to do what I never should have done and don't want Jacie doing; don't think I need to spell that out for you." She laughed.

"I'm glad you survived—all of it." Sunny's expression turned serious. "Truly, I feel blessed that you care in all the ways you do. But listen to me, Rissa. I'm imploring you not to do it again. Don't try to rope John into any more meals. I'm really afraid the third time would *not* be the charm. Not only that, despite how I feel, I'm scared to death of loving someone again. Tell me you hear me."

"Afraid it might be too late to stop the love, Sunny girl. But I understand how complicated feelings are, and I get how a person's desires can be at odds with each other. What's in your heart and what you act on can be very different things." She sighed. "Don't worry. I'm gonna behave." She glanced at the camera and waved at it. "That's just in case Rolo is watching. Hey, I was happy when John brought his friend Ben in for lunch on Monday. I played it real cool and gave them the space I give all customers. But yeah, I hear you. And I'll bitch-slap the matchmaker in me if she dares to rear her ugly head again."

Sunny chuckled. "Thank you. And you're a piece of work."

Clarissa shifted in her chair and leaned back. "What's up with the cliff house? Did you rent it?"

"Yes. I did."

"And you look so miserable about it because …?"

Sunny paused to mull over her answer. "Well, I just wish I liked the couple better. As soon as I met them, he pulled me aside while she, a young woman three decades his junior, was admiring the view from the deck. He told me she's the party who will be renting, not him. Apparently, he lives in New York *and* LA, and she's a 'friend' he will 'visit' from time to time."

"Oh, puh-leeze, Mr. Philanderer." Clarissa twisted her lips and shook her head. "Sounds like he's using his mistress's name so as not to leave a paper trail for the wife to find."

"Something like that. Anyway, she filled out the application, I checked her credit, and she signed the lease. It'll come as no surprise that *he* gave me a hefty deposit and insisted on paying me upfront for three months—in cash. There was something very controlling and off-putting about him. Even his wardrobe looked controlled. An odd thing to say, maybe, but I could see he wears tailor-made clothing and loves cuff links and Italian shoes. Oh, and every hair on his head was gelled precisely into place. And his nails were manicured."

"How about the girlfriend?"

"Bleached-blonde hair, tight clothing, too much makeup, and long red nails. Actually, she seemed rather sweet. I didn't mean to sound judgmental in my description. I just got the distinct idea that she looks the way he wants her to. Like she's his doll to dress up, you know?"

"Hmph." Clarissa rolled her eyes. "That could describe five million men in LA. And five million women too."

"You think? This man, though, whose name I've temporarily forgotten, has some kind of hubris. I saw that before he said hello. All business. Steely eyes that stared at me through black rectangular glasses. *She* was renting the home yet was all but muted after he deigned to let her say hello." Sunny exhaled in disgust. "Grey would have hated him. As you know, he grew up around the same kind of people and that's why he wrote poetry. To escape their ilk and the way they stained humanity. That's what he always said. Writing helped him to find another world to exist in, if only for a while." Sunny stopped for a moment. "In fact, I'll bet you Grey wouldn't have even rented to him. I *know* he wouldn't have."

"I don't think he would have either. So why did you?"

"Because the other prospects I met were flaky, and I didn't get the idea they were serious. I was certain they would have changed their minds had I accepted them. Or perhaps trashed the property once they did move in. When I met this couple, I just couldn't come up with a plausible reason to say no, especially as she seemed nice. That's fine.

I don't want to waste time on screening and meeting more prospective tenants. I never see these people, and I'm being a bit silly in wanting to like everyone who crosses my path. Grey used to tell me that all the time. I know that appears to contradict what I just said, but he happily rented to people who he wouldn't have had as friends. But this guy, well, different story."

"I knew what you meant." Clarissa nodded toward the door as she stood. "Here's a new guest. And hey, she looks friendly. Lots of luggage, which is way better than having a lot of baggage, right? Though some people do have both. See you later, my sweet." She laughed as she headed out the door.

"Hello!" Sunny said brightly. "You must be Harper Kinnison."

The thirty-something-year-old woman, a mop of reddish-brown hair loosely held up by a large tortoiseshell clip, wearing khaki cargo pants and a black ribbed top, smiled at Sunny. "I am. Sorry I look like such a mess. I just drove down from Vancouver, so that's my excuse. And you're Sunny Harrison, I'm guessing."

Sunny walked over, shook her hand, then hurried behind the desk. "I should have said my name before confirming yours. Where are my manners?"

Dropping a large Louis Vuitton satchel bag on the counter, letting go of the luggage she'd wheeled in, Harper looked at Sunny and sighed. "You're the nicest person I've met in a while. You have a great smile, for starters. And happy eyes."

"That's sweet. Thank you. Can I get you something to drink, Harper? You look road weary."

"Aww, I knew I liked you. I forgot to buy water when I filled up the last time. That would be so appreciated."

Sunny held up an index finger, then stooped below to grab a bottle from her minifridge. "Here you go."

"Thank you." Harper took the bottle, cracked the top, and guzzled half of the water. "So I think I was a wee bit thirsty." She straightened and put the bottle on the counter. "Now, what do you need from me?"

"ID and a credit card." Sunny reached for her reading glasses and put them on. "I'm going to put you in Suite Four. You said on the phone that this would be an extended stay, but you didn't know for how long."

"Correct. I'm from the East Coast. I'm a writer, but I can't get much done around friends and family," Harper said as she went through the items in her bag to get to her wallet, then put the water bottle in a side pocket of her backpack on the floor. "Too much to distract me." She scratched an itch on her cheek. "I've been all over trying to find a place I could chill. I went to Catalina Island, but I felt too confined there." She handed Sunny her ID and credit card. "Then, a friend invited me to rent the spare room in her Vancouver condo, but when I got there, all she wanted to do was 'party hearty.' Something I've never been into but am over it all the same. Didn't stay there but a few days." She laughed awkwardly. "So, I heard about Teal Beach and here I be, Just li'l ol' me. I have a good feeling this place is going to work out."

Sunny waved as one of the town's residents walked in and headed for his post-office box.

Turning sharply to look at him, the carefree look on Harper's face disappeared as she waited for the man to walk out again. Unable to downplay her interest, she studied the stranger with meticulous curiosity.

Sunny smiled, trying to pretend she hadn't noticed anything out of the ordinary.

"Oh, sorry. That man, he just looked like someone I know who I couldn't imagine would be here."

"As they say, we all have our doppelgangers. Just so you know, because many cottages in Teal Beach are inaccessible to the mail carriers, we have postal annexes, and I happen to run the one for Teal Beach. So, several of the residents come and go."

"Oh, that's great!"

Taken aback by Harper's enthusiasm over mailboxes, Sunny kept the same fixed smile on her face as she swiped the credit card. "You said you 'heard about Teal Beach.' We're not exactly known for our wild nightlife. Did a former visitor recommend us?"

"Well—oh, not exactly. I meant that I found it on the Internet. I was looking for quiet beach towns on the California coast, so that's how I 'heard' about this place. And this hotel had the best ratings, not to mention the view and accessibility to the beach."

"Ah," Sunny said as she handed back the cards. "I'm glad we stand out." Just as she was about to direct Harper to her suite upstairs, she was startled when her new guest, once more, craned her neck to look at yet another middle-aged man walking into the lobby.

"Guess where we're going this fine Friday?" Sunny said to Miggy, who was sprawled out on the living room rug, next to her bed.

Miggy's eyes looked up at Sunny, but she didn't move.

Sunny sat on a nearby chair and reached down to pet the dog. "Don't you remember who called your mom last night?"

Her expression unchanging, Miggy could only stare.

"John called. He invited us to have lunch at his new cottage."

Unimpressed, the dog looked down in a funk.

"You can stop moping, sweetheart. Just like I did. We're going to see *Kono!*"

Miggy, who'd been stretched out and resembling a shag rug, immediately sat up, her energetic temperament reset to normal.

"That's the bouncing ball of energy I'm used to." Sunny stood, checked the lobby monitor to see if Miranda was okay, then began to prepare for the day. "I know, I'm one to talk. Honestly, Miggy, it's been four days since we've seen those two fellas, and my feelings are clearly deeper than I've allowed myself to believe. And I think you might be a bit head over paws about Kono."

Hearing the name again, Miggy stood, wagging her tail, her eager eyes telling Sunny there was no time like the present.

"Soon, girl, we'll leave soon."

"Oh, hi. I guess you're not Sunny."

Miranda Velasquez smiled as she looked up from the register and brushed a tendril of her long dark brown hair out of her face. "No, I'm Miranda. My sister Larae and I both work here. Housekeeping is our regular job, but we also fill in for Sunny when she needs us. Like today. You must be the nice lady Harper who moved in last night."

Harper smiled as she gave the lobby a once over. "Aww. Thanks for saying 'nice lady.' I was more exhausted than I thought when I checked in. I just got up a while ago so I missed the breakfast, but that's totally okay, because I'd rather have a hearty lunch."

"Wish I could make you one. I used to cook at my *tia* Isabel's restaurant. I'd tell you my best dishes, but I might make you too hungry." She smiled. "In fact, I think I make myself hungry thinking. Especially for fajitas. 'As fresh as Tommy Lopez's mouth,' my *tia* used to say." She made a face. "That makes no sense if you didn't know Tommy, but still, you get the idea."

"I think I do." Harper smiled. "Can you recommend a nearby place to eat? I see there's a restaurant across the street, but I'm more in the mood for a triple decker club sandwich and fries, something I do *not* crave regularly, because I also don't crave wearing a bigger size."

Miranda offered a pleasant nod. Just as she was about to speak, a young man, wearing distressed designer jeans, an expensive blue-striped cotton shirt with a gray-blue sweater over it, dark sunglasses, and a baseball cap, walked up to the desk. "Um. Hi. Got a cabin I can rent? Like in the back."

"Oh, yes we do." She handed him a sheet of paper. "Here are our off-season rates. Do you know how long you want to stay?"

He glanced at the paper, looked at Harper, then his eyes made their way around the room, focusing on a woman going into the post office annex and a male guest in the gift shop. "Do I need to tell you now? Like specifically for sure?"

Nervously, Miranda reached for the tendril of hair she'd

pushed away and wrapped it around her finger. "No, we do have vacancies now. As long as you have proper ID and a credit card."

"Yeah. I got them."

Miranda attempted a smile, then looked at Harper, who was clearly scrutinizing the new guest. "Lucy's Blue Sea Diner is down the street about a mile. Across from the Kenwood Pines Motel." She turned to the young man, unaware that she was now tapping her fingers on the counter. "They're a good deal less expensive there, I should say."

"Are you trying to get rid of me? Do I look poor or something?"

"Oh, no, I'm sorry. I was just saying that ...."

"Well, people, I'm going to fly," Harper said brightly, as if trying to shake off her apprehension. "Nice to meet you, Miranda. Thanks."

Taking an ID and credit card out of an expensive leather wallet, the young man unintentionally slapped them on the counter, startling Miranda.

She picked up the ID to examine it. "Good afternoon, Mr. Dylan Coates."

He scanned the room again, then leaned forward. "Don't say my name out loud like that again, okay? Ever. I don't like people in my business. Or do you charge extra for privacy?"

"Of course we don't. I didn't mean to do that. Sorry, Mr. Co— how long do you wish to stay? You know, approximately."

"Let's start with a week. So do you have a cabin in the back?"

Miranda exhaled, drumming her fingers on the counter. "Yes."

He groaned. "Listen, I just don't like people watching me come and go. I'm not an ax murderer or anything. My luggage is outside in the Mercedes. Do you want to inspect it? For axes? Guns? Knives? Poison darts? Voodoo dolls?"

"Goodness gracious, of course not."

"So you'll tell everybody else not to blab, right? I just want some quiet. I've got a lot of studying to do."

"Oh!" Miranda exhaled, her relief obvious as she processed the cards and handed Dylan a key. "I see. Very nice. I should tell you that we have a continental breakfast in the lobby every morning from seven to ten. We also have—"

"I don't need anyone to feed me. I'm good. And so is my credit card, in case you were wondering. Brand new. Nothing on it."

"I believe you, sir." She smiled. "We're happy to have you here. Welcome."

"Yeah, okay. Whatever. Thanks."

As Dylan quickly left the lobby, Miranda was startled by the ringing phone. "Good afternoon. Teal Beach Sundial Inn."

"Ha ha ha ha!"

"Excuse me."

"Tell the bitch I'll call again."

Helplessly, Miranda hung up the phone, looked up at the camera, and waved frantically, hoping the Gardets would see her distress.

Within a minute, Rolo raced through the lobby door.

CHAPTER TEN

As if they'd done it hundreds of times, John and Sunny embraced as soon as he opened the cottage door. Looking into one another's eyes as Miggy raced past them to greet Kono, both were aware of the close proximity to their respective boundaries.

After reluctantly separating, Sunny looked down on the deck at the glazed pot of mixed succulents she'd brought with her. "It was a bit heavy to carry, so I rested it here as soon as we arrived."

"Gorgeous." John picked up the pot, acknowledging to himself that he'd purposely eliminated the word "it's" so he could compliment *her* instead of the succulents.

Dressed in a long, open sweater over her black V-neck top and slacks, wearing a sun pendant and matching earrings, she was the epitome of beauty and class to him. "Come in, please." He carried the pot to the dining table, placed it in the center, then walked back to her. "How did you know I needed a centerpiece? Thank you so much. It's extraordinary."

"You're very welcome. Hey, you've got John-Lennon glasses which I guess, are actually John-Hennessey glasses. I've never seen them before."

"Ah, yes." John closed the door and touched the gold-rimmed, round glasses. "I do need them for work and reading."

"Well, they suit you perfectly."

His tussled long hair had been nicely combed and he smelled ever so faintly of cologne. He had shaved since he last saw her, but not for at least a day. The light denim shirt he'd chosen to wear was tighter than usual and showed off his rugged physique.

Scanning the large room, Sunny smiled at the dogs playing with a knotted-rope toy. "John, this cottage is stunning. Believe it or not, I've never seen the inside before, but I can already tell you've improved it. These wood laminate floors you had installed are gorgeous. I love the muted grays and browns. Perfect choice. And this room is larger than I imagined. Oh, your walls match my sweater."

"So they do." He pointed to his left. "Bedroom here, then bathroom, kitchen, laundry room—and my office is to the right in the second bedroom. Everything else is out in the open. Just as you see it."

"Your favorite place must be this chaise sectional by the window. And you bought it in teal. Well, how sweet is that. Can we sit?"

"Of course. In fact, I was wondering if you'd like to eat lunch on the coffee table instead of the dining area table."

"Any time I can look at the ocean, that's what I choose. Every time."

"Me too."

She walked to the large sofa and sat, leaving the chaise section free. "Oh, comfy. I see you have two dog beds next to one another."

"I bought the second one on Tuesday when I was shopping for food and everything else. I figured Miggy might get tired when she comes over."

Clearly overwhelmed by the meaning behind his words, she choked, offering only a smile.

Fully understanding, and realizing that the purchase of a bed for Miggy made a powerful statement, he swerved until he was back on the road. "I'll bring lunch out. But I don't know what you'd like to drink. I have wine, sparkling water, apple cider—"

"Apple cider. And I'll pretend it's champagne. Drinking in the middle of the day, even a glass of wine, doesn't leave me as sharp as I like to be."

"That makes two of us."

Ten minutes later, with a beautiful tray of small sandwiches and cut fruit before them on the coffee table, the dogs in their beds, chewing on their rawhide-free treats, John and Sunny sat for a moment in silence, watching the waves.

"By the way, if you're wondering about these tea sandwiches, my aunt had a catering company in Scarsdale, where I grew up. I worked there when I was fourteen and fifteen and learned to do this kind of food prep which I've had almost no opportunity to put into practice until today. Which is fine with me."

Sunny turned to him. "Ah! That explains it. I've been in Teal Beach for a long time and I didn't recognize this food from any establishment in town. I was wondering where it could have come from, but I couldn't think of a polite way to ask."

He laughed. "'Did *you* make this?' would have been fine. Just don't tell anyone. Even Ben doesn't know I can make tea sandwiches. I'd never hear the end of it if he did. He can be relentless with his torture."

After returning his confession with a smile, she looked into his eyes. "Kidding aside, I do understand the need to be a private person. Because I was a flight attendant and now own a hotel, *and* am outgoing by nature, people often mistake me for someone who will happily share everything. Only they're so very wrong. What I told you not too long after we met, about Grey, well, that was because of circumstances, but still, you're far from being *anyone*, and I think I would have shared soon enough. With you. Only because the past has shaped so much of who I am today."

John picked up a stemmed glass of apple cider and held it in the air to clink Sunny's glass. "If there was ever anything more appropriate than that to drink to, I don't know what it could be." Regret filled his eyes. "Sunny, I don't want you to be afraid to talk to me. I just don't know how to get back to some semblance of the person I used to be." He replayed the words in his head. "Correction, I don't want to go into reverse, but at the same time, forward gear is a bit frightening. I'm good with the road I can see in front of me, not so good where my line of sight ends and maybe the road just drops off."

She reached over and picked up a second mozzarella and watercress sandwich. "Is that what happened to you, John? Did the road disappear when you got to the end of it?"

"One drop-off I could have handled. Probably two. But there were at least four of them that sent me flying off edges I never saw coming. So that's why I only move in small increments. It's safer. There's just been too much, Sunny." He picked up a tuna-salad sandwich and ate it in a few bites. "What you've been through losing Grey, the fact that you kept the hotel and still carry on, well, it's impressive."

"No. I just kept on running the business that Grey and I built together." She paused. "You didn't have an opportunity to carry on?"

"Everything and everyone that mattered was taken from me. I can't even count the number of people who betrayed me. No. That opportunity never presented itself. Not really."

"I'm so sorry. If I didn't have the Gardet family, not to mention my children, my brother and his wife, I'm not so sure where I'd be, who I'd be, or what I'd be doing now. They're all the reason I kept going. And I knew it's what Grey would have wanted."

"You have a lot of wonderful people who love you." He watched as the dogs got off the beds and chased one another. "I did carry on, Sunny. I'm still here, but I whittled my life down to a very small and manageable size." He touched her hand. "Hey, I really wanted to come by this week and see if you were okay, but the move and all of the shopping did me in for a few days. When I texted you that I was unwell, I meant it. I slept half of Wednesday. I think I overdid it moving in, then shopping for everything. Which is fine."

"You texted me every day to see if I was okay. And that meant a lot."

"I hate texting. I'd rather call. Just was out of sorts. I'm very happy you got the video surveillance system in. Hope that psycho hasn't called since we spoke last night."

"I hope not. I've had Miranda fill in for me three times this week, so I have to wonder, if Nancy did call, would she tell me?"

"I don't know Miranda, but your safety is paramount, so keeping that kind of information to oneself wouldn't be like telling someone you don't like their outfit. It would be a necessity for their safety."

Sunny took a sip of cider and put the glass down. "You're absolutely right."

Seeing the fear in her eyes, he put on his best smile. "Hey, you always have music playing when I come into the lobby. Would you like me to return the favor?"

She looked at him with pleading eyes.

"Sorry, Sunny. I hear your unspoken words. But the stuff I write doesn't deserve an audience. Even if that 'audience' doesn't agree."

"It was worth a silent try." She shook her head ever so briefly. "No, I shouldn't have looked at you the way Miggy looks at me when she wants a bite of my food. I was wrong. You told me how you felt about playing your music for me, and I—"

"And you're human? You're curious?"

"Something like that. But I asked with my eyes which was just as bad as having asked aloud."

"I told you last weekend, I'm not jonesing to play the mystery man, though I get why I might be perceived as one. I want to get rid of that part of me, most days, but can't seem to do it. I've punched the guy's lights out a few times, but he's like those Bozo bop bags that pop back up when you thought your right hook had annihilated him."

Sunny laughed. "Be kinder to your mystery man. He's a part of you and he's trying his best."

"Some days, maybe." He blushed. "Well, to give him credit, he keeps me sane. Most of the time."

"You know, I was just telling Miranda that I haven't played Leonard Cohen for a while. Do you happen to—?"

John stood. "I certainly do." He nodded toward the floor. "Well, will you look at that?"

The dogs, having worn themselves out quickly after their second wind, were snuggled up together on Kono's large bed.

Neither knowing what to say, Sunny grinned. "Well, guess I don't need to worry about that mother-daughter talk Miggy and I never had. I suppose things happen when it's love at first sight."

Turning to hide his emotion, John walked over to his stereo system and pressed a few buttons. Within seconds, Leonard Cohen was singing "Dance Me to the End of Love" loud enough for every passing seagull to hear.

"You didn't have to walk me back to the hotel, John, but I'm glad you did. When I said that dinner with you and the Gardets was the best time I've had since Grey's been gone, as wonderful as that evening was, it's now the second best. Today was special. As is your friendship."

"Same here," John said, choking on the sentiment as they crossed the porch and he opened the lobby door for her.

As the dogs ran in, John and Sunny looked surprised when Tyler, not Miranda, was at the front desk and Clarissa was standing there with him.

"Oh, Ty. Hello. I guess Miranda wasn't able to cover my … ahem … six-hour lunch." She smiled, then frowned. "And that's not why she isn't here, is it?"

"She had no problem staying," Tyler said. "But I just thought maybe I should guard the fort."

"You know we're all dedicated to you, honey," Clarissa said to Sunny.

John called Kono over and unhooked the dog's leash that he was dragging around the lobby.

Sunny did the same with Miggy as distress creased her brow. "Rissa, please. No prologues or disclaimers. Just tell me. Whatever it is, I can handle it."

Clarissa walked over to the couch and gestured for Sunny and John to sit down before she sat in the opposite chair. Tyler came from behind the reception desk but only stood.

Sunny turned to John. "My goodness. You don't have to be sucked into whatever this is."

"Try and make me leave," he said, tenderness in his voice and on his face.

She responded with a soft smile.

"So here's the thing," Tyler said. "Miranda had just checked a young guy into a back cabin. Same one you lived in, John. And as soon as he left, the phone rang."

"Oh, no." Sunny put the palm of her hand on her chest. "What did *she* say?"

Tyler winced. "Can't be sure who it was, now, you know that. But the woman laughed and then said …."

"Tell the bitch I'll call again," Clarissa finished for him.

"Yeah. That." Agitated, he looked around. "Good damn thing I don't have hair like my brother. I reckon I'd have pulled it all out by now. Guess that's why the good Lord saw fit to render me follicly challenged." He balled his fists in frustration. "Miranda didn't know what to do, so, wisely, she motioned to the camera, and Rolo just happened to see her while he was making the gumbo. Came running over here like a madman. He wanted to stay, but his boo" —he glanced at Clarissa— "sent him back to the kitchen and called me."

"Indeed I did. None of his staff can cook it like he can."

Sunny nodded. "I'm very glad you did that, Rissa, but you didn't have to stay here either."

"I needed to talk this out with Ty. Besides, your new guest, Harper Kinnison came over and introduced herself to us. So, Ty and I chatted with her for a good bit. Anyway, I wanted to tell you that I ran into Carolyn Wentworth yesterday, the owner of Kenwood Pines. Said she gets ugly calls from time to time—and that some other places do too. Over the last year 'n all. Don't want you to lower your guard, but maybe it's not Nefarious Nancy. But even if it's not, it's still a very worrisome thing."

John wiped the sweat from his brow as he watched the dogs play on the other side of the lobby. "Maybe it's not. But this could be a case of 'Be careful what you wish for.' It's true, though, people who run businesses get all kinds of calls from pranksters and lowlifes, but with all Sunny's been through—"

"Of course. Believe me. No precaution should be spared when it comes to our Sunny Honey. Just so you know, Miranda called Larae right away." She looked at John. "Larae is married to Sergeant Raphael Lanzo. He's on the town's police force. They've been checking on Sunny for a long time, but he asked that we let him know about every call."

Sunny turned to Clarissa. "Well, there is good news here."

"What's that, honey?"

"I already had the security system installed so I don't have to worry about a Gardet intervention on that matter." She smiled. "I say that with so much love and gratitude, Rissa. Just couldn't resist a little cheek to lighten the tension. Something I learned from you."

"Score one for Sunny. Well, I just wanted to be here to tell you what happened. It's the witching hour for dinner guests, so I do need to scramola."

Just as Clarissa stood, Harper walked into the lobby. Her eyes landed on John, staring at him intensely before turning to Sunny, then looking at them both. Feeling everyone's tension, Clarissa hurried to the door to speak to her.

"Hello, again, Harper. Did you and your muse have a good walk on the beach?"

"Oh. Lovely day. Yes."

Sizing up the stranger, Clarissa blocked her line of sight to John and Sunny. Harper squirmed as she unsuccessfully tried to get another look at them.

"Something wrong?"

"Can I ask you something?" Harper whispered. "Maybe out on the porch?"

"Yes, out on the porch sounds very good," Clarissa gently but purposefully led her by the elbow out the door. "What's on your mind? Your happily-go-luckiness seems to have taken a walk of its own. Clearly, it didn't come back when you did. Maybe you wanna go back to the beach and retrieve it."

Harper, who couldn't hide the fact that she was flustered, continued speaking. "I-I was just wondering. That man with Sunny. They look cozy—super comfortable with each other and everything. Are they an item?"

Clarissa reeled back, put her hands on hips, widened her eyes, and poked Harper with a stare. "Honey child, I'm looking at you the way my Gramma looked at me when I asked something that was none of my darn business. Which wasn't too often, I might add. Because I quickly learned better. At a much younger age."

"Oh, well, it's uh … you know … uh …."

"No, actually, I don't know. So why don't you tell me, Harper?"

Fiddling with her fingers, Harper stammered. "I'm sorry. It's just that I really like Sunny so much and so, uh, when Ty mentioned earlier that Sunny had bought this place with her late husband, I just thought it was so sad he was gone so young, and I was thinking maybe that man was her boyfriend. I'm just a hopeless romantic. See, I write love stories. Not typical romance, but angsty love."

"Well, well. I'm flattered," Clarissa said, her head turning slowly from side to side. "You just wrote a little piece of fiction for me now, didn't ya, sweetie? I mean, I don't know what you actually *do* write, though I do remember the word 'mystery' in your conversation, but that bit about just hoping Sunny was happy with a new man, well that's a crock of bullfiction. Is that a writing term?"

Harper exhaled a bit too loudly. "No, really. I meant it."

"Those were some angry eyes I saw eyeballing Sunny. That's the way I look at women who make passes at my husband. Or hold their stares a bit too long. You hear me?"

"That man *is* very handsome, but I prefer men my own age. Like thirty-five or so. Really, I swear."

"Fine then. Why were you staring like that?"

Harper looked up at the hanging pots, but they had no interest in helping her. "I was just trying to memorize his looks. He reminds me of a character I'm writing. Seeing him was like my guy coming to life. Whatever it looked like, it wasn't that. I swear on everything precious to me, Clarissa, I'm not attracted to him."

Clarissa gave her a hard look. "I have to go run our restaurant. I don't have time to play "dance around the point" anymore. You need to leave your crazy at home, or you just might find someone with more of it than you have. You dig? We'll get along just fine like we did earlier, Harper. But if you do anything to make my friends or family uncomfortable, or worse, I won't be happy. I wish you good luck with your book. Just be respectful and that's how you'll be treated. Okay?"

"Uh, yeah." Harper looked nervously toward the ocean. "I think I'm going to go watch the sun setting. That always inspires the romantic in me."

Clarissa smirked, then waited as Harper headed toward the steps to the beach. *I didn't just fall off the turnip truck. I'll be keeping an eye on you, little missy.*

CHAPTER ELEVEN

His legs stretched out on the chaise sectional, John listened while Kono lapped up his breakfast. "You know, boy, the food will still be there if you eat it slowly." As the sound of the empty metal bowl rattled on the floor, John stood, ready to embark on their morning walk. "Guess you snarf it down like that to get out onto the beach more quickly. That and well, you're a dog." He laughed. "Let's go then."

Opening the door, he almost tripped on what lay on the deck below: a bouquet of faux purple flowers, tied in a purple ribbon, with a note scribbled on a heart that had been cut out of a larger piece of paper. He picked them up and read the note: *My dearest John. Just like these flowers, our love will never die. xo*

John could only stare. A million scenarios raced through his mind, none of them making sense. He was unable to deny that he and Sunny had feelings for one another, yet they also understood one another's fears. There were both spoken and unspoken agreements between them. They respected one another, didn't they? It was impossible that he'd read her so wrong and that it had only taken one long afternoon for her to show a completely different side of herself— a side he didn't even believe existed.

Where would she get these flowers? Then he remembered. She'd told him that she regularly left a bouquet of faux flowers for honeymoon couples as a souvenir. There's no way she'd buy them on an individual basis. She had to have a stash of them. But Sunny wouldn't do this. No, it was antithetical to everything he knew and intuited about her.

As he processed his thoughts, the past, once again, came flooding back. Some of the betrayals had come from those who clearly resented him, but others, well, he hadn't expected such horrible things from them, yet those things happened.

Only, flowers and a declaration of love wasn't necessarily a "horrible thing," except under the circumstances, if Sunny had left this, and if he'd been so wrong about her, he was in one hell of a spot. But no, he couldn't be wrong and scolded himself for doubting her at all.

His mind tumbled backward, as it often did, to the time when he was twenty-one, and Juliana, who'd professed her love for him many times over, suddenly left him for another man. He hated that the memory still lingered, especially during his night walks, but yet, he wore her grandfather's old coat that she insisted he take with him. She was only nineteen when she broke his heart. Maybe her youth and inexperience had tricked her into believing John was her true love until someone else had opened her eyes to what she believed was the real thing. He never saw the breakup coming.

But this was different. Sunny was a mature woman, who'd lived through tragedy and pain and had a spirit that radiated understanding. How ironic, no matter who left the flowers, that the shattering of love and the declaration of the same both felt like a betrayal.

Many years after Juliana married, he'd heard she'd divorced her husband. But when he quietly searched for her, he learned that she'd remarried and had a child. That was the turning point, when all thoughts of reuniting were finally laid to rest. At least that's what he told himself. Clearly, she'd let the past go, something he hadn't fully been able to do. And now here he was again, contemplating her place in his heart that he had long ceased to acknowledge. She didn't leave the flowers, and she also lived three thousand miles away. It had to be the way she'd stepped out of her persona that shocked him. Just like Sunny was doing now. No, *not* Sunny. No, no, no! *Not* Sunny.

There was too much to untangle. First, he had to know for sure. But how could he even ask his new friend without offending her to the core. He'd have to find a way. He couldn't move on with anything until he'd ruled her out, despite being very sure it was not her doing. He shoved the flowers into the pocket of his jacket, grabbed Kono's leash, and left.

As he walked the beach, slowly heading toward the hotel, he remembered the continental breakfast. People always lingered in the lobby until after 10:00 a.m. He definitely needed to see Sunny alone. "Well, Konhead, I hope you're up for a long walk. I've got a couple of hours to kill, and you know I think better by the ocean.

"How did I get so lucky seeing you two days in a row?" Sunny flashed a smile as she finished wiping down the breakfast nook. "I still have a secret stash of food, so if you're hungry, fear not."

"That's very kind."

Kono whimpered as he fixed his stare on the reception desk.

"Oh, sorry, Kono. Ty is taking my girl for her morning walk. I'm afraid you'll have to be patient."

The dog looked at Sunny, then wide-eyed at John as if being

adorable would make things right.

"I can't make Miggy materialize, boy. But you are awfully cute. Like Sunny said, you'll have to wait."

"Coffee is still hot. Are you sure I can't get you a cup? Little bit of milk? Something else?"

John smiled. "Thanks. Coffee would be nice. I had something to eat earlier."

"Have a seat. I'll join you in a moment."

Walking to the couch with a stubborn dog who had his head fixed at a right angle while he stared at the gate, proved a more arduous task than John imagined. "Really, boy. You're scarily human right now. Come on. Move. Patience is a virtue. Surely, you want to be virtuous." He smiled to himself. "Maybe not."

A cup of coffee in hand, Sunny walked over with a smile. "I love the way you engage with him on such a deep level. Some people think I'm insane when they hear me pouring out my heart to Miggy." She sat in the chair across from him. "So, as the saying goes, 'to what do I owe this honor?'"

John eyed Kono, who'd slumped to the floor in a funk, then looked at Sunny, his expression similar to the dog's. "I just had something very confusing happen."

Sunny's smile disappeared. "You're scaring me, John. What is it?"

"I'm not sure how to explain this. It's on the delicate side."

"The direct route usually works the best. At least it does with me."

He took a sip of coffee to buy himself an extra moment or two, certain that his action didn't go unnoticed.

"Really, John. What's wrong? Now you're freaking me out."

He reached into his jacket pocket, pulled out the faux bouquet, and rested it on the coffee table. "I found this outside my door this morning."

Startled, Sunny picked up the bouquet and examined it, finally seeing the crudely cut heart and reading the words on it. "What on earth?" Her hands touched both sides of her forehead and pushed her hair back. "This is Teal Beach. There aren't a lot of people around. You've barely moved in. Who even knows where you live? Do you have any idea who might have left this or written this note?"

"No. Absolutely none."

Unsettled by his distress, she leaned back and sighed. After a moment, she jumped, almost as if physically shocked. "Oh, no, John. Please tell me that you didn't think I left these for you."

His expression went blank as he just looked at her. "No. I didn't come to that conclusion. Far from it."

"You didn't come to that *conclusion*." She inhaled a deep breath. "So you considered it?"

His mouth opened, and the words forced themselves out. "I didn't want to, Sunny, but it was the most obvious yet simultaneously least likely scenario. I can't even say I considered it. More like I fought with intrusive and insane thoughts. But no, I do *not* think you left anything on my deck for me. I *know* you didn't."

Wiping away a tear in the corner of her eye, she sniffled. "The fact that you considered it, even briefly, is a totally natural response. I get that. Especially since we've only known each other just shy of two weeks, despite the fact that it seems like much longer."

"It does." He took a sip of his coffee, waiting for her to

continue.

"I don't know if you're familiar with Occam's Razor, but it's a theory that suggests that without consideration, the most obvious answer is usually the correct one. Something like that." She paused. "Only in this situation, it's not. And if the situation were reversed, how could I not at the very least think about the person I'd last spent time with, and felt a strong connection with." She paused. "But this is *nothing* I would ever do, possibly not even if we were … well, you know. These flowers and this note are so far from any mindset I would ever have." She stared at the flowers. "Oh, goodness. I told you that I leave flowers for newlyweds, didn't I? That had to have crossed your mind."

"Sunny …." He felt her distress as he saw panic in her eyes.

"I can show you the flowers I use for guests, John. Come on. They're in a closet in my gift shop. And they're nothing like these. Not even close."

He put the palm of his hand up. "Sunny, please. I don't need to see them. I just need to figure this out."

She stood and turned away. "I'm sorry. I'm being totally unfair to you. I understand why you engaged the thoughts of my culpability that you did. I told you that I would have done the same. And it's not that I'm angry." She brushed the air on either side of her head away, as if banishing visible thoughts. "I'm just completely thrown by everything that's been going on. And here I am making this about my bruised emotions when some unknown person has left a creepy gift at your front door."

John rose and went to her, stopping before he could put his hands on her shoulders. "But this very well could be about you and not me, or both of us together, so you have no reason to apologize at all. And maybe it's just for me. I hope so. You've suffered enough."

"Do you think I wouldn't be upset even if that bouquet were just intended for you? Not knowing who left it, we can't know the true message. I just feel as if the universe is punishing me for opening up after Grey's death, and it's pulling me back into its dark recesses and telling me to stay put where I belong." She stopped, visibly attempting to calm herself.

"Oh, Sunny—"

"And that phone call last night. Could Nancy have left you those flowers to torture me? To torture us? I don't even know where she is now. And how would she know you and I were friends? Nobody has seen her, and we aren't even sure she made the calls. But if not her, then who? I truly do feel as if my world is spinning out of control again. How can I understand why your mind first went where it did and be hurt at the same time? Isn't that as illogical as it gets?"

"Not really, Sunny. Not at all. The stress of those phone calls, and now this has brought you to a breaking point. It makes complete sense for you to be so upset."

"Upset doesn't begin to describe what I'm feeling. And no! Nothing makes sense." Her breathing became labored as she spoke.

"Sunny, please try to calm down." Disgust washed over him. "Sorry, I know that's the worst thing I can say, but nothing else is coming to mind."

"I can't calm down. And I despise that you're seeing me like this." She paused. "Larae is working today, and I happen to know she's just finishing the last cabin. She and Rafael are saving for a new house and she's trying to earn as much as she can. I'm going to ask her to fill in for me today. At least for as long as she can. I need to go home and decompress. If that's even possible. I'm sorry, John. I can't talk to you now. I can't talk to anyone."

John turned to leave as Sunny tearfully pulled her cell out of her pocket, and Tyler walked in with Miggy.

While the two dogs cheerfully reunited, Tyler looked at Sunny, then at John. "I've only been gone a half hour. What happened?"

"I'll let John tell you. And no, I'm not upset with him so don't come to that conclusion when he explains it all. I'm just a mess. Ty, if you could just watch the desk for a few minutes, I'm sure Larae will be here shortly. I'm calling her now." She looked at Miggy. "You might as well visit with Kono for a bit instead of watching your mother fall apart." Without another word, she got up and disappeared behind the desk, then through the door to her home.

John and Tyler waited until Larae had taken over at the front desk. Leaving the dogs inside, they stepped out onto the porch and sat on the teal Adirondack chairs closest to the beach.

"Take your sweet time," Tyler said. "I know this isn't easy. I've got no idea what happened, but I get the feeling there's nothing pretty about it."

Taking care not to leave any details out, John offered a pained recap of the morning's events.

When he finished, Tyler's mouth fell open. "What in the Sam Hill? Where to start with this plumb craziness?" He softened his tone.

"On a personal note, I know Sunny will come around. She made it clear she doesn't blame you. I know you're not used to seeing her run off like that, all teary-eyed and agitated, but she hasn't let anyone new into her life since Grey was killed. Not a soul. And yeah, the two of you are similar in ways, but she can throw a person off, bubbly as she can be with some folks."

"Yes. She's told me as much."

"My family and I couldn't be happier you two are friends, but hell, even after a long time has passed, there are always kinks to be ironed out." He thought for a moment. "Imari and I are still ironing." He smiled, then turned serious. "Any way we can figure out who left that for you?"

"The only person I thought about was Nancy Nestor, only as Sunny said, nobody is sure she's the one calling. And how would she even know or think to do this?"

Tyler nodded. "One other thing. We've kept it on the down low, but it won't come as any surprise that we're checking the property for anyone poking about. None of us have caught a glimpse of anyone who shouldn't be here, and that's how we all want it to stay."

"That's good, Ty. But just to be clear, you're only able to monitor anyone who passes through *this* property, walks down to the beach, then on to my cottage. If someone is accessing the footpath from Seascape Highway, like the guys who moved me in, you have no way of seeing any activity at all. Am I right?"

"No. We don't. It's just with Nancy on our minds, we're all just thinking that she couldn't resist snooping around or trying to spy on Sunny. But your point is valid. Wish it weren't."

"Yes. Making this mystery all the more difficult to unravel."

Tyler sat up straight. "Wait. There's someone else it could be."

"Really? Who?"

"I don't believe you saw her, but there's a new guest named Harper who's staying in Suite Four. A writer. Pretty lady. Mid-thirties, I'd say. Seemed real nice when Rissa and I were talking to her, but later, she came back into the lobby, just as Rissa was leaving, and her eyes stuck to you and Sunny like super damn glue. But she was way more interested in you than Sunny."

Discomfited, John paused to search his memory. "I don't think I saw her. That doesn't ring even a distant bell."

"That's because Rissa sprung into action when she caught sight of the woman's unusual eyeball action. Pulled her out here onto the porch. Care to guess what Ms. Harper wanted to know?"

"I'm clueless." John turned to look out at the ocean, then returned his focus to Tyler. "What?"

"She asked if you and Sunny were an item."

"What the hell? A guest who's a complete stranger asked that?"

"Damn straight she did. Rissa gave her a verbal whacking about sticking her nose in other people's business. The thing is, we don't believe any of her excuses 'cause when the first one didn't take, some baloney about hoping Sunny had found happiness after losing her husband, she then told Rissa that you reminded her of a character in her love story, being that she was some kind of 'angsty' romance writer. Only she told us she wrote cozy mysteries, whatever the heck they might be. *She's* the damn mystery."

John rubbed his arms. "Well that gave me chills."

"Did me too. Rissa had to hurry back to the restaurant, but she told Harper that she needed to be respectful if that's how she wants to be treated in return."

Just as John was about to respond, Larae opened the door and stood in place. "Hi, there. Just returning Kono to you. Sunny decided she needs Ms. Miggy after all." She smiled politely "Sorry to interrupt, gentlemen."

"You didn't. Thanks, Larae." He smiled at Tyler. "Can you believe it? She thinks we're gentlemen."

They shared a much-needed laugh as John held out his arms to receive Kono, who was standing on his hind legs and kissing John's face. When Kono had finished his show of affection, he lay down on the porch, facing the ocean, and let the men continue speaking.

"Back to what we were talking about. Aside from Harper, I can't think of another soul it could be." Tyler reached to one side and grabbed the bottle of water he'd brought with him. He took a sip. "But just because I can't think of anyone else, doesn't mean it has to be either of those two."

John closed his eyes for a moment, then looked at Tyler. "I'm more worried about Sunny. She means more to me than whatever delusional stranger left those faux flowers and note." He paused. "Hey, do you think there's any chance that because I just moved in, the gift giver thought they were leaving them for the previous owner, Edward? Did he have a mistress or anything?"

"Hmm. Possibility number three. With the money he has, and all the time he spent there, could be, though I doubt it. Very decent man. I don't want to speculate or gossip. Like I told you the first time we spoke, John, we're not the nosy-ass neighbor patrol."

John hit his forehead. "The flowers and note weren't for him. Forget I even mentioned it. I feel like an ass. My name was in the note so it couldn't have been for Edward. I'm so disturbed, I can't think straight."

"Oh yeah. Forgot about your name being in the note my damn self."

Lost in thought, John slipped into a sadness he was all too familiar with. Finally, he spoke again. "I really hope Sunny will be okay."

"We're all gonna be as well as we can, John." Tyler took a long drink of water before putting the bottle down. "The stuff we live through shapes us, but it doesn't have to break us. I think this might be the opening to tell you the part of my own story that I left out of our first conversation."

"Well, I haven't exactly been open about my past, so really, there's no reason you should feel compelled to tell me anything. Even if I had …."

Tyler made a windshield-wiper motion with his hands. "I want to tell you because it feels right. Now if you don't want to hear it, that's a whole other thing."

"Please." John looked him in the eyes. "Tell me whatever you want."

Tyler took a long moment to find a starting place. "First people we ever told were Sunny and Grey. Then Imari after she and I were seeing one another for a time. No one else." He paused to breathe deeply. "I think you know that we were in a bad place when we met the Harrisons. Like I've said, coming to Teal Beach saved us."

"Yes. You made that very clear."

"To help you understand, I've gotta go back a bit. My mama, Mary Deen Gardet, was the sweetest lady I've ever known, God rest her soul. My father, Tyler Gardet Senior, was a mean and often-abusive drunk. Most of his tirades were directed at us boys, never our sister, Viola, but sometimes at our mama too. That was the worst. We would have taken the abuse any day over him talking that nasty shit to her. He didn't like that his younger son was a 'sissy cook' and his older son was a 'sissy artist' and blamed that on her raising us wrong. Rolo was working as a cook, and I was working as a bartender then, but the fact that I carved wood and sold my art just stung him to the core. And Rolo wanting to be a chef. Oh, he hated that. You'd think knowing that so many famous chefs came out of Louisiana would have opened his eyes, been a source of pride to him, but not for that macho drunk. He used to say, 'Cheffin's okay for other people, not for Gardet men. We stay outta the damn kitchen and leave the ladies be.'"

John sighed sympathetically. "Hard to get around people with that kind of chauvinistic mindset. May I ask what your father did for a living?"

"He was a construction worker. Known for taking to drink the minute his work day ended. They called him 'Ty-one-on Gardet.'" Tyler lowered his eyes. "I can't even tell you how that shamed and embarrassed our family."

"You don't need to, Ty. I get it. Go on."

"Well, sixteen years ago, I was twenty-seven and Rolo twenty-five. We all lived at home because it was a huge house, bought and paid for, and we were all still single. If the old man hadn't been so abusive, Rolo and I would have moved out long before our twenties, but we stayed to protect our mother and sister. One night, our father was more pissed than we'd ever seen him."

"Oh, no."

"Oh, yeah. And he was having a go at our mama in a way we'd never seen, meaning he'd graduated to physical abuse. Rolo and I had zero tolerance, and we were both screaming at him to stop while physically trying to push him off her. He began cussing and calling us some kind of ugly. Kicked us so we'd lose our balance, then picked up a baseball bat and swung it hard at us."

John flinched. "I'm afraid to know what happened next."

"When we ducked out of the way, just barely I should add, he went back to cussing our sweet mama while he pushed her to the ground. Again, we tried to help her, and that's when he pulled her up, dragged her to his car, shoved her in, and started the engine. Rolo stood in front of the big ole blue Lincoln to stop him, but he rolled down his window and said to me, 'I'll run the fuck over my sissy son sure as I'm lookin' at him,' and, John, let me tell you, he would have mowed my brother down in a heartbeat. So I grabbed Rolo, who had no intention of moving, and my father drove off, our mama crying hysterically in the car. Viola, who was twenty-three, was on the porch crying and screaming at us for not letting well enough be, but no way we could stand there and watch him brutalize our mama. You hear me?"

John nodded, pain etched on his face. "Completely."

"I'll make this short. About an hour later, we got a call. He was so drunk that he'd driven the car right off the Lake Ponchartrain Causeway heading toward Mandeville, and they were both killed instantly. I don't know how to even describe our grief and our rage; it was all too much. Even today, I don't have the right words."

"My God, Ty. I'm so sorry. How tragic."

"Thank you. See, after that happened, things got way worse.

Viola and our extended family blamed Rolo and me for trying to stop the abuse, sayin' that if we'd only left well enough alone, he would have maybe only killed himself, or maybe just stopped and eventually worn himself out." Ty tensed. "But I don't know how decent grown men stand there and watch a drunk like my father beat on their mama or any woman. Not something we could have or would have done."

"I understand. I would have done exactly the same thing." John looked down at Kono who had drifted off to sleep.

"When our parents died, we inherited a heap of money, most of it coming from the fortune our grandfather had made, and it was split three ways. Our sister and family didn't think we deserved our rightful shares, but they had no legal say. They never pursued anything with lawyers, knowing they had no case, but it was uglier than you can imagine. Just at that time, Rissa found out she was pregnant with RJ. So, she and Rolo got married sooner than planned, and the three of us moved into the Quarter to get away from our family. We all got jobs at the same restaurant. Server, sous chef, and me, bussing tables. There were three openings, four actually, because the owners had this thing about not treating staff so well. Great food and a charming atmosphere, but a toxic hellhole for the employees. But there was one heck of a silver lining, as that's where we met Sunny and Grey when they came in for dinner. I think you can see how meeting them changed our lives forever."

"Absolutely, Ty."

"To this day, sadly, we're still estranged from our family in Louisiana. So, several years ago, when our friends from Metarie came to Pismo Beach for four days, not only did we really want to see them, it was especially important as we no longer have a connection with anyone else from back home. But I forever regret that we went on that trip."

John looked down. "I think I know what happened next."

"I'm sure you do. And you don't have to tell me what Sunny says all the time, that we did the right thing in going, but what I just told you, about why we were hell bent on having that time away, well, all of that contributed to me feeling even more guilty about what happened to Grey."

John leaned forward. "Sunny is absolutely right. You did *nothing* wrong. You have to live your lives. You did then and you do now."

"I know, but—"

"And hear me, Ty. I would have protected my mother the same way you did. My father wasn't physically abusive, but he abandoned her emotionally, and she committed suicide when I was only seventeen. Oh yeah, and I was the one to find her—on the bathroom floor."

"Oh, John. So sorry, man."

"Thank you." Surprised that he'd revealed so much, John stopped to regroup. "Do you know how many times I wished I'd understood how lonely and troubled my mother was? That she suffered incredible emotional abuse at the hands of my father? To this day, I'm consumed with imagining the ways I might have saved her. *If* only I'd been wise enough to see her pain."

"You were a kid, John."

"That doesn't seem to matter where my guilt is concerned. I still carry it with me to this day. And this is the most I've ever talked about it." Lost in his thoughts, he paused for a moment. "Hard to believe, seeing how little I've said." He sighed heavily. "If only I'd been more insightful. If only this, if only that. Do you hear me?" He looked into Tyler's eyes. "Human beings usually live in the moment. We can't know the consequences of our inaction or action, as much time as we may spend mulling over every possible scenario in our head."

"You're right as rain there." Tyler, taking a cue from John, looked out at the ocean for a moment.

"You did everything for your mother you could. I mean that with everything I am, Ty."

Tyler offered a pained smile in appreciation. "Tell me more about yourself, if you're down with that."

John paused before continuing. "As I told Sunny yesterday, although I never told her about my mother, I worked in Scarsdale at my aunt's catering company when I was fourteen and fifteen. My father was filthy rich, but I wanted to make my own money to buy the things I wanted with money *I* had earned, not that he'd have given much to me anyway. But I still wish I'd never taken that job, much in the same way you wish you'd never gone to Pismo Beach. To this day, I still wonder if I could have saved my mother's life. Probably not. I was a teenager with an active life. I had no clue she was so deeply depressed and had suicide ideations." He looked down in shame. "As Sunny does, my mother often wore a happy face, especially because of all of the social obligations she had."

"Why do you regret that job you had at fourteen and fifteen, if she didn't end her life until you were seventeen?"

"Well, as I learned from friends, that was when she took the brunt of the abuse from him. And yeah, once I was sixteen, I was off pursuing other interests, and I've got guilt about that too. But I had to prepare myself for life after high school."

"Oh, man."

"That's all I can say about my own situation, but don't think for a moment that I can't relate to yours. You can't blame yourself, Ty. It's just so much easier to see wisdom in someone else's story than your own."

Tyler bowed his head in agreement. "Rolo and I couldn't save our mama, John, and like I just told you, we actually knew what was going on. So yeah, man. Cut yourself a break. I know I sound like a hypocrite, but as for Grey's death, just ain't no way that's gonna stop haunting me in this lifetime."

"I'll bet Grey would absolutely hate that you do this to yourself."

"Sunny says that all the time. She's right. Still can't stop myself."

"I hope you'll find a way. Oh, and one more thing: if I'd been a Gardet family member, I would never have cut you off after your parents died. You did exactly what I would have done ... what most people would have done.

"Thanks, my friend." Tyler touched John's hand. "Folks can be real good at rewriting history, telling you what would have happened if only. I never thought the estrangement would last all of these years, and now, I got little in my heart for them anymore. They're strangers to me. Sure, we miss knowing our nieces and nephew, but it is what it is and what it will be. We got new family now." He blinked the tears away. "I hate that you went through such a tragedy too. What is it with this world?"

John shook his head. "I don't know." Alarmed, he became

animated. "Ty, you don't think that Sunny would ever—"

"Definitely not." Tyler's voice grew stronger. "She's told us many times that she'll never leave until she's called home. She may wear a happy face like your mother did, but the similarity ends there. You don't have to worry."

"Good to know." He shook off the disquiet that gripped him. "I'd better be going. Sunny might be ready to return to work in a while, and I don't think she'd be happy to see me still here."

"Oh, no. I think just the opposite actually. You should stay."

"Not a chance. I'm going head off." As both men stood, John gave Tyler a hug and a pat on the back. "Thank you for letting me get to know you better. You're a good man. I'm so glad Sunny has you as her family. Take good care." Kono, awake and now standing, his tail wagging, readied himself to leave.

"She really cares about you, man," Tyler called after him as he and Kono stepped off the porch. "It'll be fine, but we do need to figure out who left those flowers."

Unable to say anything more, his back now facing Tyler, John could only raise his hand in agreement—and to say good-bye.

And Tyler, his eyes watering, understood.

The night air was chillier than usual. Standing in her backyard, overlooking the beach, bundled up in her parka, Sunny watched as John walked the beach in his old coat. Something was different. He moved more slowly, as if he had lost his purpose. He stopped more than he usually did, to look out at the dark waves, and each time, Kono would nuzzle up against his leg.

"Oh, you dear sweet dog. You know he's hurting. That's my fault." She smiled sadly and looked at Miggy. "I don't suppose *you* can nuzzle on cue, can you, girl?"

Miggy looked at her, then continued to sniff the yard.

"And John, you dear sweet man. I have only myself to blame that you didn't come back or get in touch. I feel such enormous emptiness right now. I thought I was fine, living my life as I was. I thought it was for the best. Then you came through the door two weeks ago and changed my entire world. I don't know how to go back to the limbo I was in, yet I'm scared to death to want more, to want *you*. Only I already do. I think you feel the same way, but you've managed to live the past many years with far fewer people around you, so you're better at solitude than I'll ever be. I can't let myself fall into that black hole again—the one I was in earlier. But if I've pushed you away, that's exactly where I'll be." She called Miggy and turned toward the house, offering herself one last look at John, now farther away, a mere dot in the night mist with a lower dot beside him. "Goodnight, my love."

CHAPTER TWELVE

Sitting on a blanket as the sun relaxed in the eastern sky, a Mets baseball cap on his head, dark sunglasses on his face, Dylan opened the carton of food he'd just picked up at the diner: fried eggs, hash browns, cantaloupe slices, and buttered rye toast. Just as he took his first bite of food, his cell phone played 'I'm a Loser,' the ringtone he'd set for one person only. "Yeah? What?"

"You don't speak that way to your father, Dylan."

"Why are you calling me so early? Or calling me at all?"

"Only you would think 11:00 a.m. is too early to call someone. I don't know how many times I've told you what an ungrateful little prick you are, but let's add to that number."

"Then I guess we're up to two million and one or something."

"Shut up! I just heard you quit your job a few days ago. You didn't think to tell me? You know how many people covet that position?"

"No. But I guess someone is gonna get lucky, or should I say *un*lucky, working for you."

"Ungrateful bastard. You probably sold the Rolex I gave you on your twenty-first birthday, didn't you?"

"Not yet. But I did have the GPS tracker removed that you had installed inside. But you already know that or you wouldn't be calling to ask where I was."

"Who the hell told you about the tracking device?"

"Nobody had to tell me fuck all, not that you wouldn't love to kick someone's ass over it. You think I don't see how you spy on the whole world like you're some kind of evil master of the universe? I know the stuff you do to other people, how you have your team of detectives track them, so what makes you think I'm dumb enough to think you'd leave *me* alone? I'm not like Jake. I don't bow to your bullshit and call you 'Dad.'"

"Get back to the Sixth Avenue office now! If you're not there within the hour, I'm repossessing your BMW and taking back your West Side apartment. And you know I don't play with ultimatums."

Dylan smiled. So his father thought he was still in Manhattan. Excellent. Especially after he'd slipped up and forgotten it was 11:00 a.m. in New York and not 8:00 a.m. as it was in California. "Go for it." He smirked. "Well, if that's all, I'm outta here, and heads up, I'm ditching this phone. Bye!"

"I am not finished—"

Dylan ended the call, turned off the phone, and stuck it in his pocket. He looked up to see John and Kono briskly walking west. Then he noticed a woman standing high up on the steps, also watching them. Unsettled, he went back to his breakfast.

Minutes later, Harper approached the blanket. "Hi. I saw you looking my way. Do you know that man who was walking by?"

"How would I?" Dylan said, not caring that he had a mouthful of food. "And what's it to you? Who are you? Oh, yeah, you're that person who was at the desk when I checked in."

"That's right. I'm Harper Kinnison, who are you?"

Dylan stretched his legs, leaving no place for her to sit, knowing she was waiting for an invitation. "You can call me 'Breakfast man.' Seriously, lady, does it look like I'm here to socialize?"

Flustered, she refused to give up. "So, uh, that man with the dog who just walked by. They make such a coolio kind of picturesque scene, don't they? Kind of romantic and mysterious. I'm a writer and would love to put them in my new book. Have you met him? Can you tell me anything that would make for good reading?" She gazed longingly at the blanket. "How about if you scooch over and let me park my little butt down? I don't bite."

Dylan looked up at her. "If you even try to sit your ass on my blanket, I'll pull it out from under you. And I'm not playing, lady. Man, I just came here for some morning peace and quiet, in this town that never wakes up, and here I'm bombarded with all kinds of BS on 'Grand Central 'effin Beach.'"

"Oh, really? Who else spoke to you? Or 'bombarded you?' That man with the dog? Did he come over here? What did he say?"

Shoving a piece of toast in his mouth, Dylan narrowed his eyes and transmitted his best death stare.

Putting her hands up, she stepped back. "Okay, sorry, 'Breakfast Man.' Got the message. Guess I'm not welcome here."

"Ya think?" As she walked away, Dylan mumbled to himself. "Who the hell are you, and what do you want with John?"

As he sat on the deck outside his front door, John watched the waves until they nearly put him in a trance.

"John?"

He sat up straight and looked to his right. "Rolo. You scared the sh—"

"Sorry about that. I had a feeling that no matter how I chose to catch your attention, I'd startle you." He smiled. Wearing a navy Dodo Deen's sweatshirt and jeans, his trademark braids pulled back, he carried a large pot in his hands. "I've come bearing bribes." He laughed. "It was a bit treacherous climbing down the beach stairs with this, walking a half mile at the water's edge, then across the beach and up the stairs to this cottage. Felt like a ninja on a reality show for chefs." He smiled. "There weren't many people around, but I did get a few stares. But hey, a dude with braids carrying a pot across the beach early in the morning. That's normal, isn't it?"

"I saw a guy lugging a fourteen-inch cast-iron skillet on yesterday's walk. Like it was no more than a big feather."

Rolo paused for a moment, then broke out laughing. "You got me there, John. But only for a second."

"Better than nothing. Hey, I really appreciate the kindness." He raised his eyebrows. "Might there be some of your famous gumbo in there?"

"Nah, just wanted to walk the beach with a pot." He laughed. "Yeah, there sure is. May I?" Rolo nodded toward the steps to the deck.

"Of course." John got up and took the pot from him. "Whoa. Heavy. Thank you so much."

"I hear barking. Hmm. Who could that be?"

"Someone who was too sleepy to come outside and sit with his old man, but now that you're here, he's awake and excited." John smiled. "Come on in. Mind opening the door?"

Rolo turned the knob and was instantly greeted by Kono on his hind legs. He moved to the left so John could get by, the dog moving with him.

"Just going to find a spot for this in the fridge. Have a seat, Rolo. If Kono will let you."

As John put the pot of gumbo away, Rolo walked to the large window.

"This is spectacular. What a beautiful, unobstructed view of the ocean." He looked around. "This place has old-world charm while looking like it's all decked out in new clothes."

"Something like that. Have a seat. Let me bring you something."

"No thanks. Just had breakfast. I'm good." Rolo sat on the sectional. "Nice. And comfy too."

A moment later, with his coffee thermos in hand, John sat next to him, smiling. "Thanks for the gumbo. Not certain what I can do for you, but I know it doesn't require a bribe. Not that I'm unhappy you brought one, as long as there's plenty for your customers."

A wry grin sat on Rolo's lips. "I might have made some extra for you. See, I plan my bribes in advance."

John laughed, then took a few sips of coffee before responding. "Ah ha! Well, thank you for that." His face became serious. "I'm guessing this is about Sunny. And Ty as well."

"It is. I'm concerned about both of them. Ty just hit the hay. Didn't get any sleep last night. He told me he gave you the 411 on our family, but didn't recount anything you'd shared with him. I'm not telling you this because I'm expecting you to say jack, only to let you know that we try very hard to maintain our integrity, not to gossip—too much—and not to share confidences that belong to someone else."

John took another sip and put the thermos down. "I saw that quality in all of you right away. It's very admirable."

"Thanks, friend. Just so you know, I told my big brother I was coming to see you. He said there was something he hadn't told you, only because he was 'plumb wore out,' but gave me the green light to do so. Oh, and he might have added that he plumb wore you out too."

"I'm fine. Ty needn't worry about that."

"John, why I'm here—it isn't about ancient Gardet family history. Promise. I'm just concerned about my big brother, and I thought maybe if you knew what was going down, well, I don't know, that it might be help if you were tuned in to our station. KOGD. Kings of Gar-det. Broadcasting live from Teal Beach on the sunny coast of California. And I'm your host, Rolo Montgomery Gardet."

John chuckled as he turned to watch Kono circle a few times before settling into his bed. "I like your humor. Go on. Tell me more."

"Got to put my serious face back on." Rolo stopped to gather his thoughts. "As you've no doubt seen, my brother feels things deeply. Don't misunderstand, my wife and I do too, but Tyler Zachariah Gardet Jr., well, he can hold on to guilt until it drains every drop of life out of his body. Like an octopus be strangling him to death."

"That's quite the accurate metaphor. Unfortunately."

Rolo twisted his face to signal accord. "Uh huh. As you can see, Rissa and I also worry like crazy about Sunny, but no, we don't beat ourselves up for having gone to Pismo Beach that weekend. Nobody could have known what would happen. Our hearts were broken every bit as much as Ty's, but after a while, we parted ways on the guilt thing. My wife and I are both warriors, and maybe that's because we know our kids emulate us." He laughed. "Except when they don't."

"I hear you."

"Oh, do you have children?"

Stumbling for words, John gestured toward Kono. "The four-legged kind."

"Right. So here's the thing. Speaking of kids, the big news is that Imari is pregnant, and she and Ty are finally getting hitched after way too many years. She's nine years younger than he is, but still at that age where she can't wait too much longer to have children."

John flashed a warm smile. "Congrats on the new Gardet-to-be. Is Ty going to move from the property?"

Rolo gave him a you-know-better look. "Do you see that happening?"

"That would be a no."

"Sunny gifted the backhouse to him, and there's plenty of land to build a nice extension with several more rooms. Imari makes and sells jewelry. She has a small boutique in town, but the lion's share of her business is mostly online, so she can easily set up a studio once the extension is built. We're happy he's staying. It's …."

"I think you're about to get to what's upsetting you."

Rolo nodded. "See, my brother and Imari adore one another. Obviously. But they've broken up twice because of my brother's guilt over Grey, which has him spending most nights behind the reception desk, thinking that's the only way to help Sunny. Throw in everything that happened back in Metarie with the folks, and well, that kind of everlasting soul-crushing emotion has a way of coming between people when there's too much of it. You know? So yeah, not being able to protect our mother, then Sunny and Grey, well, it's consumed him. Depleted the guy something fierce, to be honest."

John nodded in agreement. "So I take it that these calls starting again. And what happened yesterday with someone leaving me those flowers, it's escalating Ty's guilt again. Am I correct?" He picked up his thermos and finished the last of his morning coffee.

"He's wound tighter than a clock. Worried that if he doesn't handle things right, he'll have a third tragedy to take credit for. He's a damn sponge for owning shit, John."

"Not good at all."

"No. Definitely not. First and foremost, we're not going to let anything happen to anyone. We're on that like white on rice. Rissa, my gorgeous wife, if you see her acting like a guard dog, it's because she's trying to help Sunny in every way she can and also to take the pressure off Ty that he puts on his damn self."

John stood and walked to the window and looked out at the waves. "What can I do to help?" He turned to face Rolo. "Just to be clear, I'm not upset that you came to me with this. I'll admit, I never thought I'd genuinely care about so many people ever again, much less let anyone come within shouting distance of my life, but you, Ty, Clarissa, your kids, and of course, Sunny, well, you've done what I always thought was impossible."

"We're honored, John. We know how much you value your privacy, and it hasn't gone unnoticed that you've let us in the door, figuratively and metaphorically. All I'm asking is for you to keep in mind what I said, and if you see any way to keep my brother from self-destructing, I'd appreciate it. Also, and I don't want this to come out wrong, there's Sunny."

John returned his gaze to the ocean. "Beautiful, loving, charismatic Sunny."

"You planning to see her today?" Rolo swallowed a lump in his throat. "I really did *not* want to ask you that."

John took his seat again. "I want to see her, but I don't know if she needs more time because of everything … well, you know."

"Truth, man? She was ready to see you again last night. But she's so worried she's pushed you away, and naturally, that worry has found its way to my brother." He sighed. "Listen, I don't want to dictate or suggest what you should do, not even close. You do what you damn please, John. And I mean that. Only saying that if you want to see Sunny, please don't wait. She's worried your friendship is over."

Alarmed, John's eyes opened wide. "Definitely not. I'd be devastated if it were."

Rolo breathed out with relief. "Good. So right now, we've all got to find out what's going on and put an end to it. And that likely means maybe a little bit more communicating, and sticking together as best we can."

John extended his hand to shake Rolo's. Just at that moment, his cell sounded. Looking at the phone, he saw a text message from an unknown number. His face blanched in horror as he read the words.

Time to face the music, you bastard. Any day now.

Rolo looked as if his breath had been whooshed out of his body as he saw the horror on John's face. "Excuse my Cajun French, but what the fuck does that text say?"

"I think we need to keep this between ourselves." John handed Rolo his phone. "If you want to tell Clarissa, fine with me. But not Ty or Sunny. Agreed?"

"Absolutely." Rolo stared at the text. "Oh hell no." He took a moment to absorb the shock. "Seriously, what's going on? You've gotten a declaration of love and another of pure hate within twenty-four hours? Same people? Different people? Same as whoever is calling Sunny? Any idea, John? Any *at all?*"

His face tight with rage, John took the phone back and read the message again. "Nothing that makes any sense. But I'll get to the bottom of this, if it's the last thing I ever do. First order of business: to see if I can find out whose number this is."

CHAPTER THIRTEEN

John smiled as he and Kono stepped onto the hotel porch and heard Pink Floyd's "Comfortably Numb" playing in the lobby.

The moment she saw them, Sunny's face beamed. Unlatching the flip-up panel and opening the gate, she let Miggy run to Kono while she hurried to John. Just as she approached him, she stopped, remembering that as much as she wanted to give him a hug, that wasn't what they did.

As the dogs went wild, John held out his arms, and she fell into them. For thirty seconds, no words were spoken. When they pulled away, as if she were afraid he'd see the love in her eyes, Sunny looked away. "I'd better turn that music down so we can talk."

Taking his usual seat on the teal couch, he waited for her to come back and choose the seat beside him or the chair across from him.

"My sweet friend, John." She sat only inches away on the couch. "After my insane meltdown yesterday, I wasn't sure you'd be back so soon, if at all."

He glanced at Kono. "Hey! Not so wild, boy. Save it for outside." He turned back to Sunny. "I really want to talk to you, but maybe your backyard would be a wise choice" — he laughed — "for the *dogs* so we aren't distracted by their antics."

Sunny rose immediately. "Yes," she said with a nervous chuckle. "It *is* rather difficult to have a serious chat while my Miggy is smelling Kono's backside and he's about to return the favor. Goodness knows what they'll do outside, but at least we won't be watching.

Ignorance is bliss, right?" She smiled and looked at the dogs. "Come on, crazy canines. Backyard!"

The dogs, already well used to the drill, ran and followed her through the still-open gate."

Two minutes later, Sunny returned to the lobby. She waved to a local couple who had come to get their mail, then gave John her full attention as she resumed her seat.

He placed his hand over hers. "First, I don't remember any 'insane meltdown.' Sunny, you've been through so much over the years, and then, out of nowhere, you get those disturbing calls. I hope they're simply someone's idea of a silly antic, and that the unknown woman was only *pretending* to be ugly and that our collective circumstances aren't *portending* anything." He sighed. "I'm going to hope for the former. But, understanding the tragedy in your past as I do, I don't see how you could *not* be rattled. And those flowers someone tossed on my deck—I hate that you thought for a split second that I believed that you had—"

"I *know* you didn't think I'd left them. Honestly, John, it would be unnatural if my name hadn't crossed your mind at that moment. I was never angry with you. The calls and the flowers were just the perfect storm of stressors. I just needed a brief time-out from life. Thank goodness Larae was available to fill in for a few hours."

"I understand."

"And I'm very grateful that you do. I was afraid I'd lost your friendship."

"I don't see that happening."

"My new, but dear friend, I don't know what happened to make you seek the life of solitude you do, but I understand you in so many ways. Eerily so. As I've explained, if I hadn't owned this hotel, hadn't had the amazing Gardet family to prop me up, who knows where life might have led me after Grey was killed. I might be living alone in a beach cottage too. Not such a bad life at all. Believe it or not, I considered it." She paused. "I won't elaborate, but I also had some very gloomy thoughts about alternate ways to spend my days. One day, I was so down that I considered being a cave dweller. Well, not really, but close to it. I was out of my mind with grief."

"I'm glad you're doing better." John squeezed her hand again, then leaned back. "If I'd had that kind of loving support—and this beautiful place—in similar but different circumstances, I may have stayed put. But in my situation, it just wasn't possible." A look of disgust landed on his face. "Sorry, Sunny. Every time I make a reference to my past, which I just can't bring myself to say very much about, I feel like I'm taunting you. Only I'm not. I promise." He sighed, self-loathing consuming him. "You know, I have this old coat that I only wear when I walk the beach at night."

Sunny looked down for a moment, breaking the eye contact between them, then resuming it with a smile.

Noticing her momentary discomfort, he paused, then continued speaking. "I can't explain why, but the coat is comforting to me. I don't know if this will make sense, but keeping the past in a little box, locked up tight and stashed away, lessens my burden somehow. The fact that only a handful of people *in my life* know the real story is akin to a comforting hug. Just like the old coat is. Being the way I am, well, I feel less vulnerable to the world. Only the thing is, like right now, I shut out people I'd really like to let in. And I don't like that part so much." He shrugged. "Sheesh. Just replaying that in my mind sounds insane."

"Oh, no, John. Honestly, it doesn't. Not at all. In fact, the way you explained it makes so much sense."

"Thank you." He released a long breath. "I'll tell you this, though, there were a lot more people cognizant of my existence in Two Harbors than there ever will be here, which is one of the reasons I left. Yes, I had a rental cottage on the beach, but it wasn't that far from other cottages and from an entire neighborhood of homes. Not ideal. Anyway, old man Sabelli told me one day that the locals called me 'Coat.'"

Sunny smiled awkwardly. "Hmm. I kind of like that. There are much worse things to be called than 'Coat,' yes?"

"For sure. The thing is, 'Coat' came to exist because I left behind a world where ugliness thrived like a weed." He looked into her eyes. "Just to ease your mind, I'm not running from any crimes, legal or illegal. Not a fugitive from the law or my own conscience. I promise."

"Goodness. I never entertained that for a moment."

"Well, I couldn't have blamed you if you did." John smiled as "You Belong to the City" played softly. "I used to love this song. Came out in '85 if I remember correctly. I love your mixes, Sunny. When I hear the songs, it's like I put them together myself."

"You know, when these were current, I listened to the radio like a fiend, always waiting for my favorite artists to put out new music. But the year after my daughter was born, 1991, when Freddie Mercury died, it was around that time I stopped listening to the radio. Everything was just changing, especially now that I was the mother of two children."

"You stopped listening to the radio, not to music, yes?"

"Absolutely. And I still listened to many songs of lesser-known artists. I already told you about my favorite artist, but I still love King Harvest, Flash and the Pan, Golden Earring, Dire Straits, BOC, and so many others who didn't have the superstar status like Queen, Aerosmith, or Van Halen. I remember feeling sad that so many new musicians were coming onto the scene while many that I loved were fading, or had already faded, into the background. Music geek that I am, you'd think I would have embraced the new music, but I didn't. I just wanted to stay in the 70s and 80s. Every chance I got, I made mixtapes. Hundreds of them. Years later, as technology evolved, before the cassette tapes fell completely into obsolescence, I digitized everything." She laughed. "A labor of love and pure drudgery."

John cradled his head in his collapsed hands and leaned back. "Did you sell your old albums? I had friends who did that, then sorely regretted it after vinyl and turntables made a comeback."

"No way. I told Jess and Alex they can sell my collection when I die. It's still in pristine condition. I know it's silly, John, especially as the albums are sealed in boxes in my kids' former bedroom closets, but there they'll stay." She exhaled. "Whew! That was some tangent. I was trying to explain, in response to what you told me, that the music comforts *me* like an old coat but I think that ended up in metaphor purgatory." She laughed. "Be back. Phone ringing. As you can hear."

As Sunny hurried to answer the hotel phone, John stood and stretched, gazing out the window to the ocean. A minute later, his own phone rang.

"Hey, Benjo. Good timing."

"Maybe. Just wish I had good news."

"So it's bad?"

"Not exactly. I called my cop buddy, Ken Shivetta. He said the text you got came from a burner phone, so they can't trace it. Under the circumstances, the text appears to have been pre-meditated, but there's no way to really be sure."

John glanced over at Sunny, happy to see her smiling as she took a new reservation. "Well, thanks for trying. Hey, you haven't had any more objects of the sharp kind show up on your driveway, have you?"

"No. But it sucks that I have to keep looking. I did get a camera, two actually, installed outside of the garage, so I'm thinking the deterrent will work fine. Put a big ole sign up too, letting all of Long Beach know my property is being monitored 24/7."

"Damn cameras everywhere."

"What's that?"

"Nothing, Benjo. Just mumbling to myself."

"Well, my dude, when you let that rambling shit loose, not such a bad idea to mumble. Protect the ears of any innocents nearby. You know?" He burst out laughing.

John laughed. "Hey, same to you in triplicate."

"You got a point." Ben's tone became serious. "So listen, everything okay with Sunny?"

"I'm in the lobby of the hotel now."

"Oh, okay. Gotcha. Guess you can't talk then. Dodger and I gotta make a delivery to Avalon in a few minutes anyway, so I'll get going. Call if you need anything."

"Will do. Thanks." Taking a moment to process his disappointment, John put a smile on his face and walked to the desk, just as Sunny was hanging up the phone. "Everything good?"

"It is." She glanced up at the wall clock. "It's twelve-thirty. I was just about to eat lunch. I've got an extra sandwich in the fridge." She lowered her eyes. "I was hoping you might come by so I kind of made … can you stay?" She brightened. "Give the kiddos a bit more fun in the sun?"

"Sure. Why not?"

She studied his face. "I hope that phone call you just got wasn't upsetting news. You look a bit out of sorts, and that's *none* of my concern." She exhaled in disgust.

"It's fine, Sunny. I was just talking to Ben. Just business. Nothing worth repeating. I'm going to step outside for a moment. Be right back."

As Sunny smiled at him, he sensed she understood his distress as if they'd known one another for years.

Now standing by the steps, his eyes swept the ocean from east to west as he let the afternoon breeze touch his face. His mind relaxing, clarity came to him. *Who was that woman who came into the diner asking about the cottage? Did she leave those flowers? But why? That makes little to no sense. How would she know my name? Maybe I'm missing something. Or maybe I'm reaching.* He tried to shake off his distress, but it only escalated. *But that damn text.* Pulling his phone out of his pocket, he looked down at the message he received that morning. *Only one person would send me this, and after all of these years, even that doesn't make sense. What the hell is going on?*

After lovingly setting up the coffee table with sandwiches and a few extras she'd prepared, Sunny, feeling content, sat and waited for John to return as a text sounded on her private cell. Pulling it out of her pocket, she smiled to see it was from her daughter.

> *Hi, Mom. Miss U bunches. We'll talk again soon. Just want to let U know to expect a small package in a few days. Have sent something I know U will totally <3. Don't think in a bazillion yrs U could EVER guess. So excited to be the gift giver. Yay me! On set now with 75 zombies. Oh no! 2 R trying to eat me! JK. ☺ Gotta run. Love U. xo Jess.*

Shaking off his angst, John walked back into the lobby and smiled at the radiant woman waiting for him on the couch. "You look happy." Cheerfully, he went on. "Was it because I left? Or because I came back?" He paused, then broke out laughing. "Didn't know how to answer *that*, did you?"

She made a playful face. "I adore your mischievous side, and while it's definitely the latter, that I was happy you came back, I'm smiling because I just got an intriguing and lovely text from my daughter. Apparently, she has sent me a mystery gift, which should arrive the day after tomorrow. Says she knows I'll love it and could never guess 'in a bazillion years.'"

"So of course, you *are* trying to guess."

Sunny laughed. "Absolutely. Wouldn't you? By the way, any clue exactly how many years a bazillion is?"

"That roughly would describe my age."

"Hey, be careful there, old man. I think we're pretty much the same age."

"And so we are. Forgot about that. I'm not real great with numbers." He grinned, his eyes smiling as he looked at her. Solely because she was, he felt happy and glanced at the table as he sat down next to her. "This looks wonderful. But I'm thinking …."

"Oh, no. That sounds dangerous. I try to stay away from doing that."

"Don't I know it?" He smiled. "I do believe the furry ones have been in the backyard for a bit. Bringing them in at *our* lunch time, when we'll be met with doleful eyes, longing—no, begging—for a bite of our food, seems to be a toss-able idea, but another part of me thinks it might be okay to share."

Sunny rose. "Great minds and all that. Please, John, go ahead and start eating. I actually had the same idea. Miggy and Kono have been on their own long enough. I'll not only go get them, but I'll prepare a little snack for them in my kitchen, if that's okay with you. Does Kono have any allergies?"

"Not that I know about. What do you have in mind?"

"Just a bit of shredded chicken, rice, and vegetables. I make up a batch every so often and keep it handy. I'll just need to warm it in the microwave. Just small portions for each, but Miggy goes bonkers when I give it to her."

"Go ahead. That sounds like a treat. And if it's okay, I prefer to wait until you get back to attack this sandwich."

"Oh, and you won't hear the phone ring. I'm just going to punch a few numbers on the desk phone and transfer calls to my cell while I'm gone."

"Good to know." John smiled as she did exactly as she

indicated she would, then disappeared through the door to her residence. Before he could luxuriate in the good feelings he and Sunny had generated, his peripheral vision caught sight of a woman, her long reddish-brow hair in a ponytail, coming out of the dark wood door that led to the upstairs. It occurred to him that he probably wouldn't have noticed her had her eyes not immediately focused like lasers onto his face as she walked over to him. As she sat in the chair on the other side of the couch, he remembered everything Rolo had told him that morning. *Harper something-or-other. That's right. Who the hell are you?*

"Hi, there!" she said brightly … almost too much so.

Why do you look almost familiar? I'd remember if we'd ever met.

"I'm Harper Kinnison. I'm a writer. Guess you could say this is my self-made writers' retreat. I hide in my room a good deal of the day, but I also go back and forth to the beach. You know, gotta kickstart my muse 'n all, kick the dust up, create excitement that will travel from my dusty brain to the page and exhilarate readers around the globe." She laughed. "Don't I wish!"

"Uh huh." *You're way too damn cheerful, Harper.*

"So, who do I have the pleasure of speaking to, John?" Her face dropped as she realized her slip.

John could only stare at her, trying to piece a puzzle together that made no sense. "Excuse me for being overly fascinated, *Harper,* but it amazes me that I've never seen you before, yet your ebullient countenance has made a beeline for my being. And to top it off, you know my name, something you clearly wanted me to believe was unknown to you while using your enthusiasm and charm in hopes of enticing me into introducing myself." He paused. "Just taking a wild guess. Am I correct?"

"You're so eloquent. But why wouldn't you be?"

"What?"

Before she could answer, Clarissa walked through the lobby door. "Oh, hi, Harper. Hello, John." She returned her attention to Harper as she pointed at the camera above. "Just noticed you on our little closed-circuit must-see TV. Aren't you looking pretty today in your sage linen pants and blousy taupe top? My, my. Just let your tresses down in the sea breeze, and you'll be a natural for the cover of … oh, I don't know. 'Vogue' … 'Mademoiselle' … 'Stalker Monthly.'"

Agony etched on her face, Harper stood and nearly spat at Clarissa. "You've got me all wrong, Ms. Gardet. You really do. You'll see." She turned to acknowledge John. "I'll catch up with you another time. Count on it." She glared at Clarissa. "As for you, no, I won't say it. But *you* know."

Clarissa waited until the lobby door closed behind her. "That went well."

"Didn't it, though?"

"John, I don't want to give you the idea my eyes are stuck to the monitors. It's just that such a stunned look came over your face when she spoke to you, and knowing my hubs had explained things this morning, I thought an intervention might be in order. I hope I didn't misjudge the situation. And I know it sounds too convenient to be the truth, but I'd literally just looked at the screen."

Before he could respond, the dogs came bounding into the lobby, Kono all over John as if he hadn't seen him in years, and Miggy showering Clarissa with kisses.

"Hi, Rissa. I never see you here at lunchtime. Slow day?"

"Not really. I just … uh … possibly interfered where I shouldn't have. Really. I don't want you do think the Gardet eyes are monitoring your every moves. Not why we wanted these cameras installed." Distressed, she looked at everyone as she began to leave. "Hope the four of you have a good lunch. Forget I was ever here."

Dylan sat at the desk in his cabin, textbooks piled up in front of him, and punched a number into his new phone.

"Who is this?"

"It's me, Jake."

"Why the hell are you calling me from a restricted number?"

"Just because we're twins, doesn't mean we do things alike or think alike. That's been pretty obvious." Dylan took a swig out of the soda bottle he'd just gotten out of a vending machine.

"What does that have to do with hiding your number from me?"

"Because I don't want you giving it to your father, King Dick of Prickville."

"Hate to have to play biology teacher, Dyl, but he's your father too."

Dylan's face tightened. "DNA isn't everything. If you don't know that, you're lame as fuck. He may be my father, but he's not my *dad*."

"I know." Jake paused for several seconds. "Mom said you're

off somewhere looking for John. And I haven't said anything to Dad … uh … *him* … about that. I'm not gonna narc on you. You think I don't get why you hate the guy? He doesn't treat me so great either. Hello."

Dylan gave the phone a dirty look as if he were speaking to his brother in person. "Well, you get the toys you want from him, so you sell your soul. Me, I can't do that anymore."

"Yeah, I know you bailed on the job, but you never wanted it in the first place. So it was easy to walk away. No great accomplishment. Except that I'm sure he's cut you off."

"He already said he's gonna take away the car and the apartment. Whatever. I don't need them." Dylan took several gulps of the soda, then put the cap back on the bottle.

"I'll bet Mom gave you money so you wouldn't have to get it from *him*. And if she did, it was just to piss him off and to punish him more than it was to help *you*. She doesn't exactly give a damn about us, never has, so what does it matter which one of them you take money from? The money she gives you comes from the same place. So don't be so high and fuckin' mighty about me still working for Dad."

Dylan ignored the comment. "I don't even know how you can call him 'Dad.' I don't want anything he has. That's why I broke out of Dick Prison. Oh, and by the way, your *dad* put a GPS tracker in your Rolex. I had mine taken out."

"Are you fuckin' kidding me, Dyl?" There was silence on the line. "Damn! That's how he found me on Rockaway Beach last week. I couldn't figure that out to save my life! Who told you?"

"I told *me*. I used my brain. I see the bastard for who he is and

I know how he operates. I'm not blinded by the bull like you are."

"I don't wanna be," Jake said softly.

"He doesn't know and wouldn't care that I want to go to veterinary school. He didn't even notice that I lied about majoring in business and had a double major in biology and … oh, whatever. Don't wanna ramble. My point is, he's not interested in anything about us. He just wants us to do whatever he says. To be a 'him junior.' Well eff that nonsense."

Jake said nothing for a moment. "So, have you found John?"

"Yeah. He just moved to a beach cottage somewhere in California near the little hotel where I'm staying. Pretty sure he has something going with the lady who owns the place. I mean, he comes to visit her a lot. But he and I haven't been close enough to really see one another yet. I keep wondering if he'll recognize me, but I know he will. Right now, I'm wearing dark glasses and a hat so I can kind of stay anonymous. I saw him leave the lobby about an hour ago as I was heading toward the vending machines on the side of the main building. Luckily, I was able to quickly hide behind a cabin. Heard him talking to some guy who works here—Ty. John said he's going away for a couple of days to help his friend Ben with something. When he gets back, I'll think more about what to do. I'm not gonna plan anything. Plans have a way of going down the drain."

"Yeah. Do you think he'll be happy to see you? Whenever that happens?"

"I think so. Guess I couldn't blame him if he wasn't."

"He's a good man. I think he will be." Jake sighed. "I hope. So, listen, I'm still at the office. Time to go. Will you give me your number already? I'll delete every call or text. I won't use your name. Swear. I'm a techie. You know that."

"You've geeked out enough in your life to be a freakin' Trekkie like that old dork in accounting, Ross Dunworth. The one who wears checkered bowties and speaks Klingon." Dylan laughed. "Never heard of any of that until I met him."

"Me neither. So listen, you going to give me your digits or what?"

"Yeah okay. I'll text you in few. Take care. And keep your word. Later, bro."

CHAPTER FOURTEEN

"Okay, sue me for asking," Clarissa said as she approached the reception desk, "but I don't remember the last time I've seen you look so happy. John's been gone since Monday morning. Am I correct in guessing he's back?"

"He is. I heard him pull into the parking lot late this morning. He was only gone a few days, but it like forever. Haven't seen him yet. I just finished mingling with the breakfast crowd. Well, if you can call seven people a crowd."

"So this is an anticipatory smile?"

"Believe it or not, Rissa, this isn't about John at all. It has everything to do with the gift Jess sent to me. I just opened the package, and my mind is blown. She said I would love it, but that was the understatement of the century. I think I just traveled to the moon and back."

Clarissa put her hands on her hip, mock scolding her. "And you didn't bring me a moon rock or anything? How about a My-friend-went-to-the-moon-and-all-I-got-was-this-lousy-T-shirt shirt?"

"You're an original, Rissa." She laughed. "Truth is, their gift shop was closed, and I didn't want to steal."

"Oh my goodness, woman! Spill! What's the gift?"

Sunny picked up a CD from the counter and clutched it to her chest. "I'm so excited about this music that I don't dare play it."

Rolling her eyes, Clarissa laughed. "Yeah, when I really love music, I find it most enjoyable when I keep it in the case, especially with that little stickery thing sealing it shut." She paused. "Are you nuts? What'cha got there, Sunny girl?"

"One of the lighting crew members, Eddie, working with Jess on this zombie movie is a musician—guitarist. Big time contacts. Anyway, it came up in conversation that my favorite artist, who only released one album decades ago, had actually produced three. And the second one is literally *just out* today. I think they must have been lost in a vault somewhere. Who knows where or why? Anyway, when she told Eddie that said artist was her mom's number one fave, he managed to get her an advance copy. That's why she didn't Express it to me. Eddie couldn't risk anyone having it until the actual release day: today, March twenty-eighth. I'm so excited I can't even play it."

"You're torturing yourself."

"I know! I want to blare it, and I *really* don't want any guests coming in. Can you stand outside and tell them we're haunted *and* we have bed bugs? And if that doesn't work, tell them that today is 'Triple Thursday' when we charge three times the normal rate."

"You're too much. Just play the CD." Clarissa laughed. And hey, aren't you gonna share with John? Doesn't he worship music as much as you do?"

"He does. We love all of the same artists. As soon as I hear this, and verify that it's for real, I'm going to text him. He's gonna freak. I am so excited to share it."

Sunny waved, returning a hello from a local resident who had just picked up her mail. As soon as the woman left, she tried to peel the sticker from the CD. "I can't do this, Rissa. I'm fumbling like a fool."

Clarissa took the CD and examined it. "A whiskey bottle with a tiny face on the label with musical notes coming out of the top. What a strange design."

"Well, it is Whisky Devers. Just open it for me, will you?"

Clarissa quickly peeled the sticker off with the nail on her right index finger. "Here you go, fumbly girl. Happy listening! I've got some work to do. I'll be back to check on you later."

Sunny, who couldn't stop smiling, opened the tray of her CD player and slid the disk in. "Euphoria! Make yourself known. I command thee."

When Clarissa returned an hour later, she nodded to Tyler, who was kneeling on the floor, replacing hinges on the cabinet door under the breakfast nook. Seeing Sunny radiating happiness as she stood behind the reception desk made her smile too. The soft rock music was loud, but not overpowering as Clarissa approached her. "You're blissing out like I've never seen you before. I take it you're not disappointed."

"Heavens, no! The first album was beyond brilliant, made me a fan for life, and this mind-bogglingly surpasses that one. The musicality, the depth of emotion, the creative risk taking, the vocals, the guitar work— just superb. I'm gushing like a silly fangirl, and I don't even care."

"Where's John? Didn't you want to share with him?"

"I texted him fifteen minutes ago. Said he'll be here soon. He's excited to see me and to hear my surprise." She frowned. "Oh, Miggy is in the living room. Mind getting her for me? Don't want to disappoint Kono."

"Of course not." As Sunny lifted the panel and opened the gate, Clarissa walked through and immediately opened the door to Sunny's residence.

Three minutes later, just as John and Kono came through the lobby, Clarissa and Miggy were reentering. So as not to intrude, Clarissa hurried over to stand next to Tyler.

After the dogs engaged in a lovefest, Miggy initiated a chase around the lobby, Kono happily pursuing her as John stood in stunned silence.

"Do you know who this is?" Sunny asked. She smiled as her eyes sparkled. "I can see you're as surprised as I was. It's Whisky Devers!" She picked up the CD and held it up. "This was just released today. I don't think any of his fans even knew this music existed. And there's a third album coming in the future. Isn't that the best news ever? These must have been locked away somewhere, collecting dust, which by the way totally does my head in. Such brilliance. No clue why they weren't released before, but when my daughter heard this musician on set, Eddie on the lighting crew, talking about it, she asked him if he could get her a copy for her mom. And Eddie obliged. Today is the official release day in the States." She looked at John, but his expression remained unchanged. Looking concerned, she continued. "Oh, here is one of my new favorite songs. I've already memorized part of the lyrics. She sang along: 'But today I find you sittin' on my spirit, tellin' me your truths, but I don't wanna hear it. Feels like a train wreck approaching in my head, I talked; you talked; who knows what we said.'"

Without saying a word, his face reddening, John walked over

to the desk and picked up the CD. Examining the front and back cover carefully, he tensed with rage until a vein bulged on the left side of his forehead.

John, in a world of his own, an angry one, had ceased to acknowledge her presence.

Glancing at Ty and Clarissa, who were looking on in shock, the joy on Sunny's face morphed into terror.

Still staring at the CD, John finally spoke, but not to Sunny. "What the FUCK is this?" Walking away, he spoke even louder, to someone who was not there. "Son of a BITCH! You *fucking* son of a bitch!" Gesturing for Kono, who looked as confused as everyone else, he stormed toward the lobby door, the dog reluctantly following, turning every two seconds to look at Miggy as if to say he was sorry.

After the lobby door had been shut, Clarissa rushed over to Sunny, who had tears rushing down her face as she cried inconsolably. Tyler, closing the cabinet door he'd just repaired, quietly walked to the end of the reception desk, keeping a bit of distance between himself and the women.

"Oh, you poor thing! Do you have any idea what that was about?" Clarissa asked Sunny, putting a comforting arm around her.

Sunny sobbed copious tears. "I thought John would be every bit as excited as I was. I'm more stunned by his response than I was when I opened the gift."

"He really is a man of mystery." Clarissa pulled a few tissues from a nearby box and began dabbing Sunny's eyes.

"Stop, Rissa! Let me look like the wreck I am." For several minutes, Sunny wept, suddenly stopping as her face registered shock. She stood for a moment and said nothing, now in a world of *her* own.

Finally, ignoring Clarissa, she looked at Tyler. "I need you to work this desk or find someone else to do it. Or close the place down for all I care!"

Tyler gulped. "Uh, sure, Sunny. Larae is still here. I'll call her for you. And if neither she or Miranda can fill in, you know I got your back. Always and forever."

Not even saying thank you, the ever-polite Sunny just stared at him. "Do you have a box cutter?"

His stunned face stared at her. "Um, yeah. In my toolbox."

"May I have it? Like *now*!"

"Uh ...."

"Seriously, Ty. Give me the box cutter!"

"What are you going to do with it?"

"Open boxes." She sighed. "No, I'm not going to slit my wrists or cut my throat or anyone else's, though I might change my mind if you mess with me. Ty, give me the freakin' box cutter or I'll come get it myself. And if you refuse, I'll just go in the kitchen and get a big ole knife. Now! Please."

Clarissa nodded with urgency for him to give it to her. A look of fear stuck on his face, Tyler walked over to his toolbox sitting on the nook counter, removed the tool, and gave it to Sunny who was now standing impatiently beside him with her hand out.

She looked at Clarissa, then Tyler. "Do *not* ask me any questions and do *not* follow me into my home. Is that crystal clear?"

"Yup." Clarissa choked back the tears as she looked at Ty who could only nod in hesitant agreement.

Seeing that Miggy looked terrified, Sunny softened a bit. "Stay, girl. Mommy will be back."

Sunny rushed through the living room into one of the spare bedrooms that used to belong to her son. Opening the closet door, she knelt down and pulled out some shoe boxes, then tossed them without care to both sides as the shoes came flying out. Grabbing a plastic bag of old clothes, she angrily spoke to it. "I thought you went to Goodwill years ago." When it didn't respond, she stood and threw it onto the bed. "Stupid old bag!"

Kneeling again, sweat dripping down her face, she groaned as she pulled four heavy boxes out of the closet. Taking the box cutter, she angrily opened each one between the sealed flaps, nearly cutting herself on the last endeavor. Examining the record albums that she pulled out of the boxes, displeased that the object of her search was nowhere to be found, she became even more frantic. After twenty minutes, her tears having found new reason to roll down her cheeks, she stood, left the mess, then ran to her daughter's former room.

Pulling open the second closet door, pushing aside some old dresses and shirts that hung, she knelt down and pulled out three more boxes. Opening them in the same manner, the third try proved to be the charm. Slowing her breath, she carefully took out an old album, a close-up photo of a good-looking young man on it. "Meet Whisky Devers" she read aloud. "Oh, my God. Oh, my God."

The box cutter in her left hand, the album in her right, she stood, took a moment to catch her breath, then rushed out of the residence into the lobby to discover that neither Clarissa nor Tyler had gone anywhere, and Larae was standing nervously behind the desk, twirling a pen.

"Thank you, Larae. Miggy, come!" Sunny started for the door.

"Wait!" Clarissa cried. "Where the heck are you going with a box cutter, an old record album, and Miggy? Are you going to see John?"

Sunny glared at her, then walked to Tyler and slapped the closed tool into his hand. "You can have this back. Thank you."

Giving Clarissa and Ty a look they'd never seen on her face in all of the years they'd known her, she dared them to even think about asking any questions, or worse, following her. Then, with the dog behind her, she was gone from sight.

CHAPTER FIFTEEN

After making the trek to John's cottage, out of breath, she climbed the final steps from the beach to his deck. Sweaty and distraught, she stood for a moment in an attempt to settle her nerves. Unable to find any path to calm, she knocked frantically at the door. Within seconds, barking was heard, which Miggy responded to in kind, but there was no answer.

"John! Please! Open the door!"

The barking became more frantic on either side of the door, but it did not open.

"I'm not going away, John. I figured it all out and I feel like the biggest idiot in the world. I can't even imagine what you're going through. Obviously, I don't understand anything, not really, but I know now, and I should've known before. I don't regret that I didn't, because I feel certain that had I not been so dense, you would have never allowed me into your life at all. But you did. And now I'm here, and I'm begging you to open the door."

She sobbed as nothing happened.

"You think you're stubborn. Well, I can out-stubborn you any day. Go on, John, test me. I know you're in there. You don't go anywhere without Kono, and your car is still in my driveway. I'll stay here all afternoon and all night. If you don't care about me, then at least open the door so Miggy won't freeze to death when the temperature plummets."

Seeing the door open, she swallowed her fear. John stood before her, his bloodshot eyes staring at her, his face streaked with tears, pain squeezing him tight. As Miggy raced inside to be with Kono, he could only look at her face until he saw the album she held.

She looked once more at the cover, then at him. "You look so young and innocent here. So hopeful without life's defilement and the desecration of your soul." She sniffled as he continued to stare. "Like I've told you, I listened to all of my music on mixtapes. So, I'd pretty much packed the albums away for safekeeping. That's why I never saw this face more often, and that's why it wasn't burnt into my brain. Besides, it was the music that I fell in love with. I always wondered what happened to this inspiring genius who made such a profound impact on me, as I'm sure millions of other fans did. I finally came to the conclusion that he probably didn't want to share any more with the world. In my heart, I knew I should release him from my worries and simply enjoy what he left behind." She sniffled again. "I preferred that scenario over thinking something awful had happened to him." She wiped her tears away with the back of her hand. "I think maybe both of my conclusions were right."

Fresh tears rolled down his face as he listened to her.

"Please don't send me away, John. I'll never recover." She watched as his eyes filled with more pain. "I promise, I won't ask you to tell me anything you don't want. I'm just too broken to go home, and I think you're too broken to make me leave. Can't we just sit together and watch the waves until the sun sets. We can just hold one another. And if you don't want that, I'll keep my distance. Please, just let me in."

Still not saying a word, he stepped to the side so she could enter, then quietly closed the door.

Straight ahead, she saw a bottle of white wine and a glass on the coffee table. John eyed the wine as if to ask her if she'd like some. She nodded, adding a quiet, "Yes, please." Feeling awkward about the album, she handed it to him.

His immediate visceral reaction only allowed him to look at it for seconds before bitterness set in. He put the album on the dining room table, then took a wineglass out of the nearby cabinet in the kitchen. Looking over at Sunny, he knew she'd moved toward the bay window, not wanting him to feel the intensity of her stare. Only he still did.

She sat on the sectional couch and looked wistfully out onto the beach. Within moments, John put a glass on the table, poured some wine, then handed it to her.

"Thank you." She took a small sip and put it down.

Just as she was about to say something, Kono ran over to John, his front paws on his lap, furiously nuzzling his face. Touched, John pulled the dog close and returned the affection. Kono took an extra moment to study his father's sad expression, then turned to Sunny as if asking her to make John all right again. Miggy, who was having no part of being ignored, tapped Kono on the back to instigate a new chase.

"Come here." John looked at the empty space between him and Sunny, his words asking her to fill it.

Moving over, she lay her head on his chest as he put an arm around her. For a good ten minutes, neither spoke. It was John who finally broke the silence. "I feel as if I owe you so much more than I can give you—now."

"You let me in. That's all I wanted. To be right here with you."

He leaned toward her and kissed her forehead. "You're very

special."

She shivered, ever so slightly, as if the touch of his lips, even on her forehead, sent a rush of pleasure through her. Lifting her arm, she brushed a lock of his wavy salt-and-pepper hair out of his face. "You too."

He could see it took every bit of restraint she had not to caress his face, though she did so with her eyes. He knew because he wanted to do the very same to her. He held her close again as the sun began to set. The dogs settled into their respective beds while the two weary humans watched the ephemeral beauty of the orange-and-purple sky fade beyond the horizon.

Steeling himself, John took a sip of wine, then shifted his body to fully face her. "I want to tell you some of my story. All of it, well, that's not possible now." He exhaled as much pain as he could. "I don't have it in me."

"Whatever you want to share, I want to hear. I would never pressure you, John. Never."

"I know." He looked out the window at the now dark blue sky. "Remember I told you that I worked for my aunt's catering company as a young teen?"

"Of course."

"It wasn't because I didn't have an allowance, but my old-money snob of a father wouldn't allow his money to be spent on a guitar for his musical son."

"Oh, that's so sad."

"So I worked hard to buy one with my own money. And I loved the guitar even more because I'd earned it." He turned his head and nodded toward the second bedroom. "It's in my office. A treasured possession."

"Oh, John."

"It wasn't until years had passed that I figured out my aunt put extra money in my check every week, but that didn't negate the work that went into buying it. But my father's refusal to acknowledge my talent and my dream grieved me something awful, and so, when I was eighteen, I started using my mother's maiden name, which is also my middle name, because I didn't want to be associated with his. Also she'd committed suicide when I was seventeen, so it was my tribute to her."

Sunny sipped some wine, feeling his pain as he struggled to get every word out. "I'm so sorry. I didn't know."

"It's okay, but I can't digress on this story or I'll never find my way back."

"Please, go on."

"In 1978, when I was twenty, I met this girl at a party and fell madly in love with her. Juliana. And when I turned twenty-one, I decided to ask her to marry me. She was nineteen, but what we'd shared as young lovers, or so my underdeveloped brain thought then, was, well, intense. One night, I went to see her, to propose. She never even invited me inside. Standing on her doorstep, without warning, before I could recite the speech I'd rehearsed, she broke it off. I saw the love in her eyes, the hot-blooded passion, but they didn't match her words." He swallowed the lump in his throat. "She told me she had met someone else and was marrying him. That's all she would say, no matter how fervently I begged her to be honest. Then, she gave me that old coat I told you about. She'd had it waiting for me by the front door, hanging on a coat rack. It was her grandfather's. She told me three times how he used to walk the beach at Cape Cod with it, and when he'd bury his hands in the pockets on cold nights, the world would make sense."

"What an odd thing to say, much less to repeat."

"It was. She was more vehement about me wearing the coat than she was about breaking up. Or at least it seemed that way to my broken heart. But it was a cold night, so I put it on."

"Had she really fallen in love with someone else?"

"I don't think so. She ended up marrying this very rich guy, several years older than she was, a young executive who worked for his father's record company. He wanted a trophy wife, arm candy, or some gorgeous babe at his side so he could forge ahead. Her personality be damned. It was only her looks he cared about. Having a stunning wife was a special form of currency, like having a fancy sports car." He paused. "I learned much of this years later, but only bits and pieces of the story."

"I see."

"From what I was told, her new husband was a wannabe musician with little to no talent. He hated that she was in love with someone who had an abundance of what he felt cheated of— something money could not buy, and he *hated* that she never fell in love with *him*." John paused, choking on his words.

"It's okay. Take your time."

"Juliana's father was apparently a close business associate of her new husband's father. I don't know how they forced her to marry him, but they did something. It must have been powerful; that's all I know."

"You never found out?"

"I didn't try. Because I knew learning more would have made things worse, and I'd be too angry to function."

"I can understand that." Sunny offered a sympathetic smile.

"But I did move on. Music saved me—for a while. I put everything into my career and became Whisky Devers." He saw the question in Sunny's eyes. "You're wondering about the name."

"I am."

"There was a homeless man I got to know in Manhattan. Hung around Seventh Avenue and thereabouts, not far from the Sheraton Hotel, which was pretty close to Round They Go Records. We'd talk for hours and I often bought the man food and other things, when he would allow me. Very proud man. He taught me more about life than my own father ever *tried* to teach me." He paused to remember. "I never knew the man's first name. Everyone called him 'Mr. Devers.' He always told me he was married to 'Mrs. Whisky.' Sadly, that's what would kill him. No surprise, but as I never wanted to use my own name professionally, any form of it, I took his."

"How fascinating. I always assumed that Devers was the real surname of the artist I so adore."

John lowered his eyes as the sentiment of her words grabbed hold of him. He waited a bit before continuing his story. "I was lucky enough to get a record contract with Round They Go Records who had discovered me on a regular gig I played on the Upper West Side. They were almost a mid-size company and loved my work. Before the first album was even released, they gave me a contract for two more. I was on top of the world. And I put everything into those recordings. Everything I was and everything I had." He looked down. "And then some."

"I knew that the first time I heard your music. Your words, your voice, your emotion. It touched me in a way I can't explain." She let out a sigh. "This was in the mid-eighties, yes?"

"Nineteen eighty-five."

"You must be getting to the part where something awful happened." Sunny gulped and took a couple sips of wine before resting the glass.

"When Juliana's husband, knowing she still loved me, found out about my hit album, his father's company, Xavier Rox Records, bought Round They Go, just so he could control my work. It was nothing but pure jealousy, spite empowered by the all-mighty dollar. I had no idea." He poured more wine into both of their glasses.

"After Round They Go was acquired, the new management told me that my second and third albums would have to come out later than planned. I was gutted but had no choice but to wait. Eventually, the pieces came together and I learned that Xavier Rox owned my work lock, stock, and barrel. In my naivete, I still thought they'd be released. Damn fool, I was."

Horror appeared on Sunny's face. "So it was legal for them to have complete control? Didn't you have anything to say about it?"

"Unfortunately, it was completely legal. Unethical and disgusting, but legal. Round They Go had fully funded the recording sessions, so Xavier Rox, now the lawful owners, retained all of their assets. And they could do, or *not* do, whatever they wanted." John's eyes narrowed as he recalled the story. "The thing is, Sunny, this man was never in love with Juliana. His ego simply didn't allow for his wife to love anyone but him. 'Vengeance is mine,' said the bastard. And he took it. And later he and Juliana divorced."

"Oh my goodness. What happened next?"

John took a couple sips of wine. "I was devastated that my two albums were put on indefinite hold, but I was determined to wait for them to be released, so I performed gigs and worked on new material. During these years, I married a woman named Evelyn. No, I didn't love her as I had Juliana, but she was fun-loving, attractive, seemingly caring—and, I had thought, a *much* better human being than I would come to learn she was. It didn't take me too long to figure out that she'd pursued me with the hope that my success would carry her to dizzying heights and heaps of cash." Disgust covered his face. "To this day, I can't believe I let her reel me in. Anyway, in 1992, when she met a billionaire record company owner and began having an affair with him, her inner monster was revealed, to an extent that I'd never believed was possible. I mean that demon burst from her like that scene in *Alien* where the creature bursts from the guy's chest."

"How frighteningly descriptive." Sunny covered her mouth in shock, then dropped her hands. "Wait! Are you saying that the same guy who'd married Juliana, who then stole your music, came for your wife?"

"That's about it. The ego of a malignant narcissist knows no bounds. Except I would've gladly given her to him, but not knowing I'd long ceased to love her, he couldn't yank her away fast enough. And yes, he sought her out solely because he was still obsessed with 'fucking Johnny boy,' and finding out that I had a wife, well, he wanted to take every last thing he could from me. By then, I'd known for years that my albums were never slated for release, but he made a point to come to one of my gigs just to rub it in. That was the first time I'd ever met him, but not the last. Between sets, after lording his power over me, he said he couldn't wait for my star to fade to dust and crumble in the sky and for everyone to forget me. Laughed his head off and left."

"That never happened, John. Not for me." Sunny brushed a tear from her cheek. "Sorry, I just had to say that. Please, go on."

"You're very sweet." He stopped to absorb her words. "And Evelyn, money grubber that she is, was unfazed by his cruelty. She'd lost all interest in the man who'd already lost all in her. She turned out to be a monster and then she married one."

Sunny grabbed both sides of her head. "Wait, didn't Evelyn realize that her new man was the ex-husband of your ex-girlfriend and that he'd sought her out to stick it to you? Didn't you tell her?"

"It was tempting. A tiny part of me still cared about her and didn't want to lose anything more to this man—in principle. But in my heart, I wanted her to go. And even if she had known, he'd have made up some story and she'd have easily believed him because the need to eliminate internal conflict is a powerful thing. Cognitive dissonance is one hell of a coping technique, as I'm sure you know. So yeah, nothing would have changed. The money and the lifestyle reeled her in. To answer your question, I heard that he referred to Juliana as 'Jules.' And as she didn't want to hear about his ex-wife, I doubt there was little reason to mention her especially as he and Juliana had no children together. But Ev's as bad as he is and getting a billionaire husband was all that mattered." He picked up his wineglass and held it as he looked out at the crashing waves.

"Why now, John? Why did he release your second album?"

"For whatever reason, he decided it was time to torture me again. And as you can see, it worked. I no longer want the world to know Whisky Devers, and no doubt he's figured that out. Maybe he thinks the album will fail and he can enjoy a healthy dose of schadenfreude as I'm humiliated. Or maybe, if the opposite happens, he thinks I'll lose my mind seeing the money I could have made go to him. No matter what, he knows this is not what I want. He also knows I've shunned society and I'd never go public with this. But why he decided to resurrect his grudges after so many years, I don't know. Only that he wants hell to rain down on me again."

Sunny's face contorted as she replayed all he'd told her. "When you said you couldn't tell me everything, are you saying that the reason you've 'shunned society' as you just said was more than what you just told me?"

"*Way* more." John touched his throat as the words stuck in there.

"My goodness, if that alone wasn't enough." With love in her eyes, she looked at him. "I don't need to know anymore until the day you decide to tell me. If that day even comes." A tear rolled down her cheek. "And you're very certain you don't want the world to know who you are?"

John slowly moved his head up and down. "Very."

Kono, done with his nap, now stood at attention in front of John, as Miggy did the same with Sunny.

"Is it okay for Miggy to have Kono's food for dinner? I think they both eat the same brand, if I remember."

"They do. Thank you." Fighting back the tears, she dug into her pocket and pulled out her phone. "I need to text Rissa to let them know I'm okay. The way I ran out of the hotel. I scared Rissa, Ty, and Larae to death. And no doubt Rolo when he heard about it. I was out of my mind and so rude to the people who love me the most. I didn't even recognize myself."

"I'm sure everyone will be very happy to know you're all right. I know I would be." John rose and hurried to the kitchen as the dogs followed him.

Sunny composed a quick text while John fed Miggy and Kono.

Within minutes, he returned, taking his seat on the couch again. "I didn't want to tell you this, but several mornings ago, Rolo came for a visit. Right before he left, I got an ugly text." He picked up the phone from the table and showed it to her.

"Oh, no! Is this from this monster man?"

"It has to be. I thought 'face the music' was just an expression, but now I see that he meant it literally. I told Rolo it was okay to share with Clarissa, but he didn't want to worry Ty, and I didn't want to worry you. But now that I believe it was simply to threaten me about my music, I wanted you to know."

"This is dreadful. Thank you for telling me this and everything else. Believe me, I won't tell Ty. None of the details you've told me will reach anyone else's ears. They'll all know who you are, but that's it. You have my word." Lost in thought, she looked down, then at him. "You are such a fine man—in every way."

"I'm a flawed man."

"Every one of us is flawed. But not everyone is kind, impassioned, and so ruggedly and beautifully … and … well …."

"John looked into her eyes, caressing her face as he believed she wanted to caress his. "Oh, Sunny. I'd really like to fu—"

Her eyes widened as she realized what he was saying. To him, it appeared as if her entire body was unfurling after being wrapped tight for years.

"Oh, say it to me, John. Use any words you like. Be as crude and uninhibited as you want. Just, please, tell me what you want, and I'll give it to you without constraint or apprehension. With everything I have."

His face moved closer to hers, their lips only inches apart, but then he leaned back, his breathing uneven. "I can't. It would be wrong." He closed his eyes for a moment. "The timing, *not* the act. It would be wrong as things are *now*. I respect and care about you far too much. I don't want to hurt you in any way. And in my guilt and regret, I would probably distance myself from you. I don't want to do that, Sunny. I have this habit of running away, and I just don't want to do that anymore."

Together, they both looked at the bulge in his pants, their eyes meeting again.

"Oh, John."

As his eyes burned into hers, he gently kissed her lips, then pulled away. "You deserve the best of me. And that's not what I can give you today."

"I understand." Sobbing, she leaned against his chest and buried her tears, his arm holding her close and rubbing her back. They stayed that way for twenty minutes, until two impatient dogs let them know it was time to go out.

CHAPTER SIXTEEN

After a walk on the beach and the impromptu meal John cooked, it was after ten when Sunny, John, and the two dogs entered the hotel lobby. Tyler was behind the desk, and within a minute, having seen them on the monitor, Clarissa rushed in.

Seeing their emotionally drained faces, she smiled awkwardly. "Sunny, thanks for your two texts. Letting us know you were okay and again to say you were staying for dinner."

As Kono and Miggy flopped down together on the large area rug in the center of the lobby, immediately dozing off, Sunny fell onto the couch as John sat next to her. "Rissa ...."

Making a stop motion with her hand, Clarissa silenced her. "Sunny, I've known you for many years, my friend and sister girl. And while you think I saw someone today who I didn't recognize, you'd be wrong. I saw the woman who I've always known to be fiery, passionate, and unrelenting when it comes to people who matter to her. You were on a mission, and nothin' was gonna stop you. Not me, not Ty, not any darn body or any darn thing. I think I speak for us both, and probably Larae, when I say that while we were confused, and while we didn't understand the specifics, we did understand the woman. So don't you dare apologize for anything. You hear me? Not playin.' Don't even try it."

Sunny's forehead dropped into her cupped hands. After a long sigh, she looked up, first at Clarissa, then at Ty. "I wasn't myself."

"Yeah, you were," Ty said. "Just not a Sunny we've seen before. But still you. Sort of like seeing the rerun of a TV show you've seen many times, only you find you missed an episode or two." He thought. "Yeah, it was like that."

She smiled at Tyler. "What a lovely thing to say, but I was so rude. The way I spoke to you both—"

"Did you hear what he just said? What *I* just said? No apologies." Clarissa challenged her with a loving stare. "'Cause if you even try, I'm gonna have to beat you up. And I'm too worn out from dinner service to do much of anything right now."

Sunny offered a loving smile.

"May I intervene here?" John asked. "Because I wasn't exactly the person you've come to know either, even though it's only been three weeks."

Clarissa made a stop motion with her other hand. "Same goes for you, mister. No apologies. You think we didn't know you weren't cursing at us? Of course we did. I don't know who's done you so wrong in your life, but you're a very good man, John Hennessey, and we all saw that from jump." She smiled. "Y'all look like you're more than good with each other, and that's all I need to get a good night's sleep. Rolo, too."

Sunny jumped up and gave her a hug. "I love you, Rissa. So much."

"Damn tear," Clarissa said, brushing away the sentiment that rolled down her cheek. "Love you too, Sunny." She looked at John and gave him a warm smile. "Y'all be good and y'all are loved."

As Clarissa left, she nearly collided with Harper, who was heading through the lobby door after a walk on the beach. The two women exchanged only a look. As Clarissa lingered for a moment behind her, she saw Harper's eyes dart to Sunny and John and the pleasant expression on her face transform into one of anger, tinged with disappointment.

Tyler, who'd seen the exchange, winced, then buried his face into the guest register as Harper nodded a quick hello to everyone, hurrying to the door that would take her upstairs to her suite.

"Walk me outside?" John said to Sunny. He called to Kono. "Say goodnight to your girl."

As Tyler snuck a peep, he saw John take Sunny's hand. Smiling, he returned his focus to the register.

Followed by Kono, a despondent Miggy left behind, John and Sunny walked outside and stood before the steps to the beach.

His right index finger touched Sunny's lips. Understanding, she said nothing.

"When I said it was the timing and not the act, I meant it. There's too much evil, too much ill intent swirling around both of us. We need to get all of the demons and the debris out of our way. We don't want that kind of hell to bring us together. Please tell me you understand."

Sunny reached up and caressed the side of his face. "I do. And I know you're right, and I don't disagree, but I would have been okay with wrong."

John kissed her forehead. "Listen, I need to take a couple of days to decompress from all of this. And, no, 'this' does not mean *you*. Please know that."

"I think I do. I know you were way out of your comfort zone telling me all that you did. I'm so very appreciative."

"You don't need to be. I wanted to tell you, and I'm glad you know. But I've done more talking tonight than I have in years, and I've got to let the situation settle. This album being released has taken me way out of my comfort zone, much more so than the revelations from the past. Honestly, I'm still in a state of shock, not a place I tend to thrive. I just want you to know that I'll be back in a couple of days and not to worry about me or our friendship." He managed a smile. "I'm also guessing you want your record album back. I won't destroy it. I promise."

"I was kind of worried you might."

"I wouldn't do that to you, but it was tempting when I saw it again. I haven't looked at the thing in all of these years. And those times, when I came into the hotel and heard my songs playing, well, let's just say it took everything in me to play nonchalant. Hearing that music put me on the precipice of madness. Luckily, I managed to stay there and not fall off. Unlike earlier today."

"Oh, John. I wish I hadn't told—"

"Do you think I wouldn't have found out? I've had my phone off all day, and I guarantee you Ben's been trying to call."

"No doubt he has."

John looked into her eyes, certain she was fumbling to find the right words before saying more. "Sunny—"

"You know I'm always here, if you feel like resurfacing sooner than later. I just want you to do what you need to take care of yourself. And if that means I don't hear from you in a week, then so be it."

"It won't be a week. If I don't see you in two days' time, I'll call you. You have my word. And if there's any kind of emergency here, please don't feel that you can't call me. I'm unsteady at the moment, honestly, but I'm not made of glass."

"I hope what I said earlier didn't upset you." Her voice

softened. "That I'd have been 'okay with wrong.' A part of me still feels that way, but now I understand better. I don't disagree, I just ...."

He started to respond, but the words didn't want to be spoken. "Goodnight, Sunny. I'll see you on the weekend." He looked down at Kono, who was eager to make his way home. "Okay, boy, let's go."

Lying on the bed, staring at her cell phone, Harper, slightly hyperventilating, bit her lip as she tried to shake off the rage that hugged her. Punching in a number, she put the phone to her ear. "Hey, it's me. I know it's late for me to be calling, but I know you're still awake." She paused to listen. "I'm just telling you, if you're gonna do anything, if you still think you need to right all the wrongs in your life, you need to get on a plane and get out here now." She listened again. "No, two weeks isn't going to cut it. That will be way too late if it isn't already. Forget about 'getting your nerve up' and just get out here." She paused to listen some more. "I'm dying with this bullshit. I can't do anything else to help you. I've been trying for years. I don't even know who I am anymore. You think I don't have my own needs? You think I'm not in pain? If you want to get better and reclaim your life, you have to do it yourself. I can't fix it for you. I tried, and I can't. You think you're the only one with something major at stake? Well, you're not."

Holding the phone away from her ear, she cried her own tears while listening to the sobs at the other end. "I'm going to sleep now. I'm frazzled to my core. You do what you want; but don't come crying to me if your refusal to fight for *your* happiness leaves you looking and feeling like a lump of coal in the fireplace." She listened. "I'm too tired to come up with anything better. Maybe I'm a sucky writer. So what? You know what I'm saying. You decide. I can't take much more. And yeah, I love you. But goodnight."

"Hey, Benjo. Sorry to call you back so late."

"You were really starting to worry me, John."

"I had my phone off all day. I was with Sunny." John stretched out on the chaise sectional and stared at the wood beams on the ceiling.

"Nice! So things are—"

"Stay away from that subject. In case you didn't get the message, that's not up for discussion." He let out an exhausted breath. "I'm pretty sure I already know why your voicemails sounded like the world was going to end if I didn't get back to you tonight."

"You heard already. Really? Actually, there are two things. Just don't know how to find the right—"

"Let me help you out. I know the bastard released my second album. Sunny's daughter found out through a musician she knows and sent her mother a copy."

"Oh, man. So, not going into the part of this you don't wanna talk about, but I take it Sunny knows who you are."

John closed his eyes and spoke wearily. "It's a long story, but yeah, she figured it out. My expletive-laden reaction when I heard the music, followed by my furious departure from the hotel lobby, kind of clued her in that my life had just plummeted into the bowels of the earth. After I left, she put it together, dug out her Whisky Devers album, saw my youthful naïve face—and that was that. Ironically, the only place you can see my face on the CD is on the whiskey label. A very tiny old photo. No doubt to diminish me. That part, I'm actually happy about."

"Oh." There was a long, uncomfortable silence. "So, does she know everything?"

"Not ready to go there. I told her about Juliana, the record company acquisition, and about the bastard coming for Evelyn. And just divulging even that much was brutal. When you've locked the past up in a box, let it rust, and thrown away the key, prying that sucker open is painful. But I had to tell her. She deserved to know."

"I wish you'd had some warning."

"I did. I just didn't know what it meant. That 'face-the-music' text I got was literal. Bet he thought he was really clever."

"Sorry, man. I really am. Wish I'd found out sooner so you could have been forewarned."

"And what good would that have done? Honestly, it wouldn't have mattered too much, Benjo. The son of a bitch sucker punched me into the stars with this."

Another awkward pause ensued. "So, speaking of the stars, I don't know if you'll be happy or pissed to know, but that the album is selling like crazy. And it's going to be released in Europe and Australia soon."

"FUCK." John opened his eyes and sat up.

"I guess that's a no on 'happy.'" Ben sighed. "Yeah, I thought it would be. I hate that Xavier Rox is gonna make a fortune—"

"Do you think I care about the money *now*? More to the point, do you think I want to hear about it? You don't know me better than that? Seriously."

"I do."

"Then please, never say his name or the company name to me. Both chill me to the bone."

"I get it, John. I haven't forgotten. I just thought if your anger was focused on the money aspect, the rest might not hurt so much."

"Why would I want to focus on *any* part of it. You know that nothing is more important to me than my privacy—the preservation of what's left of my soul. I'm nothing like the young, naïve, dreaming fool that Whisky Devers was. He died a death harder than old Mr. Devers himself did. Maybe he deserved it. I've often thought that bastard did me a favor in killing him. I just know that I've never hoped for his resurrection."

"C'mon, dude. For one, I don't believe Whisky Devers is really dead. I mean, you're still writing songs. You've written hundreds of them since then."

"Yeah, under another name, and you've been selling them for me, for years. They're not the songs 'Whisky' would have written and they're not even the songs John Hennessey would write. They're commercial garbage—just a way for me to keep my muse from withdrawing cold turkey from my true career, and yeah, to earn an honest living."

"Do you think I don't know you still write for yourself?"

"Myself. Not for Whisky Devers and not for the world. Leave it."

"John ...."

"Hear me again, Ben Joseph Rockley. This is the last time I'm telling you. My patience is worn thin, and I have *no* desire to re-introduce myself to the world. I'm a different person. Nobody knows that more than you do. Don't try to psychoanalyze me. I've lost all desire to be known to the masses. In fact, it repulses me to even think about it. And if you don't or can't believe me, then maybe I should re-think—"

"No! Don't even go there. I'd be lost without you. You're the best friend I've ever had. You helped me find my way again and gave me my life back. Because of you, it looks like I might get my family back too. Whatever you tell me, I believe and I respect. Know that, my dude. And I would never do anything to dox you in a million years."

"That was never a concern. I just need you to respect what I've told you and stop questioning me like maybe I'm not sure how I feel about my own life. I *am* who I tell you I am. Don't look beneath the surface for more and tell yourself you're being a good friend by doing so. I'm not repressing anything. There's nothing to find." He huffed. "I'm really tired of repeating myself."

"I hear you. For real, man. So listen, there's one other thing."

"Can't wait. What?"

"I know who put the tacks under my tire."

"So the cameras worked."

"Oh, yeah. You could say that."

"Benjo, if you can't hear it in my voice, listen to my words. I'm more exhausted than I've been in years. As much as I'd love to engage in witty banter until we get to the punch line, if you don't tell me—"

"It was that bitch, 'Spiky Shelley.' No big surprise. Kind of thought it might be her, but I couldn't figure out how. See, I caught her on camera. Yeah, she was coming to put more tacks, nails, and other spiky shit on my driveway, thinking this was your house, then she looked up, saw the cameras and the sign."

"And she ran?"

"Not quite. She lifted her damn shirt and flashed her ginormous tits at the camera, followed by a very intense middle finger. Then, she spit on the ground, still flashing while she jiggled them. Then—"

"Sheesh." John muttered to himself. "I will never, ever drink as much as I did that night. Especially in such a low-lit bar. That abhorrent experience already seems light years ago, and that life is behind me." Realizing he'd inadvertently left the conversation, he returned his attention to Ben. "Sorry, what were you saying?"

"Just that she was still juggling and jiggling when Dodger and I walked out of the house. At first, she didn't even look up to see that I wasn't you. That's when she sang to me."

"I don't wanna know."

"'Givin' you the breasts that I got, honey!' Can you believe that? When she finally saw I wasn't you, she didn't even look embarrassed. Just pulled down her shirt, barely, and gave me a dirty look. Then, she walked away, doing some kind of skanky side-to-side thing with her hips."

"Charming. How did she even know to come to your house? That's a bit disconcerting, to say the least."

"Beats me. But I don't think she'll be back."

"Probably not, but still, how—"

"It's really a small community. Hey, I knew who *she* was when you described her. Wouldn't have been that hard to find out about you if she'd asked around. Your car was in my driveway for eight years, so there's that. Don't wrack your brain with this nonsense. My gut tells me she's not coming back. And you've got way more important things to worry about. By the way, speaking of things to worry about, did you figure out who sent the flowers?"

"No, and it weighs on me heavily. But I think it was some woman who was asking about my cottage in the local diner. Just happened to go there for lunch a while back before I moved in here. I had way too much on my mind to dig deeper, especially since it could have been anyone. The cottage *was* on the market for quite a while. Nothing really out of the ordinary that someone might ask about it."

"That makes sense. Listen, man, you need me for anything, call."

"Thanks, my friend." John motioned for Kono to sit beside him as he looked out onto the dark sea. "If there's nothing else ...."

"That pretty much covers it. Talk to you soon. Really sorry all of this went down. Ciao, dude."

John looked at his phone. "Do I leave you on or turn you off?" He glanced at Kono. "What do you think?" He waited a moment. "Yeah, you've got a point. Miggy and Sunny might need us. We'll leave it on."

CHAPTER SEVENTEEN

"Before you do whatever women do in there, bring a warm cloth, and clean me up." Richard Strausser, arrogant and entitled, called to his mistress, Phoebe Marcroft, from the red leather recliner he equated to his personal throne. He eyed her as the sexual toy he considered her to be, not as a woman he loved or respected but as one he hoped would believe anything and everything he told her for however long it suited him.

"But I *really* need to use—"

"Won't take you long, sweetie. You didn't quite get it all, and I don't care to wear my own secretions. Hear me? And when you're done, I have a gift and some good news for you, so don't fret, my lovely pet."

She pasted on a smile, upset that her pride wasn't the only thing she'd swallowed. "Sure."

Returning shortly with a warm wash cloth in her hands, she cleaned his manhood as he watched, moaning with satisfaction. Helplessly, after several minutes, she looked into his eyes for permission to stop.

His annoyance was undeniable. "I'm really enjoying this, in case you didn't notice, but okay, zip me up if you insist on putting your own needs first."

"I really do need to use the facilities, Richard." She smiled through her disdain as she closed his fly. "Excuse me, please."

"Go on then." He took a swig of his bourbon on the rocks, then grabbed his phone and pressed a contact. "Yeah. I know it's Friday night. And I'm glad you're still at the office. You should be. What's the deal? You got more numbers for me?" He listened, his face contorting with rage. "Really, it's actually selling? That well? I thought the loser would've been forgotten."

He took his black rectangular-framed glasses off, snarled at the smudges, then cleaned them with the corner of his custom-made Oxford shirt. "Damn it! Yeah, of course I like making money, but that was *never* the goal here." He put his glasses back on. "This loser needs to be humiliated, worldwide, and with extraordinary force. I need an unprecedented TKO to leave him flat-out unconscious and obliterated in the ring. You hear me?" As he listened some more, he finished his drink, then refilled his glass with the bottle next to it.

"Why are you changing the subject? Do I sound like I give a damn that my wife wants me to call her? We have nothing to say to one another. I haven't cut the shrew off—she's got money. It's all she's ever wanted anyway. But she can't have any part of my crowned jewels; that's for damn sure. And hear me when I say that nobody else will want her old-lady pussy, either. I don't care if she pays someone to fuck her. It's not like I'm ever going to touch that rotting snatch again."

A generous swig of bourbon slid down his throat. "Now tell me you think those initial numbers are just a fluke." He balled his fists as he listened to the response. "You know what? This isn't what I need to hear! This is *not* what I *want* to hear. And it's *not* what you fucking predicted would happen. You said nobody would remember him. How dare you be wrong about something so important to me?" He listened. "I know this isn't an exact science. But your trend-forecasting, pop-culture nonsense and your number-crunching-guesswork bullshit really ruined my day. Not to mention my tomorrow and a string of days after that. I have way too much money and power to be this unhappy and this pissed off. And you're a useless flunky." He huffed, then took another swig. "You can't quit, Rob, because I'm firing your incompetent ass. Pack up and get the hell out of the building. Oh, yeah? Well you too—and your mother! And your grandmother!"

Ending the call, he sputtered and dropped the phone on the table, fuming. Speaking softly, yet with uncontrollable anger, he addressed his true enemy in absentia. "Taking your royalties is not going to satisfy me. I'll be damned if something I've done inflates your ego or brings any kind of praise in your direction. No, if that damn album is going to sell, then I'll find another way to destroy you. You've taken what's mine too many times, and you're doing it again." His eyes bulged as his face morphed into a maniacal visage. "Yeah, I'm going back to my original plan. I came here to humiliate you, but I think I might have to kill you. Even if I can't accomplish the first, I won't fail on the last. Take that to the bank! Consider yourself dead when I decide the time is right. And it won't be long. The sooner the better. Don't you dare underestimate me. I've got lots of ideas to lure you into my trap. You're gonna walk right into it thinking you've got the upper hand."

As John, wearing his long, black coat, walked on the moonlit beach with Kono, memories of the previous day's events still chased one another in his head, taking him on a twisty trip back in time to places he'd tried so hard to leave in the shadows. Yet the most recent events weighed the heaviest on him—from the moment he heard his old music playing, to wanting Sunny so much that desire overwhelmed him and respect for her knocked sense back into his head.

He replayed the telling of secrets he'd never planned to share while the ones he hadn't yet shared sat impatiently on the tip of his tongue. He walked on. Old enemies were back. The danger was impossible to ignore. But reigning over all thoughts, at least in that moment, was Sunny. Whatever was going to happen with her would bear no resemblance to the one-night stands he'd allowed to sustain him over the past eight years.

Her demons, like his, had led her to live a controlled existence not dissimilar to his, only more people walked through her life, with only a handful of them mattering. What she had been through—seeing her husband killed before her eyes, was so traumatic, and for a moment, dwarfed his pain.

She had truly loved Grey. After two children and many years together, he had been ripped from her in the worst way. And he, John, was the first man since that time she had ever wanted, and she was the first woman he'd felt that way about since the teenager he believed to be his true love.

This wasn't a contest for the saddest story. All he knew was that everything and everyone who had been wrenched from his life had irrevocably changed it. And he would never do anything that he believed could hurt this glorious woman he felt so deeply about. Even though Juliana had been only nineteen the night he wanted to propose, he felt uneasy telling Sunny how he'd loved her. He visualized her face when he'd explained how Juliana had insisted he bury his hands in the pockets, and the world would make sense again. How odd, Sunny had said. Yes, it was more than odd. It was an enigma.

"Wait!" He stopped in his tracks and motioned for Kono to do the same.

Up on the hill, tears rolled down Sunny's cheeks as she watched him, replaying events of the day past just as he was doing. When she saw him stop, she felt a thud in her chest. Something was happening. He was having an epiphany, just like the moment she realized John and Whisky Devers had to be one and the same. Her breath diminished, she exhaled forcefully until it returned.

Kono, having sensed a major shift in his master's emotion, watched curiously as John put both hands in his pockets. Only now, rather than bemoaning the fact that the stitching had been forever loose, he pushed through it until the pockets lost all function. Immediately, his left hand felt something—a piece of folded paper pinned to the cloth several inches below where the pocket ended. Pulling it out, he stood in a spot where the moon would illuminate the words. He recognized Juliana's handwriting immediately. Being the recipient of so many love notes, he could never forget it, especially the way she drew flourishes on certain letters. Her penmanship was as pretty as she had been.

His eyes soaked in the message she'd written thirty-five years ago. His breath gave way in his throat, knocking the wind out of him and forcing him to his knees on the wet sand, the foam from the incoming waves touching him before they receded, while the sand, without remorse, adhered to the bottom front of the coat. Panting, he looked at the letter one more time. "NOOOOOO!"

His voice carried so far, that even Miggy, immersed in sniffing the lawn for scents of Kono, stopped and looked out onto the beach in unison with Sunny.

"Oh, John. I knew she mentioned those pockets for a reason. And now, you know that reason, and I can never ask you. Whatever it is, I just want to hold you. I would hold you forever and ever if I could."

She watched as he remained as he was, almost as if he was praying to the ocean or maybe the moon. "This is an invasion of your privacy, beautiful man. This is the last time I'm going to do it." She looked at the dog. "Inside, girl. We need to let John and Kono be."

"Come here, Phoebe." Richard, sitting up in bed, his bare chest signaling to her that the rest of him was unclothed as well, licked his lips as she came out of the master bathroom in cherry-red lingerie. "Well don't you look beautiful, my dear. I told you earlier I had good news and a gift. Do you remember?"

Phoebe smiled as she climbed into bed. "I do. I just thought ...."

"What? That because I had such a miserable day I'd forgotten all about you?"

"I could understand if you had."

He slipped his hand under the lingerie and squeezed her breast. "Impossible. I don't think you understand how much you mean to me. You're my feel-good baby. Am I yours?"

Phoebe lowered her eyes, hoping he wouldn't see her disappointment as she longed to be recognized for more than her sexual prowess. "Richard, I just wonder sometimes if you—"

"Guess who is going to be singing the title song for a blockbuster film? I'll give you a hint. She's blonde, beautiful, and titillates in red."

"Are you kidding? The studio picked me?"

"Of course they did. You have the voice of an angel. Congratulations, my darling. They've sent contacts to my office, but as I had to fire Rob for incompetence, we'll have to wait for someone else to send them over. No rush, though. They won't be recording for a few months."

"I can't believe it. This is so amazing! I've never had a break like this. Not ever. Thank you so much!"

Richard reached over to the nightstand and handed her a red velvet jewelry box. "And here is your gift."

"You mean *that* wasn't it?" Opening the box, she put her hand to her throat as she saw a heart made of alternating round rubies and natural diamonds, set in white gold. Recognizing the name imprinted on the underside of the lid, on satin, she knew the piece came from the finest jeweler in New York. "I've never, ever received a gift so gorgeous, not to mention such amazing news. I-I just don't know what to say, except thank you—again." She turned and kissed him deeply on the lips as his hand slid underneath her. "Oh, Richard! Now you're really spoiling me."

"Now, what is it that you wanted to say to me, my love?"

"It was nothing. I can't even remember," she lied as her face reflected the pleasure he was giving her. "Oh my goodness. This feels incredible. You're such a master at this. Oh, Richard ..."

After gratifying her for another few minutes, he removed his hand and looked into her eyes, his expression serious. "I need to talk to you about something. I'm only going to explain briefly, but I hope you'll do exactly as I ask. Anything less is unacceptable."

Seeing the abrupt change in his demeanor, she tensed. "Okay."

"I know you love the balcony off the living room."

"Oh, I do. The view is so wonderful. It's so peaceful and everything."

"Well, you can *never* step foot on it again. There's a smaller balcony off this room, quite lovely in its own right, and you can sit there as much as you'd like. But never, ever the larger balcony. Not even for a hot second."

Confusion landed on her face. "But why?"

"Why is because I said so, but I'll just tell you this much: I've learned there are cameras trained on that balcony. Very often and at times when you'd least expect it. I'm sure you understand why you can *never* be photographed here. Not even at 3:00 a.m. No time is safe. Phoebe, I need your solemn promise on this. It could ruin me, and your contract would be null and void. I need you to leave those sliding glass doors shut. Not to mention the screen doors behind them. Never open any of those doors, and never set foot on that balcony again. Do you hear me?"

Sighing in relief, she smiled. "I understand. You sounded so scary." She furrowed her brow. "But where could anyone even stand to point a camera—"

"Enough! Do I have your word? I do *not* want to explain any more of this to you! Never ever broach the subject again."

The power of his voice diminished her, and she naturally leaned back. "Okay. I'm sorry. That was stupid of me to even say. I would do anything to protect you, Richard. You're so good to me. And yes, I love the smaller balcony as well. The view isn't quite as nice, but it's more beautiful than anything I've ever had."

"Good. Settled. Now, because you've been such a good girl, tomorrow morning, I want you to take my credit card off the bureau, get in the limo that will be waiting for you, and go to the nearest big town and shop to your heart's content."

"Really?"

"Of course. I do hope you'll pick out a few outfits with me in mind."

"You're *always* on my mind, you wonderful, generous man."

"Good. And after the limo brings you back here, you can slip into something low-cut and seductive before the driver takes us north of Teal Beach to one of the finest restaurant in miles."

"I feel so undeserving."

"So no more talk about the front balcony?"

A coquettish smile on her face, she reached under the covers and took hold of him. "I have no idea what balcony you're even talking about."

Moaning at her touch, he took his glasses off, put them on the night table, and lay back to reap his reward.

CHAPTER EIGHTEEN

A smile on her face, Sunny wished her new guests a good stay as they finished checking in. Within seconds, the couple who'd been browsing in the small gift shop approached the reception desk with T-shirts, postcards, and polished shells. Relieved the strangers had no desire to linger after she'd rung up their sale, her smile disappeared as soon as their backs were turned.

As was her habit, any time the lobby cleared, music would play. But as Sunny put her finger on the stereo unit's Play button, her hand froze. Whisky Devers was on so many of the mixes. Feeling the intense pain that John had carried for years, she couldn't listen to the songs now or risk traumatizing either one of them if he came in. The thought made her insides feel sour and sick. Maybe she'd never listen to music again. Brushing her sorrow aside, she went back to writing paychecks for her staff.

Halfway through writing Larae's check, a new reservation came in over the phone. She had no sooner finished the call when the phone rang again.

"Really?" Sunny picked up the phone, having no tolerance for chatting. "Good afternoon. Teal Beach Sundial Inn."

First, she heard indistinct whispering, then slightly louder, "Hey, bitch. Did you miss me?"

Refusing to engage, she ended the call, smiling as if all were well, then walked away to hide her face from the camera. If they had been watching the monitor, the last thing she wanted was the Gardet calvary running in, but a part of her wished they would.

Forty-five minutes later, Clarissa came through the lobby with a small
plastic-wrap-covered plate and put it on the coffee table. "Hey, Sunny,
guess who made beignets today? A little lagniappe for our customers."

Looking at the square piece of fried dough, generously covered
with powdered sugar, Sunny gave Clarissa a playful dirty look. "You
know how much I love these, but you also know that the beignet
calorie count is not and never will be my friend."

Clarissa plunked down on the chair opposite. "It's not my
friend either, but an occasional treat is a good thing. I haven't made
these in months, and our customers love them. And as you can see, I
only brought you one." Her happy tone faded. "I wanted to bring
two—one for John—but it felt pushy, especially knowing you're both
having a difficult go of things now." She offered a brief smile. "Of
course, there are plenty more where this came from."

Sunny frowned. "I do love your Louisiana state donut, and I
love you more, but I'm just not feeling like I want to celebrate anything
right now." Seeing hurt in Clarissa's eyes, she added, "But why not? A
half today and a half tomorrow can't hurt anything. "After all, it's
Saturday." She made a face. "Whatever that means. Maybe that people
have permission to go wild on the weekends—calorie wise, of course."
She winked. "Thanks for bringing me one."

"That's what I wanted to hear." Clarissa chewed her lip and
repositioned herself in the chair as she looked into Sunny's eyes for
answers.

"No, Rissa. I haven't heard from John yet. Later or tomorrow, I will. He promised. I can't talk about it. I know you want to make it better and I know you, Rolo, and Ty care, and Imari too, but there's nothing to say."

"I respect that."

Both women looked up as Harper walked quickly into the lobby, purposely snubbing them both, disappearing through the door to the upstairs.

Looking at Sunny, Clarissa mimed zipping her lips.

"That was different." Sunny twisted her face. "But I've hardly got time to worry about her right now. Though as the owner of this hotel, I do hope I haven't done anything to upset her."

"Nah. She just hates *me*. So listen, Sunny girl, is everything else okay?"

"Larae is working the entire day shift tomorrow, and Miranda is working the night shift so Ty can be with Imari. And that makes me very happy—the second part. But it's way too temporary a fix. He can't go on with this insanity. I'm going to have to insist on putting a new system in place. Whether he likes it or not."

"You know we all agree with that. Especially Imari. A change is years overdue."

"It certainly is. But for the moment, I'm just thrilled he's taking tomorrow night off."

"And *he* had no trouble taking some beignets off the tray to give to the soon-to-be Mrs. Tyler Gardet and the little one she's carrying. And you didn't answer my question, Sunny girl. Everything else okay?"

"What?"

"There are many appropriate ways to answer the phone when your father is calling. 'What?' is not one of them."

"It's Saturday night. It's already ten o'clock. I'm going out with my friends. Like leaving five minutes ago. Can't this wait?"

Sitting in the red-leather recliner he'd fallen in love with at first sight, Richard motioned for Phoebe to put some ice in his glass. As she did so, he continued talking. "No, this can't wait."

Furious, he responded to the dramatic sigh on the other end of the phone. "Jake, the sooner you listen to me, the sooner you can party with whatever lowlifes you call your friends."

"They're not lowlifes. Not even close. Compared to them, I'm the lowlife. I work at my father's company."

"Which is exactly what I'm calling about." Richard nodded to indicate the bottle he wanted Phoebe to pour him a drink from. "Starting Monday morning, you'll report to my office instead of A & R. You have a new job—as my assistant."

"No fucking way! I worked in the mail room and did that crap during college so I could work in A & R after graduation. It's my dream job. I earned it. Even if you do own the company."

Richard leaned back and took a leisurely sip, then another, from his glass. "I had to fire Rob last night. So tag, son: you're it. You're now the new personal assistant to the CEO and owner of Xavier Rox Records."

"No way. I'm not leaving a great job for the worst one in the company."

"First of all, it's by far not 'the worst one in the company.'"

"Yeah, well you don't know what people really think of you, do you, *Dad*?"

Furious, Richard gestured for Phoebe, but instead of wanting his drink refilled, he unzipped his fly and motioned for her to go to work.

Pasting a fake smile over her disdain, her right hand began to stimulate him.

"Let me share something with you, Jake. Guess who I spoke with this morning?"

"Like I care."

"You should. My attorney, Henry Walters." He paused to respond to Phoebe's touch as he grew hard, taking pains not to moan aloud as he wanted to do. "And guess what I'm having him do? Oh, yes! He'll be removing Dylan from my will. Not only does your brother no longer have a car or an apartment, he won't have any inheritance once the papers are drawn up and signed." He leaned back and exhaled as he watched Phoebe in action, staring at her red, manicured nails. "I told him to wait before anything is processed ... because I might ... uh ... I might ... oh ... have to cut his twin brother out too."

"You cut Dylan out of your will because he quit his job?"

He waited until the pulsating of his groin was in his control. "No, I only took his car and his apartment away. He's being disinherited because he changed his name."

"Yeah, I know he did. And I was thinking that doesn't sound like a bad idea. In fact, I think I'm gonna do the same thing. After all, we're twins and we should have the same last name."

"*My* name!" Richard screamed, jolting forward and causing Phoebe's hand to fly off him. "I'm going to ask you something, Jake, and I want the truth. No bullshit. Is Dylan looking for John?"

"Uh … I don't know."

"Jake. I'm going to ask you one more time. Is your duplicate copy looking for that son of a bitch or not?"

"Nah. John's got a relationship with some lady who owns a hotel somewhere, I think. So no way Dylan is gonna bother him."

"WHAT? Did you say John is in a relationship with a lady who owns a *hotel*? In *California*?"

"Uh, I-I don't think so," Jake fumbled. "Definitely not. Like maybe in Mexico, Baja, or somewhere else."

"Oh, damn!" Richard could barely restrain himself as Phoebe gained control of his joystick and continued to play his game. Nodding for her to stand, he pulled her lingerie shorts down with his free hand, had her step out of them, and commanding her only with facial expressions, had her position herself on his lap, trying not to cry out as he entered her. "Oh, yes!" Richard closed his eyes and leaned back.

"Yes, what?"

Making an up-and-down motion with his hand, commanding Phoebe to ride him, he managed to hawk out a final threat. "You don't report to work Monday, you're toast, Jake."

"Oh, really. Then butter me up and slap strawberry jam on my ass. Because I'm not going to be your personal assistant in this lifetime. How about your goon, Fred what's-his-name?"

"He doesn't do administrative work, and you're never to

mention him again."

"Well, whoever you get to do it, they're gonna hate every minute of it. Because there's *nothing* good about you. *Nothing* worth selling yourself to the devil—*you*—for! Dylan figured that out way before I did. I should have listened to him."

"Oooooh, God! Oh!"

Jake took a long moment to respond. "Holy shit! Are you banging some chick while you're talking to me?" Hearing only heavy breathing, he sighed in disgust. "Man, you are one sick bastard."

Angry that he was not the one to end the call, Richard let the phone drop on the table and delighted in the last of his orgasm. After several minutes with his eyes closed, reclaiming his breath, he opened them to look at Phoebe. "How about that dinner I promised you? Is the limo still waiting?"

A pre-programmed smile appeared on her face as she climbed off him, offering only a nod. Trying not to cry, she stood before him, awaiting his approval before she dared to walk away.

Slapping her rear end harder than usual, he grinned. "Good work, doll. You've outdone yourself tonight. You keep it up"— he laughed at his unintentional joke —."and you're going to get a very good report card from Daddy."

Shame burning her face, she picked up her lingerie bottoms and hurried off to take a shower, knowing she could never wash off what was already forever stuck to her conscience.

"Hey. Dylan."

"What are you doing calling me now? Isn't it ten-thirty in New York? I thought you'd be out with your friends. I don't hear any background noise. No way you're home on a Saturday night."

"Yeah. I totally am. Just canceled my plans 'cause I've got other ones to make. Way more important. So what are you doing?"

"I'm studying for the VCAT." Sitting up against the headboard of the bed, Dylan closed the paperback study guide and put it next to the laptop by his side.

"Oh, that's the test you have to take before you can apply to veterinary school?"

"Jake. Let's keep it one-hundred, okay? You're not calling me on a Saturday night to ask me what I'm doing."

"So, well…."

"Okay, so this isn't good. And no secret who it's about."

"See, well, I did something you'll be really happy about, but I also think I might have done something really fucked up too. Except it was totally by accident, and I'm really sorry, and there's no way to fix it."

Dylan reached over to the nightstand and grabbed the open can of Red Bull next to two others. "Hit me with it, bro. Give me the bad news first because I need to know what you did and if it's really that suckworthy, then I don't care about your good news."

"C'mon, Dyl. Hear me out. Please. It sort of all runs together. See, Dad, I mean Richard, called me just as I was heading out. Said that he fired that Rob Forbes guy, his personal assistant, and that his old job was my new job starting Monday morning. Good-bye A&R."

"No way. That sucks. You didn't agree, did you?"

"Nope. I said I quit. I don't want to repeat it all, but then he started in on how he was going to take away my car and apartment like he did yours. Then, that you were going to be disinherited because he found out you changed your last name."

"So he found out, huh? I saw that coming like a Lambo on the Autobahn." Dylan chugged the beverage and put the can back. "And I don't care. I'll do fine on my own."

"Wish I could say the same. I've wanted to work in Artists and Repertoire ever since junior high. And I had just found some really kick-ass bands. Well, forget about all of that now."

Dylan crossed his legs and sat up on the bed. Pressing the speaker button, he laid the phone down. "I know how much you wanted that job, Jake, but it's all you've known. It's all we ever heard about since we were thirteen. Night and day. All the time. But guess what? There's a whole world out there. And yeah, I took the job at Xavier too so I could earn money for veterinary school, but I shouldn't have gone that route. I'll always regret it." He sighed. "I just knew I'd make a lot more money in *his* company than in an entry-level position somewhere else, especially in some job I'd be chucking anyway. You know? But I hated steamrolling over my so-called principles."

"You saw his true colors years before I did. All I could see was the glitz, glam, and green he shoved in our faces. Mom, too. And worse, I believed their lies even when nothing about them sounded right. I feel horrible about that now."

"You think I don't!" Dylan's face reddened as he remembered.

Jake sniffled. "Sorry, man. I didn't mean to sound like it was all about me. You felt bad about stuff way before my brain twigged to even a little bit of it. The thing is, I know the vindictive bastard will have me out of here tomorrow, so maybe I could fly out to where you are. Like tonight."

Dylan ran his fingers through his hair, biting his lip. "Tell me about what you did that I'm not gonna like."

"Well, he asked me if you were looking for John. I just said no, and that John was in a relationship with some lady who owned a hotel, and so you were gonna leave him alone."

"Okay, So you didn't give him any names or addresses, right?"

"No, except he got *really* riled up when I said that and somehow knew I meant California even though I said that wasn't right and I thought she was in Mexico or Baja."

"Where was he when he called you?"

"In his Third Avenue penthouse, I guess. Oh, and get this—he was doin' some chick while he was cursing me out. Moaning and groaning and shit."

"Ugh." Dylan shuddered in revulsion. "What a scum bucket. Well, he always told us multitasking was how busy people got things done."

Jake snickered. "If it wasn't so gross, and if I wasn't gonna be homeless and broke in the morning, I might laugh my ass off at that. I hate myself. I'm a fucking loser."

"No, you're not. I'm not so great, either. And yeah, you were right. I took money from Mom—Evelyn. I got myself a new credit card weeks ago, but I needed money to pay it with, you know? Oh, and when I casually asked her if he knew where John was, she dug through his desk at their Park Avenue apartment and found his secret spy journal under a fake panel in one of the drawers."

"Can't believe he still writes stuff down in a notebook."

Dylan smirked. "Mostly just his passwords and some other stuff. Anyway, Ev gave me the 411, but *only* because she likes to stick it to him for cheating on her and never being around. She didn't even ask me if I was going to look for him." He paused. "Oh, shit! That means he knows John lives here now, and he can easily find out who owns this hotel. I keep forgetting how he's always two steps ahead of everyone. And this renewed grudge against John is all because of me. Betcha he's never stopped keeping tabs on him. Ever."

"Oh, man, Dyl. I forgot to tell you because this never even came into the conversation earlier, but I found out at work that he pulled John's second Whisky Devers's album out of the vault and released it. I heard it's selling like crazy, and you know he wanted it to flatline. He's gotta be flipping because it didn't flop." He paused. "Hey, that would be a cool song. Jake began to sing. 'He's gonna flip, 'cause it didn't flop; the song said go, but he said stop. Bippety bippety, bippety bop!' Cool, huh?"

"Um, no." Dylan sighed. "Lose the songwriting and the singing. Go back to what you were saying."

"Man, you're no fun. Okay. Well, I'm kinda thinking the album kicking ass has to be why he fired Rob. He loves to blame people for shit. He's probably like a rabbit animal, all aggressive and nasty."

"Rabid."

"Whatever. Man, he's gotta be hatin' that people remember John's music after all these years and still want more. As if that's Rob's fault."

"What? Are you kidding me? John must be out of his mind over that. I know he can't be taking it well. He buried that part of his life. Deep. And then some. Look, you can come out here, but you need to stay somewhere else. If people see two of us, well, no hidin' from that. So do something funky with your hair or wear a hat and glasses. Just change something up so we don't look so alike."

"I just changed my look yesterday. Shaved the sides and got highlights on the top. That part is long and all tousled with gel and stuff. I wanted to look cool when I went scouting at clubs. Oh, and by the way, when he said he was gonna disinherit you for changing your name, I told him I was gonna do the same thing."

Dylan looked at the phone. "Good for you. I never thought—"

"Me neither. It just happened and I said it. But I meant it. I'm done with him. So how do I get out to where you are?"

"Just pack up any stuff you can't leave behind and get out to Kennedy Airport. I'm going to look online and book you a flight, a car, and somewhere that's not here to stay, but it won't be far from me. I'll get you on the first nonstop there is. There might be a layover flight leaving sooner, but you could be stuck for hours in some lame airport and have your luggage lost there too. Not worth it. Just wait for me to call. Oh. and Mom, Ev, doesn't know I'm here. I just said I was going to a friend's house in New Mexico to study. So if she calls once you get here, that's where you are. In Santa Fe. Not that either of us give a damn. She doesn't either, for that matter."

CHAPTER NINETEEN

A weary but warm smile on his face, John opened the cottage door and looked at Sunny. Their eyes locked as she handed him the lunch she'd promised to bring. "Antipasto salad. I hope you like it." Before he could even take the bowl she offered, Miggy raced past both of them to roughhouse with Kono.

"Come in, Sunny, please. He looked through the cellophane wrap as he moved aside to usher her in. "This looks delicious. Would it be okay if we wait a while to eat?"

"Of course."

John closed the door and stood for a moment. "When we spoke last night, and I told you that I felt ready to tell you more, after I hung up, I realized that I couldn't eat at the same time I was unburdening myself, or whatever you might call what I'm about to do. I mean, how can I let tales of the past come out of my mouth while I'm putting food into it." A look of embarrassment came over him. "That didn't sound right."

"Oh, but it did, John. I actually had very similar thoughts. I just couldn't imagine that whatever you feel ready to share would be anything close to lunchtime conversation. Not for you, anyway. I had a small breakfast a few hours ago. I'm more than good to wait."

He let out a nervous sigh of relief. "Please, have a seat. I'll just put this away. How about a drink? Mineral water, lemonade, …"

"Lemonade is great." Taking a seat on the sectional couch, she watched the dogs at play to avert her eyes from John.

As he walked to the kitchen, he knew she was feeling his

nervousness as if it were her own.

Two minutes later, he returned with drinks and two paper napkins. "Classy, yes? I guess buying coasters is the last thing that came to my mind before I moved here." Putting his drink down, he turned to look at Sunny. "So maybe a hug?"

Fighting tears, she moved over and held him as he pulled her close. After a long minute, her eyes glistening, she cautiously touched his face, then took her hand away. "Look at me. I'm such an emotional mess. You're all I've been able to think about. I was so relieved when you called last night."

With his index finger, he tenderly brushed her tears aside. "I told you I wouldn't let more than two days pass. There's so much out of my control, Sunny. But my word, well, it means everything to me. Kind of like …."

Although he'd swallowed the unspoken words, he believed she'd heard them, silently returning the love with her eyes: *You mean everything to me too.*

He took several deep breaths to fortify himself. "As I said on the phone, I can only give you the *Reader's Digest* edition of everything. But I think it's enough."

Sunny took a delicate sip of her lemonade, then put the glass down. "You go at your own pace and tell me only what you're comfortable with."

"Thank you." He put his hand over hers and held it. "I told you before that the bastard, whose name is Richard, by the way, came for my then-wife, Evelyn, just because he wanted to take another woman from me. He had no clue it was a miserable marriage—at least for me. And …"

Sunny waited for him to find more words.

"When she hooked up with this guy, who had been elevated to billionaire status after his father's death, I honestly don't know what she wanted more: him or his money. Probably both. Even when he was out of town, she'd stay by herself at his Park Avenue apartment. It was a social climber's dream: doorman, a luxury residence, a dazzling view of the city, a staff to wait on her, unlimited food and alcohol …."

"Did she openly admit where she was staying and what she was doing?"

John laughed in disgust. "Said she was housesitting and that she barely saw the guy. And they were just friends—yeah, right—but insisted that since things weren't good between us, she had every right to explore the possibilities. In theory, I totally disagree with that logic, but I was thrilled to have her gone and saw no reason to argue about any of it."

"Housesitting. Hmm. Haven't heard that one before."

"Rich, huh? No pun intended." He glanced at Kono who was preparing to hump Miggy." Kono, down!" He spoke softly, self-consciously. "Can't say I don't know how he feels."

Sunny smiled and touched his leg. "I know. Please, go on."

After taking a moment to regain his train of thought, he continued. "She had no idea that I knew so much about the guy and that in many ways, letting him 'steal' her from me was sweet revenge. The thing is, he's a player to the hilt, so there were times when she thought it might not work out. Each time, she would come crawling back to me. Over six months, I'm embarrassed to say she and I were together twice. And no, I'd never have taken her back, but when relationships are ending, things can still happen. Especially after a few drinks." He twisted his face in revulsion. "And then she was pregnant. She didn't say anything to me. But after she had her first ultrasound and learned she was having twins, that's when she told me they were mine as Richard had been in London at the time they were conceived."

"Oh, my."

"What she didn't tell me was that he hated pregnant women. They turned him off, were 'gross' to have sex with, and he didn't want children. Not wanting to admit to him that we'd been together again, Evelyn told him that I'd raped her in a drunken rage."

"Goodness, John. That's terrible."

"It's one of the most despicable lies she's told. But I didn't know this at the time. All I knew is that he said he'd marry her after she gave birth to my children, left them for me to raise, got her figure back, and routinely practiced vagina-tightening exercises until she had 'tightened' to his satisfaction."

Sunny's eyes widened. "Wow!" She looked at him as he waited for her to say more. "That's repulsive." She sighed. "Keep going, John."

He scoffed as he replayed the words he'd just spoken. "Yeah, he's some piece of work. Anyway, he rented a fancy apartment for her, she left, we divorced, and when the boys were born, I joyfully took them."

"I had no idea. I can already see where this is going. Oh, my."

As Miggy came over to get a reassuring neck scratch from Sunny, Kono took a moment to nuzzle up to John. Moments later, exhausted, the dogs settled onto their beds.

"It was then, Sunny, that I gave up any desire I had to keep Whisky Devers on life support. These boys were the world to me. I'd had basically no upbringing from my own father, and I wanted to give them everything I was denied: love, attention, encouragement, a solid sense of self, and everything else good parents want for their kids. But in order to do this, I had to earn money.

"It went against my grain, in ways I can't begin to describe to you, but I took an administrative job with my father, working from home, doing extensive research for his wealthy clients. I made a lot of phone calls and spoke to more people than I can count. If we'd been in the Internet age back then, it would have been a much easier job, at least to some degree. Anyway, the work was far from fulfilling most days."

"I can't even imagine you doing that. Oh, John, I hope that didn't come out the wrong way. It's just that you're such a brilliant musician. But I understand—you're an even better human being."

"You're a mother, Sunny. You know what it means to love your children with every bit of your heart. And I did. I despised working for the man, but I sensed, for the first time ever, that he had compassion for my situation. He was more decent to me during those years than he'd ever been. As long as I did the work." He paused to push away an unexpected swell of emotion. "It was almost as if enabling me to be a good father absolved him of having emotionally abandoned me. But yet, not enough to want to be a grandfather."

"Oh, I'm sorry. Did Evelyn see her boys?"

"Twice a month, if that."

"My goodness. What kind of mother can do that? I couldn't wait to see my children every day."

"If you knew Evelyn, you'd understand. Trust me."

Sunny frowned. "That's awful."

John looked out at the ocean, then, after picking up his drink and taking a few sips, the past pulled him back. His face contorted as memories overtook him. He waited a few minutes before continuing as he squeezed Sunny's hand for strength.

"When my boys were three, I put them in preschool. I had a nursing student helping me with them, and she was terrific, but my workload was intense, she had limited time, and that's when I came to the conclusion that socialization with their peers was the best thing for them. And it really was. They thrived in the atmosphere. Unfortunately, about six months later, there was an accident at the school. Not too bad, but serious enough that little Jake needed to go to the ER. He was cut and bleeding. Just as a precaution, the hospital wanted to make sure that they had blood on hand for a transfusion, if it was necessary. Because the boys were born at that same hospital, and because their mother has an RH negative factor, her blood type was in her file. The boys were type O+ and I'm AB+. Evelyn is a type A-. As was explained to me, to my shock and horror, A- and AB+ parents cannot produce children with type O+."

Sunny covered her face with her hands. "Oh, my sweet John. That is absolutely horrible. I take it Richard was type O+."

"Of course. Despite the shock, I still considered myself their father in every way. And after that incident, which was in 1996, it took me some time to come to terms with, life continued on for us for another decade. In 2006, Richard, who had sworn off being a father, expressed regret to Evelyn about not having children, especially sons, to carry on his name and legacy." He made a face. "Insert sarcasm here. Anyway, that's when he learned that the boys were his. Despite the fact that this hypocrite made his disdain for children clear, he was livid—and that's putting it mildly—with Evelyn for telling him they were the result of me raping her. She cried and said she did what she thought he would have wanted. And about that, she was right.

"The boys, then thirteen, were lied to and manipulated in the most egregious ways imaginable. I can't go into too much detail, but Evelyn told them she had only *just* suspected Richard was their father when the boys began to look more like him." His expression turned to one of disgust. "For the record, they don't resemble him at all. Anyway, she told them that after taking DNA samples from their hair brushes, she was able to verify her suspicion.

"John, I'm trying to imagine how all of this must've hit you. I can't … sorry, please go on."

"Richard, a man who wants what's his and everyone else's, with no regard for how the boys might feel, now deciding that sons were a benefit to him, began telling them the most despicable lies about me as he showered them with outrageous gifts I'd never have given them. The boys were told I raped and beat their mother every chance I got, and that out of fear I might kill her, she left me to raise them. The entire spiel was devoid of logic, but to thirteen-year-old minds with no adult life experience, the deafening sound of adults shouting 'truths' at them took on the vague but conflicting appearance of it. I remember Jake asking 'How come Dad never yells at us if he's so mean?' to which Evelyn told him to shut up and not ask any more stupid questions." Tears rolled down his cheeks. "Sunny, I never fought so hard for anything in my life. But there came a time when their young minds had been so twisted and tortured that I saw them disappearing into themselves. Over and over, almost robotically, with flat emotion, unconvincingly, they told me that they wanted to be with their 'real father.'" I knew they were being forced to do so, but I worried about their mental health if the strain on their sanity, the push-pull, continued. So finally, out of love, with greater reluctance and sorrow than I'd ever experienced in my life, I let them go. I was always grateful that I'd had ten years to deal with the heartache of knowing they weren't my biological children. Somehow, my brain prepared me for what was to come. Had I not known, well, I don't like to think how I might have handled things. But I have never gotten over the pain of losing them, and I never will."

Sunny, having no words, hugged John as he sobbed quietly. "It's impossible for me to know what that might have been like. My poor, dear man."

After composing himself, John went on, reciting the speech he'd prepared the night before. "In the work I did for my father, who was a high-powered New York attorney, I located a lot of people hiding out in beach cottages, small European cities and country hideaways, and for some reason, the idea of living a solitary life on the beach began to tug at me. With each passing day, it became more appealing. After all, Whisky Devers was dead and buried, and the children who I loved with every cell of my being were long gone. That's when I made the decision to lead a very different life." He smiled uneasily. "I'm not unhappy as I am. My life isn't for everyone, but it's worked for me. Being Whisky Devers is something I remember as if I were accessing a past life through hypnosis. That's how far removed I am from everything I was and wanted to be."

"I'm so glad you're still here, John. All of that would have been enough to convince some people to stop living. I get why you'll never stop missing them."

"Never." He spoke quietly as he gazed out to the sea. "Never ever." He turned to her. "Do you understand, after finding my beautiful mother dead in the kitchen, having Juliana leave me the night I was going to propose, having my music stolen, then finding out that my children were not mine biologically, then losing them, knowing they believed the most flagrant, vile lies, well … I just needed to keep my world as small as possible within what I perceived as my control." His face flushed with rage. "As I told you the other day, I have no idea what caused this son of a bitch to release my album, but evil is hardwired into his system, and whatever the reason was, it's not good." He paused. "I don't mean to sound mysterious, but since then, another mystery of my past was revealed to me. I can't even touch it myself … much less share it. But I hope you understand."

Sunny started to speak, but he wasn't finished.

"I just have to say … what you went through … losing Grey as you did, well, that was horrific. I'm not saying I've been through the worst pain. People go through far more. But only having myself to answer to, I made the choices that worked for me. This isn't a woe-is-me declaration, Sunny. It's just my story. Nothing more. Nothing less."

"I understand." She thought for a moment. "How old would the boys be now?"

"Twenty-one. Not too far from twenty-two." He stopped to catch his breath. "Wherever they are and whatever they're doing, I hope they're happy and nothing like their biological parents. With everything I am, Sunny, I pray that in the thirteen years we had together, I gave them something to change what I never want to believe is inevitable."

Sunny eyes radiated compassion. "Have you ever considered—"

"Looking for them? Now that they're twenty-one, yes, of course I have. But every time I've entertained the thought, I end up back at square one. There's just no way I would ever risk pulling them back into any kind of trauma or do anything whatsoever to upend their lives. I love them far too much."

"John, I am so grateful that you trust me enough to have shared all of this." A sheepish look crossed her face. "I should confess; your friend Ben told me that one day, when you unburdened yourself, I should make sure you tell me how you saved his life."

"Big mouth told you that, did he?" John rolled his eyes as a slight smile formed. "He told me I should tell you one day, but he didn't include the part where he'd said anything to *you.*"

"I'm afraid he did. But if you're uncomfortable—"

"Very short version. Okay?"

"Absolutely."

"Well, Ben was married, and when his daughter Avery was three, he came to New York by himself to see a musician friend, Dante, who's also a friend of mine. Ben's a drummer."

"Yes, he told me that when we met." Sunny smiled. "Go on."

"Well, I liked him immediately, but as the father of two boys, I wasn't happy to see the father of a young girl, not to mention a husband, partying hard in clubs three thousand miles away from home."

"Oh, no."

"It was none of my business, but we got to talking, and I saw the extremely stand-up guy underneath the party animal. He told me his wife wanted a divorce, that he was losing his job because the owner of the freight company was retiring, and he admitted he was doing everything wrong in trying to deal with his problems."

Sunny smiled compassionately. "It's tough when the sky falls on you."

"It is. Cutting this short, we stayed in touch. Although it was too late to save his marriage, Ben immediately stopped partying and went to look for work. After a while, I decided to offer him money to buy the freight company he worked for. He accepted, with the caveat that he work for me to pay his debt. He's made me proud ever since. And as he hinted, he and his ex may be getting remarried. He plays in a band a couple nights a month, handles my songwriting, and I'd say he's come to my rescue every bit as much as I came to his. It wasn't too long after I met him that I lost the boys. Knowing I had such a close friend here was one of the main reasons I came to California."

He gently ran his fingers through her hair. "I need to change the subject now. I told you more than I'd planned because leaving you with only part of the story no longer felt right." He sighed. "I'm as emotionally depleted as I was the other day, but I wanted you to know at least this much. I hope you understand."

"Of course."

"How are you, Sunny? Is everything okay? How about those calls? Please tell me they've stopped."

Looking guilty, Sunny sucked in a bit of air through her teeth. "Actually, I got one yesterday afternoon. 'Did you miss me, bitch?'"

"Oh, no! Did you tell the Gardets and the police?"

Sunny bit her lip, then gave a wry smile. "You mean the Gardets aren't the police?"

John laughed. "I think they'd find that quite funny."

"They would. Especially Rissa." She exhaled. "Speaking of whom, she came by three-quarters of an hour later. I'm going to be honest, I was so distraught about you, that for the moment, I didn't have the strength to deal with the call. More to the point, I didn't think I could take Rissa's alarm on top of the agony that was ripping me apart inside." She sighed. "But after Miranda took over for me later, I worried. And so I slipped into the back door of the restaurant and I told Rolo. And then I called the Teal Beach police who really can't do anything more than they've been doing." Sunny put her hands at his temples, letting her soft caress slide sensually down his face. "I honestly don't know what Rolo chose to do with the information, and I feel as if I've abandoned my responsibility somehow. But how can I not be honest with you after what you've just shared with me. Oh, John. I just want …."

"Me too, Sunny. More than anything, but we can't. I've seen where life goes when I have no control, so I'm damned if I'm going to destroy things when I do. Not that I'm fully in control now. You are pretty much impossible to resist, but I think the only thing we can do is …."

Making a sad face, then hinting at a smile, she looked at him. "Have lunch?"

He leaned over and gave her a slow kiss on the lips, despite knowing what it would do to both of them. "I think so."

"Oh, John."

"I shouldn't have even done that. But I had to. You need to know …."

"I'm so glad you did." She closed her eyes for a moment, then looked at him. "It's the timing, not the act."

He stood. "Something like that. Despite those being my own words, they stick in my throat." He nodded toward the kitchen. "Let me get lunch on the table."

Richard walked over to the balcony door off the living room and slid both the glass and screen doors to his left. Stepping outside, where he had forbade Phoebe to go, his steely eyes inspected everything in sight.

Phoebe, who'd just been turning the corner to enter the large living room, stepped backward into the hallway, out of sight, a split second after seeing him on the verboten wooden deck.

Rotating his head slowly from left to right, then repeating the process, a barely discernable smile landed on his lips as he closed the doors and returned to the recliner he'd grown to love.

As she heard him settle into the chair, something stopped her from making an entrance. Within seconds, she knew her gut had been right as she heard him on the phone. "Fred, it's me. First, good job yesterday. Brilliant engineering. I need something else—pronto. The woman who rented this house to Phoebe—her name is Sunny Harrison and she owns the Teal Beach Sundial Inn. I want every last detail about her life that you can dig up. Everything. Her past and everyone she sees now. Especially on a romantic basis. No detail is too small." He listened. "Yes. That's right. I need you to move on this yesterday. You're still in Teal Beach, yes? … Good. Do *not* fuck this up. Do you hear me? Get on this yesterday!" He listened, his impatience revealing itself in his heavy sighs. "No, Fred, you haven't disappointed me. Are you some little kid who needs to be reassured? Then stop fishing for compliments, or I'll wind the line around your thick neck." He huffed his annoyance. "Glad we understand each other. Tomorrow is April Fools' Day. Make sure not to be one and I'll give you a fat sum that's way more handsome than you'll ever be. Now get on it." He put the phone down. "Phoebe!"

Walking backward until she reached the bedroom, she called to him as if she'd been there the whole time. With heavier steps than usual, she walked into the living room, hoping he would feel secure that she'd been out of earshot.

"Don't you look dazzling in that burgundy dress. I can't wait to show you off at the restaurant later." He smiled as she stood by his chair. "I'll let you pick the place. It feels good to indulge in pleasures I can't stop thinking about. You know?

"Uh, yes."

"Were you just in the bedroom?"

"Yes. My sister called from Vermont so I was talking to her."

"Her name again? Never mind. I don't care. Phoebe, you didn't hear me on the phone just now, did you?"

She wrinkled her brow in confusion. "No, I was talking to my sister."

"Right. Does she know how I feel about you?"

She stammered. "Oh yeah. Every time we talk, she reminds me."

"That's good. Because you are truly my goddess. You're so beautiful. Did you know you're my best friend?"

"I am?"

"Who else in this world do I treasure the way I do you?"

"Um … I don't know."

"You really like the balcony off the bedroom, don't you? It's a special place."

"Yes. It's beautiful. And it's the only one I'll go on. I promise."

He slowly got off the recliner and gave her a kiss. "My love, I wasn't even thinking about that." He took her hand. "Let's go onto the bedroom balcony and look out at the ocean. The moon looks so beautiful on the water after the sun has set. Don't you think?"

Stunned by words she wasn't used to hearing, she could only whisper her agreement.

Richard walked her down the hall, into the bedroom, and onto the deck. He put an arm around her and squeezed tight. "I love these romantic moments we share, don't you, Phoebe?"

Wary, she looked at him. "Of course."

"Why don't I help you out of your dress and your unnecessaries? I can't think of anything hotter than you standing here, the moon throwing light on your naked body."

"And then I'll help you out of *your* clothing, right?"

"No, sweetie. I just want to enjoy a moonlit snack on the balcony." He began to undress her. "When we go back into the bedroom, you'll have yours. I've been thinking of new ways to spice up our relationship. It's important to keep things interesting, don't you think?"

"I wish we could talk about more things. I don't think you know very much about me, Richard. Not really."

Taking off the last of her clothing, he tossed it into the bedroom where it landed on the floor. "I know you like *this*," he said fingering her.

"I do, but …."

"But what, darling? You want to tell me your sister's name and the things you did as children? Is that what you think pleases a man?"

"I just want you to know me as a person." She looked down on the deck, unable to meet his eyes. "You know, how I feel about life, events in my past that made me who I am today. What I envision for my future … besides singing."

"Give me a lousy break, Phoebe. And look up the word 'aphrodisiac.'" Angrily, he grabbed her and pulled her into the bedroom. "Fuck the moonlight. We're going to enjoy some things in the dark you've never known in your twenty-five years."

"I'm only twenty-two."

"Even better. Further from your expiration date. Longer shelf life." He thrust his hardness against her body, then gave her an incongruous and gentle kiss. "You are extraordinarily beautiful and you want me to be happy, right?"

"I do, Richard. It's just that I really …"

"I want you to be happy too, sugar biscuit. Quiet now like a good little girl. And just to show you that I care about what you want, you may remove *my* clothing now, just as you wished." He winked. "See how attentive I can be to your needs? This is what makes our relationship work so well." A lascivious grin dripped from his lips. "Now, I want you to kiss every ounce of my flesh as you unwrap me. Enjoy your gift, my dear."

Hand in hand, John and Sunny walked the beach, the dogs happily enjoying their togetherness every bit as much as the humans.

Stopping at the water's edge, John put his hand on her shoulders. "In all of these years, I've spent so little time with people. I don't regret it either. But today, we've been together over eight hours, and it feels like eight minutes. I've never been so comfortable with any human being. And I've never known anyone to understand me the way you do."

"I cherish every moment with you, John." She played with the ends of his hair. "There's nothing about you that I would want to change. Do you know that?"

"I do."

"Good. I hope that it won't be long before …."

He looked into her eyes. "We have to figure some things out. I hate being obsessed with this garbage every bit as much as you do. There are some sick people out there who wish harm to both of us, and I'm not quite sure how we sort that all out and fix it, especially only knowing for sure who one of them is, and having a good guess about another. And I hate not knowing how many people we're dealing with. But I promise you, Sunny. I will find the culprits if it's the last thing I do."

"Oh, John, please don't phrase it like that!"

"Sorry. I didn't mean it to sound that way. I will get to the bottom of this, and we'll be good. Very good. I didn't wait my life to meet you for it to turn out any differently." He smiled as best he could. "Life will always throw things in our direction, but this is something else, something sinister. We can't find happiness being the target of sick minds."

Choked up, she could only offer a slight shake of the head.

"So, let me escort you home, okay?" He lifted her chin and looked at her. "It will be all right." He took her hand again as they began walking.

Ten minutes later, they arrived at the hotel. Looking through a porch window, John saw that Tyler was behind the desk. "I'm going to say goodnight to you out here. So I can do this." Embracing her, he kissed her more deeply than he ever had.

"Oh, John …."

"Ty's inside. I'm sure he'll be happy to see you and have a chat. I'll talk to you tomorrow, okay?" He motioned for Kono to come to his side as he addressed Miggy. "You too, girl."

"Until then, sweet man." Looking at him one last time, Sunny walked through the lobby door with the dog as John and Kono walked toward the beach stairs. No one, not even the dogs, saw the large man who stood in the shadows by the cabins, watching their every move.

CHAPTER TWENTY

Looking right, then left, wearing his Mets baseball cap and dark glasses, Dylan knocked softly on the door to Room 18 of the Kenwood Pines Motel.

Bedraggled and exhausted, wearing a designer sweatsuit, his hairstyle undiscernible as the long hair on top of his head hung wildly in front of his eyes, Jake opened the door. "Damn, bro. That hat. Those glasses. You look like a criminal on the lamb." Confusion landed on his face as he brushed his hair to the side. "What does that mean anyway? Why would a criminal be on a sheep?"

"It's lam … with no 'b.' Not lamb like a sheep." Dylan walked in the room, eyeing the old floral bedspread and matching drapes. "I told you—don't use random expressions you hear if you don't know what they mean. Speaking of words that end in a silent 'b,' it makes you look like a dumb ass." He smiled crookedly and hugged his brother. "Good to see you. Man, you're a wreck."

Jake flopped onto the bed. "You think? Luckily I got to JFK in enough time to catch that red-eye you booked me on. Slept the entire way too. Thank God. I never would've been able to pick up that car at LAX and drive up here if I hadn't. But I made it. GPS lady brought me right to the door." He grinned. "But when I asked her to come in for a drink, she told me to go 'recalculate myself.' Ha ha. Oh, and I drank the Red Bull like you told me and only had one."

"Good." He eyed his disheveled brother from top to bottom. "What a trip you are." Taking off his cap and glasses, Dylan laid them on the nearby desk before sitting in front of the headboard, facing his brother. "I'd like to tell you that's a cool new hairstyle, which I'm sure it is, but I can't be sure looking at you now." He smiled. "But I get the idea. Bet it looks great."

"Thanks." Jake yanked a loose thread from the old bedspread, then twirled it around his index finger. "So I've got stuff to tell you." He twisted his face uncomfortably.

"Oh, no. Every time you do that, it's bad."

"Yeah. You know me. So the first thing, which I'm not crying in my beer over, Dad, I mean Richard, left a bunch of nasty texts for me. As soon as we landed, I turned my phone on and saw them. The first two were from last night, telling me I'd better show my ass up Monday morning to his office. Then, when I didn't, he sent me three more telling me I'm the biggest April fool he knows, and I'm fired. And other stuff I won't repeat. There were a few voicemails, too, but I deleted them without listening."

"Did you text back and tell him you'd already quit?"

"Nope. I've got nothing else to say, plus, ignoring him pisses him off more than anything."

"I know."

Jake glanced at the phone on the nightstand. "It's off now." Illustrating the relief he felt, he made a loud blowing sound.

"Thanks for that great impression of a nor'easter. Now tell me what the second thing is."

"Oh, yeah. It's gonna shock you. Sorry I'm all over the place. I'm just so tired."

"Yeah. Not your usual sharp self, are ya?" Dylan burst out laughing.

"You want to hear this or what?"

"Yeah. Tell me."

"So, after I checked into this palace, I was so freakin' hungry. I went over to that Lucy's Blue Seas Diner, especially because you told me not to step foot in the Dodo bird restaurant." Jake brushed his hair out of his eyes.

"It's Dodo Deen's, but whatever."

"Holy shit, Dyl. It was really good you told me to disguise myself. Guess who was sitting at the counter flirting with the pretty server as he shoved a double bacon cheeseburger and fries into his big mouth?"

"Well, that doesn't describe John, so no guess there. This is Teal Beach. So who else could you possibly know here except me?"

"Exactly, dude!"

Dylan rolled his eyes. "You're the one that just flew here from New York, but if you keep dragging this out, I'll be more exhausted than you are."

"Richard's goonmeister—Fred Glopperman!"

"It's Gooberman. But who cares about his name? Are you serious? More to the point, how sure are you that it was him?"

"The guy is like three-hundred pounds, wears that Jets jacket everywhere." Jake offered his best gangster impersonation. "He talks in that raspy grunt-kinda New Yawk accent like he's ready to shoot someone in an alley and shove 'em in a trash bin. Or maybe put a pair of cement shoes on 'em so dey can swim with the fishies. Hey, that really sounded like him." Jake laughed and continued his story. "So, because this woman was really pretty, he's doing this sexy macho thing to impress her. Man, it was pathetic! He's a joke. I wanted to say, 'Oil & water, man. Forget it.' It was just funny listening to him for a few seconds, not that she wanted anything more than a good tip. I know I mess things up, but trust me, it was Glopperman. Besides, there's more to prove it if you don't believe me."

Dylan was riveted as he leaned forward. "Go on."

"So as you come into the diner, there's this old green box on the left. You know, the kind where you lift the lid, and it had these free Teal Beach newspapers. I grabbed one and hurried to the last booth I could find. I think it kind of pissed off the other server lady that I made her walk so far to wait on me, but she didn't say anything. I ordered a bowl of clam chowder and a turkey club on rye toast. I told her to just bring the soup first. No way I wanted to finish before him—because he always orders dessert —so I knew I had to eat real slow."

"Is there a 'good part' you're gonna get to?"

"Chill, Dyl. I'm getting there."

"Anyway, even from a distance I could see he finished everything. Then, he pointed to this apple pie that was in one of those pie-display things that are up on a pedestal with a see-through plastic top. They're like standard on old diner counters. I only know what kind of pie it was because I noticed it when I first walked by. It had those crisscross pieces of crust on the top with the baked apple peeking through. Like "Hi, there! Recognize me?"

Dylan's mouth fell open as he stared at his brother for a few seconds while shaking his head. "Once again, you're a fucking trip, Jake. I don't even know where you get this weird stuff from. He laughed. "Go on."

"Okay, but does that expression 'Shut your piehole' come from guys like Fred shoving pies in their mouths at diners?"

"Tell me you're joking."

"You just told me to ask about expressions I don't understand."

Dylan rolled his eyes. "Just go on."

"Then, he pulls his phone from the side pocket of his jacket and starts walking back to the men's room, which isn't far from where I was sitting. I put that paper up like I was reading it. It's called the *Teal Beachcomber*, if you want to know. Anyway, even though he was talking low, I had no problem hearing him."

"And maybe this century you'll let me know what you heard."

Jake laughed. "This isn't funny, but you are. Yeah, so he's talking to Richard. He said he could confirm Richard thinking that John's in a relationship with the Sunny lady because he saw them in a deep kiss outside the hotel last night. Then he said something crude like they're obviously, you know, and that as soon as he finished lunch, he was hitting the road for the Los Angeles area and would visit Catalina Island on Tuesday."

"Whoa. That's where John used to live for eight years. That's not a coincidence."

"I know! And then the Glops said he knew exactly what to do. Oh, and that he won't come back to the house Richard's renting from Sunny, but that he wants some money transferred into his account today. Then he said, 'I know you're good for it, but that ain't the point. I need it now. And don't insult me again like you did on the other call, or you can find someone else to do your shit while you swim in some.' It was heavy."

"Do you realize what you just said?"

Jake scrunched his face. "You need me to repeat it?"

"No. Once was more than enough, but it's the part about the

house Richard's renting from Sunny. I didn't know anything about that, except fuck! The old man is here in Teal Beach. He has to be."

"Damn. You're right, Dyl."

"I could barely sleep last night. And I was only thinking about that Whisky Devers's album. I went online and found it. I downloaded a copy from iTunes and wow."

"Told you. It's the real macaw."

"McCoy. Anyway, Richard's resurrected John's music for not-a-good reason. And when he's on a mission, he doesn't stop with one thing." Dylan paled. "I think he wants to kill John. I do."

"C'mon, Dyl. He's the prickiest of the pricks, but he's not a murderer."

"Are you gonna tell me that you never heard Richard say he'd 'see the em-effer dead one day?'"

Jake gulped. "Um ... oh ... yeah. Like too many times. But I thought that was just his way of hatin' on him. But still ...."

"Don't you remember the threats he made before we came to live with him?"

"Oh, man." Jake contorted his face. "I must have seriously blocked that out. Why does the brain even do stuff like that?"

"Self-preservation, I guess." Dylan continued. "You think he hires people like Fred Gooberman because they're law-abiding citizens? You're the one who just did that imitation of the guy killing people. What makes you think Richard hasn't hired *him* to kill John?"

"Oh, man! I don't like how much sense that makes." Jake took a moment to think. "But why now, after all these years?"

"I think it's my fault. Well, it's because we've both pissed him off, but it definitely started with me, not you."

"What do you mean?"

"Remember last night when you said to me on the phone how I saw through Richard's lies years before you did?"

"Before I was honest enough with myself to admit I felt the same way." Shame washed over Jake's face.

"Well, I was also the one who started talking about how much I missed John and wanted to be his son again." Dylan leaned against the headboard.

"Oh, yeah."

"You know how well that went over. So what better way to make John pay for being missed—what a sick bastard—then to do everything he can to destroy him?"

"And now we've both quit Xavier Rox and he knows I'm going to change my name too."

"Right."

Jake frowned, looking as if he were going to cry. "So what should we do?"

"I think we have to go see John. This really isn't what I wanted to share after eight years, but he needs to know this. Like Richard always says: yesterday. I also think Richard's planning to kill John, and maybe Sunny, too, at that house he's renting. Or have someone like Gooberman do it. He'd never go anywhere that someone could pinpoint his location. Especially if there are cameras like in the hotel lobby. Never ever."

"You're right, Dyl. Not his style. That's exactly what he's planning to do. You should go to see John first. If it comes out that you were on top of Richard's bullshit way before I was, or before I could admit it, John might not like me so much."

"I seriously doubt that. In fact, I'm sure you're wrong. You told me the same thing when I was worried about seeing him again. Remember? Anyway, there's no time to hash anything out. I'll go alone. This really can't wait."

"Seven-fifty-nine on the dot and ready to work." Tyler smiled at Sunny who stood glumly behind the reception desk. "You look like someone I know, except she doesn't usually look as sad as you do right now."

Sunny, wearing a sundress with a lemon motif, took her reading glasses off and laid them to the right of the guest register. "Am I that transparent?"

Smiling, Tyler squinted. "Well, I can't see through you if that's what you're asking. But you can be a pane." He laughed. "Just a little smile for a tired old joke?"

"Why are you always so sweet to me, Ty? I don't deserve it."

"Come sit with me a quick spell. I've got some news, and I want to hear how you're doing."

"Okay." Sunny lifted the panel and walked into the lobby. Miggy, who'd been lying listlessly on her bed, had no desire to follow her mother.

Tyler gestured toward the couch. "After you."

Once Sunny had settled comfortably, he did the same.

"On behalf of all of us, thank you for telling Rolo about the latest call. That's the third one, yes?"

"It was. Actually, it was the second one I got—personally. I know it's ugly, Ty. But I can't even be sure if it's Nancy. And if it is, somehow, I have the feeling she's just playing with me. It's uncomfortable, but I feel more hassled than I do threatened, despite her crimes. And no, I don't want to be naïve; that's just my gut talking. And for the record, I don't consider 'hassled' to be benign in any sense of the word. The woman is evil, if indeed it is her."

Spotting a travel brochure that had fallen to the floor, Tyler picked it up and laid it on the table. "But the sad face I'm seeing has nothing to do with the calls, does it?"

"No." Embarrassed, she looked away. "John called to say he need to immerse himself in work today, and I'm embarrassed to say that it devastated me. He's so much better at this solitude thing than I've ever been. Even one day without seeing him, well, it does me in." She sniffled. "Oh, Ty, I never thought I would ever feel so deeply for another man again, but John is not 'any man.' I think he knows himself better than I know *my*self."

Tyler took both of her hands. "I would never say this if I didn't believe it with every bit o' my Louisiana heart, but he has great love for you. We *all* see it."

Sunny tried to smile. "Believe it or not, I don't disagree. I just wish I did better when he wasn't around. And now it's time to shift gears. I want to hear your news."

Tyler took his cell phone out of his shirt pocket and hit Send on a pre-written text. Within two minutes, Imari, a tall, stunning Black woman, with flowing dark hair, wearing a long white linen dress, walked through the lobby door.

Seeing Tyler's face light up, Sunny touched her hand to her

heart as she stood to greet her. "Oh, Imari. How I've missed you, lovely woman. You look more radiant every time I see you."

Imari, her arms wide open, wrapped them around Sunny as she came to greet her. "Well, once I'm here permanently, I don't know if I can radiate exponentially." She smiled warmly. "I truly can't wait until the addition is built." She glanced at Ty. "They're starting a week from today. April ninth, right?"

He nodded. "That's the promise I was given, sweetie."

Sunny nodded for her to sit in the chair as she took her seat on the couch. "I am ecstatic that you've chosen to live among us."

"Which is why I'm here tonight. As you know, there'll be a new Gardet man in six months."

Sunny beamed. "I do. And I can't wait to spoil him."

Imari gave her a devilish smile. "Wouldn't you like to know what he'll be called?"

"You've chosen a name! How exciting."

Tyler gestured for Imari to continue. Putting her hands gently on her stomach, she spoke. "Aunt Sunny, meet Grey Alexander Gardet."

"Oh my goodness. Are you serious? I'm so touched. I don't know what to … but why not Tyler Zachariah Gardet the third?"

Tyler shook his head as a smirk crossed his face. "The Gardet family didn't do so well with the original Tyler. Yeah, the second one, yours truly, turned out to be a gem. But lightning only strikes once most of the time, so to play it safe, and because we loved Grey as we love you, we couldn't think of a better name than Grey Gardet. Has a rhyme and a ring to it. Ah, speaking of rings." He jumped up and ran behind the desk to answer the phone.

As the two women excitedly chatted, he turned his back to them, desperate to hide his despondency over the ugly words that he'd just been told to relay to Sunny.

CHAPTER TWENTY-ONE

John closed the laptop, placed his glasses on top of it, and put it on the coffee table. He turned to Kono who'd taken over the chaise sectional. "You do realize I bought that for *me* to stretch out on, right?" He laughed as Kono's guilty eyes looked up at him. But the dog wasn't budging. "Yeah, I can see you're all broken up about it, doggo. What's that? Oh! You get the chaise on Tuesdays? Funny thing, I don't remember making that deal."

He watched the few people below on the beach as they strolled and played in the midday sunshine. *Oh, Sunny, I haven't seen you since Sunday night. Not even forty-eight hours ago, and I miss you like crazy. I should come visit you today or invite you for dinner. I just don't know how to do this anymore. I'm so afraid of hurting you despite that being the last thing I would ever knowingly do. I just haven't figured out how to be the man I am and the one I want to be at the same time. I really do want to clear a path to us. If we're going to give ourselves to each other, it has to be healthy. We've both been through so much. I'm afraid if I give too much, then it will hurt you if I can't continue. I hate being so conflicted. But I do feel good about us; I really do. So why do I feel like I'm hurting you. Maybe I should give you a call and ....*

Startled by a knock at the door, John sat up. He turned to the dog who was already standing. "Well, I know how to get you off the chaise. Just get someone to knock on the door." He smiled as Kono ran in excited circles. "You think Sunny had someone take over for her so she and Miggy could pay us a surprise visit, don't you? Let's go see."

He walked to the door and opened it. When he saw the young man standing before him, John's mouth dropped open, but only silence and shock filled the air around him. His eyes welled with tears as he soaked in the details of the visitor's face, his height, his clothes, and most importantly, the look of trepidation and love in his eyes.

"Hi, John." He paused. "Dad …."

"Dylan. I never thought … oh my God … Dylan." John stepped forward and hugged him with an intensity that encapsulated all the years of pain and loss. After a long minute, teary-eyed, John stared into Dylan's watery eyes. "There aren't a lot of people who would come to my door, but you're the last person I ever expected to see and one of two people I'm most happy to see. There aren't any words to adequately describe how much I've missed you both. And how much I love you." He stroked his hair, just like he once did as a father.

"Oh, man, I missed you so much. We both did." Dylan looked down at the dog.

"This monster jumping all over you is Kono. Please, come in." John moved out of the way so he could enter. "I'm ecstatic to see you. This is the best thing that could have happened to me."

His eyes sweeping the large room, Dylan looked around, then focused on the large window with the ocean view. "You know, this is just how I pictured you living. It's really nice and Zen. Not all of that tacky look-at-me-I'm-rich crap in every square inch of space."

Still not over the shock, John paused to allow some air into his lungs. "Is Jake with you?"

"He's nearby, but he was afraid of how you might react, so I came alone."

John's brow wrinkled. "Afraid of how I might react? In case you can't recognize the emotion on my face, it's utter euphoria. I love you both more than life itself. But I have no words for how much I've missed you."

His cool collapsing, Dylan burst into tears and threw his arms around John. "I'm so sorry. I'm really sorry. We were stupid kids, and they're both evil liars."

John, tears streaking down his face, led Dylan to the couch. "Please sit, son. Let me get you something to drink. And maybe you'd like something to eat."

Taking a seat, Dylan yanked at his arm as he'd done as a child. "No, not yet. I just want to sit with you." He sniffled. "I can't even believe I'm acting like this. I didn't expect to sound like a freakin' kid all over again." He looked into John's eyes. "You're the *only* father we've ever had. They said horrible things about you and came up with this bogus ways to 'prove' what they were saying. And they bribed us with stuff that doesn't mean fuck all. I know we were thirteen, but isn't that old enough to have a working brain and the ability to tell good from evil?" He started to hyperventilate.

John cupped his hands around Dylan's shoulders. It's all right, son. "My God, I can barely speak." He paused to calm himself. "Listen to me, please. I never thought you'd both be taken from me—"

"Only we weren't! We told you we wanted to be with our *real* father! We were so cruel to you! You're the only real father we've ever known, and you were never anything but amazing to us."

John's hands fell to his sides. "Dylan. You were traumatized and brainwashed the same way thinking adults are pulled into cults.

What better way to take you away than to make you think it was what *you* wanted. Yeah, you were taken from me and from your own lives—in the most insidious way possible." Noticing that Kono was jealous, John motioned for him to come over, gave him a quick neck scratch, then, with insistent eyes, pointed to Kono's bed.

Reluctantly, but not before shooting another jealous glance at Dylan, Kono lay down.

Gently, John continued. "I thought I'd be able to raise you boys as I saw fit. I wanted you to have happy childhoods, free of as much ugliness and pain as possible. You already had a strike against you with a mother who saw you twice a month at best."

"She's the *worst*. The only reason he won't divorce her is because he doesn't want her taking his money. They hate each other, and they've always hated us. He's been cheating on her for years, and I don't know who she's doing, but it's someone, or probably lots of men. And I don't care." Dylan reddened. "Sorry."

"Hey, you're not a kid anymore. No apologies necessary for speaking as an adult."

Dylan tried to smile as he brushed his tears away. "I'm sure acting like a kid."

"Tears do not a child make, Dylan. Hear me. Do you not see that wet stuff coming out of my eyes too?" He paused to take another breath. "The point I'm trying to make here is that I wanted you to enjoy as much of your youth and innocence as possible. Just at the time Richard and Evelyn disrupted our lives, well, that was just around the time I would have started to teach you, in more depth, about the joys and perils of adulthood. You can't blame yourself for what you didn't know. And hell, even when we do know right from wrong, we don't always make the best choices. There's a saying that experience is the best teacher, and it's true, but certainly no guarantee. Not to mention that emotions are complicated buggers, and when you've got people like those two, doing *all* that they did to try and mold you into whatever they wanted or needed you to be, well, you cannot blame yourself. Ever."

"You make more sense in a few minutes that either of them did in eight years. So you don't hate us?"

John closed his eyes and exhaled. Opening them, he looked at Dylan. "I hope that neither one of you ever believed I hated you. I love you as much right now as I always have and then some. Why was Jake afraid to come with you?"

"Because I was the one who saw through Richard's bullshit first. Or maybe the most clearly is a better way to say it. And I started missing you even more and talking about you. A lot. It's a long story, but I know Jake missed you too. I used to catch him looking at photos of you we'd hidden. But he really wanted to work in the record business, so he pushed that aside and went on with the ruse—that he gave a damn about Richard."

"How did you find me? How long have you been in Teal Beach?"

"I just really needed to connect with you again. I'm hoping to get into veterinary school, which is really hard, so I thought I'd go somewhere and study for the VCAT. That's the Veterinary College Admissions Test." He sighed in distress. "I hate saying this, but I knew Richard's had his goons keeping tabs on you for years. So I asked Evelyn if she knew where you were. I just pretended to be mildly curious, but not like I wanted to see you. The prick was gone, like he is most of the time, but she knows where he hides this secret password notebook and managed to access some file on his computer. She found your address for me. It's one of the only decent things she's *ever* done, even though she didn't do it for me. It was totally just to stick it to *him.* She said you'd bought a cottage here and left Catalina Island. So I got on the first flight I could, rented a car, and took a cabin at your friend's hotel. I've seen you a few times, but you didn't see me. I've been wearing a Mets cap and dark glasses, so I doubt you would've recognized me, especially at a distance. Oh, and Jake just got in yesterday, and he's staying at that motel up the road by the diner."

"I see. And today you decided to make yourself known? Was there a particular reason?"

Dylan, noticing that Kono was watching him, smiled. "Hi, Kono." He turned to John. "We were never allowed to have animals. I used to go volunteer at the shelter all the time, but they never knew. I want to help animals more than anything. The prickmaster always said animals are useless. But you know what *was* important to him? He wanted us to see prostitutes on our sixteenth birthday so we wouldn't be 'loser virgins.' You'll be happy to know we both said no … and uh … we're not. With no help from him." He offered an embarrassed smile and began to hyperventilate again. "So listen, there's like a bazillion things to catch up on. Like I changed my last name to Coates."

"Oh, Dylan."

"Are you mad? Do you want me to change it back?"

"No. It's just all so ironic. I gave you both my family name, even though I had been using Hennessey, because I wanted us all to have the same name. Then, after you and Jake were gone, and I knew you weren't coming back, I changed my name legally to Hennessey, knowing that your names would be changed to Strausser. And now you're Coates again." He smiled as he brushed away a stray tear. "I can't tell you how touched I am."

"Jake told Richard he was changing his name too. We should all be Hennessey then. But only if you really want us back in your life. I couldn't blame you—"

"I blame you and Jake for nothing. And yes, I really want you back in my life. If you believe anything, believe that. Have a look in my bedroom later. There are several photos of you both on my dresser and one of the three of us on my nightstand. A day hasn't gone by when I haven't missed you both terribly."

"I need to tell you something." Dylan put his fingers in his mouth as if he were about to chew his nails.

Gently, John pulled his hand down. "I see you still make a snack of your fingers when you're nervous."

Dylan looked at him sheepishly. "I try not to. Old habits and all that." He squirmed in his seat. "I want to catch up on everything. There's so much. I don't even know where to start, but I came today because I've got some really upsetting things to tell you—like to warn you about."

John's eyes went dark with alarm. "I do know that your fath… I mean, Richard, is trying to destroy me. I know about my album, of course, and I'm miserable about it, but I'm just trying to stay out of sight, even more than usual because I've been told by a couple close friends that the music media, not to mention old fans … literally old" — he managed a laugh — "want to find me. I suppose I should be flattered, but I have no words for how much I hate it. Most musicians would be thrilled. I'm not one of them."

"Yeah, I understand. That's gotta be super stressful, but I can almost guarantee Richard's not going to broadcast your location. In fact, I think he'd do the opposite, like try to steer people to the North Pole or some other place where they'd never find you."

"I don't understand, Dylan."

Agony covered Dylan's face like a mask. "Because … um … it's much worse. I think he might want to kill you and doesn't want anyone around who cares about you or will try to protect you. And also, he might be after that Sunny lady who owns the hotel. She's your girlfriend, right?"

John's body tightened with fury. "What the hell do you think that monster is planning to do? Tell me *everything* you know. Please."

"I will. Promise."

John said nothing for fifteen minutes as he listened to every word Dylan relayed about his talk with Jake the night before. Being as precise as he knew how to be, Dylan took care not to leave out even the smallest detail.

Trembling, John watched his hands become fists as he felt the sting of his nails digging into his palms. "Wait. Your father and his girlfriend are renting Sunny's house up on the cliff?"

"That's what Jake heard Richard's goon, Fred say."

Unfurling his fists, John pressed the palms of his hands into his forehead. "Of course! Sunny described him to me recently, and she told me she had an instant visceral dislike for him. The more she described him, the more I thought it sounded like Richard. But only his *type*, not *him*, if you know what I mean. Damn. Why didn't I ask her more questions?"

He shook his head in disgust. "Know why? Because Sunny wanted to forget about him since she never sees the renters, and I didn't want to upset her by talking about the guy anymore. And for some reason, I got the idea it was a Hollywood film mogul with a young actress, so that threw me off his foul scent. If only she'd mentioned his name." He looked at Dylan, remembering how he used to do so when they were children, and he wanted to be firm but kind. "If you're right about this, which I fear you could be, it's neither your fault nor Jake's. That said, there are no circumstances under which it would be your fault. I'm so proud of you both for seeing the light and taking your lives back. And so grateful and happy you came to me." He smiled. "Why don't we have something to eat, talk some more, and see what else we might be able to figure out? I'm worried about your safety and Jake's as well."

"Oh … yeah. He might disinherit us by death instead."

"I won't let him hurt anyone I love."

"Same here."

John smiled as there was a knock at the door. "Dare I hope, Dylan?"

"Yeah, Jake probably figured out everything is cool since I didn't come tumbling out on my ass all bloodied and shit." He laughed. "Just kidding. Hey, looks like Kono's all excited. He's doing a circle dance or something."

The tears rolling again, John opened the door. Jake, already blubbering, looked into John's eyes, then threw his arms around the only man who'd ever been a father to him. "I'm so glad to see you! I wish I didn't have his blood in my veins. Don't hate me. Please don't hate me!"

John pulled away, meeting his eyes again. "Never, Jake. I love you both more than ever. And thanks for coming here so I didn't have to send my dog to track you down."

Jake wasn't sure whether to laugh. "Really?"

"Yeah, he means it," Dylan said with a grin. "This dog is some kind of sensitive. And smart. Oh, no. Look."

Kono, who was now standing by the door, looked at Dylan, then Jake, then repeated the process several times before looking quizzically at John.

"They're identical twins, boy. I'll explain it to you another time."

"We're your human brothers," Dylan offered. He shrugged and turned to Jake. "At least we can share the dirty looks he's gonna give us. He's kind of an intense woofer, but really smart."

Walking over to Jake, Kono rubbed against his leg. Then, he strolled over to Dylan and did the same thing. When he had finished, with only love in his eyes, he sat before John and looked up at him for approval.

"Good boy," John said, wiping away another tear as he petted Kono. "Very good boy."

"Good evening. Teal Beach Sundial Inn."

"Good news, bitch. I'm not going to call you anymore. I'm bored."

"Who is …"

Sunny's face wore a distressed reaction as the call ended just as Tyler was walking in.

"Oh, no. Not again. Shit!"

"Oh, Ty. I hate it when you get so distressed over this. And why are you at work so early. It's only seven."

He leaned on the reception counter nodding toward the phone. "What did *she* say?"

"Oddly, that she wasn't going to call me anymore because she was bored. I'm not sure what to make of that."

"Well, I'm *not* relieved." Tyler bit his lip as his face tightened. "Not relieved at all. Did she call you a bitch?"

Sunny gulped. "I'm afraid so. You didn't tell me why you're here so early."

"It's not important now."

"Actually, it's more important than ever. Please, Ty. Tell me."

"Because I wanted to give you the good news that I'm finally going to listen to you and stop working the night shift and just be your assistant manager and the artist you're always telling me to be. Not to mention the most important job titles I'll soon have: husband and father. I've contacted a company who can put in the new security grille and install the entry system you've always wanted. Except now …."

"Except now nothing! That's wonderful, Ty." Sunny lifted the counter panel and walked to the couch. Miggy, still dejected, stayed in her bed.

"Come on, sit, Mr. Gardet."

Agitated, Tyler sat in the chair across from her. "I've got a very bad feeling, Sunny. Not likin' this."

"Will you first tell me about the security system and anything else you came here to say?"

Distracted, he looked around but said nothing.

"Tyler Gardet. Talk to me. I want all of the details. Please."

Nervously, he scanned the room again, then looked at Sunny. "It can wait. I have all of the literature at my place, and I've memorized it. I researched a few systems, spoke to friends who work in other hotels, and I believe I've picked out what will work best for you. But this isn't my hotel, so of course, you have the final say. I just wanted to do the legwork so you wouldn't have to be bothered."

"This is the answer to a prayer. Mine and Imari's." She smiled. "Whenever you want to show me the material or have me meet with someone from the company, I'm ready."

"Exactly what I wanted to hear, only I'm not leaving my night spot until this madness is resolved. Not playin', Sunny. I will *never* let anyone hurt you. I promised Grey that on the day of his funeral and I'm not going back on my word."

Just as she was about to respond, she looked up, stunned to see John and Kono walk through the door with Dylan and Jake. Loud whimpering sounded from behind the desk, Tyler jumped up, opened the gate, and let Miggy run to greet Kono.

Standing, Sunny put her hand over her mouth. Her eyes filled with tears. Letting her arm drop to her side, she looked at the boys, then at John. "These young men can't possibly be who I think they are, can they?" She looked at Dylan. "You're staying in one of my cabins, aren't you? But we haven't met."

Glowing with pride, John watched as both boys introduced themselves to Sunny as his sons. "It's a good thing I just told you about the boys, or you'd be really confused."

"I still am. Very." Her watery eyes sparkled. "But I'm ecstatic." As she went to hug John, Dylan and Jake introduced themselves to Tyler.

"So look, Sunny, I know this is all quite a shock, but we've got to talk to you. Rather urgently, I'm afraid." He turned to Tyler. "Are you coming on at eight?"

"If it's important, I can work right now."

Concerned but still smiling, Sunny looked at John. "Would you all like to come to my place? You've never even seen where I live yet. I can cook dinner." She turned to Dylan and Jake. "Or perhaps everyone would prefer to go across the street and have Rolo fix up something for us."

Anxiously, John scanned the room, not even realizing paranoia was setting in. Hoping no one noticed, he offered a nervous smile. "I'd prefer to go into your home and have Rolo prepare some take-out. This isn't a conversation we can have in any public place."

Tyler bit his lip and moved his head from side to side, his facial muscles tightening even more. "I know this mess is all connected. Not likin' it one bit."

John nodded. "Ty, I promise you. After we talk to Sunny and have dinner, I'll fill you in on everything. And yeah, whatever your worries are, I share them. I think something very ugly is escalating and we're going to stop it."

"Yeah we will," Dylan said.

"You've got an army now," Jake added. He looked at Tyler. "So you got a cabin near my brother's I can stay in? My stuff's down the street at the Kenwood. I can grab it later."

Tyler walked behind the desk. "I'll take care of the cabin, Jake.

Meanwhile, you'll need these." He reached under the counter and pulled out four paper menus for Dodo Deen's and handed them to him.

Sunny looked at John, Dylan, and Jake. "Come on. Let's go into my place where we can talk." She lifted the counter panel and ushered everyone through.

Tyler, doing his best to stay calm, tried to smile. "I'll be here. We'll get this right. And it sure is a pleasure to meet John's sons."

As everyone but Tyler disappeared through the door to Sunny's place, Tyler turned to see Harper standing at the desk, her face burning with anger. "Did you just say those guys are John's sons?"

Trying not to lose his cool, Tyler narrowed his eyes. "I think my sister-in-law told you to be minding your own business, Ms. Kinnison. Now *I'm* tellin' you."

Pulling her phone from her back pocket, she typed in a numerical code to unlock it, then quickly scrolled through her contacts. As she walked toward the doorway to the second floor, she snarled at Tyler. "Why don't you take some of your own advice?"

As soon as she closed the door behind her, Tyler ran over and put his ear to it. "It's me. You need to get here right away. Or don't bother coming at all."

"Damn," he mumbled as her voice quickly faded. "What the hell is going on?"

CHAPTER TWENTY-TWO

"And that's the whole sordid story," John said wearily.

"My goodness. I'm in absolute shock. Are we one-hundred percent certain it's Richard in my cliff house?" Sunny leaned back on her seafoam-green armchair and looked upward, taking a moment to calm herself.

Dylan, who was sitting on the large overstuffed couch with John and Jake, swiped through his phone to pull up a few photos. He stood, walked to Sunny, and showed her the images on his screen. "This is Richard. Is this who's living in your house?"

Contorting her face with revulsion, she glanced at the photos, then looked away. "Yes. Not even a speck of doubt. Same glasses, same hair gelled in place, and same arrogant look. And now, when I think about it, of course I remember his name. I must have repressed it because he unnerved me so, though logic dictates I should have done the complete opposite." She exhaled a long breath. "It's very unlike me to forget the name of anyone I rent to. But as his girlfriend was the official renter, and she's the one whose credit I checked—well, that's my excuse." She sighed. "But that's him all right."

"Yeah. Thought so." Dylan resumed his seat.

Sunny buried her face in the palms of her hands. After a moment, she looked at the three of them. "I'm a complete idiot. Everything about this man disturbed me the moment I saw him. And the young woman, Phoebe, in whose name the house was rented, didn't say a word unless she was prompted to speak. She looked completely intimidated by him as if her only purpose was to do what he wanted."

"Uh, yeah!" Jake blurted out. "Word! She must be the one he was banging when he was talking to me. He was moaning and shit while he was cursing me out. Took me a moment to realize he was having an or—"

Dylan elbowed him hard in the ribs.

"Ow!" Jake looked at Sunny and then John. "Oh, sorry. TMI, I guess."

John suppressed a smile, wanting to laugh at the boys, but not at the situation.

"No apologies necessary." Sunny exhaled in disgust. "That doesn't surprise me at all. Which is why I'm livid with myself for renting to them. As I told my friend, Rissa," she addressed the boys, "Grey, my late husband, would have never rented to him. I wanted to turn him down, but I didn't because I learned a long time ago that I cannot be in this business and like every person who rents a room or a house from me. Also, because he had the money, and her credit was excellent, I saw no reason to say no, especially when the other people who saw the property seemed like big-time partiers to me—and probably are." She thought for a moment. "That's no excuse. I'm a fool." She looked at John. "I should have seen more prospective tenants, but I was impatient and just wanted to get the whole process over with. And in my haste, I rented to a man who made your life hell and now, quite probably, wants to kill you and maybe me too.

"Sweetheart …."

Sunny gulped. He had never called her that before.

"I know Richard Strausser, and so do the boys. If you had turned him away, that would *never* have stopped him. If he wanted that house, he might have paid off whoever you did rent it to—or found another place nearby. He not only would have had a Plan B, he'd have a plan for every letter in the alphabet. And he's very good at knocking over obstacles and kicking them out of the way to get what he wants. He has no conscience whatsoever."

"Totally," Dylan said as his brother nodded in agreement.

"So what's he going to knock or kick over to kill us?"

John jumped up from his seat and hurried over to Sunny, who stood and buried her face in his chest, sobbing. When she looked up, he kissed her forehead and stroked her hair. "I didn't mean to frighten you, but that's exactly what I did. I was trying to tell you that this is not your fault. In fact, maybe it's a good thing you did rent to him because he would have been harder to find."

Sunny nodded, wanting to kiss him, but remembering the boys were there. "I'll be okay. Please, sit down, John. Just tell me what we do now."

"Well, first, I hear Kono barking, so I'm thinking it might be time to bring the dogs in from the yard and feed them." He gestured toward the menus on the coffee table. "It's also time to figure out what we want to eat and call across the street. I'll have a shrimp platter with a side salad. While the three of you order dinner and get to know one another better, I'm going to have a chat with Ty, provided there are no strangers within earshot. The first thing I want to do, aside from notifying the police, is to get someone from the force to guard the place."

"There are a few who would be happy to moonlight," Sunny said.

"Good. We'll need a man at all times who can patrol the

grounds."

"Yes. And Ty is going to freak out. He already is. Best you go out and talk to him now."

Jake waited for John to leave, then leaned forward and spoke softly to Sunny. "Don't tell him I said this, but I can totally tell he loves you something major."

Too choked up to respond, Sunny smiled as a lone tear escaped.

"Ow," Jake yelped as Dylan elbowed him again. "What did I do now?"

"Dad can speak for himself, Bozo."

"I *know*." He looked at Sunny, then at Dylan again. "I just thought she looked sad and hearing that would cheer her up."

"It did, Jake. Very much. Thank you."

Richard walked over to Phoebe who was sitting on the sofa leafing through a pile of sheet music. "I'm going out for thirty minutes. Do not call me." He looked at his Rolex. "It's almost eight. I'll be back at eight-thirty. Oh, I want you naked by the time I return." He paused. "I'd like you to be sitting on the red recliner, perhaps with your legs open, just a bit ... as if you were teasing me. Yes, that sounds perfect."

He hurried to the door without a good-bye. Phoebe snarled behind his back as she gave him the finger. *No way. No more, you fucking pervert.* She waited until he left, then carefully took a peek out the front window, watching as he climbed into the back of a limousine.

Once it was out of sight, she walked toward the living room balcony.

Turning on the light, she quietly opened both the glass and screen doors, just enough to squeeze through. Carefully, she walked where he had forbade her to go. She looked down. "No way anyone is out there with a camera, and what is there to take a photo of? Gotta be something else." Using the flashlight on her phone for extra light, carefully, she looked at every inch of the deck and railing in sight. "Nothing! Why can't I figure this out?" Repeating the process, the second time, she saw something unusual at the end of the deck." Squatting, she took a closer look. "Oh, my God. No way. Please tell me I'm wrong."

Distraught, Phoebe quickly left and ran into the bedroom to call her sister. After twenty-five minutes of frenetic conversation, replete with old and new warnings, newly energized with a fierce determination to do things differently, she promised her sister and herself she would stop the vicious cycle of abuse. Before she could finish, she heard the front door unlock. "It's him, Tillie. Gotta go."

"PHOEBEEEEEEE!"

Hearing him scream her name made her shudder.

"Where the hell are you?" He rushed into the bedroom, furious to find her clothed and sitting on the bed. "Do you know where I've just been?"

"No. How would I?"

"I was with the producer of the movie you're going to sing in. He was on his way to LA from San Fran and had his driver take a detour so we could talk. Know why? I insisted that we speak in person to ensure everything was in order and that you'd be getting a contract soon. Yes, Phoebe. That's what I just did for you. And what did you do for me? You came into the bedroom, probably to gab with your silly hick sister, and you haven't removed a stitch of clothing." He stared at her. "Now would be a good time. Take it off."

"Oh, I was going to, but then I found out it was that time of month, you know, so I can't."

"Nah. You had 'that time of month' two weeks ago. I remember because menstrual blood sickens me. It's like a monthly crime scene. Women should have yellow tape around their pussies until every last drop is gone. But that isn't necessary now, is it? Phoebe, my darling, take off your clothes unless you want me to do it for you." He smiled as he studied her face. "Oh, so that *is* what you want me to do. That turns you on, does it?"

"No. It *doesn't* turn me on. I don't feel well. I don't want to have sex."

His furious eyes stared at her. "Take your clothes off NOW. I'll rip them into pretty little shreds if you don't. I'll enjoy it too. I never tire of finding new ways to get off. I love to experiment. And you and I haven't begun to explore. So far, our sex life has been grade-school level. But not for much longer. You're going to skip middle school and go right to high school. And then college. I've got things planned you're going to love. Oh, yeah, sweet cheeks!"

Terrified, Phoebe said nothing.

"Do you fucking hear me? Take off your clothes!"

"But … uh … why would you want to be with me when you're so angry?"

"Anger makes me hard. Always has. Haven't you figured that out yet? Stop stalling, and do what I tell you! Do you have any idea how much time and money I've spent on you?" He huffed. "Wasted is more like it."

Shaking in fear, she did as he commanded, unable to pretend she enjoyed anything about him, no longer caring about career opportunities he might offer her. "Richard, I really don't want to do this anymore. I'm saying 'no.' And I mean it!"

"Ah, did your silly sister coach you to say that?" He laughed. "You're hardly convincing, Phoebe. I know you want me. And you know what, I almost believed you for a minute. But then I realized you just soaked in my words, and you're trying to please me. You catch on quick, trying to piss me off with 'no.' And you know what, I like it. You've got a fiery side I haven't seen before."

"No, stop!"

"Ah, you want me to get *really* angry so I'll be rough with you. Okay! What other surprises do you have? Maybe you're not the little girl I think you are." He walked over and grabbing both of her breast in his hands, biting one at a time, ignoring her cries of pain. "Enjoy this, my pretty pussy. I know I will."

"Richard, no! I mean it for real."

Twenty minutes later, after he had raped her and called it 'the best sex we've ever had,' he abruptly jumped off the bed and hurried to the bathroom.

Traumatized, she got up and walked to the bedroom balcony, grabbing a blue chenille blanket she found on the floor at the end of the bed. Naked, her face wet with tears, she wrapped the blanket around her shoulders. The sound of the shower teaming down wasn't loud enough to mute her sobs. She knew he had rushed into the bathroom to deny her the opportunity to clean herself, to humiliate her like she was discarded trash, and was purposely taking way more time than he usually did. Her mind's eye tortured her with a replay of the licentious smile on his face when he'd finally removed his body from hers, licking his lips in satisfaction. How dare he think she'd wanted to be raped. She collapsed on the deck, sobbing loudly now. It was all her fault. What else did she think a man like Richard Xavier Strausser would ever want with her? She didn't know who he'd gone off in a limo to talk to, but it had nothing to do with her singing in a movie. That was a conversation easily had on the phone, but he played on her naivete every day. How stupid she had been to move to New York City with the dream of becoming a recording star, then tell herself she got lucky when she met the CEO and owner of Xavier Rox Records in a trendy East Side club. She remembered the way people looked at her the first night as she walked out with him. Twenty-one at the time, being a naive young woman from Vermont, she told herself the onlookers were envious. But no. They all knew what lay in store. At least the older ones did. They knew who Richard X. Strausser really was, and they felt sorry for her.

But Phoebe could not accept her naivete as an excuse for all that had happened to her. Even at her young age, somehow, she should have known better. She deserved everything that she got. He'd made her watch porn to learn how to please him. He'd taken her to an expensive Fifth Avenue salon and had them bleach her hair and teach her how to wear more makeup than she felt comfortable in. He sent her shopping in boutiques and high-priced department stores with an older woman named Carol, someone who worked at the record company, who picked out everything she knew Richard would want Phoebe to wear. Not once, did the woman ask Phoebe what she liked, nor did she engage her in any unnecessary or pleasant conversation.

Phoebe remembered feeling like a store mannequin Carol was dressing to stick in the window.

The life she had now was not what she'd ever dreamed about. A year ago, she'd tried to excuse herself for being a dumb girl from rural Vermont and came close to leaving him. But then her young girlfriends drooled over her "good luck," telling her how envious they were that she got to play with the big boys and that she would become a star. And so, she convinced herself she was indeed lucky with the perverted record mogul sixteen years her father's senior who dictated nearly every waking moment of her life when he was around.

And now, she hated herself more than she hated him. So what if she'd flown around the world in a private jet? He'd defiled her on every flight. The crew members knew it. She'd even caught them watching. She gasped as she remembered something she'd made herself forget. He'd *paid* the flight crew to watch. He got off on that. How stupid she was. All of that had to be recorded too. She could never escape what she had let happen to herself. She was tainted and dirtied for life. Nobody would ever want her now. Who could ever respect her? She couldn't respect herself. What life would she have now? Where could she possibly go?

For twenty minutes, John stood in the lobby and filled in Tyler and Clarissa on everything he knew. The Gardets not only agreed that someone should patrol the grounds to protect Sunny, along with Dylan and Jake, but also that a second person should patrol John's cottage.

Sighing in agreement, just as he was about to return to Sunny's place, John's cell sounded. Seeing the call was from Ben, he relied on his better judgment and answered it. Waving good-bye to Tyler and Clarissa, he walked out of the lobby, across the porch, and stood by the beach steps, making a three-hundred-and-sixty-degree inspection of his surroundings as he did so. "Hey, Benjo. I don't even want to know why you're calling so late on a Tuesday night, do I?"

"Oh, man, John. I was so afraid you were gonna send my ass to voicemail hell. I'm really glad you picked up. I think I've figured some things out, and I also owe you an apology."

"Before you tell me, I want you to know that my boys are back."

There was silence on the other end.

"My sons."

"Are you serious, my dude? Jake and Dylan?"

"Yeah. They are. And I couldn't be happier, but I don't have any time now for in-depth commentary or any at all, for that matter. And for now, that's a secret. We're all in danger, and I've got to get back to them and to Sunny. So no mysterious teasers, just tell me why you called."

"Well, great news about the boys, and you're not gonna like this."

"Benjo, did you even hear what I just said?"

"I did. Sorry. So listen, I was just out in Two Harbors with my crew. We're moving an older couple to the mainland. Outta nowhere, my sort-of new guy, Mateo, tells me about something that happened almost a month ago when they came for the rest of your things."

"Gee, I can't wait. Because things aren't fucked up enough as they are. What?"

"Well, he was standing by your rental cottage and being super meticulous with checking boxes off as I'd showed him. Then, he said this hippie-like woman, late fifties, pretended to be oblivious to his presence as she did this weird fairy dance and crashed right into him, knocking his hands really hard so that his clipboard fell to the ground."

John looked out to the ocean—the only thing that halfway calmed him. "How special. And I have no idea what a 'fairy dance' is, but go on."

"I don't know what it is either. She told Mateo she liked to dance like a Celtic fairy."

"Yeah, I hear Celtic fairy dancing is all the rage on Catalina. Seriously, what the hell …."

"Well, the thing is that Mateo didn't pay too much attention to it at the time. He thought she was some new-age nutjob, so he took back the clipboard, and she apologized and moved on. Real quick like."

"This isn't good."

"Not so much. So when we were on the job earlier, some neighbor came to say good-bye to the couple, and they mentioned this older hippie woman, saying that she was living on the campground and nobody really knew who she was."

"I think I do. Unfortunately." John shook off his rage.

"That's when Teo said how she knocked the clipboard out of his hands, but now that he thought about it, before she handed it back, she looked really hard at it."

"Peachy keen, Benjo."

"So, um, yeah, I think it was that Renata woman. Sabelli's daughter. Sounds exactly like how you described her. And I think she got your address off the clipboard, so I'd bet she left you those fake flowers and love note on your deck. She must have parked on Seascape Highway like we did. Otherwise, someone would have seen her."

John clenched his fists as he looked around again. "That makes more sense than I want it to. She has to be the one who came into the diner asking about the cottage."

"And I'm thinking, John, if she saw you were staying at the hotel for the first week, she might have been jealous, and so it could be her calling Sunny, not the crazy Nancy bitch who killed Sunny's husband. I thought you'd want to know."

"I can't believe this."

"I'm a wreck over it. I'm really sorry. Especially if one of my guys, even unintentionally, put you in this kind of jeopardy. I really wish Teo had piped up before now, but he didn't think it was a big deal at the time."

John walked around the cul-de-sac as he talked. "No big deal. I mean hey, you're on the remote part of an island, no crowds around, and some hippie woman does some weird dance smack into you, says she's a Celtic fairy, and knocks your clipboard to the ground. Then, she stares at it, burns whatever she wanted to know into her brain, flies off, and yeah, nothing to see there, huh?" He huffed in disgust. "What the fuck is wrong with that guy? Why would any of that be remotely normal about that to him?"

"I don't know, dude. It's California? What can I say?"

"Yeah, well there is that." John said nothing for a moment and ran the information through his head. "I appreciate you telling me, Benjo, but I'm a little more than enraged, you know?"

"Yeah. I can hear that."

"Anything else?"

"Um, 'fraid so."

"I was kidding." He looked around again. "Go on. Tell me."

"So um, my cop friend, Ken, the one who sent Shelley home when her black hair dye inked his sheets ...."

"I remember. What about him?"

"Well, he knows someone who's a regular customer of Her Spikiness at that hair salon she works at. And Shelley was bragging to her how she memorized your license plate number and that's how she found your home here in Long Beach. Only it's not your home, it's mine, as she apparently figured out after she saw me and Dodger. And so I'm really hoping that you haven't changed your address with the California DMV yet, because she's planning to get someone to look again for her. To find you."

"Damn." John sat down on the top step. "Unfortunately, I'm a law-abiding citizen, and I changed the address within ten days like they tell you to do on their website."

"I was afraid of that. So the thing is, I've thought about this for over an hour, and it really could be either one of those psycho chicks who left you the flowers. Shelley wouldn't know to harass Sunny, but it wouldn't be too hard to find out you'd been staying there. And then she might be the jealous kind and all. I'm thinking it could be either one of them."

"And why's that?"

"Because the other night, the spiked one came onto my

driveway and held up a big white sign to my camera written with a Sharpie or something. Uh, it said, 'Tell Sleepy John he owes me a good fuck, and I intend to collect.' She stood there for a good minute, mooned the camera, then left."

"Sensational." John's stomach turned. "Is there anything else? If there is, no matter how small or insignificant it seems, please tell me."

"Just that I got a voice mail from our buddy Dante Massimo the other day. He didn't sound too upset or anything. Just asked me to call him when I had time. He said that he hadn't had any new songs from you in a while and wanted to know if you'd sent me any to pass onto him. Oh, and he mentioned the Whisky Devers album and that he didn't think you'd be too happy about it. Asked me if I knew anything about how all that went down, and he hoped you were okay and doing well in your new home. Then he just said to call him when I had a free minute."

"Okay. Well, when you talk to him, just tell him I'm working on some new music, but not to expect anything too soon." He sighed. "I don't want him to know what's going on here. He's one of the few friends I have, besides you, and I've known him since I was a teenager, but the fewer people who know anything right now, the better. So maybe wait to call him back so you don't let anything slip, and he doesn't make you uncomfortable by pressing you for more info. You hear me?"

"Loud and clear."

"I'm not happy about anything you told me, Benjo, but I appreciate that you did. And that you've got my back. Sorry for any sarcasm. I'm just at the end of my very frayed rope."

"Just don't hang yourself with it, man. I'll be in touch."

CHAPTER TWENTY-THREE

John and Dylan laughed as Jake rolled on the floor with Kono.

"He loves me," Jake told them. "I'm his new best friend." He looked at Dylan. "Maybe I'm the one who should be the veterinarian. Or we could have like a twin practice."

"Hey, Jake-O, have a seat," John said. "I want to talk to you about something."

"Woof," Jake barked to Kono. "Guess I've got to get up." As Jake sat on the couch, everyone was surprised to see Kono jump up and sit next to him. "Told you. Brotherly love."

John smiled. "I'm so grateful to have you both back in my life. Jake, just hearing how you've been so immersed in Richard's world, and how happy you are to be out of it, I'm wondering if you've given any thought to what you might like to do next. Or, if over the years, you might have had other goals. Wondering is the operative word. No rush. In fact, taking a break right now is probably the healthiest thing you can do."

"Yeah, I know. But you know what I *don't* know? What it's like to be asked what *I* want to do instead of being groomed for a future that's already been mapped out for me." He frowned. "I'm really happy you care about me. More than a breath of fresh air when you've been breathing in pollution for eight years. I feel so freakin' lame having let myself get sucked in."

"Don't even go there. Richard did a number on the two of you. Big time. Besides, the recording business can be very glamorous. At one time, as an artist, it was to me too." He cringed as he thought about it. "What appeals to you now? Same work, different company? Something else?"

Jake frowned, his playful expression gone. "So, right after I quit and split from the SOB, right before I flew out here that same night, Dyl and I were talking …." He made eye contact with his brother. "Remember how you said the record business was all I'd ever known and how everything about it was drummed into our brains since we were thirteen?"

"Sure. Especially since the convo was only the other night."

"Right. And you said there was a whole world out there. I've been thinking —"

"I know that's tough for you," Dylan said with a smile. "Thinking."

"No, seriously, bro— and Dad. I just realized that I never thought of anything *but* the record business. And I only wanted to work in A & R because it was the coolest department. And because it's how he lured me into the business. He made me want it. I can't think of one single time he ever asked me what *I* wanted to do. He just told us what would happen with our lives: where we'd go to school, what we'd major in, and on and on." He turned to Dylan. "Funny how he never even noticed when you switched your major."

"Yeah. Because he thought his job of molding our futures was done. Go on with what you were saying."

Jake continued. "Just that him controlling our lives reminds me of when we were kids and had those toy pirates and superheroes. Dyl, remember how we'd make up stories for them, and they'd have whatever adventure we wanted them to have?" He looked at John. "And you bought us a pirate ship and built that cool superhero headquarters out of wood. Painted it and all. That was awesome."

"I still have them," John said, trying not to tear up at the memory. "They're in my friend Ben's garage. I stored them there, and well, let's just say I didn't bring them with me because it hurt too much to look at them, but I couldn't throw them out. They're too much a part of both of you."

Jake brightened. "Well, now you can bring them here. And that's really awesome you saved them." Sadness covered his face again. "So like I was saying, Richard treated us like toys, only not in the fun way that Dyl and I played with ours. I mean, no, we never asked the toys what they wanted to do with their lives, because uh ...."

"They were toys?" Dylan said, laughing. "But you're right. I see your point. And it's smack on, bro."

Jake looked at John. "When I was a kid, did I ever talk about what I wanted to do when I grew up?"

"You did."

"I can't remember. It's like it was all washed from my brain."

Anger settled on John's face. "Brainwashing does that."

"So what did I say?" Jake looked at his brother. "I remember you loving animals. And in the sixth grade, you said you wanted to be a vet, but I don't remember squat about myself."

John clasped his hands and rested his head. "You've got to remember how much you loved going to the New York Aquarium in Brooklyn and the one in Camden, New Jersey, right? Those weren't the only two we visited, but they were your favorites. Dylan loved them too, but you were intrigued by the underwater society." He laughed. "You didn't quite use those words, but you were fascinated with how the animals communicated and said that when you grew up, you wanted to study them. The sea creatures, plants, the coral—all of it. Your favorite animal was the bioluminescent octopus. You asked me if you could have one for a pet."

"Ha ha ha!" Dylan lovingly punched his brother in the arm. "And you cried when Dad said no. Waaaaaaa!"

Jake gave him a dirty look. "Whoa! I totally forgot that. It was. I wanted to be an oceanographer. Or something like that. I still love marine life, actually. I had all of those underwater photos in my room—like plastered all over the walls."

"You did. I learned a lot from them and from you, Jake. I think having a son who loved the ocean so much has a lot to do with who I am today and where I live. Just wanted you to know."

"Oh, wow. I only thought I left you with pain. Not anything good."

John smiled lovingly at the boys. "You two were the very best part of my life. And I hope you always will be."

Touched, but too embarrassed to answer, Jake looked down. "So um … you think I could still look into the oceanography thing?"

"Absolutely. But take your time. There are a lot of choices."

"I wanna think about them, but not until this bullshit is resolved, and I don't constantly have to think about what that sicko Richard might be trying to do." Worry distorted Jake's face. "It's been almost two days since we met Sunny and told her everything. Now we've got a cop out on the deck, another one patrolling the hotel, and no one has seen anything. But I hear this voice screaming in my head to be careful. I mean, it's 'effin loud. I need to listen to it. I don't think I should be talking about a career when I feel like everything around us is about to explode."

"Yeah," Dylan said. "Same here."

"Believe me, boys, I'm no different. But the short breaks to get reacquainted has been good for all of us. And productive. Trust me, though; my fear hasn't gone anywhere. I understand; it's hard to plan your future when the present is toxic and bubbling under the surface."

"Is that why Sunny isn't your official girlfriend yet?" Jake asked.

"Something like that."

John stood. "Rather than sit around here any longer, I think Kono could use a play session with Miggy. Also, Rolo and Clarissa's kids, RJ and Jacie, really want to meet you both. Ah! I just remembered. I hear Jacie has an amazing fish tank in her room. I bet you'll love it, Jake. And RJ wants you to hear some of his Louisiana blues collection. He grew up in California but got his love for the blues from his parents and his uncle Ty. Why don't we drop Kono with Sunny, visit with the Gardets, and then we'll have dinner with Sunny when she's done working?"

"Sounds like a plan," Dylan said. "Only I don't think it's going to play out that way."

"Nope," Jake said without thinking. "It won't."

"And by the way," Dylan added, "the guy outside should stay here. Leaving this cottage unattended could be really dangerous."

Silencing his own foreboding, stone-faced, John nodded and walked to the door. "Come on, everyone. Let's go."

"It's nice John's boys are spending time with my niece and nephew," Tyler said, as he stood next to Sunny behind the counter. "Glad that John is too. The kids dug him from jump. Just like we did." He smiled as he tried to control his nerves. "Hey, just like you too."

Sunny blushed. "Just like me."

Tyler bit his lip as he looked around. "Sunny, I'm trying hard, but I can't do this small talk. I'm a wreck. Something's really not right about Jeff having to leave in a hurry when he's the only cop guarding this hotel. I can't blame him for rushing home, but I'm trying to understand what kind of crim does a home intrusion in a cop's house in broad daylight?"

"I had the same thought, Ty. Maybe the criminal didn't know a cop lived there. Maybe he just picked the first house that looked good to him. And why do criminals do what they do no matter what time of day?"

"Yeah. You have a point, but my gut tells me he did know and that it was a ruse to pull Jeff away from here. All part of a bigger plan. Sounds like Jeff's wife was scared to death when that masked intruder burst in with a gun. Hope he didn't hurt her."

"Me too."

"And now we don't have a cop here."

"Larae said that her husband, you know, Rafael, will take Jeff's place until he can find a replacement, and she's coming with him just in case Sunny needs her. They should be here in ten minutes."

Tyler was frantic as his eyes darted about the lobby. He stopped to listen. "Usually, only Kono barks at other dogs down on the beach. Miggy never barks unless something is wrong. Maybe you should go check on them." Tyler pushed the small pile of invoices to the side.

"Something's off."

"My goodness, Ty. I was just thinking the same thing. I tried to tell myself she was just copying Kono, but I've had the two of them out there together many times, and I've never heard the commotion I'm hearing now. I'm going to see what's going on."

Just as Sunny turned to go into her home, the loud sound of a car engine revving startled them both. Looking at her for a split second, Tyler ran outside, only to see the dust from a speeding car that was too far away to identify.

Seconds later, Sunny stood by his side. "Ty, what's going on?"

Tyler looked down the road. "What in the Sam Hill was that? Why would someone come down this way, to a dead-end cul-de-sac, then turn around and gun it outta here?"

"Oh my, I have no idea."

"This just isn't sitting right with me." Agitated, he twisted his hands together. "When Jeff left to go home, he told me his wife said the intruder just grabbed something at random from the mantle. A wooden elephant statue, I think. She said it seemed like he just needed to take *something* to give the appearance he was robbing her, but that she thought his true motive was to terrify her before he hauled ass outta there. Just like that car did here. Only it couldn't have been the same guy. Jeff lives some twenty minutes from here. Like I said, an organized plan. Something real bad …."

Just as he was about to say more, Clarissa came charging out of the restaurant. "What the heck was up with that car? Rolo and I heard that engine from the kitchen. I don't think John or the kids did; they're upstairs showing off our turntable and blasting their great-grandmother's favorite, Lead Belly." She paused. "You sure you don't know who could have been in that car?"

"We don't know, sis. Anyone skip out on their check?"

"No, not at all." A look of panic swept over her. "Only there were a few customers having long meals recently … *men*, actually, who didn't look like they were here to chill at Teal Beach, if you get my drift. Men who sat by the window where … ugh … where they kept looking at the hotel, now that I think of it. One today, and two guys a few days ago."

"Not good, Ri—."

"Oh no!" Sunny blurted out. "I can only hear Kono now. Even he doesn't bark nonstop like this! Not even close. I was on my way to check on the kids when that car went racing up the road." She hurried to the west side of the hotel. "I've got to see if my Miggy girl is all right. And Kono too!"

Clarissa ran after her. "I'm going with her, Ty. You stay here in case that car comes back."

Before he could argue, she had followed Sunny to the backyard.

"Oh my God, Rissa!" Sunny screamed as she saw Kono, who was barking and agitated, come running to her. "Whoever was in that car took my Miggy! They took my baby!"

"Oh Lord Jesus!"

Before Sunny could decide what to do, her cell rang. Not recognizing the number, which was a rarity, she answered in despair. "Who is this?"

"Mrs. Harrison?"

Rattled by the soft feminine voice, Sunny slowed her breathing. "Who is this?"

"Um … this is Phoebe Marcroft. You rented your house to me.

I have you on speakerphone and I need to tell you that I think your dog got lost and ended up here. I found your name and number on her tags. And oh, Miggy is such a cute name."

"My dog didn't get lost! She was just stolen out of my yard as I'm sure you know!" Sunny held in her anger as she could hear Richard in the background telling Phoebe what to say.

"So, you'd better come get her, but you need to come alone. And don't tell anyone where you're going."

"What does that man want? It can't be money! He's a billionaire."

"You better hurry because...." Her voice faltered. "Because, well, your dog might fall off the deck onto the rocks if you don't."

"No! Don't let him hurt my Miggy! Please! I'll be right there." Sunny ended the call and turned to Clarissa. "Please take Kono back to John. Poor boy. He's every bit as scared about Miggy as I am."

"Sunny, where are you going?" Clarissa followed her into the house only to see her grab her car keys from a hook in the pantry and run back outside again.

Sharply, Sunny turned to face her. "Don't follow me, Rissa!"

"But you're more hysterical than the day you figured out who John was. And you're getting into to a car, crazed. You're going to get Miggy, right? I know you're scared to death, but you should wait for John. You're no match for that psychopath, and Lord knows who else is there with him. Please, don't—."

Before Clarissa could say any more, Sunny had jumped into her Honda CRV and was gone. Within seconds, she drove past Tyler, just as Rolo stepped outside to join him.

Overwrought, Clarissa, with Kono at her side, returned to the road between the hotel and the restaurant. "Someone's kidnapped Miggy! I'm sure it's that monster who's living in her cliff house because I heard Sunny ask what he wanted and that it can't be money because he's a billionaire. So that means he had someone do it for him. It could have been that crazy Nancy woman who killed Grey. I'm not sure. I'm just so scared; I have no idea who called Sunny just now, but I know she's headed right into a trap."

Kono, barking loudly, looked around for John and Miggy.

Tears trickled down Clarissa's face. "I'm afraid that maniac Richard will try to kill her to hurt John. And if I'm wrong and it *is* that lunatic Nancy, she'll try to kill Sunny to get revenge for having to go back to prison after *she* killed Grey. I think I heard a woman's voice on the phone. I'm so scared. I'm so confused. Maybe it was Nancy. I don't know anything except we can't lose Sunny—or Miggy! Where's John? Someone, please. Get him now!"

"On it!" Tyler said as he ran into the restaurant.

Rolo put his arms around his sobbing wife. "I don't want John to get hurt either, baby, but I'm afraid he's the only one who can save her. Doesn't mean we can't help him though. And believe me, we'll do everything in our power."

"Oh, Rolo!" She turned to see John, Dylan, Jake, and Tyler running breathlessly out of the building. "I don't want any of you getting hurt—or worse."

"All is gonna be good," Rolo said as he held her, hoping his reassuring words would convince himself as well.

"We'll call the cops from the car," Ty said. "Let's get going."

Rolo looked at his wife. "You stay here, honey. Don't let any new dinner guests in. Close the place after the last ones leave."

"It's Strausser behind this," John shouted to them as he reunited with Kono. "He set this up so I'd follow Sunny to save her life and then he could kill me, and possibly her first, to watch me suffer. I'll follow all right, but that son of a bitch isn't going to hurt me or anyone I love. Never again." John scratched Kono's neck, upset that the dog was more agitated than he'd ever seen him. "Boy, you've got to stay here with Clarissa. We're going to get Miggy and Sunny."

Kono barked loudly in protest, jumping up and putting his paws on John's chest.

"I know you want to come with me, but you need to stay here."

Clarissa patted her thighs. "Come on, boy. Stay with your Auntie Rissa." She looked up at John. "If you can get Miggy out of the thick of things, not that I have an idea what you're going to find … oh, please Lord, let them be okay. Just call or text, and I'll come get Miggy. In fact, I've got a better idea. Kono and I will park down the street from the cliff house. Just in case anyone needs help or a fast getaway. As soon as Rafael gets here, that's exactly what I'll do."

"That sounds good. Thank you. But please, Clarissa, be very careful." John turned to Tyler. "Okay, let's go. You know where it is, right?"

"Sure do. Twelve Cliff Road!" Tyler shouted and ran toward his truck as John, Rolo, Dylan, and Jake followed.

Clarissa sobbed as Kono frantically barked his desire to go with John. "Oh, Lord. Please watch over them all." She spoke gently to Kono. "Don't worry, boy. We'll be hot on their trail soon. Security patrol and all that. As soon as the nice policemen come to make sure everyone here is safe."

Just as she was about to go inside to check on her children, she noticed that Harper had been watching the entire incident from the far corner of the porch, and a redhead, one she'd never seen before, was standing outside of an old beat-up car she'd just parked in Sunny's hotel lot.

CHAPTER TWENTY-FOUR

Sunny let herself into the cliff house and raced up the stairs to the living room. To her horror, she saw Richard standing to the left of the open balcony doors, an evil grin on his face, while a horror-stricken Phoebe trembled by his side. To the right side of the doors, a woman dressed in Bohemian garb, hands behind her back, her long, wavy, gray hair in disarray, flashed a macabre smile at Sunny.

With no understanding of the odd positioning, her enemies standing as if they were soldiers guarding the balcony, Sunny shook with fear as a chilling sense of déjà vu discomfited her. As she looked to her right, she saw Miggy shivering on the floor behind the red-leather recliner. She noticed the strange woman's eyes following her gaze. In horror, Sunny watched as the woman burst out laughing, her right hand coming from behind her back to reveal a gun that she immediately trained on the dog.

"Oh my God! Nancy." She looked at Miggy. "My sweet girl. I know how scared you are. I'm so sorry."

As soon as Sunny spoke, the dog made a move to come over to her.

"Don't you dare move!" Nancy shouted. "Tell your mongrel to do the same, and then don't open your fucking mouth again, bitch."

As all she had feared stood before her in human form, Sunny gulped and followed orders. "Stay, Miggy." She put her palm out in the stop motion Miggy understood. "Stay, sweetheart. *Stay!*"

Confused, the dog's eyes asked her why but obeyed her command.

Nancy laughed. "When I told you I wouldn't call you again, it was because I knew we'd be seeing each other. Don't think you recognized me at first. I've had to make some changes for business reasons. Anyway, hey, fancy meeting you here, huh? Gosh you've aged. You look like a wizened old hag. You simply must share your skincare routine with me. Oh, wait, you probably don't have one, hagalicious bitch that you are."

Richard, a salacious grin on his face, turned to Phoebe. "Oh, I've been looking forward to this. I told you I had things planned for us. Give me a new high any day. And this is one hell of a turn-on."

"Huh?"

"Take me out of my pants and suck me hard while these two older ladies watch and weep," he growled at her. "Do it!"

"My goodness! Leave her alone!" Sunny shouted. "You sick, twisted predator!"

Richard's eyes transmitted fury. "Unless you want me to throw your pathetic pup onto the rocks, Mrs. Harrison, you'll be wise to shut your mouth and watch the opening act." He turned to Phoebe. "What part of 'take me out and suck me hard' didn't you hear? Do it! Now!"

Taking a deep breath, Phoebe glared at him. "I called Mrs. Harrison against my will. And that was the last horrible thing I'm ever letting you force me to do. I heard every word of your order, you demented, perverted, fucking piece of scabies-ridden contaminated pond scum that the toilet won't flush to the sewer because it doesn't want to offend the excrement! Jerk yourself off if you want, but I'm *never* touching you again. *Ever!* And if you want to try and force me to put that little boy in my mouth, I promise you, I'll bite it off and spit it out."

As Phoebe found her voice and her courage, Richard's wrath grew. "Nothing little about me! And you know that. Tell them!"

"Oooooh," Nancy said. "Lemme see, pretty please. Phoebs can hold the gun on this shaggy pooch and her mama, and I'll do you good. Right now."

His face burning with rage, Richard spat onto the floor. "No part of my flesh touches any broad with an odometer higher than Methuselah can count, not to mention one with your craggy-ass face." He gave Sunny a once-over. "I'd do this shivering blonde long before I'd do you." His stare returned to Nancy. "Talk about a wizened hag!"

"How dare you!" Nancy squinted as she screamed at him. "You've got to be the same age I am. And I was only trying to be nice."

"I don't need your kind of nice. I had my man bring you here for one reason. You do what I tell you, without *any* improvisation, and you'll get your very generous reward. Don't you talk back to me again!"

"Maybe you're forgetting you gave me the gun," Nancy countered. "Ha!"

"Are you truly dumb enough to think there isn't a gun trained on you? Two for that matter. Do you have any idea who you're dealing with, you walking cadaver? Don't even think about testing me."

As Nancy fumed, she brightened at the sound of several footsteps pounding up the stairs. Her face lit up when she saw John, but she briskly stepped to her left, behind a faux leafy green floor plant to partially obscure her identity.

John stepped into the room and surveyed the area, his eyes locking with Richard's after so many years. Sunny stifled a gasp as she saw Richard's steely eyes focus on John, but seeing John return the stare, one of fury, she felt certain that he was not about to back down nor show his nemesis fear.

Just as Richard opened his mouth to speak, he caught sight of the Gardet brothers. But he quickly returned his focus to John. Seeing his calm countenance, he seethed. "You're not going to leave here alive, you bastard." He laughed. "But you know that, right?"

Sunny knew John wouldn't give Richard the reaction he was hungering to see, or a reason to kill her or Miggy. She watched as he fought back every instinct to lunge toward the man who had bulldozed so much of his life and his joy.

"Did you hear what I said, Johnny boy?"

John said nothing, offering only a look of hostility as he stood his ground.

Her heart racing, feeling sure John's was as well, Sunny locked eyes with him and knew he was assessing the dynamics of the situation and formulating a plan.

"What the hell?" Richard screamed, realizing that Jake and Dylan had come with John. "Why did you bring my sons here? How dare you even speak to them, for that matter. I hope you're not delusional enough to think their presence will stop me from taking care of business. Making them miss you was the last straw! They've been too spoiled and far too happy to have thought of you by their lonesome. You had to have been calling or e-mailing them— brainwashing them with your lies. And that's why you're going to die today. They're my sons, not yours!"

"We're not your sons, sleazebag," Jake told him. "John's the only real dad we've ever known. He didn't contact us at all, we haven't been 'far too happy,' and we've always missed him. And don't accuse him of brainwashing or lying to us. That's your game."

"Ditto, dirtball," Dylan said. "And he's never done anything to you. Ever. It's the other way around. What kind of maniac wants to kill someone because he's always been jealous of him? You're sick!"

"How dare either one of you address me that way. What part of 'I'm cutting you off' didn't you hear?"

"You can't buy love or respect," Dylan told him. "It's not for sale. People pretend to stomach your presence. I can't think of anyone in the world who likes you."

"Me neither," Jake said. He looked at his twin. "Though maybe the dirt under his shoes might find some common ground. Nah, don't think so. Dirt has all kinds of useful purposes. It feeds plants and flowers, for one." He scowled at Richard. "We're so done with you, and we don't need your money."

"You mean any *more* of my money! You've both been spoiled rotten. Let me know how a life of poverty works out for you. I'll make sure nobody hires you anywhere." Steaming mad, Richard paused for a moment. "Besides, I've given you way more than money. I've been one hell of a role model."

"Yeah, of who *not* to be," Dylan said, snickering.

"Totally," Jake said.

"Shut-up! I've done *everything* to mold both of you losers into real men. Only you're still losers."

"Yeah, that's rich. Only not your kind of rich," Jake told him. "You don't have a clue what a real man is. You wouldn't be terrorizing this nice girl if you were. And you wouldn't have treated us like shit for eight years."

"Oh, really. I treated you boys like shit, did I? A fancy home to live in, expensive cars, college educations, Manhattan apartments, Rolex watches, jobs at a prestigious record company. Yeah, you illegitimate street urchins have really had it rough."

Dylan started to speak, but he froze and stared. Nancy had stepped into full view, her gun pointed at Sunny.

After exchanging looks with Sunny, John stared at the woman holding the gun. "Renata? What the hell? I never did anything to hurt you. Why and how are you involved in this twisted plot?"

"Hey, there soul mate. You should have never tried to get away from me. Really, John, darling, you should've known there'd be consequences. Especially moving to Teal Beach where the weeping widow lives. That got all of my angry juices flowing again. Oh, boy, I sure was steaming mad. Also, I don't take very kindly to rejection, especially when I have so very much to offer. You spit in the face of what could have been, and will still be, the greatest love of your life. Me!"

"She's not Renata," Sunny squeaked out. "She's Nancy Nestor, the monster who killed my Grey!"

John's face paled.

"Oh, yeah," Nancy said. "There's that little matter of my name. Renata Sabelli lives somewhere in Italy. Tuscany or wherever—running a winery and making more euros than she'll ever know what to do with. Stingy rich bitch. I went to UCLA with her. We became friends, but when I got into a bit of trouble and asked her for some help, Ms. Deep Pockets wouldn't give me fuck all. She wouldn't even listen to me, for that matter. Told me we were mere acquaintances and nothing more." She struck a defiant pose. "When you hang out twice with someone and share your stuff, well, that's a friendship. Damn bitch!" She grumbled as if in physical pain. "So yeah. I keep tabs on everyone who's done me wrong. And I make them pay. I'm powerful good at it too."

Jake and Dylan kept their focus on Richard while the Gardet brothers and John watched Sunny.

"Sounds like Dick here is your psychic twin," Dylan said.

Nancy giggled. "Maybe. Except he wouldn't let me do him a very special favor, and then he insulted me."

"I'll happily do it again if you don't shut your fetid trap!" Richard snapped.

Jake and Dylan exchanged confused looks while Richard kept his stare anchored on Nancy, who had no intention of keeping quiet.

"I'd been planning to take what Renata owes me ever since I saw her photo in some alumni magazine online. Still looks like a damn hippie, so I figured I'd let my hair grow, stop coloring it, and wear these colorful rags like she wears in her vineyard. Had a feeling my new look would come in handy. And sure enough, about a year and a half later, when I heard her *padre* 'bought the farm,' so to speak, and she hadn't come to collect, I thought, Why not pay a vizz to some forger buds from prizz, get some fancy new ID, and see what I can see. Mm hmm. And, mostly important, collect Renata's estate." She looked at Sunny. "So don't feel bad you didn't recognize me at first. I've gone through quite the metamorphosis." She paused. "Appearance-wise, anyway. Ha ha ha!"

Her flesh crawling, Sunny said nothing as angry thoughts raced through her head while fear consumed her.

"What part of 'shut your fetid trap' didn't you understand?" Richard spat.

Sunny tried to remain as calm as possible while Nancy, ignoring Richard, alternated the pointing of the gun between her and Miggy. She noticed that John was about to speak.

He looked at Nancy and spoke slowly. "How'd that estate thing work out for you?"

Her eyes gobbled him up from top to bottom. "It didn't. Got word the real Renata was heading to Two Harbors. Damn bitch. So I hadda skedaddle from the island. The timing was serendipitous though. Got a much better offer that brought me right where I wanted to be. With you. And *you're* going to work out for me just fine, Mr. Sexy. As soon as we get rid of Blondie." She turned to Richard. "Don't you worry; I'll keep up my end of our deal. You'll get what you want."

"Ren ... Nancy ... please," John said, desperately trying to subdue her and appeal to the better side she lacked. "Let's talk this out. I'm not a violent man. You've seen the very quiet life I've lived. Yes, I'll admit it. I was attracted to you the moment you introduced yourself as Renata Sabelli, but I just wasn't used to having anyone in my life. Adjustments are hard for me." He paused to regroup, looking nauseated as he listened to himself. "You're quite the ravishing seasoned beauty and your inner spirit has touched mine in ways I can't bring myself to describe."

Nancy swayed her body as if to show it off. "You likey?"

"As lithe as a Celtic fairy."

"I don't know how he doesn't choke on those words," Dylan whispered to his brother. "Look, he's gonna say more."

"You see, I just didn't feel my chakras were balanced enough to deserve you and that I needed time to meditate on the love I felt, so deeply and intensely, that would enable me to guide you into my life the proper way. You know, to ensure us both everlasting happiness."

"What a fucking crock if I ever heard one," Richard said. "You should have set that bullshit to music." He burst out laughing. "I'm sure it would have had enduring appeal—unlike you."

"Yeah, he wishes Dad didn't have enduring appeal," Dylan whispered to Jake.

Phoebe, opening her mouth to speak, was immediately dissuaded as Richard's penetrating eyes warned her to stay quiet.

"Ooooh," Nancy cooed as she continued to ogle John. "Me likey likey."

Across the room, only one step down from the twins, who stood on the top step, Tyler and Rolo exchanged looks of agreement that John was handling things well, as the twins appeared to be planning a synchronized vomiting display.

Richard snarled at Nancy. "This bullshit is a stalling technique. I thought you were smarter than to fall for this loser's garbage. Do what you're supposed to do! Now!"

Nancy turned to Sunny. "Get on the red chair!"

As Sunny began to hyperventilate, sitting down as ordered, Miggy came around from the back, wanting to jump on her lap.

Seeing an opening, Tyler stepped forward. "You need to let me take that dog away. She's a wild card."

"I don't know about that, big fella."

"The dog could really take a bite out of your plans." Tyler wiped the sweat from his brow. "You should have seen—"

"Okay! Take the four-legged bitch then. Only brought her here to lure the two-legged one anyway." She shot Sunny a menacing look. "And *she* stays."

Sunny, relieved to have Miggy safe, looked at Tyler with gratitude as her breathing slowed.

"Here, girl. Come to Uncle Ty." Miggy glanced up at Sunny, then reluctantly ran to Tyler. Rolo grabbed the dog and quickly took her outside to see if Clarissa had arrived yet with the rescue vehicle.

Richard watched with rage, angry that Miggy was gone, but let the battle go as he focused on his war.

"Hey!" Nancy said loudly, staring at Sunny, still holding her at gunpoint. "If I shoot your hair, do you think it'll come out in bangs? Ha ha! Always did love that joke." Her visage grew deadly serious. "Don't think I've lost my concentration, bitch." She looked across the room at Tyler. "Hey, dumbass. You think you did her a favor by taking the dog, but all you did was make it easier for me to focus on my target. I never did thank you for going out of town all of those years ago. I stalked the place forever. wearing my clever disguises, and waiting for a good opportunity. Even dressed like a guy a couple of times. Ha ha. I was in your restaurant when I overheard you talking about plans to go away.

"That's when I moved in for the kill and came for this bitch and her husband as soon as you left town. I only pretended to be startled when some idiot walked in, saw my gun, and screamed. Dimwit Grey Harrison thought he was convincing me to put the gun away. Nah. I just took advantage of a golden opportunity. When I got to court, my lawyer played the she-got-scared-and-the-gun-went-off card. Killed the bastard and got a reduced sentence. I love people who inadvertently make things easier for me. Like you're doing now."

A wicked smile crossed Richard's lips.

"Oh, my God!" Sunny cried softly. Horrified, her heart

breaking all over again, she clutched her chest. Tyler, beside himself with rage, appeared to be ready to tackle Nancy, gun or no gun.

But Sunny, despite being retraumatized, knew Nancy had found Tyler's Achilles' heel and was an expert at torture. She begged him with her eyes to stay calm.

He fumed, his body tightening, but relaxed a bit when Rolo came back to whisper that Miggy was now safe with Clarissa and Kono, giving Sunny a thumbs-up so she would know too.

As all parties were assessing the situation and frantically trying to formulate their respective plans, a voice nobody expected was heard at the bottom of the stairs.

"Where is he? Where's John? I've waited thirty-five years!"

John, confused, yet looking as if there was something oddly familiar about the voice, froze.

Running up the stairs, with Harper behind her, the woman in her early fifties, her auburn hair piled on her head revealing the gray underneath, and wearing a loose-fitting rose-colored pantsuit, rushed into the room. Approaching John, looking eager, if not desperate, to hug him, she held back as it was clear he had no desire to embrace her. "Oh, John, my love. I didn't know if I'd ever see you again. You look even more handsome now than that night I had to send you away."

"What the hell is my pathetic ex-wife doing here?" Richard screamed. "And the throw-away daughter I put down the trash chute years ago."

"I hate you!" Harper screamed at Richard. "More than I've ever hated anyone. And believe me, I never wanted to see you again! Ever!"

"It was mutual, sweetie. I see you're just a super-sized version of the same loud-mouthed brat you were all those years ago."

Harper bit her lip, clearly restraining the urge to scream at him.

Startled by the unexpected visitors, Nancy moved to her left again, now fully obscuring herself behind the faux plant, lowering the weapon, but still keeping it trained on Sunny through the green leaves.

"John could only look at Richard with bitterness, then turned back to the woman. "Juliana … I …."

"I know it's a shock, love of my life. But I lied to you that night because I loved you so much. You weren't wrong. My feelings were forever ones."

Richard bristled as Juliana spoke, checking Nancy to make sure the gun was still pointed at Sunny. Phoebe, standing next to him, suppressed a smile. His plans were derailing and he was imploding with Juliana's every word.

"Did you get the message I put in the left coat pocket? I tried to tell you over and over again that the world would make sense when you put your hands in the pockets … as it did for my grandfather. Only I made that last part up. But the coat really was his, and he did wear it to walk the beach at Cape Cod. Oh, John. Please tell me you got my note."

Speaking with every ounce of calm he could muster, he stood before her. "Juliana. It's wonderful to see you again. And no doubt, we have much to talk about. But you and Harper need to leave *immediately.* I can't say it more strongly: this is the worst possible timing. Do you hear me?"

"But I've waited thirty-five years. I don't want to go anywhere that you're not!"

"You need to go!" He appealed to Harper. "This isn't a safe environment. Please, take your mother out of here now."

Unlike Juliana, Harper saw the fear in John's eyes and understood that something was very wrong. "Come on, Mom. We're leaving."

"But I don't want …"

Harper tensed. "Can't you just, *for once*, pay attention to something besides your own selfish needs?" She grabbed her mother's arm as she scanned the room. A shiver cascaded down her back. "John said he'll talk to you later. He didn't say no. He just said 'not now.' We're leaving. It's not safe here. I can feel it."

"Oh, come on? Don't be silly. It's not like someone is going to shoot us! This isn't fair …." Juliana cried as Harper led her downstairs and out the front door.

"I would've enjoyed shooting both of those bitches," Nancy mumbled, making herself partially visible again.

Before anyone could say a word, the redhead who'd been at the hotel, who had been waiting for her moment in the spotlight, boldly stepped into the room. She looked at Sunny. "You can all do what you want with him, but before anyone makes any long-range plans, he owes me a good …." She drove her fist into the palm of her other hand and twisted it. "You know, dudes and dudesses!"

John, once again twisting his face as if something familiar was tweaking him, turned to her. "Who the hell are you?"

Reaching on top of her head, she yanked her red wig off, exposing her dyed black spiky hair. Throwing the wig on the ground, she ripped open her blouse, exposing her oversized bra-less breasts. "Remember me now, John?"

"Oh, for fuck's sake ...."

As every eye in the room widened to take in the sight, Tyler was not having any of it. "Oh, hell no. I don't know who you are, nasty lady. But I'm escorting you from the premises." As she turned to give him a full view, he cringed. "Cover your damn bosoms up. If I wanted to set fire to my eyes, I'd pour kerosene on them and light a match. Button your blouse already!" He shrugged. "Nasty!"

"You don't tell me what to do, whoever you are. And don't pretend you're not enjoying it."

"Like a damn root canal or prostate exam, I am. Out!" Tyler said. "Smarmy exhibitionist."

"Ditto, brother man," Rolo said, making a face. "Sheesh!"

Shelley turned to give John one last glance as she jiggled her breasts. "You could have had all of this, but you walked away. Your loss, another man's gain." She turned to Rolo. "I dig those braids, cutie. Who might you be?"

"You sure can make a man's stomach rise," Rolo told her. "Like my brother said—out!"

As the Gardet brothers escorted her downstairs, Richard burst out laughing. "This is your life, John Hennessey Coates. You're one hell of a hag magnet. She's exactly what you deserve, Johnny boy. But I can't claim any credit for her impromptu appearance. And I certainly didn't bring my mentally unstable ex and her throwaway daughter here either. Like flies to shit these women are to you." He fastened his stare on John, then on Sunny. Looking panicked, as time was of the essence, he screamed at Nancy. "Intermission is over. Now! Do it now!"

"And I'll get my reward?"

"I've told you ten times already!" His face burned with anger.

"Okay then. Showtime!" Nancy turned to Sunny. "Get off the chair and go stand out on the balcony. Take a nice look at the pretty view of the ocean."

Taking a deep breath, Sunny tried to downplay her panic, hoping it would somehow deter Nancy from pursuing her reign of terror. "I-I …"

"Move your ass, bitch! If anyone knows I can shoot a gun, it's you." She burst out laughing as she watched Sunny quake with fear as she stood. "Oh, sorry, methinks you might have a little PTSD happening. Well, I can end that for you forever if you want. Right this minute in fact. I'll pull this trigger right now if you don't get your bitch ass on the balcony."

Sunny looked despairing at John, Tyler, Rolo, Dylan, and Jake as she turned to walk onto the balcony. Standing in the middle of it, tears rolled down her face.

Terrified, but laser focused, John watched as Sunny prayed he would find a way to save her.

Following Sunny with the gun, Nancy screamed, "Go right up to the railing, bitch!"

"NO! Don't do it!" Phoebe screamed. "Richard's had the whole thing booby trapped. I found sawdust at the far end of the deck. If you stand next to the railing and even touch it, you'll fall onto the rocks!" She turned to Nancy. "He lied to you! He's not giving you a red cent, and you're not getting John. He wants you to commit *his* crime while he walks away scot-free, and you go back to prison forever! Did you really believe that one-hand-washes-the-other bullshit he fed you? He was investigating people in Mrs. Harrison's past because that man,

John, who he wants to kill, cares about her. So he wanted to find someone who could hurt her and watch him suffer before he killed him too. He's that big of a vindictive prick. Hit the jackpot with you. Struck shinier gold than he ever expected to find. However you want to say it. But hear me out. When he heard you're an ex-con with a serious criminal record, one who was already harassing Mrs. Harrison with phone calls and fake flowers, he had his personal tough guy bring you here. He thinks it's a cinch that you'll pay for his crimes—already having so many of your own."

Richard snarled at her. "Shut-up, Phoebe! I'm warning you." His eyes narrowed with rage. "Should have gotten rid of you a long time ago." He mumbled to himself. "So much good pussy out there. Just waiting for a prize specimen like me. And I've given you all of my treasures, you undeserving slut!"

Refusing to make eye contact or say anything in response, Phoebe winced as she continued to address Nancy. "Believe me, you fit more perfectly into his plans than he ever imagined. Think about it." She gestured in John's direction. "Everything you were already doing made his deadly plan way more believable."

For the first time, Nancy looked unsure of herself. "I don't know. I—"

"Please listen to me!"

"No! *Don't* listen to her," Richard barked. "She and her hick sister made up this entire story."

Phoebe turned sharply to face him. "I'm not making anything up."

Richard looked as if he might explode with rage but said nothing.

Phoebe glared at Nancy. "Are you getting any of this?"

Nancy could only stand there, her mouth gaping wide open.

"Ugh!" Phoebe said despairingly. "How many times do I have to tell you! Wake up already! This man is a sociopath, and he's using you. This whole thing was carefully planned out. You're his fall woman. Got that? There's nobody in the world he won't manipulate. Believe me; I should know!"

"Enough with these fucking lies!" Livid, seething with rage, Richard turned around and grabbed Phoebe with both hands, shaking her hard. "SHUT-UP! You stupid little twat. You're just like my ungrateful sons. I've given you the world on a silver platter, and you have the gall to betray me like this! You've been listening to my phone calls, haven't you? Don't even try to lie. I know you've been skulking around the corner with those elastic ears of yours, pretending you'd been talking to your country-bumpkin sister when I questioned you. You'll pay for this, you backstabbing piece of ass! Do you hear me?"

"Please," Phoebe screamed to Nancy, undeterred as Richard shook her, "Don't harm that lovely woman! You'll pay for it; he won't." She stared into his eyes. "You can't even keep your story straight! I'm lying, but then, oh no, I got all of this from eavesdropping. You're pathetic."

"You filthy untalented whore-for-hire," Richard screamed at her. "No good man will ever want you! I can't believe I let you use me the way you have!" He slapped her face as hard as he could, and then, exploding with rage, shoved her against the wall.

As the expression on Nancy's face turned to wide-eyed anger, it was apparent that the depth of Richard's deception had finally registered with her. Without missing a beat, she moved toward him, taking her aim off Sunny and moving to within inches of the back Richard's head.

In the split-second Richard's attention was diverted and Nancy had the gun directed elsewhere, John rushed past them both, onto the balcony. Shielding Sunny with his body, just in case a shot was fired, he pulled her back into the living room and headed toward the stairs.

Tyler and Rolo quickly got in front of them. Looking into Sunny's eyes, John whispered in her ear, then put his arm around her, holding her tight as she let the tears fall freely.

Nancy now held the gun on Richard, who, having turned around, was now fully aware of the threat. "Nobody tells whoppers to Nancy Nestor and gets away with it. I'm sick of people betraying me and not giving me what I deserve. First Renata Sabelli, then Grey Harrison, a gazillion other fuckers, and now *you*, who thinks his dick is too precious for me to suck. You go stand against the railing. If your little blow-up doll girlfriend is lying about everything being booby-trapped, then prove it."

"I don't prove anything to anyone, never have. Not my ball of wax, my cup of tea—however you want to phrase it. People prove themselves to *me*. Never the other way around." He stood firm, staring her down. "You do anything to me, I can guarantee you a grand return to the old iron homestead for life. Maximum security. Or maybe even Death Row. No way to see your enemies suffer if that happens." Glancing in Sunny and John's direction, only to find them barely visible behind the Gardets, he fumed to see them safe. "Those two hiding behind their henchmen will be happier than pigs in shit to see your criminal ass locked up. Is that what you want? For that failed musician and his blonde bimbo to have the wonderful life together that's eluded you, that should have been *yours*—while they have the world's biggest laugh at your expense?" His merciless eyes attempted to browbeat her in concert with his words. "I am Richard Xavier Strausser, and I've got more money than you can imagine. My lawyers can easily buy your way out of this, and I'll give you a beautiful new life anywhere in the world you choose. But you pull that trigger on me, sweetums, and your life will be over too. It's pretty simple."

"Stop trying to confuse me! I have to think."

Richard, certain his tactics were working, pressed on. "Do you really like the idea of those two having wild sex in his fancy beach cottage while you wither and rot behind bars, having it on with Big Mama?"

"If you were locked up as many years as me, you'd do 'Big Mama' too! Don't you dare judge me for finding pleasure where I can, you loser."

He laughed. "Ah! I've hit the bullseye, have I? So how was she? Good enough to give up your freedom for, or was she *so* good you'd give it up to have her on a daily basis?"

He had her now. As Nancy pondered his words, Richard took advantage of what he perceived as a diminishment of her concentration by making a grab for the gun with both hands. But Nancy's quick reflexes unpleasantly surprised him.

"Oh no you don't, Richard Xavier whatever. You're not wrangling this gun from my very pissed off and capable hands." She snorted. "There aren't any other guns trained on me, liar. You wouldn't be spewing so much crap trying to make me put this one down if there were. Just how stupid do you think I am?"

Playfully, Nancy waved the gun above her head. "Want the piece, big boy? Let's go out there and have some fun." Stepping backward, now on the balcony, she giggled with childlike glee. You let me have some fun with dick on the deck, Dick, and maybe I won't kill you. Hey, that's a real tongue-twister." She giggled. "Ah, but do I want to give up killing you for a bit of oral pleasure? Nope. Don't think so. See, I can tell by looking at your hands. Nothing too much behind the zipper. Pity, pity!" She roared with laughter. "Anybody have a microscope so I can magnify little willy in there?" Pleased with herself, she guffawed. "Such a shame you're so tiny. You must shrivel up to nothing in the cold weather, huh? Come to Nancy, itty bitty boy!"

"You don't know what the hell you're blathering about, you reptilian old bat!" Furious and desperate to prove her wrong, Richard unzipped his fly and let his erect manhood answer for him. "There! You can cancel the microscope!"

Phoebe dropped her jaw, mesmerized by Richard's capitulation to psychological warfare, succumbing easily to the tricks he played on others. She watched as he slowly moved toward Nancy, smug and confident that his lower half would be received like red meat to a hungry tiger, and he would be able to get the gun. "You wanted this bad boy. Well, I'm giving him to you. Go on, put me in your mouth and show me what you can do. He snorted. "If you can shove it all in."

Nancy, miles ahead of him, smiled, moistening her lips to indicate her readiness. "Oh, I likey! Not so tiny after all." Pretending to be distracted and all in, she moved a half step toward him.

Thinking he had her exactly where he wanted her, Richard lurched for the gun, but she was too quick. Hitting him over the head with it as best as she could, even though slightly off-target, she smiled victoriously.

The left side of his forehead now bleeding, he staggered, determined not to fall. "Give me the gun, you miserable ex-con!"

"Nobody treats Nancy Nestor like a fool and lives to tell about it!"

Standing, but unsteady, he swayed back and forth as he fought to keep his balance as Nancy stepped backward, closer to the railing, her right hand still firmly in possession of the gun.

Determined to show no fear, he walked up to her. A Cheshire cat smile on her face, she knelt down on the balcony in front of him, opened her mouth, shoved him inside, stroking him vigorously with her left hand as she did.

"Fuck no!" he screamed, wanting to pull away, but as she tightened her grip by lightly bearing down with her teeth, he hesitated.

"He's freaking that she's gonna bite his dick off," Jake whispered to Dylan. "Scared stiff."

"Totally. Oh, and great choice of words, bro."

Jake gave a quick lopsided smile. "Oh, yeah. Didn't mean it that way but whatever."

Perspiration dripping from Richard's face broadcast to everyone that his plans to take the gun from Nancy, while she still consumed him, was trickier than he imagined, especially after a blow to the side of his head.

"Man," Dylan said. "Check out his sweaty face and bloated eyeballs. There's that sinister nostril flair. Man, haven't seen that for a while. Look at how twisted up he is. Pissed doesn't begin to describe him. He looks like a boxer dancing in the ring trying to figure out how to permanently punch his opponent's lights out. He thinks he's gonna get the gun, not to mention his dick back in one piece. His timing had better be perfect."

Jake nodded. "No way it can be that easy. Dude is outta control. He just doesn't know it."

Outside, two policemen hurried out of their cars and up the stairs, pushing aside the six humans, not even noticing Phoebe who now stood to the far left of the room. "Police! Drop your weapons!"

In one quick movement, Richard made a successful grab for the gun, appearing overjoyed that his precious hostage was released unscathed. Nancy, still on her knees, but now the one in jeopardy, grabbed a balustrade to right herself, punching his genitalia with her free hand as she did so. In that moment, the look of horror on her face revealed that the balustrade and the ones to either side of it were breaking. Accepting that she was going to fall to her death, seeing Richard doubled over and moaning in pain, she clutched a fistful of his monogrammed Oxford shirt and pulled him to her with all of the strength she had left. As he toppled onto her, both of them caterwauling and shrieking in abject fear, the booby-trapped balustrades fell away, clearing the way for Richard, Nancy, and the gun to make a rapid descent to the boulders below. Within seconds, Richard, near death as he lay on top of a lifeless Nancy, begged for help, cursing everyone for his undeserved fate.

The two policeman ran to the balcony, quickly halting their chase as they saw the missing pieces of the railing and surmised the fate of their quarry. Keeping a safe distance from the edge as they peered below, they could hear Richard's faint cries for help. Just as they were assessing the situation, a huge wave crashed against the rocks, sweeping two take-away shark dinners out to sea as it receded.

"Man, Mike," the younger officer mumbled to the other. "Wonder what went down here. Looks like some headline-grabbing fuckery for sure. Can't wait to take the statements. I'm gonna be in serious need of a triple shot of Scotch after this shit."

"Me too." Mike said, revealing an ever-so-slight smile. "Right with you, Leo." He nodded toward the sea. "Only I'll have mine on the rocks."

CHAPTER TWENTY-FIVE

Sunny stood under the porch light and knocked gently on Tyler's door.

Opening it, he smiled through his sadness and let her in. "I know I look terrible, Sunny. What an ordeal today was." He tried to lighten the mood. "But at least I'm not having a bad hair day, right?" He gestured to the couch. "Please, have a seat. What can I get you?"

"Thank you." She spoke softly and sat. "I want nothing but a few minutes of your time, my dear friend and family member." She glanced around at the photos of the Gardet family, including several of his beloved mother, Mary. Aside from his immediate family, there were many of her own family, and a few of friends in Louisiana she didn't know. Each photo sat in a unique wooden frame that Tyler had handcrafted. "There's so much love in this room. Even if I didn't know you, just seeing all of these photos would tell me that you're a man who feels deeply."

"That I do. Too much at times, you all tell me. Did Ro and Ris send you?" Weary, he fell into a nearby armchair.

"Absolutely not. You know I can worry about you fine all by my lonesome."

"You went through a far greater hell than I did. So why are you here checking on me, lovely lady?"

"I'm quite sure you know the answer, Tyler Gardet. Because I don't want you owning anything that isn't yours to own. You know exactly what I mean."

Stressed, his breathing was slightly erratic. "I'm truly trying not to go there. Tough not to." He wound the clock back several hours. "I knew something was off. The gut didn't fail me."

"No, it didn't."

"It took the police two and a half hours to take all of our statements. And if more hadn't shown up, we'd still be there. It was exhausting. Imagine when you've actually done something." He turned his head in a failed attempt to mask his pain. "You should be with John and the boys. Forget about me. Today had to be the second worse day of your life."

"Yes, except it had a way better outcome than the worst day of my life." She took a moment to regroup. "I'm in tremendous pain, Ty. But I'll deal with it. First, I need to talk to you. No excuses."

"I've let you down."

"Oh, anything but, my dear man." She gave him a hard look. "Do you trust me, Ty?"

"Of course. Do you even have to—"

"Then listen to me. When that monster laughed about the day she killed Grey, and her stalking that preceded it, I could feel her talons clawing at my heart. All of the pain I'd worked so hard to tame was an open wound again, becoming more infected by the second. But when I saw the look on your face, that's what broke me because I know the same was happening to you."

"Oh, Sunny. You shouldn't worry about me."

"Try to stop me." She gave him a hard, but loving look. "We all love you so much, and for years, we've tried to drum it into your head that nothing was your fault. Nothing. And today, as that psychopath babbled so maliciously, and I saw all of that guilt returning to us both, I panicked. I know how to recover, but there's no way I'll stand by and let you go back to that cage of hell you put yourself in. Those two horrible people are dead, and while I'm not someone to celebrate anyone's death, I have no sorrow or mercy for their souls.

"You have a new son on the way and a woman who's beautiful on the inside and out. Someone who loves you with all of her heart and who you love with all of yours. You've almost lost her a couple of times because you let guilt shut you down and steal the time you should have been with her. That can't ever happen again."

"I just wish I had—"

"Stop, Ty. Unless you're going to confess that you're not a mortal man and that you have powers I don't know about, nothing was your fault. In fact, today you saved my Miggy, and despite what that creature said to make you doubt yourself, you have no idea how much better your actions made me feel while that gun was still pointed at me. You're my hero, Tyler Gardet."

"I don't feel—"

"What? You don't feel like one or you're undeserving of my words? Tell me what you've got in here that I can bonk you over the head with. Something hard enough to knock sense into your head."

Tyler smiled.

"You know me, and you know I am passionate about the people I love. You also knew Grey Harrison, and that means you know exactly what he would say to you now if he could."

"Pretty much the same thing as you, only with some colorful language you rarely, if ever, use."

"Exactly. So, if you want to help me move on, realize that I can't do that if you're not there with me. You need to focus on Imari and little Grey—even before he's born. Guilt, Ty, especially undeserved guilt, makes nothing better. *Ever.* Can you imagine how happy that horrid woman would be to know that her cruelty lives on?" Sunny looked to her right and smiled as Imari came out of the bedroom. "Oh, sweetheart, I had no idea you were here with Ty."

"I was going to come out, but I knew you were going to say everything to him that he needed to hear, so I didn't want to interrupt." Imari smiled as she hurried over to hug Sunny, who stood and put her arms around her. "And thanks for the sweet things you said about me."

When the women finished embracing, they sat next to one another on the couch, Sunny squeezing Imari's hand.

"So what do you have to say, big guy?" Imari smiled at Tyler.

"Just that you two ladies make a fine tag team, even unintentionally. And the fact that two evil people destroyed themselves makes a statement to me that sometimes things work out as they need to." He grinned. "But learning I'm only a mortal man, well, that's gonna take some getting used to."

Imari laughed. "You don't always have to act like one. I don't mind having fun with Superman." She touched her belly. "How do you think this happened?"

"You're the best, baby. What Sunny said just now and what you said earlier makes a whole lot of sense. It's true, even thinking about being a dad changes my perspective. There's no way I'd encourage my son to carry around guilt, especially for someone else's crimes. Absolutely not." He shook his head. "Man, little Grey's not even born yet and he's already teaching his old man a lesson or two." He winked at the two women. "Maybe with a little help from his aunt and mama."

Sunny stood and walked over to hug him. "That's what I wanted to hear. And listen, I can tell you honestly, I'm not going to recover from the horror of today overnight. We may need to have a good cry together sometimes. Dealing with trauma is one thing; blaming yourself for it is another thing entirely. One that has no place in your life." She offered a gentle smile. "Everything is going to be okay; it has to be. We're both surrounded by so much love."

"You're going to be the best aunt to our boy," Tyler said as he turned to Imari. "Isn't she, baby?"

"You know it. She already is. And don't let me get all sloppy and sentimental now. I cried enough today just praying that everyone would come home safe."

"Thank you again, Ty, for saving my Miggy girl." She hugged Imari who was standing by her side. "I love you both so much, and I'm thrilled you're going to make your home here. I'd better get going."

"Hope John and his sons are okay," Tyler said. "This can't be easy for any of them."

As Dylan sat on John's sectional couch and looked out at the ocean, Jake, sullen and depressed, sat next to John. Kono and Miggy, nearly as emotionally worn out as the humans, lay sleeping on their beds.

"Where's Sunny," Jake asked.

"She just needed to see Ty; then I think she's going to stop by the restaurant and check on everyone there. Or maybe she did that first." He paused to take a good look at them. "How are you both doing?"

Dylan shrugged. "About as good as I look. Or worse."

"The same," Jake said.

"You know, guys, emotions are tricky things. It's not unusual to have conflicting sentiments at odds with each other. It's only been a few hours, so I don't know how either of you are processing Richard's death, not to mention his actions, but if you mourn him, it's okay. Don't feel you need to hide your grief."

"Fuck no!" Jake said. "No grief here. Yeah, I'm not feeling so great at the moment, but that bastard wanted to kill you and Sunny, and he would have if it worked out for him. I hate that he's our biological father and not you. And man, the way he treated Phoebe like a sex slave and the sick shit he did to get off. You know, what he wanted her to do before we all got there, then later finally getting to take his dick out for everyone. Did he think he was the only dude who's got one? Ugh. Just everything about that SOB is worse than I thought it was. I knew he was a sexual pervert, but damn. It was so embarrassing telling all this to the cops. I felt they were thinking we had to be the same way. Only we're not. How do people even get to be like he was?"

John cast his eyes down. "I don't know."

"I don't wanna state the obvious, but there's mega poetic justice in the way he died. You know, hanging out of his pants like that," Dylan added. "And no way I'm mourning that scum. I wonder how many pieces he's in now. And that murderer Nancy who he died with."

"How is Phoebe, anyway?" Jake asked. "I feel really bad for her."

"Sunny's given her a suite in the hotel for as long as she wants it. Beyond that, I don't know *how* she is, only *where* she is."

"I feel like I want to talk to her," Jake said. "Try to help her. But me being that bastard's son might just make it worse for her, you know? But I just really want her to know it's not her fault."

John gently touched his hand. "That's kind of you. I think after she gets a good night's sleep, maybe you'll be able to gauge. I'd just play it by ear. I'm sure she's very confused. It's quite likely she has no idea what she wants."

"Yeah. I guess. Has anyone spoken to that woman who gave birth to us?"

"*I'm* not calling her." Dylan made a face and shifted to sit cross-legged facing John and Jake. "I don't ever want to speak to her again."

John locked his fingers and stretched his arms out. "I'm not advocating for either of you to call or not call. Your decisions have to be your own."

"She's worse than you know," Jake told him. "You don't even want to know the stuff she did *after* we went to live with her."

Shivering, as if he could imagine, he turned to the boys. "No matter what she put you through, I'm always here for you both. Don't ever hold back anything you need to discuss, about either of them, to protect me. Ever. And conversely, don't ever feel pressured to share what you don't want to talk about."

Dylan looked at Jake. "I think maybe we should tell him the one thing now. You know, about when they took us away."

"Yeah, I was thinking the same thing."

As the twins' faces paled in unison, John's stomach flipped. "What is it, boys?"

Jake cracked his knuckles. "Yeah, I still do this when I'm nervous. Um, he did a lot of nasty stuff, but he kind of told us that you might die if we didn't come live with them."

"What Jake said," Dylan said more forcefully. "He threatened to kill you and made up so many lies about you. One on top of the other. Evelyn too. They really did our heads in. But Richard saying you might not live if we didn't cooperate, that's the main reason we weren't so nice to you and why we said we wanted to go with them. We were afraid he might be for real. When we got older, we thought it was a bullshit scare tactic."

"*You* did," Jake said. "I blocked it out like some wuss."

"Don't beat yourself up for that." He sighed. "Today, well, I guess we learned it wasn't." Dylan's face reddened as he remembered. "And Evelyn was good with all of it. And you know what? She was a worse mother seven days a week than when she came by two days a month. So, no, we don't need to call her."

"Do you want me to? I'd do anything for you both. I can handle it."

"Thanks, Dad, but no way," Dylan said. "Besides, since she's his legal wife, someone's already called her. Maybe the police. Or she heard it on the news. She's probably partying it up, counting his money."

"Except," Jake said, "he told me last year she was getting the Park Avenue apartment along with three million bucks, and that everything else was going to us. By this point, that'll be chump change to her and she'll cry poor. Who cares? And I'm sure he never got to write us out like he was planning. For someone that rich, that's not something you do quickly. We probably own the record company. We're probably billionaires. Man, that sounds surreal even saying it."

Nervous, John stayed quiet. He watched Jake and Dylan—waiting for them to speak.

"I don't want the record company and I don't want his billions." Dylan turned to his brother. "Maybe you want to go back to A & R, now that he's dead and maybe you want his money too. Go for it if you want, but leave me out."

"No way," Jake said. "I don't want that. Besides, I'll always be labeled as his son. You too. And everything would remind me of him. Especially living off billions that I didn't earn. Not that he did either. I don't want the record company. If it *is* ours, I want to sell it and help make the world a better place with the money from a bastard who hurt so many people."

John attempted to smile. "This has been one hell of a day. This isn't something you even need to deal with now. I'll just tell you something I've never shared with anyone."

"Nobody?" Jake asked.

"Not a soul. As you both know, my father was no prize. He emotionally abandoned me and my mother, which tragically prompted her to take her own life, but he was nothing like Richard. When he died, he left a massive part of his estate to me. Money was his way of apologizing. But I never wanted it. I kept a small amount to survive and started a private foundation with the rest, *not* in my name."

"Wow," Dylan said. "That's so you."

"Yes. It's me. But it doesn't have to be you. You're both going to have a lot of decisions to make. Today isn't the day, and tomorrow isn't either. I'm far more worried about your emotions than your money."

"Do you want that album taken off the market?" Jake asked.

"I would. Yes. Thank you. And I'd like the third one to never see the light of day. But I'd like Sunny to have a copy."

"Man, you put everything you are into that music."

"No, Jake. I put everything I *was* into that music."

"Oh, yeah." Jake slumped. "I didn't think of it that way."

John reached over to the coffee table and picked up his phone. "It's Sunny."

Hearing her name, the boys got up and hurried out onto the deck to give John privacy.

"Hi, there. You doing okay?"

"I feel like I could sleep for days, John. How's my girl?"

"Asleep. Did you talk to the Gardets?"

"Every one of them. I'm home at the moment. I stopped back to the hotel to talk to Larae, and Juliana was waiting in the lobby, demanding to see you."

"Oh, no."

"Unfortunately, oh yes. I told her it was late and I didn't think you'd have the energy to talk to her tonight." Sunny paused. "Of course, she has no idea that we were almost murdered today, but somehow, John, I get the impression she might not care. She just kept saying you'd promised to talk to her and thirty-five years was long enough to wait. Meanwhile, Harper kept telling her that you didn't mean 'later tonight.' Juliana is one stubborn woman. I can see on my monitor she's still in the lobby arguing with her daughter."

"I'm so sorry. If you're up to it, tell her I'll meet her at noon tomorrow in the lobby. There's no way in hell I'm getting into this after what we've all been through. I couldn't if I wanted to." He paused. "Are you coming to get Miggy? If you are, I'll send the boys up to walk you down here."

"Those poor young men. They must be in terrible shape after all that happened."

"They've got a lot to work out. It'll take time. I don't think they've quite grasped just how much, nor do I think they're prepared for the enormity of what may be an emotional tsunami. But I'll be here for them."

"You're such a good man. And yes, I'm coming to get my girl. Unless she wants to stay close to Kono tonight. I couldn't blame her."

Standing in the doorway of John's cottage, Sunny hugged Dylan, then Jake. "Thank you for walking me here. Hope you both get a good night's sleep."

"We've got our own cabins," Dylan said with a crooked smile. "That increases the chances that we will."

"Believe him, Sunny. These boys could babble on through the night. I had to get a place with a third bedroom so I could get them to school on time."

"He's totally exaggerating," Jake said. "He just put my bed in the walk-in closet."

John's eyes widened in shock.

"Ha ha. Just kidding." Jake laughed.

"Yeah, but he did call our room 'Babylon,'" Dylan added.

"Man, I forgot that."

"Me too," John said, smiling. "It was appropriate, yes?"

"It was." Dylan offered a brief smile, then frowned. "We were too sad to talk a lot when they took us away. And we would cry but try to hide it from each other."

"But we both knew," Jake said. "There was nothing to be happy about and a whole lot of reasons to be miserable."

Sunny put her hand to her heart, not wanting to say anything, but unable not to react to what she'd heard, as Miggy stood by her side, craving attention.

John hugged them, one at a time, as hard as he could. "I love you both. Words are inadequate to express how blessed I feel having you back in my life."

Blushing, both boys offered similar sentiments and left.

The moment John closed the door, he and Sunny embraced, holding each other as tight as they could until the dogs nosed their way in between them.

"Hi, Kono. Hey, Miggy girl." Sunny hurried to the couch where she could properly reunite with Miggy. As she sat, the dog enthusiastically pushed her back, jumping onto her lap and kissing her as if she hadn't seen her in years. "Oh, girl, you already gave me this wonderful greeting before, and now I'm getting it all over again. Aren't I the lucky one?"

"You are loved," John said, cuddling with Kono. "Miggy can't use words to tell you what it was like to be kidnapped and watch her mom being terrorized, but she sure can show you how relieved she is that it's over."

"So true." Overcome with emotion, Sunny let the tears fall. "Okay, girl, you've made your mommy feel so good. Those bad people will never hurt any of us again. You go back to your bed, okay?"

Miggy, who pretended not to understand English, continued to shower her with affection, only stopping when Kono went back to his bed.

"I've got you all to myself now," John said, moving over on the couch and running his fingers through her hair. They kissed for several minutes, neither wanting to stop as they pulled away.

"I love you, Sunny. I never believed I would ever find someone like you, but the moment I met you, even though I fought it, I knew there was a greater reason I came to Teal Beach, one that had hidden itself from me until that moment."

"I love you, too, John. So very much. I wondered if I would ever feel your lips again or be able to tell you how I felt. When that horrid woman had the gun trained on me, I thought I might have to scream it at you before she pulled the trigger. But I didn't want those to be my very last words, and I believed they might hasten our death. Oh, what a horrible thought."

"I had the same thoughts—that Nancy and Richard would have taken those words as acquiescence to their wish that we die."

She gently touched his face. "We were thinking the same things—good and bad." She smiled. "Would it be twisted of me to segue to a slightly funny thought I had when I went back home?"

"Not at all."

"Well, when I sat on my couch, right after I'd left Miggy with you, I decided to check my email. I have no idea why. Probably because my brain was on overload, and I needed something else to focus on. Anyway, some of the charities I contribute to include one that helps to rescue dogs and cats and another that works to restore the ocean. Every time I purchase something from the animal-rescue site, it will say, 'This purchase feeds fifty-three dogs,' or something like that. And the ocean donations tell me how many pounds of trash are removed. I couldn't help but think of Richard and Nancy now somewhere out to sea and a subsequent email reading, 'Thank you for your generous contribution. It will help feed seventy thousand fish.'"

John burst out laughing.

Relieved he found it amusing, Sunny did the same.

"Nothing like dark humor to help salvage a very dark day, beautiful woman. I think I love you even more for that."

"Oh, I almost forgot something. You'll probably think I'm superstitious, and silly too, but this morning, before the hell that ensnared us, I was walking along the beach when Miggy became extra playful and wanted me to chase her. I was running after her like a crazy woman and felt something under my feet." She reached in her pocket and pulled out a silver dollar. "It's from 1973 ... and there's President Eisenhower."

John stared in disbelief.

"I've found some different things on the beach over the years, but this was special. I decided it was my new good luck charm, and I just put it in my pocket." She smoothed two fingers over it. "When that gun was trained on me, I told myself that maybe I'd found a magic coin that would protect me."

Still saying nothing, John just listened.

"And maybe it did. See, I told you, silly, huh?"

Cupping his hand over hers that held the coin, he smiled. "I found this coin when I was eleven. On my way home from school. I picked it up, and very much like you, believed that if I carried it with me, it would protect me. It was in my pants pocket for years. But after the boys were taken, I didn't feel so protected. Like maybe the coin had betrayed me. So I put it away."

"Oh, John."

"After the years went by, I had a good think and came up with the idea that maybe the coin had greater powers, and I should make up with it." He made a face. "Ever known a grown man to reconcile with a silver dollar? I took it out of the drawer I'd stashed it in and decided to carry it in my old coat."

Sunny's eyes sparkled as she waited to hear more.

"Well, a while back, walking the beach here one night, I reached into my pocket and realized I'd lost the coin. I was angry at myself for not getting the loose stitching fixed. I couldn't fully admit how devastated I was. And now, the coin having found its way to your pocket, I think it had all the powers that I attributed to it at age eleven. And then some."

"Which is exactly why you must take it back."

"Oh, no. Absolutely not. Finders keepers. It's yours now."

"Thank you. I'll cherish it as I do you. Such a magical story, John."

"It can't hurt to believe in a little magic, can it?"

As Sunny went to lay her head on his chest, she gasped in surprise. "Oh, my, will you look at that!"

Following her gaze, John saw Miggy curled up next to Kono

on his bed. Opening her eyes for just a moment, she shot Sunny a don't-even-think-about-taking-me-home-now look.

A loving smile on his face, John took Sunny's hands in his. "While we're both too tired for anything tonight, and while I think neither of us want to consummate our love on this ghastly day, even though in another way we do, I sure would hate to upset Miggy or Kono, wouldn't you? I think they've got the right idea. We've been running on pure adrenaline, and I think we're both far more tired than we know. How about if we go into the bedroom and fall asleep in each other's arms?"

"Nothing in the world would be better," Sunny said. They rose and left the dogs to enjoy a long night's snuggle. She turned to wink at Miggy. *Thanks, girl.*

CHAPTER TWENTY-SIX

As John, with Kono at his side, walked into the lobby at noon on the dot, Juliana, who could hardly contain herself, ran over to squeeze him as tight as she could.

Not wanting to hurt her feelings, he offered a quick and compulsory return embrace, then gently pushed her away. Her face fell, and she stared at him, disappointment heavy in her gaze.

Harper sat on the lobby couch looking utterly depleted. She could only roll her eyes as her mother began gabbing to John without even waiting for him to take a seat.

Before he could respond to anything, Miranda, who was working the front desk, called him over.

"I'll be right with you ladies," John said, hurrying over to Miranda with the dog. "Is everything okay with Sunny?"

"She's fine. And very happy you're going to leave Kono with her and Miggy. She's asked me to work the next several days for her. Larae and I are glad to help. I called you over here, not just to get Kono, but because Harper asked me to. She said it's urgent that she tell you some things privately after her mother gets done with you." She scrunched her face. "And I should probably tell you, she looked a bit squeamish when she said those words: 'gets done with you.'"

John sighed. "I'll bet she did. Is there more?"

"Oh, yes. She said that after she walks her mother back to her room, she'd be grateful if you would meet her at the bottom of the steps to the beach. She said there's a place down there that's out of view. She must mean that little cave where you can speak privately and where her mother can't see anything should she look out of her window … since she does have the end room with the view." She paused. "Oh, one more thing. From what conversation I could hear, I don't think the mother has any clue what happened at the cliff house last night. It's like she's in her own head all the time. The daughter knows, but I get the idea she's trying to shield her. At least until they're away from Teal Beach." She sighed in frustration. "If I've overstepped by telling you this, I apologize."

"Absolutely not, Miranda. Your instincts are on the money. That's very helpful to know, and I understand even more why Sunny appreciates you and Larae so much. Thanks for delivering both messages. And don't worry, I'll take these ladies for lunch. I won't subject you to any more histrionics in the lobby."

"That would be appreciated." She laughed uncomfortably. "It's been … well … challenging."

"A good word for it, I'm sure."

She laughed. "I try. I'm sure taking them to lunch will make Sunny happy too." Raising the counter panel, she called to Kono. "Come here, handsome fella. I hear your girlfriend is waiting for you. At least that's the word about town."

"Go on, boy," John nudged him. "I'll see you later. Miggy, boy, Miggy!"

He and Miranda laughed as Kono's ears perked up, and he hurried toward the door to Sunny's home.

Before John could reach the couch again, Juliana was already speaking. "Oh, John. We've lost so many years."

"Juliana," he said, holding up his palm. "First, while I'm happy to talk with you, I don't have the time I'm afraid you may be expecting me to spend with you. Please understand that. Second, this public lobby isn't the place for a private discussion. Why don't we go across the street for lunch? My friends have set aside a private booth, far from the other customers. Can we hold the conversation until we get there?"

"Oh, if we must," Juliana said as if the weight of the world had just been put on her shoulders.

Harper made a face. "Are you sure about Dodo Deen's? Ms. Gardet and I haven't exactly hit if off too well."

"All that's changed, Harper. And Clarissa's the one who suggested it."

As soon as a server seated them and put three menus on the table, Juliana released the first of her pent-up and well-rehearsed love sonnets. "Oh, John, my true love …."

He shuddered. "Juliana, let's make the best use out of the time we have together. Please. Can we do that?"

"Oh, darling, I have all the time in the world."

"You may. But I don't. I *really* don't."

She pouted like a child who believed a sad face and fluttering eyelids would ensure she got her way.

Already feeling the stress, John inhaled a calming breath. "Do you mind if I begin with a question?"

"Ask away. Anything."

"There was no time to ask you this last night." *Much less to listen to your answer.* "How in the world did you find me here?"

"Oh, that's an easy one. I was listening to this oldies station last year. And I heard this song, and I memorized it:

> We met at that party neither wanted to be,
> Til I looked at you, and you looked at me.
> Out on the porch, we talked for hours,
> Unfazed by Autumn's raging showers.
> After that, we were rarely apart,
> As if we were destined to love from the start.
> But then you said, but your eyes didn't agree,
> That you loved someone else who wasn't me.
> Your eyes don't lie, babe,
> They never did,
> Don't know where you went, where you done hid.
> No clue why you left me that night in December,
> Then burned our love, till there was nothing but embers.
>
> All I know's that our love was real,
> And I've spent too long wonderin' how you truly did feel.
> Yet I still gotta wonder, do you still think of me,
> Or has time erased what was destined to be.
> Your eyes don't lie, babe,
> They never did.
> Don't know where you went, where you done hid.'

"Oh." Distraught, John had no better words. "That horrible song."

"No! Don't say that. It's beautiful. It was our story, John. I knew it. I checked to see who wrote it, and it said 'J. Coat.'" I knew that 'Coat' was the last gift I gave you and also a shortened version of Coates."

John didn't try to hide his confusion. "I still don't understand how you found me through those terrible old lyrics that I wrote in the dinosaur age." He took a drink of his water. "I was commissioned to write a relatable pop song, *many* years ago, and given a few hours to so. So how did those words lead you here now?"

Juliana's eyes filled with love as she gazed longingly at him. "Well, my darling, recently, when I felt the urge to see you again and rekindle our love,"— she smiled as her eyes twinkled — "all I could find out was that you'd disappeared and wanted to hide your identity from the world. Then I remembered that Dante Massimo had produced that love song you wrote for me, that you two were good friends in high school, and that he was a musician who later became a producer. I figured you were probably still friends." She tapped her head as if to indicate her smarts. "So, I called his home, and his wife, Tamara, answered the phone. I was so relieved to hear her say she remembered me. When I explained why I was calling, she cried and said we just had to find our way back together."

John held up his finger to hold off a server who was on her way to their table. "Tamara never should have said …." he mumbled under his breath.

Ignoring his obvious distress, Juliana continued. "Also, she told me that your friend Ben Rockley was your manager and that he was the one who dealt directly with Dante. That's when Tamara told me she'd heard you were moving here to Teal Beach but wasn't sure if you were still living on Catalina Island. I would have come myself, but Harper insisted because I've been unwell. She even went to Catalina Island first."

John fiddled with the fork on the table, picked it up, then ground the prongs into a napkin, ripping it. Realizing what he was doing, he stopped and put the fork down. "Before we go any further with this conversation, Juliana, you do understand there is zero possibility of us reuniting, yes? We were children when were together. I was still a kid that night I was going to propose. I just didn't know it then."

"Not to me you weren't. Oh, John. We can get back there."

"No, we can *never* go back there. I have no desire to go back there. Ever."

"But didn't you get the note I left in the old coat pocket?"

John looked at Harper, who was visibly uncomfortable, then at Juliana. "Believe it or not, it was only a few nights ago that I found it."

She made an angry face. "For real?" Making a quick recovery, she flashed a bright smile. "Then you know Harper is your daughter!"

Harper ever-so-slightly shook her head to indicate otherwise. Noticing, John addressed Juliana again. "I'm confused. I heard you'd gotten married after you and Richard divorced … and that you had a child."

"I did, but Harper was eight when that happened. You see, my darling, I broke up with you that night because I was pregnant with your child and my father forced me to. He was a brute of a man; you know that. He told me that if I had your child and if I stayed with you, he'd make sure you never played a note of music again. 'He'll work under my strict tutelage and get a business degree,' he said. Ugh. I hated that horrible word: tutelage. That's when he told me that unless I wanted to destroy your dreams, I'd marry his colleague's son because, get this, he 'owed him a huge favor, and I'd be lucky to marry into that family.'" She tensed with rage. "So my arm was twisted to marry that horrible Richard, the son of another horrible man, Xavier R. Strausser. Can you believe it? Richard treated me like a cheap prostitute. It was no more than an arranged marriage negotiated by two unprincipled men. Richard didn't care about anything but his twisted and constant sexual gratification, not to mention having a pretty wife to show off—and his father's money."

"I believe you. And I'm so sorry your father colluded with Xavier Strausser. I know Richard was a very sick man; I didn't know much about his father."

"A devil who spawned another, he was. Xavier wanted his colleague's daughter as some kind of sick payment for facilitating a big financial deal. Probably shady, knowing my father and Xavier. Immoral, twisted monsters."

"That's awful. It must have been devastating for you."

"Oh, it was. I'm so thirsty!" Juliana waved down the server, then turned back to John. "You see, my love, that's why I forced my grandfather's old coat on you ... because I wanted you to find the note in the pocket and come claim me and your child. I kind of made up that thing about my grandfather putting his hands in the pockets so that the world would make sense. You know, to get you to think there was something spiritual about it and try it for yourself. I even loosened the stitching in the left pocket. I pinned it pretty far down, but I figured you'd have found it way before now."

Harper groaned, but Juliana was so animated, she didn't even notice.

"Go on, Juliana. Please."

She shot John a loving gaze. "Well, after my divorce, I married a wonderful man named Kyle Kinnison and he became Harper's dad, even legally adopting her. Kyle and I tried twice to have a child, but I miscarried both times." Her face looked as if tears were going to roll, but none appeared. "My husband was everything that barbarian Richard was not."

After the server came over and took drink orders, Juliana continued without missing a beat. "But Kyle died last year, and I've been grief-stricken ever since … as has been Harper. Truthfully, I've been wallowing in a deep depression, and yes, I've been suicidal at times and even gave it a go once. But my darling daughter intervened and saved me. Lately though, thinking about you brought me renewed hope. This is why Harper came to find you instead of me. Such a heart of gold. She's so upset seeing me languish in depression. We have a wonderful daughter, my love, and now we can be a family again. It was our destiny then, and it still is now."

John looked up and saw Clarissa across the room shoot him a sympathetic glance as Juliana's loud voice had carried farther than it needed to.

"Mom! We can *never* be a family. Did you hear what John is telling you? You were nineteen the last time you saw him. You're fifty-two now. John doesn't want you and he can't take away your grief from losing Dad. You're deluding yourself. Dad was the true love of your life, but you think your childhood sweetheart, who is a complete stranger to you now, can fix your broken heart. That would never work for either one of you. Don't see you how skewed your thinking is?"

"No, honey. I don't. I think it's providence."

Practically hyperventilating, Harper waited as the server placed drinks in front of everyone. As no one was ready to order, the server hurried away. Harper turned to John as Juliana chugged her iced tea. "I'm so sorry for everything. I came here because I hoped that if my mother spoke to you, she would realize how irrational she's being, and yes, a part of me thought you might want her again. And no, I wasn't happy when I learned you were with Sunny. I apologize for that. I was momentarily blinded with my desperation to end this madness and reclaim my life." She turned sharply to Juliana. "I only wanted you to be happy, Mom, because your depression makes my life utterly impossible, not to mention miserable."

"I've said I'm sorry. You've told me many times what a burden I am, and you're right. Is that what you need to hear, sweetie?" She reached over to hold Harper's hand, but Harper angrily snatched it away.

"You're not sorry about anything. Those are just empty words, Mom, because knowing you've been a burden has never stopped you, has it? Even after I saved your life, you quit therapy after two sessions, adamantly refusing to go back. Let's see, how did you phrase it? Oh, yes, unlike 'the stranger with the psychology degrees,' I 'understand' you. Actually, Mom, I really don't, and nobody should use their children as therapists. You never gave that woman, who was one of the best, who I begged to take you despite her full roster, a chance to know you at all. I love you, but you've been really selfish, and I can't do this anymore. Now *I* need therapy, but unlike you, I'll get better."

She nodded toward John. "And I can't make this man want you and neither can you."

Juliana's mouth dropped open. She looked at Harper, then at John. "Please, tell our daughter she's got this all wrong."

"Harper doesn't have anything wrong." John's patience was wearing thin as he fought to remain kind. "I'm truly sorry you lost your husband and that Harper lost her father. I don't love you, Juliana. I don't even know you anymore, and I have no reason to change the status of our acquaintance. I'm happy to buy you lunch, but there's really nothing else for us to say to one another."

Stunned, she snarled at him. "Do you have any idea how much energy I've put into our reunification?"

"He didn't ask you to do that, Mom. And I told you a thousand times it was a terrible idea. Don't blame anyone but yourself. Not me, not John."

Juliana looked at him again. "I snapped. I'm sorry, my darling. I see now that I've had a lot of time to contemplate things and ruminate on my feelings whereas you're only getting started. I need to be more patient and give you time."

"Once more," John said, surprising himself as his voice grew louder, "I have no interest in any kind of relationship with you. Never ever. You're a complete stranger to me, and whether you know it or not, I am to you. Please, stop already."

Juliana froze. After a few moments, she stood. "Well, there's no reason to stay here only to be rejected time and time again over a Cajun seafood lunch. I'm going back to the room to pack. And Harper, you'll need to make arrangements for us to fly back to New York as soon as possible. Goodbye, John. I'd like to say today was a dream come true, but you've made that impossible."

As Juliana stomped out, Harper turned to John before running after her. "I'm so sorry you had to go through this. I just need to make sure she settles in her room. I'm guessing Miranda gave you my message. Please, meet me at the bottom of the stairs in about a half hour, and I'll tell you the real story."

When John reached the bottom step, he heard Harper calling to him from the cave where Sunny had been. Sitting on a beach towel, an empty one across from her, she waved.

"For me, I presume?"

"Of course. I hope you don't mind. It just seemed weird for us to stand under the stairs. Better to be here—comfortable and out of sight."

"I agree. This was thoughtful of you." He sat, then crossed his legs. "Harper, before we get into everything, can you just tell me one thing: are you my daughter? It's been weighing heavily on me since I found your mother's note recently, but of course, I didn't know who you were then."

She looked down before meeting his gaze. "No, I'm not your daughter, John. I wish I were. You'll understand after I tell you the whole story."

His eyes widened. "So your mother made that up to win me back?"

Harper dug her fingers into the sand. "No. She believes you

are. I'll explain in a minute, but please understand that as honest as I am with her about everything else, if I awaken the truth in her about my parentage, which has lain dormant for years, I think she'll go completely insane and probably end her life."

Taken aback, he waited for her to take a breath and continue.

"Most of what she told you was true, but she's not in the best state of mind, as you saw for yourself. She's long repressed what happened to her and replaced it with something far more palatable. My grandfather Gus Garfield's sister Joanne, who is the very kind person he was not, is the one who explained everything to me many years ago." She brushed some sand from her thigh. "Where to begin?"

"Anywhere you can. This can't be easy."

The corners of her mouth turned upward in appreciation of his words. "You met my mom at a party when she was eighteen, right?"

"That's right. We were at a fraternity party our respective friends had dragged us to, and we both commiserated on our less-than-willing desire to be there by sulking on the porch where we met. Under the circumstances, we bonded pretty quickly."

"And you dated for about a year?"

"Right again."

"So that night you came to her house and were going to propose, you'd just been away for a while."

"I had." John scanned the beach to see if anyone was around, but saw no one except a couple of strangers far in the distance. "It was the first time I'd started playing gigs in Manhattan. I should add that I'd left Scarsdale to stay with a musician friend in the Village, where he'd booked me into several coffee houses and small bars. I missed your mother a lot and called her every chance I got." He hesitated. "Harper, I don't want this to come out wrong, but despite my best efforts, I haven't seen even a trace of the young woman I used to know. I kept looking, but she's gone."

Harper nodded. "The old, or should I say *young* Juliana was really sweet, wasn't she? And funny."

"She was. Loving and extraordinarily beautiful too. I had dreams about her for many years ... her long auburn hair flowing down her back, a cluster of freckles on each cheek, and her joyous laughter."

Harper smiled sadly. "That's nice to hear. That's who I remember as a child, but that person began to fade a very long time ago." She shook off the memory. "I'm sorry, John; you don't need to hear me dwell on the past." She straightened out a lump on the towel, then smoothed her hand over it. "This is a bit awkward, but that night you came over to her house to propose, you hadn't had sex with her in three months, right?"

"Definitely not. I never left the city the entire time I was gone, and she never came to visit. Her father wouldn't allow it."

"Well, I was born approximately a year after the last time you and my mother were together."

"I see." He paused as a look of horror came over him. "Oh, no! Please tell me Richard's not your father."

Harper straightened, steeling herself before speaking. "He was my half-brother and my uncle. And no, I don't think he ever knew."

John's jaw dropped. "What!?"

"Let me explain. See, the night you came over to propose, Mom hadn't even met Richard yet. But she'd met his father, Xavier.

My warped grandfather let his warped friend Xavier 'test drive' my mother to make sure she was good enough to marry, or to be more precise, I should say 'satisfy' his son."

"Xavier raped Juliana?"

"Worse, actually. Let me start from the beginning." She took a handful of sand and let it fall gently from her closed fist. "You may remember that Mom loved fashion."

John thought for a moment. "Of course I do. She had dreams of becoming a designer one day. Our creative aspirations were a big factor in what bonded us."

"Right. Anyway, she used to put her favorite magazine photos on her bedroom wall. There was one glittery red dress that she coveted. Her father took the magazine page and gave it to Xavier. Mom was hysterical when she noticed her prized picture was gone but overjoyed, albeit confused, to learn it had been taken so the real thing could be purchased for her. When the dress arrived by messenger, her father gave her the 'good news' that she was going into Manhattan with his 'special friend' who wanted to meet her and who had 'kindly' bought the designer dress for her." She made a face. "Sorry for the air quotes. I know how annoying they can be. My friends tell me that all the time. Anyway, back to the story."

John momentarily closed his eyes. "I feel sick. Really sick."

"Yeah. You and me both, John." She waited before continuing. "So Xavier took Mom to dinner and a Broadway show where they went backstage afterward and met the actors. Then, as if that weren't enough, he took her to some private club where celebrities hung out and made her feel like she was one herself. No doubt, this was where he started to ply her with drinks."

"How in the world do you know this?"

"Xavier told my grandfather the whole story. After all, Gus had willingly offered up his daughter, so he was eager to hear how it all went. Xavier was bragging, as if he'd had done a decent thing by showing Mom such a nice time before dragging her to the hotel room." She stopped to catch her breath. "That's where he got her really drunk and made her think that she was a willing party to whatever happened."

"Oh, Harper, that's appalling. I don't have the words to say how sorry I am. Everything that comes to mind is completely inadequate."

"S'okay. I understand." She exhaled. "My aunt said that her brother was thrilled that Xavier Strausser thought his daughter was good enough to marry … ugh … and to *pleasure* his son. I can't even fathom it."

John began to tremble, but stopped himself. "That's vile. Again, I just can't say how sorry I am."

"I know you are." Harper played with another handful of sand, annoyed that a wet patch was sticking to her fingers. "It's kind of hard to find the right words. I get it." She rubbed her hands together until the sand was gone. "Sorry, I'm super fidgety."

"I get it." John smiled. "So how do you think your mother ended up believing I was your father?"

"My aunt thinks Xavier got her very drunk and that she likely blacked out, and afterward, she repressed the entire incident. So, when she discovered she was pregnant, you were the only man she remembered being with and the only one she loved."

"But the time thing doesn't add up. How did she justify that?"

"She insisted that you'd only been gone three weeks, not three months, and it went downhill from there. Denial is a powerful thing. Maybe somewhere inside, she knows the truth, because my aunt Joanne said that she lost all interest in fashion magazines and a designing career after that night. While Mom knows Xavier was a monster, as she said back at the restaurant, and that her marriage was arranged, we think it's doubtful she has any memory of the horrid night she spent with him." She paused. "But who can know for sure? Most of us probably have repressed memories of one kind or the other."

John furrowed his brow. "Earlier, your mother said she let me go because her father insisted I'd have to get a business degree if I married her. He had to know the truth. I was gone for three months, if not several days more."

"Of course he did. But when he saw she was lost in fantasyland, he happily used her self-deception to his advantage—to get her to break up with you in order to save you and your career aspirations from his evil clutches. Mom hated to do it, but she saw it as a great act of love for you, and yeah, it was. My aunt Joanne said her brother was positively euphoric that Mom was so confused yet willing to let go. So of course, he never got her any help. That would be far too decent ... too lovingly paternal. Too selfless."

John gently put his palm up. "Wait, what about your grandmother? Helen, right?"

"Yes. She had no say and was never consulted on anything of significance. Gus and Helen Garfield had nothing remotely resembling a real, or should I say, equitable marriage."

John lowered his eyes. "It was somewhat similar with my

parents, though not entirely."

"Oh, my goodness." Harper put her hand over her mouth. "I completely forgot. Mom told me about your mother's suicide when you were only seventeen. And that you were the one to discover her. I'm so sorry. I didn't mean to stir up any heartache for you."

"It's fine, Harper. And while my father would never have done what Gus did, I've certainly never sought to emulate his character. I can only tell you that when I was dating your mother, my pain was too raw to compare family dysfunctions. When Juliana asked how my mother died, I told her the truth and asked that we leave it there. For one, I didn't want her to think the same fate would befall her own mother, and I had no desire to elaborate on the death of my own. So I suggested we just focus on our relationship and on the future."

Harper frowned. "Again, I'm so sorry about your mother."

Feeling vulnerable, John paused a few moments before speaking again. "Please, continue with your story."

"Well, after Gus made it clear that my grandmother should look the other way about Mom's mysterious pregnancy, she did as she was told without argument, though my aunt thinks she knew exactly what happened. Gus then handed Mom over to Richard, who was told, rather instructed by Xavier, that he would be a father to the child she was carrying. Xavier knew it was his, but Richard, who was already bursting with resentment, was told it was yours."

John put his hand to his forehead and held it there for a moment. "So much makes really ugly sense to me now."

"Yeah. Richard *hated* that he was marrying a woman pregnant by the talented man he was denied of being, but his father's influence on him was immense, in every horrible way, and he did what he was told. Not to mention that he did find Mom, and his father's billions, to be exquisitely beautiful. Not necessarily in that order."

John shivered in revulsion, then looked out at the ocean as he replayed all she had told him. He turned back to her. "I hope I'm not prying, but I'm curious as to when your aunt told you all of this and if she had a specific reason to do so."

"Well, Mom was married to Richard for eight years." She made a face." He filed for divorce the second his father was pronounced dead and the will was read. Still thinking I was your child, he hated me, because he hated kids, felt he had carried your 'burden' long enough, and by that point was consumed by toxic jealousy that your talent had brought you so much acclaim. He was happy to have his father's billions, but he didn't exactly love playing Daddy. He despised it … and me. But the fact that Mom never got over you really chafed his ass. Or should I say his ego. When they divorced, he told me in the nastiest way he could, with a huge smile, that I was not *his* 'idiot child' and that my real father, *you*, didn't want me either." She paused to catch a memory. "Oh, and that I should pretend the nearest trash chute was a sliding board and go play on it."

"Son of a bitch."

"To answer your question, John, I was eight when my aunt first told me that you weren't my father. She only did so because Richard had been so brutal, and she wanted me to feel better about my biological father supposedly rejecting me. But that's about all she told me as she needed to keep things as age appropriate as possible. It wasn't until I came to her at sixteen that she agreed to tell me everything."

"That must have been devastating for you. Especially having

to keep up the pretense with your mother."

Harper stroked a gold heart pendant she wore. "It was, but by then she'd met and married the wonderful Kyle Kinnison." She lifted the pendant to show John. "He gave me this for my sixteenth birthday." She let the heart drop. "He nurtured us both in ways we'd never known. My mom was deeply in love with him. And that's easy to understand. I've never known a gentler, kinder soul. Somehow, he knew how to make her happy. Maybe because he was a clinical psychologist. Mom blossomed again. Like she was a brand-new person. So did I. And well, you see where life took us after he died."

"That's tragic, Harper. I'm so sorry. What a devastating loss for you both."

"Thank you. It was." She exhaled. "So, you see, after a while, Mom resurrected *you* as her true love because his death has left her so irrevocably broken, and somehow she's justified all of this because she believes she's the mother of your child."

"That makes a lot of sense in a tragic kind of way." His guilty eyes looked at her. "I feel awful that I've been so harsh, but I didn't know how to get through to her."

Harper's distressed visage quickly morphed into an angrier one. "Don't feel awful. Listen, I'm very sorry for what happened to her. But she makes my life hell, and it gets worse all the time. Like I said, I'm sorry for the way I acted. I know everyone here thought I was nuts. I was so desperate to tame the beast and relieve my own burden that I played games with strangers and told one silly lie after another. I don't blame anyone for not taking a liking to me."

"We just didn't know what to make of you, Harper. We knew there was something else going on, but people get defensive. Nobody likes being played."

"I deeply apologize."

"Not necessary. I get it, and I know you didn't have to tell me all of this."

Harper leaned toward him. "I couldn't let you think I was your daughter. I grew up with lies, and I still enable *some* delusions but for a good reason. When I heard about what happened last night, I can't even imagine how freaked you must have been when we showed up at the cliff house. Talk about bad timing. Thank you for asking us to leave so promptly. I never even saw that crazy woman with the gun."

"I was afraid for *everyone.* I had no idea what those maniacs would do. It must have been awful for you seeing Richard again. And for Juliana too."

"It was. To say I was stunned to see him sounds trivial. My mind was blown wide open. Mom dealt with her shock by focusing on you." Harper picked up a small shell and threw it as far as she could. "We only showed up because we knew you'd be there. Before you left with the Gardet brothers and your sons, you shouted out the address. 'Twelve Cliff Road.'" She paused. "It was so wrong of me to follow you there, I know. It was crystal clear that something was terribly wrong." She stopped for a second. "I guess I can take on my mother's bad habit of ignoring the inconvenient truth when my needs feel greater. I need to work on that. I'm sorry; I'd just waited so long and really wanted to get the reunion over with and to get my mother off my back. But I never imagined anyone's life was in danger, John. I really didn't. And I never would have gone anywhere I thought Richard might be."

He offered her a reassuring smile. "I believe you."

"Oh, and I was so happy to hear you were all okay and that he wasn't." She looked curiously at John who was watching the ocean again. "You still with me?"

He turned back to her but waited to speak as his thoughts continued. "Yes. Sorry about that. I'm trying to process all of this, and something just occurred to me. You're an aunt to my boys."

"I am. But I don't think they should know. Definitely not now. 'Hey, guys, guess what? Your grandfather was a sexual pervert too.' Ugh." She looked down. "You're their dad. And if one day, down the line, you think they should know, give me a call, and we can discuss." She reached into her jacket pocket, pulled out a card, and handed it to him. "Honestly, considering the circumstances, I think it would be better forgotten."

John looked at the card. "So, you *are* a writer. A ghost writer and a freelance one as well."

She smiled. "Yeah, only I'd rather write about actual ghosts than books for famous people who take the credit. But hey, it pays well. And I can work from anywhere." She sighed. "One more thing. My mother doesn't know this, but I'm not going back to New York with her. I've got a former boyfriend who's living on the coast of Oregon, and I'm heading up to see him and to try and clear my mind. And hey, maybe one day, we'll find our way back to what we used to have. Or not." She shrugged. "I hope you don't think I'm horrible for not going back East with her, but I've spent years trying to help, and she has psychological disorders that I can't handle. She's killing me, John. It didn't take you long to see that."

"No. Definitely not." He offered a sympathetic frown.

"I've arranged for top-notch professionals to step in and help care for her. She won't be alone. Oh, and I'm not going to tell her about my plans until we leave Teal Beach. Our presence has caused enough drama on top of drama. I'm also not going to ask you for your number."

"Are you sure, Harper?"

"I am. I owe you that much. I'll call the hotel if I ever need to find you. I know you value your privacy, especially now that your sons are back in your life. Not to mention there were some reporters poking about, but that Ms. Gardet, wow, I thought she came down hard on me, but she chased them away something fierce. That woman was on fire!"

He smiled. "So I heard. Clarissa's a feisty one, for sure. I'm sure more will turn up, and I'm grateful knowing she's there for me."

"You can definitely count on her— on her husband and brother-in-law too."

"I know. I'm very lucky. You sure you don't want my number?"

"I don't. Like I said, I'll call the hotel. I have this not-so-crazy feeling that you and Sunny are going to be a forever thing. So there's that."

He smiled, his eyes brightening for the first time. "Yeah, there is that. You're right, Harper. That's exactly how I see it."

CHAPTER TWENTY-SEVEN

Feeling lost, Jake walked from his cabin, past the hotel, and toward the stairs to the beach. In his peripheral vision, he saw Phoebe sitting on one of the teal Adirondack chairs, on the right side of the porch, looking hopeless and disoriented.

He stopped, then retraced his steps. Once on the porch, gathering his courage, he walked over to her. "Hi there. I'm Jake. You probably remember me from last night. And I'm sure you know, I'm the biological son of that piece of now-dead slice of crud pie who treated you so horribly. I'd really like to talk to you, but if you want me to fuck off, I won't hold it against you. I swear."

Saying nothing, she stared at him as a large tear rolled down her face.

"Do you want me to leave you alone? I totally get it."

Phoebe nodded toward the chair next to her.

"You sure?" Jake asked as he sat down.

"I don't blame you for anything." She spoke softly. "I heard the way he talked to you and your brother. I know I wasn't the only one he tortured and abused. It's just that …."

"What?"

"I don't really know who I am anymore. Or where to go."

"Where are you from?"

"A small town outside of Windsor, Vermont." She twisted her lips. "I don't know if you've even heard of Windsor. Don't feel bad if you haven't."

"Sorry. Nope. But I've heard of Vermont."

"You're funny."

"My brother tells me that all the time. Except it's never when I'm trying to be."

Phoebe tried to smile. "So you're kind of quirky, huh?"

Jake beamed. "That's an awesome way of saying it. I'm totally quoting you on that!" He paused. "Like if that's okay."

"You really are funny. You're the kind of guy I would like if I hadn't been abused by that bastard. He took so much from me."

"I'm really sorry. He was good at taking stuff from people. If it meant something to you, kiss it good-bye. That's who he was." Jake tried to meet her gaze. "I'm not sorry he's dead. And now we can be with the best dad in the world, John."

"You're lucky." Phoebe looked up at the cascading plants hanging above. "Do you think these plants ever worry about anything?"

"Probably about being watered. But not much else."

"Jake, can you tell me what to do now? Because I have no idea."

He searched her deep-blue eyes, but saw nothing but sadness, tugging at the sleeve of her fading sense of self. "You don't want to go back to Vermont, huh?"

"No. It's really boring there. I'm close to my sister, Tillie … Matilda, but she's married with a three-year-old and another kid on the way. Plus, she told me exactly who Richard was every time we talked, but I kept on taking the abuse and making excuses for him until the very end. For a long time, I told her she didn't see the 'good side' of him.'" Phoebe made an embarrassed face, then looked away as she continued speaking. "I know, he didn't have one. Tillie knew that. She was so frustrated and kept begging me to leave him. She hated that

I stayed, but she never wrote me off because she was my only lifeline, and she loves me. I stayed because I didn't know where to go or what to do. Going home was never an option."

Jake cracked his knuckles. "Can I ask why you were with him? I mean, when you thought he had a 'good side?'"

"In the beginning, I believed that I cared about him, even though inside I knew I really didn't. Doesn't say much about me either, does it?" Her shoulders drooped. "But he was never nice enough to *let* me care, you know?"

"Yup. Sure do. Go on."

She angrily waved a fly away. "This sounds awful, but I was also with him probably because I never want to live in Vermont again. It's pretty there, but so what. You know?" She looked at Jake as if to see if he was disgusted with her.

"We're cool. Keep talking."

"Also, I guess because he was important and sometimes he said nice things but only about my body or my looks. He didn't want me for anything but sex, but he'd make up lies to keep me with him, like saying I was his best friend, that he got me a job singing in a movie, and how I'd be a star someday." She paused. "I used to be a singer."

"I'm sure you still are."

"No. I'm just a lost girl who let a scuzzy creep use her up by the ripe old age of twenty-two."

"That's how old we'll be. In a month." Embarrassment unsettled him. "Man, that was a dumb-ass thing to say."

"I like that we're the same age."

"Yeah, me too." He laughed. "And in case you're wondering, yep, I'm always this fascinating."

"Like I said, you're funny."

"Phoebe, I don't want this to come out weird or anything, but I want to help you. In whatever way I can. I just don't want you to think I'm hitting on you or anything. My brother Dylan and I are nothing like that bastard. The first thirteen years of our lives, John raised us, and luckily, we're a whole lot more like him."

She listened with interest, then finally replied. "My father is a minister, and my mother is kind of old-fashioned. She tutors kids with math and reading, does bake sales at the church, and never curses—like I do now. And she loves the Bible. They would freak their you-know-what if they ever knew what happened to me. That's another reason I can't go back now, even for a visit. They'd notice how depressed I am and how much I've changed. I can't hide it. I'm afraid I'd slip and tell them way more than I should. They're super charitable … always helping and consoling people who are hurting, but I'm afraid they'd judge me for letting stuff happen, even more than they'd judge him." She thought for a moment. "I don't know if they could be as understanding with me like they are with others. It would just be too personal … not to mention shocking for them." She paused to mull over her words. "Yeah, after they picked themselves off the floor, they might just get super angry and shame me even though they're nice people. I don't really know. But that's what I worry about the most."

"Do you *have* to go somewhere?"

"No. Sunny said that we paid for three months' rent on the house, which is like six months' rent in a room here. But she said that even if that weren't the case, I can stay for as long as I want. She said that I was brave and saved her life and John's by speaking up when I did."

"I was just going to say that. I think you did too. I can't thank you enough. Not ever. I hated seeing Richard slap you around, but I knew you were getting through to that crazy woman. You were super fierce when it mattered the most."

"I don't feel very fierce now. Or like I deserve any thanks. But Sunny said she would be grateful to me until the end of time and always be my friend."

"She's a sweetheart. No wonder my dad is in love with her."

Phoebe turned to face him. "I still can't believe Richard and that spirit psychopath of his almost killed both of them last night." She fumed. "I'm *so* glad I got to tell that bastard off before he died. Just so glad." She slowed. "Oh, sorry."

Jake reached over, just enough to touch her arm. "For what? Being a hero … or um … heroine. Just remember, *they* died. The bad guys. And we're all still here."

"Yeah. We are. But I don't know who I am, just that I'm no Superwoman. I feel like it should say 'loser whore' on my driver's license and my passport."

"No way, Phoebe!" Jake's face twisted in pain." Please don't go to that dark place Richard put you so he could control you. Seriously, the guy was a one-trick horse … donkey … ass … pony … whatever they call it. He didn't know how to do anything but promise stuff to people and trash them when he didn't get exactly what he wanted *when* he wanted it."

"That's so true."

"So look, I'm gonna hang around Teal Beach for a while because I've got a lot of stuff to figure out, plus, my brother and I want to spend time with John. We were separated for eight long years." He smiled. "You and I can be friends, or I can get lost at any time."

She laughed. "You know what, your fath… I mean, Richard, he never made me laugh, not even once."

"Seriously, he had no sense of humor. Just a fucking pervert. I never told John this part, but when we were seventeen, Richard made us watch him with a prostitute so we'd know what to do. I can't unsee that shit and it really bothers me. Dylan too. Sometimes I even dream about it."

"Sounds just like that scum. He just got off on being watched. Even by his sons."

Jake's cheeks bloated with disgust. "Gross. I never even thought about that part. Makes even more sense. That's way worse than the other reason." He exhaled. "So listen, maybe we can hang out together and figure out what's next. And look, I'll have some money. So if you decide where you want to go and need some help, I'm your man. No strings. In fact, I'll give you a pair of fuck-off scissors so you can cut all ties. Swear to God."

"You're awesome, Jake."

"Yeah, I am." He laughed. "Just kidding. You are too, Phoebe."

Alone, John sat on the sectional couch and watched the sun as it began to set. Before Sunny could knock, Kono barked to be let in.

Smiling, John got up and rushed to the door, overjoyed to see Sunny standing there. Never taking his eyes off her, he petted Kono and Miggy. As he and Sunny walked toward the couch, the dogs took a suspicious detour into his office.

"Thanks for watching the boy while I met with Juliana and Harper, then Harper again. Wow, I'm still in shock from it all."

With her back against the chaise, Sunny motioned for him to sit beside her. "I hope you're okay. Thanks for telling me on the phone the gist of what transpired. Especially with Harper. That's a whole lot to take in on top of everything you've just been through. I can see why you needed a bit more time to sort out your thoughts before I came over."

"After all these years, wondering about Juliana, the things I learned about her from Harper were the dead last things I ever expected to hear." He managed a weak smile. "And it's not just what I've been through, it's all *we've* been through, Sunny. I wanted to tell you the little I did on the phone, mostly so we can push that business aside for now. There's more I want to share in much greater detail, but this is our time. Finally."

"It is." She brushed her palm against his cheek. "It truly is."

Feeling as he never had in his entire life, he tried to soak in the moment and the love, which was uncannily brand new. "This feels incredible, Sunny, with everything finally in sync, that we are free to feel and to act without the threats and ugliness that taunted us. Nothing is holding me back. In other words, I can't wait to go at you with reckless abandon." Alarmed, he paused. "But I don't just mean physically. I mean emotionally as well. And that's always been the most difficult for me—as you well know." He smiled. "How are you feeling? I don't want to make any assumptions, especially after all you've been through. I won't assume that what you wanted yesterday is what you want today."

Her eyes soaked him in as she caressed his leg. "Nothing is holding me back. But I do want—"

"Tell me. If I can give it to you, I will."

"I need to be sure I'm not keeping you from chasing the dream that eluded you as a young man, because that Whisky Devers was a pretty cool guy."

John cupped her face in his hands. "Sweetheart, I don't know if you believe in reincarnation, but I do. Know why? I've been reincarnated before I died." He took his hands away to briefly squeeze hers. "Whisky Devers was me in another life. But I'm not him anymore, and I don't want to be. Even imagining it unsettles me. I like my life just where it is now. When I heard reporters had been snooping around the cliff house story, mostly because of Richard's notoriety within the record industry, not to mention my second album emerging, it gave me chills. I pray they leave me alone. I neither want to be known nor seen by the masses. But I must say, it fascinates me to learn how truly hated Richard was, especially that he was dubbed 'Rx for Disaster' by his colleagues."

"Fascinating, yes. Surprising, no." She spoke tenderly. "I just wasn't sure that his demise might not motivate you to go after all that was taken from you. There was so much."

"Not even for a split second." John kissed her lips. "I have my boys back in my life. And now you. Trust me. I'm exactly where I want to be. I've never been happier."

Sunny sniffled. "My heart is smiling because I don't have the words tell to you what that means, John. Thank you for reassuring me about Whisky."

He looked her in the eye. "Hear me, Sunny. Losing Dylan and Jake was the worst thing that ever happened to me. I could have gone on with music, but I was consumed with grief. I worried about them every day, praying they would be able to survive whatever Richard and Evelyn were doing to them. My desire to sing, much less to perform, pretty much evaporated into thin air. I didn't want any obligations that weren't utterly necessary, and writing music under a pseudonym for other artists was all I could manage. Those years changed me."

She lightly touched his cheek, then took her hand away. "Can you tell me how?"

"Well, I had time for excess contemplation, to say the least. And I told myself that I would dig deep, remove myself from any denial I might be submerged in, and get to know myself better, if that was possible."

"How introspective of you. And did you succeed?"

"I think so. I realized that even as a young man, chasing the bright lights of fame wasn't my dream and that I'd never really had the chance to work out what I *did* want. But my father insisted that seeking a career in music was idiotic and told me many times that my talent was mediocre at best. And I thought, Well, I'll show him, I'll be a star." He closed his eyes for a moment as he remembered. "That fueled my ambition with a vehemence I'd never known. I played club after club, doing everything I could to be discovered, as I eventually was by Round They Go Records. I wanted to perform where people would cheer for me ... adoring crowds clamoring for more." He squeezed her hand for a moment. "But now I know that my appetite for fame was really an obsession to prove my father wrong. Don't get me wrong, I wanted to use my talent and be successful, but not as a recognizable celebrity. I would have been happy being a writer, producer, and studio musician. Just the fact that I went by the name Whisky Devers ought to tell you something."

"John, there's something I don't understand. Was your father tone deaf? Did he have no appreciation of the arts? You're absolutely brilliant on so many levels."

"Thank you, sweetheart. As I learned after he died, he *did* think I was talented, very much so, which is exactly why he was afraid for me." He paused to reflect. "Or more accurately—for himself. Apparently, Morgan J. Coates didn't think I'd be able to handle the fame or the many temptations that come with it. In his mind, if I ascended to stardom, I'd quickly fall and go on to live in some never-ending bacchanal, which would have embarrassed him to the core." He sighed. "Nice vote of confidence, huh? Anyway, he never told me all of that. His partner's wife did."

"Why did he think so negatively?"

"Because he was a high-powered entertainment attorney and had many clients who were living, breathing, not to mention deceased examples of his fear. I'm far from perfect, but I never did anything to give him the idea that tragedy would prevail if I succeeded. Once in a blue moon, I drink a bit too much. And I've never done drugs—minus a bit of weed here and there."

"So your father thought it was better to tell you that you had no talent rather than have a strong talk with you about the pitfalls of fame?"

"Affirmative. As I've said, interpersonal relationships were not his strong point, to say the very least, and consequentially, he pushed me further in the direction where he didn't think I'd thrive and where

I didn't necessarily want to go."

Sunny shook off the shock of his words. "Please, continue."

"What I'm trying to say is that my many years of solitude, in the rare moments when I wasn't thinking about the boys, helped me to find my true self again. And now that they're back and I've met you, life makes sense for the first time. I've never been happier. Was I miserable, not to mention enraged, when Strausser took my music? Of course. And it still enrages me because it was so evil. But that act of cruelty paled in comparison to taking the boys, because they were the true victims."

Sunny followed his gaze out the window. "You've had a lot of time to contemplate your life, my sweet man."

He turned to her. "What I've just divulged to you took me many years to figure out. My quick summary of events may have made it all sound easy and obvious. But it wasn't. I didn't know who I was or what I wanted. My life was cloaked in obscurity of my own making."

Sunny looked at him with guilty eyes. "What you just said …."

He smiled. "I know; it sounds like a Whisky Devers' lyric. What can I say?"

Sunny kissed him. "Thank you for telling me all this. I promise, I'll never ask you to bring him back. Believe it or not, after Jess gave me the CD, I never told her that you and he were one and the same. I'd like to, now that things are okay, and request that she doesn't share the information, which she won't, but I thought it best not to get into it with her at the time. She would have had way too many questions that I was in no frame of mind to answer, much less *have* an answer *for.*"

He smiled. "Speaking of Whisky, that young fool, he has one more album in the vault. And guess who's going to get one of the few copies that will be made?"

"Really? You're sure?" She laughed. "I mean, is *he* sure?"

"Very. I used to be pretty tight with the guy. I know he'd want me to give his biggest fan the last of his music because his alter ego is an even bigger fan of hers."

"Oh my." Sunny ran her index finger over his lips. "I'm just sad that it's the last of your music."

John smiled. "It's the last of Whisky Devers, Sunny. But I'm hoping you'll be a bigger fan of John Hennessey's. In fact, I have it on good authority that he's written a couple of songs for this woman named 'Serena Sundial.' Imagine having a name like that? Hmm. I wonder what kind of songs he'd write?"

Sunny beamed. "Every time I think I've seen it all, you surprise me in the most incredible way."

"I may still do something with music, but I'm very sure I don't want to be in the public eye."

"May I selfishly say that I'm good with that?"

He traced a heart on her forehead. "You may. I love you, Sunny." He crinkled his brow. "By the way, where in the world are the dogs?"

"Not far. But do we *really* want to know?" She winked and returned the heart on his forehead. "How do I tell you, without being all gushy and mushy, that I never, ever thought I would be happy again? I was sure the best of my life had long passed me by. Some friends and family encouraged me, *pushed* me, to get out there and look for love again. I adamantly refused. I told them all that if there was someone out there who I could love, he'd find his way to me. They told me life doesn't work like that, but they stopped pestering me, and here we are. Life *does* work like that. Here I am with you in this gorgeous cottage, imaging all of the ways I'm going to, well, you know."

He smiled. "I do."

"I feel ecstatic about life again. Those cretins are long gone, Imari and Ty are having a baby, and the other Gardets are here as well. It's our family compound. So special. And Dylan told me that he and Jake aren't going anywhere for a while. I know that makes you very happy."

"It does."

"John, I hope this doesn't upset you, but I know Grey would have really liked you. And as much as I once thought that moving on would be a betrayal to him, after meeting you, I believe he sent you here somehow. I do."

He smiled. "That makes a lot of sense to me. And I won't say I'm not glad to hear it. I know how much you loved him, that you still do, and that he will always be a part of you."

"He will. But I'm truly ready, and I don't believe it was any coincidence that you ended up here. I'll just leave it there."

"Thank you. I've been wondering, about what you just said about Grey, but I didn't know how to ask."

"I know." Sunny squeezed his hand. "That's why I told you."

Overwhelmed, he said nothing and just looked at her, choked up by her intuitiveness.

"Oh, and I'm having my realtor put the cliff house on the market once it's repaired and spiritually cleansed. I have no need for it. I have everything I want. I can't wait to know you better. Thank you for letting me into your life."

John stroked her hair. "Those gorgeous heart-shaped lips look like they've still got something to say before, well, before we chase our ecstasy."

Her fingertips tapped their way down his face. "Just that I've done nothing but think about you and what we might have. I have many fantasies but no expectations. I just want to love you and get to know you even better. To see how we roll and how we ultimately decide to live. And you know what, if we stay just as we are in this moment, I'm good with that. I'll say it: I hunger for you."

"As I do for you."

An embarrassed look landed on Sunny's face. "While we're on the subject … gee, this is awkward. I just thought it was so odd that two sex-crazed women were there in the cliff house on the same night. I know that was the least important thing going on, but still, what are the chances?"

John laughed. "Oh, Sunny, I'm not laughing at the presence of those two ghastly females. But it crossed my mind, in those moments of horror, that I was thankful there were *only* two. When I was touring as Whisky Devers … how do I say this without sounding full of myself? I met more women like that on a nightly basis than I could count. That was yet another reason Strausser was so jealous. Women only lined up for his money."

"Ah, so I take it women regularly undressed for you whether you wanted it or not."

"Yeah, I had some real shockers backstage, not to mention women in the front rows disrobing while I was performing, then throwing their underwear at me." He paused to acknowledge the passing nausea. "It actually made me sick. I wasn't trying to be sexy. I was trying to share my art, and having to bat bras, thongs, and other things away from my guitar strings, and my face, wasn't exactly something I welcomed or appreciated. But I couldn't exactly show my disgust."

"If I'd seen you way back when, before I met Grey, I would have understood their attraction, but certainly not their actions. However, I must warn you," — she smiled — "I am a bit sex crazed, but only for you. It feels so good to be able to say that, rather than just …. "

He smiled crookedly. "Rather than just watch me from way up high in your backyard, looking down at me and wondering what I was thinking? Who I was?"

Sunny's face reddened as her hand covered her open mouth.

"It's okay, sweetheart. While you were looking at me, I was thinking of you. Wondering pretty similar things, I'd imagine."

Taking her hands away from her mouth, she gulped before she spoke. "I'm mortified with embarrassment. And I did eventually stop. You know that, right?"

"Yeah, and I missed you when you did."

Sunny exhaled, a look of both amusement and shock on her face. "Oh, John. How in the world did you know?"

He laughed as he squeezed her hand. "There are these things called light bulbs. They come in all shapes, sizes, and wattages. When you illuminate your backyard with a string of them, and then stand underneath, it's not impossible that someone on a dark beach below might notice, especially as said person approaching from a distance could see without looking up. I saw you the first night we arrived."

Sunny closed her eyes and her chin dropped to her chest. "Well don't I feel like the silliest woman ever."

John laughed. "Don't you dare. You're far from it." He paused. "One night, I had this overwhelming urge to wave to you, or take out my phone and call you, but I was afraid it would destroy our burgeoning friendship, and I didn't want to risk it—or embarrass you. Not to mention how insanely conflicted I was about everything."

"I've felt so guilty about invading your privacy." She laughed. "But you don't mind embarrassing me now, huh?"

He grinned. "Nah … not too much, no."

As the light danced in her eyes, she looked lovingly at him. There's just so much more to learn about you."

"Then I suggest we have our first lesson, considering I feel the same way about you." Taking her hand, John rose and escorted her to the bedroom. As they reached the side of the bed, his hands slid up her shirt and touched her, gently, sensually.

She moaned, his touch far more pleasurable than anything her fantasies had allowed her to imagine. "Oh, John."

"You said before that you hunger for me. Well, I hunger for you, too, Sunny. Thing is, I told you old Whisky was gone, but it seems he wants to meet you before I take over. Okay to let him?"

She fell backward onto the bed and put her arms around his neck. "Oh, my. Yes. My inhibitions have run off, and I don't expect them to return in this lifetime. You're both free to take me to paradise, and please, take me now."

As Whisky and John merged into one, pooling their talents and soaking in the love she had for them both, they carried her far, far away to an idyllic wonderland of their own creation far from the waves that crashed outside the cottage window and the momentarily dim memories of the night they almost lost everything.

THE END

Dear, Reader:

If you enjoyed this book, I would be deeply grateful for a short review on Amazon or whichever site you downloaded this book from. It really helps. Thank you!

ABOUT THE AUTHOR

LISETTE BRODEY was born and raised in the Philadelphia area. She lived in New York City for ten years and now resides in Los Angeles.

She is the multigenre author of twelve books. Her titles include: *Crooked Moon; Squalor, New Mexico; Molly Hacker Is Too Picky!;* The Desert Series (*Mystical High, Desert Star, Drawn Apart*); *Hotel Obscure: A Collection of Short Stories; Love, Look Away; The Sum of our Sorrows; The Waiting House: A Novel in Stories;* and *All That Was Taken.*

She has also published two short stories in an anthology called *Triptych's (Mind's Eye Series, Book 3).*

All of her books are available in both Kindle and paperback.

Website & contact: lisettebrodey.com
Amazon author page: Author.to/lisettebrodey
Twitter: twitter.com/lisettebrodey
Facebook: facebook.com/BrodeyAuthor
Instagram: @ca_lisette
Pinterest: pinterest.com/lisetteca/

www.ingramcontent.com/pod-product-compliance
Lightning Source LLC
Chambersburg PA
CBHW070907260626
47162CB00007B/2589